THE

ORCHID

THRONE

THE
ORCHID
THRONE

Jeffe Kennedy

St. Martin's Paperbacks

This is a work of fiction. All of the characters, organizations, and events portrayed in this novel are either products of the author's imagination or are used fictitiously.

First published in the United States by St. Martin's Paperbacks, an imprint of St. Martin's Publishing Group.

THE ORCHID THRONE

For information, address St. Martin's Publishing Group, 120 Broadway, New York, NY 10271.

www.stmartins.com

ISBN: 978-1-250-19431-2

Our books may be purchased in bulk for promotional, educational, or business use. Please contact your local bookseller or the Macmillan Corporate and Premium Sales Department at 1-800-221-7945, ext. 5442, or by e-mail at MacmillanSpecialMarkets@macmillan.com.

Printed in the United States of America

St. Martin's Paperbacks edition / October 2019

10 9 8 7 6 5 4 3 2 1

For Darynda Jones,

Who roomed with me, patiently
put up with my emo ramblings
for a week as I finished this book,
and helped me find the answers,

And who is the best of colleagues,
the loveliest of friends, with a truly
kind and generous heart.

~Acknowledgments~

Many heartfelt thanks to Grace Draven, who helped me think through this ending—and who is always there, whether for gossip, brainstorming, or helping to plan world domination.

Thanks to Jonathan Brazee for the limerick and the guy perspective.

Much love and gratitude to my agent, Sarah Younger, who helped me to work up this idea and polish it until it shone. You are a fireball of amazing. To many years and books to come!

Huge thanks to my editor, Jennie Conway, who told me she obsessed about Lia's dresses, which is one of the loveliest things for a writer to hear. She's been outstanding every step of the way on this book's journey. Communicative, supportive, thoughtful, and insightful—the best kind of editor to have.

To everyone at St. Martin's Press: thank you for making me feel welcome and valued in small ways and large, and for working so hard on all aspects of this book. It's such a privilege to be part of this team.

Love to Margaret, and to Kelly Robson, for devoted friendship and daily chats—you bring sunlight to my life. To Thea Harrison, Jennifer Estep, Amanda Bouchet,

Elizabeth Hunter, Ilona Andrews: you inspire me and I'm ever so grateful for your friendship and support. To Eric Wolf, Ed Khmara, and Matt Reitan—gratitude for feedback on early iterations of this book. Special thanks to Sage Walker and Jim Sorenson for sticking with me. Love to Megan Mulry for being the okayest friend ever, and for emergency margaritas and Fab Finds. Also love (but no hugs) to Minerva Spencer for coming into my life at the right time and being the loudest of cheerleaders.

Many thanks to my professional writers organizations, the Science Fiction and Fantasy Writers of America (SFWA) and the Romance Writers of America (RWA)—especially my local RWA chapter, the Land of Enchantment Romance Authors—for being a port in the storm, a rising tide that floats all boats, and fellow travelers on the sea of publishing.

As always, thanks are inadequate for my fantastic assistant, Carien Ubink, who keeps the balls in the air and me out of my trees. You're the best.

Finally—first, last, and always—love to David, who makes everything possible.

~Prologue~

Fragment from the unfinished
History of a Tyrant by Ambrose Daluna

The oldest records and recollections agree that it all began with the discovery of vurgsten. The records aren't cohesive across the many kingdoms, or even particularly coherent within the same document, as the immediate results of that discovery quickly shattered lives and governments so few people spent their time writing things down.

So exactly how the devastating power of vurgsten was discovered and who first applied it have been obscured, perhaps deliberately so. Most likely whoever identified the power locked inside the rock mined from the depths of the volcanic island of Vurgmun died for the privilege. They could've perished in any number of ways—from the ash-laden air of Vurgmun, to toxic fumes emitted by the rock vurgsten itself, to an accidental explosion of the volatile stuff, or at the hands of those who took that knowledge for themselves and used it to defeat magic, forever changing the balance of power.

Vurgsten wasn't new or unknown to the many kingdoms. Theatrical productions used it to create lightning or mimic magical spells and enchantments. Street magicians used it to counterfeit actual magic. Mischievous children used hoarded bits to startle unpleasant relatives, in the time-honored fashion of all children. All more or less harmless.

The history-changing impact of vurgsten came from a volatile combination: the creative application of an unusually pure vein of the ore from a chasm on Vurgmun opened by volcanic activity and the ruthless intelligence of one man, Anure Robho.

Robho had been a landowner in Aekis, though not born to it. With no elemental blood, no true attachment to the land, he somehow acquired it anyway—and was later granted a minor title for unspecified reasons. It gave him legal rights without the true understanding, the mystical connection and bone-deep commitment to stewardship of the land that blood ties bring.

Of course, other landowners, noble or not, have acquired their properties in similar ways, but those people sacrificed their life energies to the land they held, raised their families on it, and created the needed ties according to ritual and the ancient laws of magic.

Anure Robho ran with a set of new thinkers who scoffed at the old ways and called all magic fake superstition. Records in Aekis that survived Robho's abrupt departure for greater fortunes reveal him as greedy in his decisions and petty in their execution. His lands, captive to his uncaring stewardship, failed to flourish. Setting the pattern for his rule, he ruthlessly extracted their wealth, leaving nothing behind. When and how Robho ascended to the actual throne of the kingdom of Aekis is less clear. All we know is that the records from neighboring Oriel showed the former king gone and Anure Robho crowned in his place.

Soon after becoming king of his rapidly declining kingdom, Robho claimed that Ejarat and Sawehl were false gods who'd failed to protect their people, that the court wizards were frauds pretending to have magic that consisted of trickery and sleight of hand, and that the people had revolted against the corrupt king and queen of Aekis and placed him on the throne.

From Robho's later conquests, we can extrapolate his methods. He used well-placed vurgsten charges to assassinate magic workers and break guardian spells. Castle and city walls fell to the destructive explosions no one had before experienced or could predict. Taken by surprise— and perhaps lulled into complacency by their soft lives— court wizards failed to muster the appropriate defensive spells. The people, betrayed and enraged, turned their fury on anyone with magic, executing them for conspiring to trick the people. Priests and priestesses were exiled for fulminating superstitions. And the royal and noble families disappeared.

Many went to unmarked graves. Others went to Vurgmun to mine more of Robho's unstoppable weapon.

One by one, the kingdoms fell to the great and grinding wheel of Robho's hunger. Those who cooperated were rewarded with power—under Robho's control—while those who resisted were treated with utmost cruelty before they disappeared.

By the time he took the title of His Imperial Majesty Anure, Emperor of All the Lands, only fair Calanthe remained as a free kingdom. Calanthe, island of flowers and pretty pleasures—and possessed of the most ancient heart of magic—offered no overt resistance to Anure's arrival. Old King Gul met Anure's ships with garlands, not arrows, and welcomed the upstart to savor the many delights of Calanthe.

Though the oppressed and often enslaved folk of the many scattered and forgotten kingdoms decried Calanthe's self-serving cowardice, King Gul managed to send Anure away again believing he'd won—with only a promise of marriage to his daughter and sole heir—and the false emperor built his citadel at Yekpehr.

The defeated kingdoms subsided into servitude, Anure temporarily satisfied to enjoy his power. Until the balance shifted again.

Set here by my hand, Ambrose Daluna
16th Year of the Reign of Emperor Anure
Year 2037 of Sawehl's union to Ejarat

1

"Arise, Your Highness. The realm awaits the sun of Your presence."

The ritual words cut through the thick smoke of the nightmare, bringing me awake with a start. A bad omen that I hadn't come out of the dreams on my own—and a sign that gave the images the power to linger in my mind, stains refusing to be scrubbed clean.

The wolf fought its chains, howling in hoarse rage, shedding fire and ash.

The sea churned, bloodred and crimson dark, bones tossed in the waves, white as foam.

The tower fell into a pile of golden rubble, then to fine sand, the grains sliding against one another with soul-grinding whispered screams.

I loathe dreaming, where I have even less control than in the waking world. Calanthe Herself sings sweetly to me of the seas, the plants, and the creatures that walk Her soil. But outside our fragile island, the abandoned lands beyond cry like frightened children in the night. I can't help them. It's all I can do to protect Calanthe, and most days I despair of being able to do even that.

Still, with no one else to hear them, they call to me in chaotic images, the nightmares dashing me from one dark scenario to the next. No matter how the dreams plague me, I usually wake when the light of the rising sun reddens my eyelids. I keep my eyes closed, pretending to anyone who checks on me that I'm still asleep. Pulling the pieces of my composure together, I listen to the morning song of Calanthe. The birds sitting high in the canopy to catch the first warming rays of the sun show me the sky. The fish swimming in the sea speak of clean water and plentiful food. Even the trees, the flowers, the small insects in the soil all hum to me of their lives.

All reassure me of the balance, that Calanthe, at least, is peaceful and vital.

Only I and the land I'm tied to exist in that time after sleep and before true waking, in what I call the dream-think, an almost enchanted bubble where I belong entirely to Calanthe. The emperor does not own me. The crying lands he's orphaned are silent. My ladies have not yet woken me to wrenching reality and the trials of the day ahead.

Dreams always seem to me a terrible price to pay for the succor of sleep. Neither my naturalists nor my physicians seem to be able to explain the purpose of such dreams. And of course, Anure killed all the wizards, so I have none to tell me if magic can answer those nighttime screams. So without answers, and like the exorbitant tithes I'm forced to send to the emperor, I do pay the price, and nightly. The dreamthink is my reward, my time with Calanthe. A gift arising from waking Ejarat of the earth welcoming the return of Her husband, Sawehl of the sun. In the dreamthink, in Calanthe's sweet communion, I can believe the old gods are with us still, that they haven't abandoned us. That I have reason to hope.

"Euthalia, wake up. We're ready," Tertulyn whispered in my ear. My first lady-in-waiting, doing her duty as always. She couldn't know she'd woken me from the nightmare instead of the dreamthink. Or that starting my day this way meant it would be certainly cursed.

No one believes in omens or curses anymore. Or hope, for that matter. In this, too, I am alone.

Euthalia is a mouthful, but no one calls me that except for Tertulyn so it doesn't matter. Only Emperor Anure has the rank to address me by my given name, and I avoid conversation with His Imperial Nastiness to the best of my ability. Tertulyn has called me by my name since we were children, but only when no one can overhear, as etiquette demands.

As if she'd whispered them into my ear along with my name, the concerns of the realm immediately flooded my mind. The emperor's emissary should have returned in the night and would want an audience with me—something I'd been dreading, as he never brought good news. Rumors had spread of slave uprisings, possibly even rebellion, as unlikely as that would be, that had the emperor both angry and insecure in his power. The worst possible combination in a man like him.

If I believed a rebellion could succeed, I would rejoice in the battle to come. But I had no hope of that. No one could defy Anure's vast power and ability to destroy the least whimper of resistance, as all those kingless and queenless lands testified, crying their hopelessness to me every night.

No, such rumors meant the Imperial Tyrant would only tighten his fist—one that already strangled us nearly to death. The prospect of worse to come made me inexpressibly weary, and I hadn't even gotten out of bed yet.

Nevertheless, I had to face the day. A realm awaited the sun of my presence, after all.

I opened my eyes and pasted a serene smile on my lips.

Tertulyn—already wigged, gowned, and decked in fresh flowers—stood a decorous three steps back from my bed, hands folded over her heart. All equally polished and lovely as morning dew, my five junior ladies awaited in a ring around her. They'd all been up since well before dawn to dress themselves before attending me. And yet their eyes sparkled as brightly as the birds that had shown me the sun on the sea, pretty painted lips curved in delighted smiles.

Though I was only twenty-six, they made me feel old. If a witch offered me a magic potion to remove the last ten years and restore my youth—and the innocent belief I'd had then, that my life would be a good one—I'd down it without question. Even if it meant my death the next day.

No, that was a lie. I would never shirk my duty to Calanthe, not even for such a fantasy. Not without an heir to take my place. No matter how old and tired I felt.

Making sure my smile matched my ladies', I sat up. "Good morning, Tertulyn, ladies. Who is our guest today?"

The ring of women parted and Tertulyn swept a gloved hand at a young girl wearing the cascading sky-blue wig and gown of a Morning Glory, curtsying with a practiced deep knee bend. I'd kept my father's custom of inviting a maiden from one of the outlying villages to attend my morning ablutions, though only because my adviser, Lord Dearsley, had insisted. In those dark days following my father's death, when I'd first taken the orchid ring and throne, the song of Calanthe so startlingly loud in my thoughts, I'd been less sure of myself and my decisions.

"The people regard it as the highest honor," he'd urged. "They hold competitions at festivals to select these girls. Think of it: every town and village, even the tiniest islands, choosing the loveliest girl, the brightest and most talented, all vying for the privilege of sending *their* Glory to the capital, to the palace itself, to attend the queen! For most of these girls, this will be the one and only time in their lives they will leave whatever humble place birthed them. And You and I understand it's more than that. You have your connection to Calanthe and Her people." He paused meaningfully, to allow room for the truths we didn't speak aloud. "But You know that not everyone feels it. Certainly not those who come from refugee families. You cannot take this away now, Your Highness, especially at this time, with their king so recently relegated to the waves, particularly for no reason."

"I *do* have a reason," I'd told him, resolved to meet the uncomfortable subject head-on, no matter that he was a man much older than me. "I understand that this 'privilege' came with . . . an unsavory price." Though I'd been only a girl myself—and a thoroughly protected one at that—I'd also never been ignorant. The land herself spoke to me, and the Flower Court gossiped incessantly. The sport of information exchange in the palace might as well be one of those village competitions, the way everyone vied to be the first to know some bit of news.

All knew the Morning Glories who'd attended my late father, King Gul, left again with their petals more than a little bruised. And many whispered that more than a few villages celebrated new citizens three-quarters of a year later, Calanthe delighting in the births of more of Her children. Something that had *not* occurred since I ascended to the throne, for obvious reasons. Disconcerting, I can tell you, to know that though I am the only legitimate child of the late King Gul, my part-blood half-siblings might number in the tens, if not hundreds.

Not that it matters, as I am the only child of my mother and thus the only possible heir to the orchid ring and throne. Unless I can find another. When I was but sixteen, that bothered me far less than it does now.

"The girls will suffer no bruising at Your hands," Dearsley had pointed out.

"I have no use for them."

"The custom is old," he'd said, with a meaningful dip of his head to the sea. "You risk making Your people fearful and unhappy. Calanthe will feel that and respond to it. You are new to having sole responsibility for the land, but this custom is important. Change it at Your peril."

"Even if I don't draw their virgin blood?" I'd asked sweetly, my sarcasm far more overt in those days.

"A queen has other ways."

I knew full well, in my bones, that Calanthe didn't care about the Morning Glories and the rituals of men like my father. But I keep Calanthe's secrets and She keeps mine. Dearsley had a point that the superstitions the people observed had weight, whether they affected Calanthe or not. I kept the custom, despite the inconvenience. And I kept up appearances. The Morning Glories were not the only virgins in service to the arcane requirements of the Orchid Throne.

"Welcome, Glory," I said. "You may assist Me from My bed."

An earnest, if awkward young thing—weren't they all? Though surely I'd never been so innocent—she tripped a little over her lavish hem in her haste to oblige. That's what came of dressing a simple girl in an elaborate confection of a gown for the space of a few hours. Ridiculous how the styles had billowed in imitation of my own.

Accustomed to such bumbling, one of my ladies snagged her by the elbow, preventing her from careening headlong into me. A fortunate catch, as I would have had to be severe with her over the lapse. I'd already begun the day with bad luck—I didn't need to add ruining the best day of this young girl's life. Never mind that attending me shouldn't be anyone's best anything.

"If I may, Your Highness?" Recovered from her near disaster, though blushing prettily—and as only those who've never suffered severe consequences for their errors can—Glory offered a gloved hand to me. I took it with my left, letting her see the famed orchid ring, a treat possibly greater than any other. It hadn't left my hand since the day my father took it from his and threaded it onto my finger with his dying breath. What would happen to it— and Calanthe—upon my own dying breath didn't bear considering.

I simply had to survive until I found an heir. Promised to Anure, I couldn't conceive a child without bringing his fury upon me and Calanthe. And I'd die before I'd have a child of his abominable blood mixed with Calanthe's. A pretty prison I found myself in.

I gave Glory a moment while she bent her head over the ring in stunned admiration—who could blame her?— breathing in the fragrance of the living orchid. True Calantheans sense the magic in the gorgeous bloom, even if they don't know what it is they feel, and the encounter is nearly a religious experience. Perhaps Calanthe Herself whispers to them. No one has ever said, and I won't ask. I try not to rush the moment.

But finally I set my feet on the stone floor and used the leverage of the Glory's grip to rise. More to snap her out of it than because I needed to. I wasn't *that* old. Court rituals, however, have taken the place of the magic spells we practiced before Anure killed all the wizards. Though empty rituals like welcoming the Morning Glories argu- ably do little to protect us, we nevertheless cling to their assiduous practice to fend off disaster.

I suppose it makes us feel better, though disaster seems to find us regardless. Magic had deserted us, leaving us only with science to fight the monsters. I sometimes entertained the notion of skipping some rituals—or even controverting them—as a test. But the risk of finding my way into even worse trouble always seemed too great, especially just to satisfy my curiosity.

So I followed the dance steps, allowing the Morning Glory to take my head scarf, which she would keep as a memento. In my rare whimsical moments I imagined thousands of my scarves, stained from the oily sweat of sleep, enshrined in towns, cities, and villages across the realm. I really didn't want to know what they did with them.

I only wished the nebulous comfort of the orchid ring had enough magic to silence the rest of the world, to banish the nightmare images that clung to my thoughts in sharp-edged fragments, refusing to disperse.

As my ladies and Glory helped me into my bath, I used the quiet to clear my mind. They washed, dried, then oiled me from toe to scalp. A practical aspect to the custom—the Glory could attest to my continued good health, my nakedness hiding nothing, dispelling the rumors that I was anything but a human woman for those spies of Anure's in my court. Not that any Glory would say so if she detected otherwise, which was why every one was carefully chosen for her connection to true Calanthe. A discretion and loyalty that cannot be shaken.

The daily sameness of the bathing ritual usually allowed me to order my thoughts—and my plan of attack—for the day. But missing the dreamthink left me in the grip of the nightmare images. If only I could wash them away, too, along with the sticky dregs of the night.

These dreams had been more specific than usual. A wolf fighting heavy chains, howling in hoarse rage, shedding fire and ash as the sea churned beyond, bloodred and crimson dark, bones tossed in the waves, white as foam. Then the tower that fell into a pile of golden rubble, then to fine sand, the grains sliding against one another with soul-grinding whispered screams.

I often got fragments like that—memories of the forgotten empires and abandoned kingdoms, mourning their lost kings and queens, forever replaying their deaths and destruction.

But in these dreams, I'd been present. I'd stepped close to the wolf, ignoring the falling tower, the distant cries of the flowers as they burned, shedding crimson petals into the sea to stain the waves, and put my hands on the wolf's chains. He savaged my bare hands with his fangs, my blood running into the sea also, staining it. Screaming with the pain, Calanthe fell in fire and ash while I ignored Her cries and persisted in my foolish task. Breaking my fingers on the wolf's manacles, I tried to free it, knowing it would be the death of me, the ruin of all I loved and had vowed to protect. Then, in place of the wolf, a voiceless man stood, holding out an empty hand. A demand. A question.

None of it made any sense. There was nothing I could do to help the world.

I'd considered asking my diviners for their interpretation, but some quality of the dreams made me afraid to describe them aloud. If I knew any wizards, I'd ask them. Calanthe spoke to me in Her own ways that even my brightest philosophers could never understand—especially those not born on the island. No matter how many invitations I sent to bring the best, brightest, and most creative to Calanthe, no one had ever answered the call who could answer my questions.

The land communicates in images and symbols, in the

blooming of the flowers and the fall of the rain, the songs of the birds and the swish of fish through the waters, whispering into my dreamthink self, sometimes in the florid movements of the orchid ring. My father only hinted at how I'd have to learn to interpret what Calanthe tells me before he died so precipitously. In this, as with so many things, I was on my own.

I had to consider that the change in the dreams meant something dire.

An omen. A warning.

But of what?

2

The imperial soldier screamed as I swung my hammer in a remorseless arc. The sound stopped, silenced by the satisfying crunch of his skull collapsing. Mad joy filled me, along with the taste of blood and grit—and the sweetness of vengeance.

But only until I sighted the next target. Leaping, I used the momentum to swing my bagiroca and punch it into the soldier's kidneys. The thick leather bag filled with heavy stones dropped him to his knees. I brought round the rock hammer in my other hand in a counterswing to the head that crumpled the man. With him down, I took out another soldier trying to sneak up on Sondra's back, cleanly crushing him with the same one, two strike. Freed to focus on her opponent, she launched into a sequence of furious slices, her sword flashing in the sun, reducing the soldier to a bleeding pile to join his fellows.

"Thanks, Conrí!" she called, flashing a satisfied smile. A feral, lethally sharp smile, and one that mirrored my own, no doubt. After all the years of chains, labor, and lashings, none of us tired of this—the freedom to strike back. The clean rush of retribution and victory. If only for that moment.

I roared, pointing the army behind me to surge forward,

and we both wheeled to find the next volunteer to die. A phalanx of soldiers approached from the off side and I launched myself at the nearest of them, muscles singing with power. Here was the strength they nurtured by forcing me to labor for them in the mines. Here was the hammer they handed me to crush the rocks they coveted. They created me, all that I am, and I relished using it to beat their evil brains from their useless bodies.

Sweat ran in hot cracks through the dust coating me, hair whipping into my face driven by the coastal wind. Ignoring all of it, I chewed through their ranks, mentally howling the mantra of my revenge. *Rocks. Hammer. Rocks. Hammer.* Like a hero of the old tales, except there was nothing good or noble left in me. The child prince called Conrí had died when he'd been imprisoned and then escaped from the mines as the King of Slaves. They meant to mock me with it, but I owned the title. *Rocks. Hammer. Rocks. Hammer.*

The imperial soldiers fell before my might like wheat before a farmer's scythe. The Slave King's gruesome harvest, making the worthless into fertilizer.

One sweet day it would be Anure returning to the shit he sprang from.

A boom crashed over the landscape. False thunder shook the already faltering ranks of the enemy. Weak as well as worthless. Only the spineless and morally corrupt could stomach working for the false emperor, especially since we'd offered them the honorable alternative of joining the rebellion. The defense broke, imperial soldiers scattering. Some ran for the forest bordering the Keiost plain. Others for the city that would no longer be their haven.

To my right, Sondra streaked after one group, golden hair streaming, looking like a lioness running down her hapless prey. Her warriors followed, ululating their terrible glee. If the soldiers surrendered in time, they might be given a chance. A single opportunity to convert.

I took a moment to assess the positions of my people and theirs. Calling out the orders, the shout grating painfully in my throat, I sent units to run down the soldiers fleeing for the woods. The ones hoping for protection of the city walls would be taken care of soon enough. They'd neatly trapped themselves for us.

The wind shifted, bringing the tang of vurgsten in billows of sulfurous yellow, thick with the grit of exploded rock. My scarred lungs spasmed at the searing contact. I hated the accursed stuff. And not only for the way it made my chest tighten and my lungs labor to draw air. Even after all these months out of the mines, the smell reminded me of slow suffocation in the close tunnels, body aching in every joint from the hard labor. Still, I made myself inhale it, sucking in its foulness as if breathing the sweetest of perfumes, letting it fuel my rage and resolve.

After all, how delicious that we used the emperor's vurgsten—his own secret weapon that he'd nearly killed us to mine for him—to fight the war to destroy him forever. *He who controls vurgsten controls the empire.* Not one of the wizard's mystical bits of obscure advice, but my own hard-won insight.

Anure had controlled us with his vile rock. Now we'd destroy him with it. Nothing like taking the arrow meant for you and sending it back on your assassin. Anure had orchestrated his own demise. The false emperor made me into his slave and his enemy when I was only a child. He bestowed on me the brutal training that forged my body into the weapon that would bring down the empire. He'd forced us all to mine the toxic rocks, thinking to use and discard the children of the nobles he'd crushed. But we were a tool that turned in Anure's hand. We became his doom.

Another boom, rolling out and thundering back. Right on schedule. The walls should be down now. I climbed a small hill, legs pumping with strain after battling since before dawn, and squinted into the lowering sun that glanced off the sea beyond Keiost. The walled city stood in silhouette, dark and stolid amid the green coastal marshes. Its famed golden tower gleamed against the sky. As poetic in reality as in the songs and paintings, the Tower of Simitthu speared like a ray of sunlight beaming out of the squat stone castle beneath it.

Most of the city hid behind its high walls, once a nearly perfect circle. But there, on one side, the line broke, the neat architecture crumbling as if impacted by a giant rock hammer swung by Sawehl Himself. Not at the well-defended, grand entrance, but on the poor side. The Slave Gate.

One more way to use imperial blindness against them.

A third boom, and the rest of the wall fell. Where the gate had been, a hole gaped as wide as a toothless mouth. Led by General Kara, our reserve army rose from the mudflats, lethal weeds sprouting from the tall grasses, and poured through the opening to take the city. Below me, the soldiers our battalions had drawn away from the city's defense—the ones who hadn't already fled to the woods in terror—turned in response to the shouted commands of their leaders. They broke into a run, hurrying to defend walls that were no longer theirs.

Yes, the vurgsten fumes smelled sweet, indeed. I inhaled, savoring the burn.

Then I raised my hammer for all to see, calling the charge to chase the hapless troops. With a roar, my army surged past, racing for the final kill. The imperial forces in front of the main gates moved, but sluggishly. *Too late*. They tried to cross the bridge over the brackish moat, to escape the lethal pincer we brought down on them. Loosing the last chains on my restraint, I charged downhill, leading all those we'd recruited to share in vengeance to smash the city's defenders. We became the hammer that crushed the soldiers, pinning them between their erstwhile servants and the no-longer-friendly walls.

I spotted my own people on the parapets, dropping vurgsten charges on the soldiers below. Those too close to the explosions died outright, while those who tried to flee found themselves mired in the moat embedded with more vurgsten planted with subtlety in the quiet of the nights before.

Our curse and cure in one, the vurgsten rocks enabled us to destroy the imperial forces wherever they posed any challenge. We'd started small, as we'd been few—but far from weak. Toughened by years of hard labor and emptied of compassion, we conquered and took over first one deteriorating estate. Then another. After that we conquered poor villages, then barely more prosperous towns, one by one. Guile in one hand, might in the other, we created our own empire of revenge.

In truth, it had been easier than I'd ever expected. Far more than the initial rebellion and escape. Doing that had been ascending the mountain, and we'd fully expected to die in the effort. After that, each new target had been a risk, and we'd been just as glad to perish. Better to die free than live in prison. No one had been more surprised than I that we kept winning.

Now we hurtled downhill, an avalanche of rage and revenge that none could slow, much less halt. Not that we met many obstacles worth the name anymore.

In his confidence—his megalomaniacal complaisance—Anure had let his forces in the outlying countryside thin to the point of fragility amid the broken scattering of the kingdoms he'd consumed and virtually discarded once he bled them dry. In his paranoia, he refused to stock them with vurgsten, hoarding it all for himself at his citadel in Yekpehr. Complacent and greedy, he cared only for the goods his vassals tithed. In that forgetting, he'd made yet another mistake.

A man who took loyalty, who manipulated, tricked, and forced it from people, had acquired a worthless commodity indeed. People's memories were short for being intimidated, and long on the bitterness from the horrors of conquest. Even the imperial soldiers had little to motivate them. Most of those soldiers—often conscripts to begin with—had been exiled for poor attitudes or worse performance, then also forgotten. Corrupt, incompetent, or disloyal, they either threw in with the rebels or died at the hands of those they'd brutalized.

Before I could count them, my group grew from less than a dozen desperate escaped fugitives to a small, committed army. Even the greater defenses at the minor seaports of Esaq, Irst, and Hertaq fell quickly to our determination and the judicious use of vurgsten. Once I possessed a navy of fishing vessels and sailors more than willing to try for bigger fish, I figured it was time to do something truly ambitious.

And lo! There fell the walls of Keiost, the golden city by the sea, struck down by our hands. The imperial governor for this entire region would be squatting somewhere inside, a tender morsel to be plucked from the bones. *He who controls vurgsten controls the empire.* I sent a prayer to my father's spirit, the victory missing only his presence. Vurgsten killed him and now became my own weapon.

How he'd laugh at that. All I could do, however, was send his restless spirit more blood. More men to die for all those of lost and forgotten Oriel who'd followed their king to their doom.

I swung the rock hammer, mining more of Anure's men to pay for all the horrors they'd wrought. The wolf prince had grown up and broken his chains, thirsty for vengeance. One day it would be Anure himself, and then it would be enough.

As much as anything ever could be.

3

"If Your Highness will look to the sky," Tertulyn coaxed, breaking into my dark thoughts and affixing the crystal-tipped black silk lashes to my lower lids. The glue itched already. Small pains. Requiring nothing more of me than this simple compliance, Tertulyn returned to her muted conversation with the other ladies and the Glory. I let their soft words tinkle in the background, relaxing as the fall of water—a peace I was unlikely to have again until the end of the day.

For the moment I wore a simple silk shift, to protect me from the bite of the corset I'd soon be encased in from hip to collarbone. A queen mustn't slouch or sag, no matter how long the day, and this one promised to be endless. Until then, for a short time longer, I could enjoy the freedom of movement and cooling breezes before the sweltering commenced in earnest.

Ibolya, one of my junior ladies, filed my toenails, hiding their true nature with glued-on bits of abalone shell, while Nahua did the same to my fingers, though those would be covered with fitted, jeweled tips with long, wicked points. I'd had to give up the simple expedience of gloves when I took the orchid ring. I liked the curved metallic thorns, however. They suited me and gave a message: I guard my blossoms of all kinds with wicked barbs.

Tertulyn painted on my makeup personally, covering my skin to smooth perfection. She's done it since we were girls together and is an artist beyond compare in creating the mask I wear for the world. Once she finished, my ladies would dress me in the costume I'd chosen the night before. The day called for virginal white, if one ever did, with Syr Leuthar returned from his extended consultation with the emperor.

His absence had been like a holiday and I now faced a return to the onus of dealing with him. His ship's sails had been spotted out beyond the barrier reef at sunset—though the seas around Calanthe had murmured to me of the foreign ships' arrival for some time before that—along with several more. If I could sink those ships and guarantee the emperor's men never again set their foul feet on Calanthe's soil, I would.

As it was, all I could do was continue my father's desperate game. When I'd been only twelve years old, King Gul had betrothed me to Emperor Anure—a clever plan, if one of last resort. He'd made Calanthe and myself into the emperor's concubines—but at a protected and cherished remove. Coy and virginal, allowing ourselves to be viewed from a distance. As princess of Calanthe and sole heir, I'd known from childhood that I'd have to marry for duty.

Barely a woman, I'd been terrified of the loathsome Anure and the way his gaze crawled over me. Even then I'd worn the elaborate gowns and makeup, but he'd made me feel naked and helpless. Only my father's repeated explanations and reassurances helped cool my panic, and I locked my fears away with my girlish heart. If I stayed smart, Anure might own me and my island paradise in name, but he'd never fully possess either. Not while I lived.

Could the manacled wolf in my dreams represent the emperor and the danger he posed? The blood could symbolize the loss of my carefully guarded virtue, the breaking of my fingers on its chains my attempts to resist the captivity I could never escape.

Somehow I didn't think so. Anure had cast a chilling shadow over my fate and Calanthe's for most of my life. The nightmare of the chained wolf was much more . . . acute. Violent. Disastrous. Full of terrible omens. Especially coinciding with Leuthar's return.

I had to consider that the portents might be connected to the rumors of the rebellions. They thickened in the air like a hatch of flower flies—equally irritating and without substance, easily batted away until they returned to buzz in one's ears. I was keen to discover how much truth the rumors contained, which was one positive of Leuthar's return. His ships brought information more detailed than dream images, small compensation for his insidious presence.

Usually Tertulyn would have mentioned gossip to me by now, cloaked in niceties to spare the Glory dangerous or upsetting information. Tertulyn's reports helped me calculate what the day ahead would hold, as she heard what I could not at the late-night parties I couldn't attend, not and maintain the reputation of virginity that protected me. I still allowed the more licentious customs of the Flower Court to flourish. Another of the concubine's costumes, Calanthe's abandoned revelry. We appeared carefree. Surely we kept no thoughts of resistance in such frivolous hearts, no secrets in such empty heads.

We had our rules for daylight, and other rules for night. Once I, the eternal virgin ever faithful to her betrothal, retired to my apparently innocent bed, the court cut the bonds of propriety. The wine flowed, sensual games commenced, and tongues loosened. As I possessed my network of Calanthe's denizens who reported to me on the doings of the realm and the lands beyond, Tertulyn had formed her own web of informants among the courtiers. At her own waking rituals, the ladies who dressed *her* reported on the nocturnal events of my palace, which she faithfully related to me.

That she'd said nothing so far that morning could mean there was nothing to say . . . or something else. If the dreams were true portents, I needed more insight into what news Leuthar would bring to his audience with me. He liked to catch me by surprise. I liked to make sure he didn't.

Surely Anure hadn't decided to send for me and make me his bride in fact. The thought sent a shiver up my spine, and Tertulyn noticed.

"Your Highness?" she inquired.

"I hope the entertainments were enjoyable last night," I remarked, as if in idle conversation.

"Not so, Your Highness," she replied immediately. "Many hostesses were quite deflated to have their parties poorly attended without their guest of honor."

Aha. No wonder she hadn't yet shared the gossip with me. Leuthar hadn't made it in last night. They must have arrived too late for the tide and anchored beyond the barrier reef. My dreams had been too dominated by the cries from far away for Calanthe's waters to speak to me of that. Also, a ship at the reef or in our harbor seemed much the same to the vast and shifting seas.

"Has the emissary's ship yet docked this morning then?" I pretended I didn't know he'd brought more ships with him. What Calanthe confided in me I kept to myself.

"It hadn't when I woke You, though it might have by now." Tertulyn briefly met my gaze as she drew the rose-pink lines for my lips and cheekbones. Reading my intent, she flicked a glance at Calla, who curtsied and glided out of the dressing chamber. Tertulyn switched to a brush to black my eyebrows. Wielding her palette of precise tools, she painted in all the definition the alabaster paste concealed.

Calla returned with several folded letters and the news that not only had the emissary's ship docked, but three others with it. Surprise, surprise. The former meant court would begin on time. Not that they could start without me, but I'd rather tweak the emperor's nose with something more important than keeping his emissary waiting while I dallied with primping. The latter . . . I didn't know what it meant except that more ships meant more of the emperor's men, and another indication that the tides of events had shifted. I couldn't have gone on forever at my precarious stalemate, but I snarled internally like that nightmare wolf at feeling the bite of my chains.

Sorting through the intricately folded letters, Tertulyn set most aside, for her or my royal secretary to deal with, but one she gave to me. That was something. One of my spies in the emissary's party had sent news in the guise of a letter from a friend.

Tertulyn proceeded apace with the rest of my cosmetics while I read, and the other ladies distracted Glory with trimming flowers for my gown and wig. The letter rambled on about the romantic intrigues of the emperor's court, before settling on a long description of the fashions imported from Keiost. An involuntary murmur of unhappy surprise escaped me. The portents positively rained down.

Tertulyn's gaze snagged mine in mute question. Now was not the time for outside ears.

"Thank you, Glory, for your service to Me." I raised my

voice, keeping my tone as kind as I could, even as my heart beat wildly, assimilating the impossible. Never had the long-distance wails of foreign lands proved to be so accurate. Time to send the girl away. "Will you stay awhile in the capital?"

"Your Highness, yes." She curtsied again, deeply, speaking barely above a whisper. "My family is with me. We hope to visit the map room and see other sights."

"Enjoy some on Me." I nodded to Calla, who gave the girl a gold coin stamped with my likeness. Anure had "gifted" me with a treasury of the things. I would've commanded her to spend it—the price it would fetch could likely feed her family for a full year—but many of the girls kept them, along with their souvenir scarf folded in the queen's style, on my specially dyed paper, with a personal note of thanks from me. My ladies penned those for me, but each evening I affixed my signature for the next morning. Another of my little rituals, planning for the sun to indeed rise once more.

And that Calanthe would still be whispering harmoniously when sunrise came.

Calla led the Glory out of the chamber to hand over to the guards to be escorted away. As soon as she was out of earshot, I relieved their suspense. "It seems that the latest styles from Keiost are all in shades of red."

Tertulyn's hand trembled, pausing in her task of gluing the tiny jewels to their proper places at the corners of my eyes and mouth. She closed her eyes, lips moving in a prayer for the family she had in Keiost, the other ladies falling into furious whispering, relaying the information to Calla when she returned. They were intimate enough with me to understand the codes. Red for blood. The rumors of uprising were true. And as always, it was the common people who died.

My father had taught me this. The emperor didn't suffer when war ravaged his empire. He stayed lazy and overfed on his throne while we tore one another's throats out fighting to get to him. Why trouble himself if we killed one another? Another of the many reasons that rebelling against him harmed only ourselves. My father's untimely death only proved that point.

I touched Tertulyn's hand to steady it, for a moment seeing an overlay from the dream, of my own fingers, broken and bloody from the chains. An escaped wolf leading an uprising. It couldn't be coincidence. But who could this mongrel leader be? For he had to be common. None of the old royalty were left outside their genteel captivity in the emperor's citadel at Yekpehr. Besides me.

"We'll find out more," I told Tertulyn. She nodded, her face, clear and lovely as a doll's, showing no concern. All of my ladies were exemplary, and Tertulyn the best of them.

Her hands steady again, Tertulyn finished, then invited me to stand. Even with the Glory gone, we observed our ritualistic formalities. The ladies all gathered round, fastening the structures to support my gown onto the rigid corset. Six ladies assist my toilet, and not because I love having a crowd around me. It takes four of them to support the jewel-encrusted material while two sew it into place—one on each side, to ensure symmetry.

A courtier attempting to rise in prominence through his wit once jested that my court gear weighed more than a soldier in full armor headed into battle. I hadn't found it at all funny. Let him wear my gown for even an hour. There's a reason my parade steed is the same stalwart breed as those the armored warriors ride.

And though my armor consists of jewels and flowers, I am no less resolved than those dandies in metal shells. It protects something precious to more than myself. What happened to Keiost would never happen to Calanthe.

As the final step, the ladies lowered the day's wig, white to match my gown, onto my bare scalp. Tertulyn added spots of glue to hold it in place, although most of that would be up to me—and to the years of posture training ingrained in me. The other ladies circled me with baskets of fresh flowers, studding the elaborate ivory tresses with blossoms of all kinds.

Then they affixed the crown of Calanthe. Fortunately for my neck it was remarkably light for all its jeweled glory. With sapphires, aquamarines, and diamonds set in a frame of shining loops and arcs of purest platinum, the crown evokes the sea that surrounds Calanthe. It is the waves and the light upon the water, and all who live within.

My ladies presented me with the looking glass and I surveyed their work, though I hardly needed to. I looked as I always had, preserved like a blossom under glass, perfectly groomed to present the perfect image. The Flower Queen of Calanthe. This set of five ladies had been with me for nearly three years and knew their business well. Tertulyn had been with me for over twenty years—ever since she came from the court at Keiost to foster with us at the beginning of Anure's rampages—and we knew each other like the insides of our own hearts. I'd have been lost without her. To show it, I plucked a flower from my hair and tucked it into her canary-bright wig.

She produced a smile for me, perfect in every way. Good girl.

Suitably clad in my flower-strewn and jeweled armor, I descended from my chambers to battle to keep at least my small, unspoiled paradise in the light.

4

"Good morning, Your Highness," the young squire blurted. "I'm pleased to report that Keiost is yours. General Kara asks me to inform you that our wounded are being tended, their wounded dispatched, and the survivors assembled, awaiting your arrival. Victory is ours," he added unnecessarily. Clean and wearing a fresh set of clothes, General Kara's squire grinned with the cheeky triumph of one too young to understand the cost of war.

I nodded at him, not yet ready to test my voice, scanning the camp and the battlefield beyond. What did I hope to see? Confirmation that the bloodshed had been worth it, perhaps. Now that I'd come down from the battle rage—and up from the sleep of exhaustion—seeing what we'd wrought only sickened me. I'd rather feel the glee, the savage satisfaction. Vengeance tasted best hot. In the unflinching light of what should be a beautiful morning, I had no stomach for such a cold dish, or for celebration.

But Keiost was mine, at long last. Hopefully it would hold the information the wizard promised.

"Your Highness?" The squire made the question a reminder. The boy's name escaped me at the moment. Brad? Bard? Names mattered, but I'd passed the point of being able to keep track of everyone in my growing armies. And today I'd more than double that by adding the people of Keiost.

Depending on how many chose not to be added.

Enough of dark thoughts. Kara and the others waited on me. Stripping off my shirt, I dunked my head in the waiting bucket. The cold water helped wake me, too. Dragging a hand through my hair, I tried to dislodge the worst of the blood and grime. Not easy. This was the price of not bathing before exhaustion claimed me.

Of course, it was also the price of refusing to cut my hair ever again. Call it pride. Call it superstition. When I'd been Prince Conrí, I'd worn my hair as I pleased until the day Anure's soldiers clapped me in chains, shaved my head, and dragged me off to the mines. I'd promised myself—the vow of the boy I'd been, with all the certainty and passion of childhood—that one day I'd break the chains and never again cut my hair.

That boy had seen and suffered so much, I owed him that much, to keep that promise.

I made quick work of dunking my head—the icy water clearing the dregs of dead sleep from my brains—and splashing water over my face and chest, then donning the clean garb Kara's squire brought me. No time to shave, but my grizzled appearance would likely go a long way toward hammering home the message I must to deliver to the people of Keiost. At least no one expected a king of slaves to be pretty.

Slicking back my wet hair, I tied it into a queue with a strip of leather, then snagged my "crown" and donned it. Finally I slung my cloak over my shoulders. I looked like no king of old, by any stretch. But then, I wasn't one. I'd lost Oriel, lost the land of my father, forever, both of us cut adrift.

"Let's go," I said, my voice gruff from sleep and not

speaking, throat sore from pushing out shouts of command. Even at my best, though, I sounded like a dog chained so long that its manacled collar had strangled its voice into a hoarse parody. "You did well yesterday," I added, to sound less curt, though the words snagged, burning, and I couldn't suppress a cough. The boy's grin widened, happy to be so honored, unperturbed at being unnamed. A good lesson there, that what I considered important didn't always matter to everyone else.

Or often, to anyone else.

Soldiers sprang to their feet and saluted as we passed, the tang of vurgsten hanging still thick in the air, and my lungs tightened with familiar pain. Surely this would be enough. With possession of Keiost—and its famed tower—no matter what the wizard Ambrose did or didn't find, this victory should at least give us the forces, and more important the ships, to get me to Anure. The emperor sat fat and greasy on his stolen throne beyond that sea, and so that's where I would go.

Take the Tower of the Sun,
Claim the hand that wears the Abiding Ring,
And the empire falls.

Ambrose's words—albeit obscure and poetic—had become my mantra these many months. Another irony, as I distrusted magic and disliked poetry. My father, King Tuur of Oriel, like so many kings and queens that fell before Anure's might, had believed in and followed the advice of his wizards.

It hadn't saved us or Oriel. That's the problem with prophecy—too much is left open to semantics. The court wizard of Oriel had seen death in the cards, but not how or when. And my father . . . maybe he simply couldn't envision the fall of his kingdom. Certainly not to the upstart would-be emperor. King Tuur had been convinced that the "death" the wizard saw represented transformation.

Instead it had meant our utter destruction. I'd been only a boy then, not privy to political discussions, particularly ones that dire. But my father had spoken of it often enough in the mines, hashing and rehashing every wrong turn and least decision that led to that terrible day we lost everything. My father had no throne to leave me, but he did have his stories still.

So I never—almost never—argued with Ambrose. The wizard had attached himself to me, begging physical protection in a world where wizards no longer existed, in return for his advice and guidance. No one but Ambrose had predicted I'd see this day. Keiost of all places. And yet here I was, guided by poetry and magic. How my father would laugh at his recalcitrant son.

How I wished I could hear him laugh—or remember my sister's face smiling instead of contorted in those last screaming moments of horror and pain—just once more.

I shook off the dark thoughts. No one would be laughing if the "Tower of the Sun" turned out not to be the one here at Keiost. Once Ambrose had spoken those words, I'd been sure of it—at least in that moment—and the memory had come back to me, the poetry read in my tutor's voice during that childhood when I'd been privileged enough to be soft and bored. *Built entirely with marble as golden as the sun.*

Like most memories of that brief and shining boyhood, however, I'd taken them out and pored over them so many times that they'd become worn, tattered, and full of holes. They'd also taken on a sheen I didn't trust. Surely I hadn't been that happy and carefree.

Sometimes it was easier to tell myself I'd made all of that up. Otherwise remembering what I'd lost became more than I could bear. And I had promises to keep before I crumbled.

Spotting us, Sondra strode up. Her hair streamed, defiantly unbound, pale gold in the sunlight. Like so many of us, she'd relished letting it grow, so I hardly blamed her the indulgence. But it made for an incongruous effect, the rippling hair of a young maid around her ravaged face.

The sight never failed to stab at me, though I'd never tell her so. The mines had left their stamp on all of us, leaving us dark and pockmarked like a permanent burn corroded into our skin. Sondra had been a lovely girl. Older than me by five years, the daughter of one of our nobles and my sister's best friend, Sondra had ruled all the hearts at court with her sweet face and sweeter voice. She'd lived through that terrible day, surviving when so many, including my sister, died from their injuries.

Sondra had knelt beside me to have her glorious hair shorn, her delicate limbs placed in manacles, to work in the mines with us. Now those elegant bones, which had once portended that she would become one of the great beauties of Oriel, had sharpened into blades threatening to pierce her leathery complexion. Even her eyes had toughened somehow. No longer softly full of laughter, they'd hardened like the rest of her. As we all had.

Harden or die was the lesson of Vurgmun.

"Conrí. My king." She bowed, stiff in her armor, helm tucked beneath her arm. I bit down on the reflex to tell her not to call me that. She wouldn't listen. She returned my scowl with her fierce, flesh-eating grin and paced alongside. "*Take the Tower of the Sun.* Who'd have thought we'd make it this far?" She didn't wait for an answer. She was the one whose faith had never flagged. Instead she gave me a piercing look. "Did you sleep? You don't look like it."

I nodded, not planning to waste breath on convincing her. "Casualties?" I asked.

She lifted a shoulder, rotating her sword arm in a half shrug, half reiteration of the pitched battle. "Ten percent or so. Mostly imperial soldiers and fat slugs of the governor's staff. No great loss."

For whatever reason, her voice had survived better than most, though the nightingale soprano she'd been famed for was forever lost. She spoke with a whiskey burr that might give a sultry sound to the old songs, but the world would never know. Sondra refused to sing ever again, saying that girl had died. I understood that. Our younger selves had all died in the mines, and we'd emerged as hard-shelled but empty versions of those children.

I didn't care for her cavalier attitude, however. Sondra's black humor had helped her survive, but killing innocents was no joke. I didn't have much in the way of morals, but I didn't kill without offering the choice. We always gave them the opportunity to change loyalties. The accountants and secretaries that served the imperial governors wore chains the same as any of us, just invisible ones that imprisoned them at desks. Insane that this war of ours required so many to suffer and perish, while the man who caused it all dined on delicacies.

"We killed staff?" I asked, growling the question I'd hoped to keep neutral.

"Us or them," she replied with impatience.

"Fat slugs were a threat?"

She scowled. "You'd be surprised at the stings some vermin conceal beneath their jeweled robes."

I said nothing more about it. It was done. No sense in reviving a stale argument, and I wouldn't want to trigger any of her old memories. Aside from a decided tendency to kill certain men in the most painful way possible if they reminded her of the wrong sort, Sondra kept her most vicious thirst for vengeance mostly under control. We all had our festering wounds and managed them the best way we could. The escaped slaves and other victims that couldn't wrestle their demons . . . Well, most of them had imploded—or exploded—early on. The ones who managed to keep going I treated like packages of vurgsten: carefully handled and pointed only at the enemy. Sondra included.

"Any sign of the former king's bloodline?" I asked, hoping to steer her away from brooding down a dark path. We never found any descendants of the former ruling families, no matter whose realm it had once been. As much as Anure scoffed at the old ways and sneered at the superstitions of blood ties to the land, he'd been thorough in killing or imprisoning the old families. Still, I always asked, some part of me unable to believe they'd all been obliterated. Part of me childishly longing to restore rightness to the world that my adult self knew was forever lost.

"Nowhere to be found," Sondra replied. "Conflicting rumors regarding them—some say dead, others say fled. Could be even worse than that, you know. The young princesses would have fetched a high price in the underground flesh markets, if Anure didn't simply keep them for himself." Sondra shrugged in a show of callousness far thicker than mine. "That trail would be years cold. Can't save everyone," she added.

It might as well be our credo. If I had a crest—which would be a set of broken chains like those that had choked me and killed Father—the cynical motto would fit perfectly. But I hadn't sunk that far. Not quite yet. "That doesn't mean we won't try," I said, and it came out as a growl again, not only because of my sore throat.

Sondra flashed me a surprised glance. I shook my head,

dismissing her concern. Not enough sleep, that I'd spoken that aloud. But she inclined her head in agreement. "That's why we saved the *ex*-imperial-governor"—she emphasized that with relish—"for you to interrogate. Though I may have softened him up for you." She smiled, not at all nicely. I restrained a sigh, almost feeling sympathy for the bastard. Hopefully she hadn't terrorized the man past coherent speech.

"And Ambrose?" I asked.

"Found the alchemist's library and workroom *in the tower*." She tossed her hair over her shoulder with some glee, a vicious triumph in what had once been a flirtatious gesture, sweeping her hand toward the golden tower that stood out against the sky.

"And no," Sondra added, "before you ask. We didn't have to kill the alchemist. To all appearances, the place has been abandoned for years. Probably dead along with all the other magic workers. Ambrose says he'll send for you when he has information—or a new insight into the future."

Oh joy. I only hoped it would be useful information, like the kind that would have me taking a force to kill Anure.

"Take the king through there, Bert." Sondra pointed as we arrived at a narrow tunnel. She handed me a flask that contained the honeyed herb infusion Ambrose brewed to soothe my throat long enough to last through a speech. "Better entrance for the rabble to first glimpse their new and forever king. I'll guard the rear."

Bert. That was the boy's name. I made a mental note before throwing Sondra a reproving look. "These people you call rabble will soon be your companions at arms."

"You might change your mind once you see them," she retorted, adding a crooked smile.

She was trying to cheer me up. Which meant I'd failed to lead. So I drank deeply of the unpleasant brew, then toasted her with it, trying to appear as if I savored this victory. She saluted me, looking relieved, so I'd been at least partially successful. I followed young Bert through the shadowed portico and into the bright sun of the open stage. Trumpets blasted, the ringing tones encouraging me to feel as majestic as they proclaimed. My officers ringed the stage at attention, all clean and neatly attired. They saluted in unison, a striking maneuver, one we'd practiced many times—though we'd never before defeated a city this size—and I acknowledged them curtly, my role in this elaborate staging.

We all know that any performance requires a costume.

The leather cloak I'd stitched together with my own hands over many nights by the campfire streamed from my shoulders. No, it's not made from the skins of my enemies, though that's a useful rumor. The crown weighed heavy on my brow. The crown is a deliberate inversion of tradition. Made of silver, we looted it from minor nobility who'd thrown in with Anure and thus kept their lands and wealth. Until we relieved them of their greedy gains bought with the blood of the land and people they'd been supposed to protect.

It had been one of the first estates we captured. The more minor the house, it seemed, the more elaborate the badges of office. When Sondra showed the crown to me, I'd rejected it immediately as too gaudy and uncomfortable. She insisted I had to have one—and when did I plan to find another?—so I'd conceded as the easier path. But I'd wrapped the sparkling thing in leather strips left over from the cloak, to at least help keep it on my head. Also, we'd needed the funds from the jewels more than I needed a flashy crown, so we prized those out to be sold for supplies. I'd rather liked the gaping holes left behind, as they seemed appropriately symbolic.

Kara had been the one to suggest filling the holes with polished black stones from Vurgmun. We all had our supplies of them that we'd collected—bitter souvenirs of a time best forgotten—so we'd spent an evening in someone's looted salon, drinking their excellent contraband liquor, laughing at the fine joke as we refitted the broken crown with stones gathered by prisoners in the mines. The perfect crown for a king of convicts.

And it was nothing like my father's crown, which had been set with the jewels of Oriel, handed down for over a thousand years, a magical totem symbolic of the king's connection to the realm. Anure had said from the beginning that magic didn't exist and he proved it to be true by relentlessly destroying every aspect of it, merely symbolic or not. The crown was lost—along with the realm—and rumored to have been melted down to serve as part of the emperor's chamber throne, where he shat his final insults to those who'd resisted imperial aggression.

In the end, they were all empty symbols. Crowns and costumes. Magic, too, if it had ever been real. But I'd use whatever I must in order to win my vengeance and put the restless shades of my family and kingdom to rest at last.

At center stage, I stopped, surveying the throng crowding the extensive escarpment below. As Sondra had snidely implied, they did not impress. The people looked ragged. Too thin and too poor for denizens of this prosperous capital city. Regardless, they looked better off than we had when we escaped the mines and taken our own lives back. I'll never forget that first glimpse in the mirror, its too-bright reflection wiped free of dust. How that soft-faced boy I'd remembered had somehow swelled into a hard-faced monster of big bones and ropy muscle, a scarred wraith of burning anger.

I'd avoided mirrors ever since. Judging by the uneasy silence of the crowd, their aghast faces as they stared at me, not much had changed. I forced down the insidious doubts, the brutal mockery of the overseers, the whispers of all the dead, my father's lifeless and accusing gaze, my sister's dying whimpers as the soldiers had at her.

I raised my fists, though I hardly needed to silence the defeated and suspicious gathering. They waited, braced for the worst. No matter how many times I'd given this speech, unease crawled down my spine, and not just in anticipation of the discomfort of projecting my voice and speaking so many words in a row. I cleared my throat, hoping Ambrose's brew had done its work.

"People of Keiost." My voice boomed out, raspy, but carrying reasonably well. "I offer you a new day, a new life, if you choose it. Though we have all passed through a long night of death, destruction, and misery, let us put that in the past and forge a new direction, together. I am the Slave King." A murmur through the crowd at that, though surely they'd known. Perhaps they simply wondered at my audacity in owning the insult. "*Your* king. The ones who called themselves your imperial governors, the puppets of a distant and uncaring empire, they are dead or imprisoned. Your lives belong to me now. I grant each of you a single choice, which you must make today. Give me your allegiance—swear it by Sawehl and Ejarat—or give me your death."

Utter silence settled at the grim words. The words of a tyrant, of an autocrat as ruthless as Anure ever was. They didn't know I had no choice in this, either. I was a fraudulent king. One without lands, castles, dungeons, or camps in which to keep prisoners. Even if I had, I could spare no one to serve as guards, much less supplies to sustain them. We struggled to preserve the supply chain back to Vurgmun, to keep possession of it and our precious supply of vurgsten.

I couldn't afford to have enemies at my back, as I faced entirely forward. A lethal arrow pointed at the emperor's heart. Nothing else mattered.

I let them absorb that blow, then offered the salve. "Give your loyalty to me and I will restore your kingdom to you. If any remain with the blood of the royal family of these lands, come forward to take your rightful place, to resume guardianship of your people and your realm. I have no desire to rule. I ask for your warriors, your supplies, your ships. Make your choice. You will leave this assembly as my vassal or as a body to be burned with those already dead."

Finished, I walked away. We'd refined the speech to the bare minimum, to spare my ravaged throat, but also because nothing more could be said. Through no fault of their own, these people faced the same choice as any prisoner. Submit or die.

5

There's a trick to walking in the elaborate gowns of the Flower Court. The spine must be very straight, with shoulders centered over hips and chin tucked slightly so that the point of the skull aims at the sky. *Imagine standing under a waterfall so that the cool torrent flows into your head, through the column of your neck and down your spine to fill your legs.* My teachers made the practice into an art form that is nearly a religion, complete with the requisite philosophical mantras. That particular lovely image was meant to teach me to carry the immense weight in the legs, rather than in my fragile back.

A woman's strength is in her legs, after all.

Also the chin tuck is critical to balancing the wig and, for me, the crown. And lest you think the brackets at hips and shoulder are simply frames to display the extra jewel- and flower-studded veils, cloaks, and trains, those work to distribute the load, too. Witness the maids of the villages carrying their yokes across their shoulders, buckets of milk or grain dangling from either end. Peasant laborer or queen, we are not so different. Except, perhaps, in the burdens we carry.

I'd never be so trite as to wish to be one of those maids, but I sometimes envied the simplicity of their burdens.

I confess I like the way court waits for me. One of my petty pleasures. When I enter a room, they fall silent in deference to my arrival. After that moment, they relax to some extent, as people familiar tend to do. Besides, I am not so exacting on such protocols. But in that first moment when I enter, they all hold their collective breath, ladies and gents alike keen to see my gown for the day.

Tertulyn has regaled me with the court theories on how my attire and choice of flowers reflect my mood and thus the prospects for the petitions I'll review and for the state of Calanthe at large. Political forecasting based on feminine frippery. There's an underlying truth to it that the older generations remember—that as I am, so is Calanthe—but the younger think it's all my whims.

Courtiers even offer my ladies gifts to slip them hints ahead of time on what I plan to wear. I don't know if they accept those gifts, as it doesn't matter to me. I suppose it's no more flimsy a magical theorem than casting stones or ripping open the innards of some innocent animal that deserved better than to be wasted so.

Still, those courtiers would better spend their time in the study of science. The wizards are dead and the final truth is that no one can know the future because it is fundamentally unknowable. It doesn't exist to be known because *it has not yet occurred*. Simple logic. It baffles me that anyone with wit can think otherwise.

Besides, if I dressed according to my mood, today I'd be in dread gray with accents of days-old blood. Ha! Now there would be a fashion trend to set.

The buzz of court echoed down the back hall, to which I descended each day via my private stairs. I paused there before stepping through the velvet curtains on the dais. A bit of showmanship never hurts. My father, regardless of his other faults, set the bar high there, and I emulate him.

My most junior lady parted the curtains, and those courtiers watching for the movement with the sensitivity of the dependent sycophant—there is no more alert or more desperate creature under Ejarat's gaze—dropped their conversations instantly, the ripples of silence spreading faster than through any other medium. My naturalists inform me that sound travels more quickly in water than in air, because fluid is denser than gas. I, myself, have observed that the air of court is the densest by far of any other human-occupied medium.

A word. A reaction. All ricochet with blazing speed. The reverberations only catch up later, like the tardy thunder chasing after a lightning bolt long since vanished from the sky.

One by one, my ladies preceded me into the bated anticipation of the throne room, in order of seniority and my favor, which amount to the same thing as I give rank to those I trust, and whom I like. A minor exercise of my royal muscles that at least smoothes my daily life. They are my vanguard, my frame, and my first and last line of defense. Never underestimate the blossoms of the Flower Court. We all have our thorns.

I counted to three after the last of Tertulyn's train swished through the doorway. Then I entered, pausing a moment, both to let the gossips assess my outfit—many of them actually jotting down surreptitious notes on the bound pads of paper it had become fashionable to carry and tuck in the various hidden pockets of court garb—and for me to breathe in the tenor of court.

Tense. Fearful, though not fully afraid. Anticipatory. Scanning the faces, I wondered how many had heard the news from Keiost. A few, perhaps, but not many.

Taking small steps—not mincing, *never mince, glide*—I moved to my throne, pausing to rest my hand on Lord

Dearsley's forearm while Tertulyn and Calla arranged my train and skirts. After a decorous moment, I lowered myself onto the hard seat. Dearsley bowed and backed off the dais, though remaining close at hand. He'd been my father's adviser before he was mine, and I valued his experience. For his part, he valued that I actually listened to him—for the most part—as my father had not at the end.

With one last survey of the assembly, letting the moment stretch out, a small public flexing of my power— *never let them forget they sit and stand with* your *permission*—I finally lifted a hand, granting them the opportunity to rest themselves. Tertulyn lowered herself to a chair a step down, at my right hand, the others of my ladies on stools ranged below.

The emperor's emissary remained standing. Of course. He was never one to appear to follow my dictates in any way. At least he'd left his Imperial Guards at the rear of the assembly.

Grandly garbed in the emperor's somber grays and rigid gold armor, Syr Leuthar inclined his jaw ever so slightly but did not bow. He enjoyed special status in my court, and I pretended to be fine with it. My court, my palace, my kingdom even—my land in the most profound way—but all of that belonged to Anure, by force and fear. So did I and so did the emissary. It made us siblings, of a sort, both beholden to a mad parent more likely to starve us or deny our privileges than to care for or guide us. Like those siblings, too, we'd knife the other in the back if it meant our survival.

I could have him killed with a gesture, but that would risk spilling blood in violence on her soil—anathema to living land like Calanthe—and also bring unholy retribution down on us from His Imperial Nastiness. Leuthar could make things difficult for me with Anure, whisper in the emperor's ear of vague treacheries—or, worse, insinuate that I no longer possessed the virginity Anure so prized in his blind certainty that no man in my bed kept me sexually innocent—but that would lose him the plum job of emissary to the wealthiest, loveliest, and most pleasurable of all the emperor's subject kingdoms.

My father had preserved Calanthe in all her pristine beauty, much as he had his daughter, to be Anure's prized possessions he dared not touch lest he ruin them. Leuthar enjoyed the privilege of pride of place, entrusted with those things.

So I made certain that the emissary's spacious rooms with a breathtaking view of the hanging gardens and the sea beyond were always well stocked with his favorite foods, wines, and willing companions of all genders. In return, he reported only glowing tales of my loyalty and behavior.

I wouldn't call us friends. In truth, I had no real friends besides Tertulyn. But our congenial détente served us both.

"Syr Leuthar," I said, allowing the sound of delight to infuse my voice, a sweet jasmine touch. "We have missed you these last weeks. What news do you bring of My old friend, His Imperial Majesty?" I like to try out lies of varying sizes and to see how well I can make them sound sincere.

Syr Leuthar swept off his elaborate hat, less a helm and more a confection like those the court ladies wore perched on their wigs. Some unfortunate bronze bird had given up a significant portion of its tail feathers for the cause.

"His Imperial Majesty sends his regards to the rose of his empire, and also a box of the candied dates You so favor, which I'll have delivered to Your rooms, once the ship has been unloaded. He's also sent a special message of affection for Your Highness." He reached into an inside vest pocket and produced a folded letter on the emperor's stationery, Anure's symbol clear even from that distance. Embossed in deep-gray tones on paper shades lighter, it was a stylized image of the citadel at Yekpehr, the rocks jagged and menacing. Someone had added a pink ribbon to decorate the missive—which I imagined Anure's desiccated heart had thought romantic—but that only made the stark symbol look more grim. Maybe that was just me.

Leuthar vanished the envelope again with the deft sleight of hand practiced by con artists of all types. "I'm to place it in Your hands only," he added with a sly twist of his mouth that insinuated a great deal.

To make a point, I nodded to Tertulyn. Anticipating me, one of her particular gifts, she'd been watching and sprang to her feet as if her gown weighed nothing and drifted light as a petal on a breath of summer wind to the emissary. She curtsied to him with perfect respect, holding out her gloved hand in patient demand. He only flicked a brief glance at me before producing the letter again and laying it in her palm. She brought it to me, her eyes full of lively mirth once only I could see her face, one brow cocked in a way that clearly communicated both her disgust and her amusement.

We both knew what the missive would likely say, and I would read it aloud for her later so we could laugh at it and pretend we weren't afraid of what Anure would do. Such were our bedtime stories. I only hoped it was his usual vague promises and not what I feared.

For the time being, I tucked the vile thing away in one of my own hidden pockets, this one guarded by a cluster of indigo blossoms. The advantage of my grand gowns being so full of air is that I have multiple secret spaces to choose from. "My gratitude." I bestowed a smile on Leuthar with the words. "If that is all, then—"

"I beg Your pardon, Your Highness," Leuthar interrupted, "but I'm afraid I am tasked to bring You distressing news." He paused with great significance—then he had the actual balls to simper at me.

I made sure to seem surprised. It served several purposes to have him think me a blissfully ignorant and loyal vassal. Not the least because sending spies beyond Calanthe made me a traitor. I like my head attached to my neck, thank you. I blinked, long and slow, the glittering crystals on my lashes falling, then rising again. They gave me a sleepy-eyed stare, as if everything that occurred bored me beyond belief. Also a useful impression to give. "Oh?" I cooed. "Not too distressing, I hope. Don't say His Imperial Majesty is unwell!"

We should be so lucky. I liked to suggest it often. If only I'd been born a wizard, I could make it so by repeating it enough. In that case, however, even Anure's lust to possess me wouldn't have preserved my life.

A quicksilver grimace creased the corner of Leuthar's mouth before he smoothed it, shaking his head. "Your concern for the emperor's health does You credit, Your Highness. Not everyone wishes him well as sincerely as You do."

"Well," I said, adding a vague finger-flutter that had Tertulyn suppressing a smile, "I have no quarrel with the emperor. He has always treated Me with tender care." I even produced a simper of my own, far better than curling my lip in contempt—or fear.

One day, no doubt, Anure would find a way to wed me in truth. A dire fate I'd managed to stave off by pretending to wish for it with all my heart, all the while reminding him of his existing stable of wives and citing his own

vows to make me empress. As queen of Calanthe, my rank
fell second only to the emperor himself, but if I became
his fourth wife—no, it would be his fifth wife now that
he'd married the Lady Ibb, practically on the battlefield of
Derten while standing over the corpse of her former husband and king—I'd be lower-ranked than the previous living wives by ancient custom, and unable to be empress.

In destroying magical law, Anure had bound himself to
man's law, and that kept us at an impasse, which had so
far saved me.

I wrote lavish replies to Anure's stomach-turning love
letters. Much as I *loved* him and *longed* for us to be joined,
I just *couldn't* risk angering the ancestors so—or destabi-
lizing the empire by violating the emperor's own laws—
and bringing the wrath of ill luck down on his empire, and
so on and so forth, ad nauseam.

On a less melodramatic note, I frequently reminded him
that compromising my rank that way would make inheri-
tance of the throne of Calanthe problematic, as if it weren't
already. What imperial governor could be trusted with
Calanthe's bounty, which I kept pristine for him and from
which I tithed so generously? I'd managed to continue my
father's gambit and the stalemate that, if tenuous, at least
let me remain on Calanthe. The entire empire viewed me
as the emperor's fiancée in essence, if not reality, which
worked fine for my purposes. And they viewed the endur-
ing beauty of Calanthe as testament to the stability of
Anure's rule.

Syr Leuthar had been blathering on, assuming a grave
expression, using many words and saying very little. He
toyed with the feather on his hat. Nerves? Interesting.

This trouble worried the emperor far more than I'd have
predicted. The news from Keiost mattered to Tertulyn,
thus it mattered to me, but it was a small kingdom with

relatively little wealth, especially after Anure pillaged it. Beyond his propensity to want to own all land and people in existence, the emperor shouldn't be so bothered by a small rebellion. In fact, he enjoyed bloodshed and visiting punishment on those who dared resist. Whatever had happened in Keiost, though bloody, shouldn't reach as high as Anure's seat of power. Not unless something monumental had occurred.

"I must inform You"—Leuthar finally came to the point—"that Keiost has been overrun, fallen to a craven enemy of the empire."

The court gasped as one entity at the words that were tantamount to treachery to even voice aloud. *Enemy of the empire.*

The orchid ring on my finger tightened, petals flexing to send a scent wafting up. The smell of broken iron, old ashes, and new burns. A wolf, dragging its chains.

Whatever the dreams foretold, it had begun.

6

I left the plaza and its conquered populace, swallowing down the grate of ash burning my throat. General Kara quickly caught up and paced alongside me, subtly directing the angle of my escape. "I have the imperial governor confined to his treasure room," he said. "You'll want to interrogate him."

Want wasn't how I'd have phrased that. "Treasure room?" I inquired instead of saying as much. Surely Anure hadn't left much "treasure" behind to be hoarded in Keiost.

"You'll see. The room has the great benefit of being secure." His smile made a lipless slash on his sere, dark face. "In fact, if you want the man to answer any questions, you might hurry, as I can't guarantee the air supply now that we've sealed it."

Sondra bowed as she joined us, Kara's words hanging in the air, her grin as tight and toxic as his. "Your prisoner awaits, Conrí," she said by way of greeting.

I ask only to hold the torch. She didn't speak the words aloud, but I heard them like the day she first spoke them to me. They resonated in my memory like the striking of steel against stone, lingering like the stench of sulfur in the air. Even though it had dissipated in the breeze off the ocean, the vurgsten smoke lingered in the ache between my eyes and the burn in my lungs.

My father had felt that burn as he died, as the vile shit slowly suffocated him. His death had been foul, not fitting for a king. His blood would never return to the soil of Oriel. There had been no state funeral with solemn crowds and violet-stained horses drawing his draped casket. Instead the fallen King Tuur had died bald and emaciated under a cloud of gray ash falling around us like burning snowfall. Knowing the man barely clung to life, the guards and even the overseer had watched from a healthy distance. Dying men brought bad luck, according to the old ways. The specter of mortality swung its weapon in wide arcs, happy enough to take bystanders along with the chosen. Anure might've declared all that to be untrue, but the old superstitions die hard. The guards were hardly enlightened men. They'd left us alone.

And I'd held my father at the end. I'd put my back against a rock, the dying king propped upright against my chest, lying against me like the son I'd never have. An ironic reversal of our roles. Keeping him at that angle let the fluid of infection in his lungs settle to the bottom as much as possible.

Still, he'd drawn in each breath with terrible effort. He strained to inhale. If he'd had air to give voice to the pain, he would have. But he had no breath for screaming. His mouth contorted with it, a wide hole, gaping nearly toothless after years of his body weakening. The hearty grinning father from my youth, the arrogant, untouchable king who'd defied prophecy, boomed orders, and wielded a mighty sword had collapsed into a wraith, a bare skeleton wrapped in weakened parchment, blackened from fire and ash.

The only thing that remained of the father I remembered were his eyes, the fierce blue rheumed and milky, but something of his ferocious spirit still shining within. I'd tried to calm him, but he'd stared up at me, his only remaining son, gasping for life like a dying fish out of water. Desperate to speak a last message.

I'd bent close trying to hear, weeping shamelessly, not caring who witnessed the accursed weakness. Even if I had cared about anything but watching my father die, I couldn't have stopped those tears. And it took so long, the wait unbearable, each racking breath, each grating shudder seeming to be the last. The air would leak out. His body going still. And I'd think it was finally done. Until, impossibly, the man breathed again. Fighting, always fighting. He'd never known when to quit, when to surrender to the inevitable defeat.

If he had, maybe the emperor's retribution wouldn't have been so severe. Wishes like ash on the wind.

In the end, he vanished in one of those long pauses between one breath and the next. It seemed death should arrive with more fanfare than that. Instead the last remnant of the man inside the desiccated husk simply evaporated. I kept waiting for that next labored breath that never came. Finally, it became clear the old king would never breathe again.

"The king is dead. Long live the king."

The quiet voice burned through my vigil. Sondra crouched nearby. She must've crept over to share my vigil. She'd smeared ashes in lines over her shorn skull. More lines of ash trailed down her cheeks in the traditional style, something she'd done purposefully, rather than the standard grime that coated us all. Even in my stunned grief I'd had the thought that if she wanted to recognize the old man's death, to demonstrate in the old ways that it mattered, she'd have washed. But that would've meant

squandering precious water rations we needed to keep
ourselves alive.

"The king is dead. Long live the king," she intoned
again with somber gravity.

"It's not a time for jesting." Even then her humor had
been black and twisted. The ashes grated between my
teeth.

Her dark eyes fixed on mine, rage in them. "You insult
me, Conrí."

A laugh, harsh and bitter, escaped me, painfully scrap-
ing out of a throat choked with unmanful tears, and jos-
tling my father's corpse. He weighed nothing, and I fancied
his bones rustled in a mocking reply. "Don't call me that,"
I bit out. "That's not my name. Oriel is gone. My family is
all dead. I'm king of nothing. I'm only a slave, as we all
are."

"Shall I call you the King of Slaves then?" Sondra
sneered. She'd meant to taunt me, but it sounded right.
With my father gone forever, the boy prince I'd been had
died with him. Conrí, a boy who would never be king, had
finally and utterly ceased to exist.

"Apt," I replied, staring at my father's slack face, dead
eyes finally devoid of the last piece of the king he'd been.
"A slave to lead slaves, and with one future. I'll lead you
all to the same death, perhaps one step ahead of you. Call
me Con."

Easy to slice away the honorific *rí* for a king. My father
should never have given me a name that assumed so much.
The court wizards had been wrong in that foretelling, too.
No throne awaited me. The kingdom that would've been
mine shattered into pieces and consumed by Anure. Our
borders erased, our people enslaved or scattered, the royal
line of Oriel—and with it the land we'd tended—had ended

with my father's last agonized breath in the stinking fires of Vurgmun.

"This is a time for grief." Sondra closed her eyes, bowing a face gaunt with sorrow, and making the ancient sign consigning the old king to the afterworld, to Sawehl's shadow sister, Yilkay. Then she lifted that burning, raging gaze to mine again. "But not for despair. The bloodline of Oriel lives in you. Long live the king," she repeated, implicit demand in her voice.

I'd had to look away from that, look at anything but her. The jagged black peaks around belched their smoke and flame, broken craters spilling liquid rock. Beyond that, the bleak and ragged land that had never yielded life forever shifted between molten and solid, crimson here with fire, grayed there with ash, steam billowing. Farther down the rockslide, the guards crouched, passing a skin of water and watching us only obliquely. A stretcher lay beside them, not to rescue a dying man but to drag away his desiccated corpse, to ship it to the emperor. Proof that his old enemy had died at last, and not by his hand. Proof that Oriel would never reclaim the blood and bones of her last king.

It was bad luck to kill a king; even Anure wouldn't dare that much. Besides, murder didn't require a direct blow.

Something hard shifted inside me, and a resolution formed to deny Anure his prize, his satisfaction in subduing the claims of the land he falsely possessed. The upstart emperor wouldn't have his peace, nor his evidence that he hadn't struck a blade to King Tuur's heart himself. I would deprive him of that—and strike a blow of my own.

"Help me with the king," I said, not realizing in that moment that it was my first royal command, the first step in a long campaign.

Sondra had known it, though. I'd never forget the

severe slash of her grim smile, or the way she inclined her head in eager compliance. "Always, Conrí," she averred.

I gathered the old king's corpse against me and rose to my feet, stealthily so as not to draw the guards' attention. Then, quickly enough that they had no time to stop us, Sondra and I scuttled to a vent nearby. The heat seared my eyes, burning away the last of my tears. Meeting my eyes, Sondra took my father's feet and helped me swing his body up and out, flinging him into the abyss. With a sigh and a scrabble of loose rock, the body fell away, bursting into flame before it hit the surface of the molten pool below.

The guards shouted. Began climbing the long slope.

And the old words came to me. I grated them out, that prayer I'd have sworn before that moment that I didn't remember. Another voice, sand to my gravel, finished it with me: Sondra, chanting loud and with determined rebellion.

"I will avenge you," I told him. *Avenge them.* We never talked about my sister, what happened to her and all the others. We couldn't.

Sondra nodded as if I'd spoken to her, as if she'd expected it all along. "*We* will avenge him, and all the others. You will lead us."

"I can't lead my father's people."

"Your people now, Conrí." She threw the words at me.

"No." I shook my head. "His people. The last of Oriel died with him. I am a ghost. I only want to watch Anure choke for breath, die, and burn."

"I ask only to hold the torch," Sondra replied. Then she bowed.

The guards reached us then. They dragged us away to flog the rebellion out of us. They hadn't thought we had any left. Neither had I, and I embraced the pain. It felt good, in a twisted way, right and justified. And I hadn't shed any tears, not even when they flayed the skin from my back, grinding ash into the wounds so I'd forever carry the black scars of Vurgmun.

Somehow I'd not only lived through it, but also found a way to live up to that ill-conceived vow born of rage and grief. And Sondra survived what they did to her, her relentless gaze holding me to those promises, that rage. The blackest passions spur one on where nobler notions fail. The mines crushed nobility along with all the finer emotions. But the need for revenge, gritty and sulfurous—that flourished in the dark, suffocating tunnels.

We held the rage in our hearts, feeding it diligently.

We'd conspired with the other prisoners, encouraging them in terse whispers and silent gestures to pilfer and hide some of the vurgsten rock we mined for Anure. The information passed from one to the next, and we stockpiled our vengeance tithe, as we came to call it. It took years, but the day came that we surprised the guards, killing them and taking command of the resupply vessel. Shocking ourselves that we triumphed.

I ask only to hold the torch.

Sondra offering her fealty and challenge. Vurgsten dragging at my lungs with every breath, the sound so like my father's, evoking his dying face. I'd never escape any of it. Not until Anure breathed his last, too.

As if reading my thoughts of the past, Sondra flashed a grim smile now and stepped forward to open the door. "Through here, Conrí." She refused to call me anything else, every use of my title a pointed reminder.

Giving her a nod, acknowledging what she said and what echoed between us, I passed her and entered the extensively fortified addition to the original palace, which might have been as elegant as the Tower of Simitthu at one time. Of course, the castle and surroundings were much the worse for their encounters with vurgsten, a disarray uneasily reminiscent more of the jagged landscape of Vurgmun than any human dwelling. I'd shed my blood on Vurgmun, my barren kingdom, and I brought that legacy with me wherever I went.

Kara had been right about the security of the so-called treasure room—and the staleness of the air. Deep in the interior of the governor's castle, the vault sat within stone walls an arm's length deep. There the former imperial governor, Salvio, squatted like a dragon from an old tale on his literal pile of treasure.

Immediately the bloated, pitiful lump of quivering terror began bleating at me, offering protestations of innocence in between promises to aid his new overlord in any way. It soon became clear that the greedy slug—Sondra had been accurate in her description, too—knew nothing of the fate of any of the members of the previous royal family. Unfortunately. Though they insisted on calling me king, I had no intention of ruling anything.

That meant that someone else would have to be found to govern Keiost. Not any of my officers, either. The campaign couldn't afford to lose them. Besides, none of them wanted to govern, which meant I'd have to force it on them. I had only so much stomach for that—and preferred not to do it to people I liked. This business of conquering created more headaches than it was worth.

Looking the worthless man in the eye, I gave the order for his execution. That was a responsibility I took entirely on myself as Father would've expected. I might not swing the executioner's ax, but I always assumed responsibility for the cool-minded decision to end a life. My father taught me that, long ago when he thought I'd make those weighty decisions in the throne room of Oriel, not in some stinking airless room beneath the rubble of a city I'd taken without remorse. Having done my job, I turned and left, hoping for a measure of time. Perhaps to finally and completely scrub off the blood and stink.

Kara followed me out of the room, however, pacing me, a grave expression on his dark face. "My king, we'll have to brace for counterattack. We have multiple confessions and other associated information that Salvio and his staff sent missives to Anure, alerting him to the situation here—including a final messenger bird that made it safely away at dawn announcing their defeat."

No surprise there. In fact, we'd been extraordinarily lucky it hadn't happened before this. And while luck played a larger role in our campaign than I cared to examine, it seemed unreasonable to believe no news had made it to the false emperor. Which made me think he either underestimated us or dissolved his fear in denial. "Let Anure attack."

"You say that now because you welcome the opportunity to kill him. But we both know he won't come in person. If he's smart, he'll bring the hammer of all his forces down on Keiost. He could destroy us in our own trap."

"Good for us, Anure isn't smart." And he wasn't. But he did possess an almost magical talent for victory. That would be the smartest thing to do, crush me and my armies before we grew any larger. Kara knew well that I'd trade all our advances for the opportunity to throttle Anure with my bare hands. Not an admirable quality in a king—and just another measure of how I didn't deserve the title. King of Slaves. King of Nothing. No king at all. "How long do you think we have?" I asked.

Kara rubbed his stubbled chin. "A week at worst. Ten days at the outside."

I nodded, my lips cracking with a sharp split as I smiled. Exactly what I'd thought. "Plenty of time."

"For what?" Kara looked exasperated. "We've decimated

the fortifications in taking the city. There won't be enough
time to rebuild the walls to the point that they can—"

"Kara." I halted, gripping my friend's arm to stop the
flow of words. He commanded troops like no other, and
he'd never failed to carry out a mission for me, but Kara
sometimes didn't look past the battle to see the war. "Plenty
of time for us not to be here."

I pointed in the direction of the sea meaningfully, not
to be cryptic, but to save my words. I'd hoped the fall of
Keiost—and the close ties between its imperial governor
and Anure—would be sufficient to catch the false emperor's
attention. If he sent the bulk of his forces here, then we'd
find him less defended when we slipped around them to
Yekpehr to topple the throne. Fortunately Kara, like all
my officers, knew me well enough that I didn't have to
waste words explaining all of that.

His eyes widened in understanding, and he nodded
slowly. "We'll meet this evening then—a conclave to plan
the next direction."

I agreed. I knew how I wanted it to go, but they'd all
feel better for talking it out. Sondra came jogging up, grinning with a fierce delight that reminded me of her carefree smiles, back before. "I have word from Ambrose,
Conrí!" she announced. "He asks you to attend him. It
sounds like good news."

Knowing Ambrose, he hadn't put it so nicely, but Sondra did still fall back on court etiquette. We all had our
cracks where the lords and ladies we'd been glimmered
through the rough skin we'd acquired. I gestured for her
to take me to the wizard.

No time to bathe and recuperate just yet. Hopefully
Ambrose had determined that we'd satisfied the terms of
his precious prophecy. It could be that claiming this Abiding Ring would require nothing more than plucking it

from whatever niche in the tower it rested in, and we could move on to attacking Anure.

Another week, possibly two, and I could finally kill the tyrant and be done.

Forever.

7

"A craven enemy of the empire?" I echoed Leuthar, letting my voice tremble. Tertulyn handed me a scented silk, which I pressed to my septum, careful not to smear my makeup. While I appeared to recover from a near faint, I thought hard and fast on how to respond. So many possibilities and ramifications. I needed more information. "With armies capable of taking Keiost?" I waved a hand, laughing, and my ladies laughed with me. "I can't imagine."

"No armies, Your Highness," Leuthar replied, a hint of impatience beneath his dulcet tones. The poor man, faced with such dithering frivolity. "Nothing so organized. They're merely a small band of criminals, escaped slaves, not even worthy of being called men. They are more like former livestock gone feral. Still, they are desperate creatures. Against all probability they've taken temporary control of Keiost. Word is they plan to execute the imperial governor, along with all the helpless denizens of the city."

Good riddance to Governor Salvio. He'd been unremittingly self-aggrandizing and ambitious. On top of his less-than-average intelligence, it had made him a cruel ruler who'd squandered Keiost's meager remaining resources. My father had been great friends with old King

Panos, and many times I'd heard him counsel Panos not to fight when Anure turned his acquisitive appetite on Keiost as a portal to her wealthier neighbors. Panos in turn had castigated my father for rolling over to the tyrant, for giving up without that fight.

In the end, Anure had defeated Keiost's formidable navy and dethroned King Panos, sentencing him to slave labor for his temerity in resisting. My father . . .

Well, difficult to say whose fate had been worse.

No, I'd hardly mourn Salvio—I'd even thank these criminals for ridding the world of his blight—but for them to slaughter the innocent populace? Like feral dogs indeed. The dream image of the wolf, dragging its broken chains, nudged at the edge of my mind. I pushed it down to the depths, where it belonged. I needed to *think*, not feel. Conjuring images from nightmares wouldn't help me protect Calanthe.

The news didn't bode well for Tertulyn's family in Keiost. It seemed a foregone conclusion we'd lost them, but I'd made her a promise to discover more. It wouldn't be politic to ask after the former royal family, as the emperor's official policy dictated that slaves were not people. A queen could not inquire about slaves any more than she'd ask about how the rats in the cellars had fared. Except to wonder if they carried disease, perhaps. I could only inquire tangentially.

"I greatly regret that Keiost has suffered such a devastating loss." I made sure to sound as if I recited rehearsed polite phrases. "If you would, give Me word of the imperial governor's wife and children."

Leuthar paused, quickly changing his prepared reply. He hadn't expected me to say that. "Your Highness, I regret that I do not know."

In other words, no one had bothered to discover their

fate. Tertulyn didn't betray her reaction by the slightest twitch. Time enough for that in private. Perhaps my spies could find out if her family yet lived, and go from there. Prisoners, especially those of the unimportant female and juvenile variety, could often be discreetly smuggled out as servants. They had not been responsible for Salvio's cruelty and deserved a chance to make or break by virtue of their own decisions, if I could manage it. Much there would depend on this army that held the city.

"Who are these 'criminals,' then?" I asked, fanning myself with the scented cloth, disguising my keen curiosity. "Escaped slaves, you say. Surely they are no match for trained imperial forces. From what prison did they escape?"

"No prison, Your Highness, but mines."

"Mines," I echoed, as if befuddled by the entire concept.

"To the north." Syr Leuthar flicked that away as inconsequential, which it absolutely wasn't. Mines to the *north*. I knew of none such. Though that explained the appearance of new players in the game. Hmm. I would have to inquire with my scholars. The many kingdoms and forgotten empires had included lands distant and varied. Before Anure had brutally thrown us all into one stewpot over his fire, we'd had little reason to know much of the far reaches. Calanthe had enjoyed a historic insularity for good reasons that hampered me now. We'd never needed the rest of the world before.

With so much riding on me and the decisions I made, I needed all the advice and information I could gather. All the more reason to offer sanctuary to the learned and the artists. I'd long hoped that perhaps a wizard who'd escaped Anure's notice would answer the call. My father would laugh at me, calling me unwise and insecure in my rule for seeking advice. A king or queen should depend only on themselves, he often said. But he was gone, and I had my own ways of protecting Calanthe.

"The imperial forces are indeed moving to retake Keiost," Leuthar continued in the same breezy tone, "which should be the work of a moment."

Anure wished it would be so easy, though he'd accomplished far more uncertain victories in the past. I doubted it would be the "work of a moment," especially as he wouldn't have his emissary speaking in my court about it if he weren't invested in making us believe that.

It served the emperor's interests to present an image of unassailability. Still, he would—easily or not—undoubtedly manage to squelch this uprising. Then he'd make an example of all involved, which would include most everyone in Keiost not already slaughtered, no matter their affiliation. After that, he'd likely sanction the rest of us, to spread more fear and make himself feel better. The prospect made me feel ill, and I took a moment to look out the window at the shining sea, so blue and calm. No blood or fire. Not yet. How could I avert that?

"The ships that brought me here will continue on to dispatch this vermin," Leuthar added, solidly in his prepared soliloquy again. "I've a list of required supplies before they depart in the morning."

I glanced back to see Dearsley take the scroll with the list of supplies, a line between his silver brows for the additional demand. We'd already tithed more than three times our due this season. Why the imperial toad couldn't use his own vast supplies, I didn't know. Oh wait, yes I did—because he had so much more fun reminding me of his power to demand I give whatever he wanted. His way of making me pay for denying him his ultimate desire. At least the warships wouldn't be lingering. I'd likely pay more than whatever Anure asked to remove their taint from my waters. Even awake, I heard the muttering of Calanthe's seas, unhappy about the old violence soaked into the wood of the warships.

"I'll see it done," I replied in a bored tone. "If that's all . . . ?" I let the question trail, raising my brows ever so slightly.

"Not quite, Your Highness. The emperor wishes me to relate a warning and deliver a charge."

Finally we got to the crux of it. I couldn't sit straighter, but a line of sweat crawled down my spine beneath the corset. Leuthar tugged just a bit too hard on the feather, a few of the barbs coming loose in his fingers. The situation had him far more concerned than he wished me to know. I gestured to Calla, who handed me a cool fruit juice to sip while I waited for Leuthar to spit it out.

"Your Highness, His Holiness, the Divine Emperor, bids me warn You to guard Your shores. And should any of these ferals escape the net of the Imperial forces, You are to make certain they don't travel past Calanthe. At any cost."

I made certain to show no reaction, even as the court fell into a frenzy of whispering—silenced when I flicked a quelling gaze over the room.

"I see no problem with that, Emissary. Surely a ragged band of escaped slaves can hardly pose a threat to Calanthe."

"They are . . . uncommonly organized, Your Highness. They supposedly defeated the walled city of Keiost in only two days by all accounts, unlikely as that seems."

That confirmed the time line in the coded letter from my spies. A piece of information I'd hoped wouldn't be corroborated. "How could they accomplish such a feat? Keiost is small, but hardly indefensible. Their fortifications

are like none other." Certainly Calanthe had no such physical barriers. The juice had gone sticky in my mouth and
I handed it back.

The emissary hesitated, chewing over his reply. "It's . . .
rumored that they have obtained some sort of weapon.
They use a fire that rends stone from stone."

I giggled through my jeweled nails, hiding my instant
horror. My ladies laughed with me, leading the court in
the joke. Fire that rent stone from stone. Like the secret
weapon Anure had used to subdue all the realms that we
all had to pretend we didn't know about. We knew he'd
been getting it from somewhere. Mines to the north, perhaps?

"Oh, Leuthar!" I exclaimed, silencing the laughter but
keeping my merry smile. "Surely you don't mean to imply they use *magic*." I made the word scathing, to remind
him that we lived in the emperor's world now.

"Not magic, no, Your Highness," he bit out. "A product
of nature, twisted to their purposes."

A rock that produced fire with the force to rend stone.
It made sense it would come from the ground. Coupled
with these "mines" I'd never heard of, the information had
me wondering what our devious emperor had been up to.
Escaped rebels from mines with explosive rock.

"They do sound more organized than your typical cluster of criminal elements," I observed. "Somewhat more
intelligent than feral livestock."

He nodded, once, sharp and concise, missing or ignoring my barb. Oh yes, they were concerned. Was Anure
afraid? That would be something, though a frightened emperor meant more pain for us.

"Your Highness, they are led by a man known only as
the Slave King, a brute of a creature, reported to be a ruthless rapist and murderer. He conquers through terror, then

torture, laying waste to all in his path and leaving devastation behind."

My ladies exchanged apprehensive looks, two falling into whispers, which I allowed this time. The court, taking the permission, also began to murmur among themselves again. Let them talk. The conversations would stimulate chance overheard remarks and rumors to surface in their minds, so Tertulyn could later ferret out what they knew.

"And does this Slave King have a purpose?" I asked, shading it so I sounded amused, as if I believed such a thing to be impossible. But a group organized enough to take Keiost in two days had their sights set on more than that battle. Keiost was far too poor to be an end in itself, which the emperor knew as well as I did. He might be a corrupt tyrant, but he wasn't stupid. Alas for that. "Surely this feral mutt doesn't think to take Calanthe." I waved my jeweled nails at the astonishing and unblemished view out my windows.

Syr Leuthar shrugged, his confidence that he'd bamboozled me regained. "Who knows what motivates such a depraved creature? The craven desire for whatever power he can grasp, lust to possess treasure and captives."

I pressed my long nails to my lips, hoping to appear dismayed while I restrained any smirk that might escape— or, a far worse indiscretion, remarking aloud that Leuthar might as well be describing the emperor himself. I was not stupid, however, so such foolhardy and treacherous words would never pass my lips, even in privacy speaking only to Tertulyn.

"These sorts are not the kind of men You'd understand, Your Highness," Leuthar explained in all earnestness, clearly pleased to have upset me. "Make no mistake but that they call him king out of deepest irony, out of mockery. He possesses no nobility, no refinement. You cannot credit his type with purpose more than You would a hound gone mad from disease. He knows only his endless hunger to consume more and more and more."

"Even hunger can't make a mad dog swim," I declared with a carelessness I didn't feel. "His Imperial Majesty is kind to be concerned for Me and the safety of Calanthe, but I don't see how this Slave King can even get here if he has no ships—"

"But he does." Syr Leuthar clenched his jaw. "Your Highness," he added, as if to wipe away the rudeness of interrupting me. "Before Keiost, he took Irst, and Hertaq. His Imperial Majesty had no great concerns over those minor losses, as those seaports are little better than fishing villages that have no strategic value, but . . ."

"But they do have seaworthy boats," I murmured, momentarily forgetting myself in my astonishment at Anure's blindness. Or ignorance. It could be he actually hadn't known. It could be he was showing cracks at last. A huge mistake on his part that might give me hope, if I were capable of hope still. Tertulyn cast me a glance, a flash of powdery blue behind sparkling lashes.

"Indeed, Your Highness. Fishing boats, but they do now belong to these ruffians."

"So." I tapped my nails on the arm of my throne, the orchid ring's petals swaying, a bit of sinuous fluttering of its own accord. Tertulyn sent me an inquiring glance, and I took the reminder to heart and focused on Leuthar instead. "So, His Majesty suspects this King of Slaves might sail across the inland sea to sate his hunger here?"

"Not as a final target, Your Highness," Leuthar reassured me, all paternal concern and full of shit. "Calanthe is precious to His Imperial Majesty, the jewel of his empire, but much as we love it, it's but a pretty paradise, of no interest to a villainous scum such as he."

A reversal of his claim that this Slave King wanted only to sate his immediate desires. My pretty paradise of a realm always held attraction for those sorts, including Leuthar, whose own appetites were well known.

No, the emperor suspected—or knew of—a deeper purpose in this rebel who'd managed to take Keiost. *Anure is afraid. This is your opportunity.* The knowledge whispered through me, scented with orchids. In the corner of my eye, the orchid ring's petals seemed to unfurl as it murmured in a voice only I could hear. "And yet the emperor asks Me to act as guard," I mused aloud, to prod Leuthar and test the ring. It didn't respond. Hmph. "Calanthe is, as you say, but a pretty paradise. We have no navy, no standing army."

"But You do have seaworthy ships," he returned. "Your Highness."

"Fishing boats and pleasure skiffs, no more." I made sure to look mournful as I lied. We made sure they appeared to be only that. Calanthe's power did not lie in those sorts of weapons.

"No worse than this Slave King has procured. Surely a ragged band of escaped slaves holds no great threat for the stalwart men of Your realm, Your Highness." Leuthar's eyes glittered as he stroked the feather of his helm. Mocking me by throwing my words back at me. He'd become incautious of offending me, which meant he knew something. Probably he'd read the letter Anure had sent me or had inside knowledge of the contents.

Either that or Anure must be afraid enough to sacrifice me and Calanthe in the hope that in devouring us, the escaped wolf would die of poison before it reached the emperor's throat. I was not interested in making a sacrifice of either myself or Calanthe. Certainly not to protect Anure. Quite the opposite. "We shall be on watch then," I declared, entirely done with coaxing Leuthar along. "I assume we'll be sent word if His Imperial Majesty's net proves to have holes in it?"

"I advise You not to rely on such an eventuality, Your Highness. Be on the alert, such as You are able. His Imperial Majesty was most clear on this point, and wished me to express this onus to You where all might witness."

I allowed my lids to droop as I toyed with a blossom on my gown, caressing its petals when I wanted to tear them off to vent the savagery in my heart. "What onus might that be?" I sounded oh-so-very-bored. Inside, I recited the vilest of curses.

"You are the final barrier. Your Highness will not allow this Slave King to pass. The emperor calls upon You personally to fulfill Your vows of fealty to him, to repay him for the indulgences that have allowed Calanthe to flourish independent of his hand all these years."

"Flourish," my virginal ass. We'd clawed to feed our own and still fulfill the tyrant's exorbitant tithes. Still, he had me. I had no choice but to do as Anure commanded or find my leash yanked up short. Not that I would've aided this rebellion in the slightest. They had no chance of succeeding, and would only draw out the emperor's worst. The beast that was Anure had more or less slumbered, fat and sated. A rebellion of escaped slaves could do nothing more than sting the emperor's nose and send him into a rage that would have him scouring the lands of "rebels," which would mean anyone he and his scourge of soldiers fancied killing.

Legions of innocents would die, and the lands would

cry to me incessantly of their deaths. If they managed to make it this far, I would stop this ill-advised rebellion that endangered us all.

"Of course I serve His Imperial Majesty's will." Fully ready to be done, I held out a hand to the emissary, smiling with all the warmth I could manufacture when he bent to kiss the orchid ring on my marriage finger. It symbolized my wedding to my true family: my kingdom—husband, wife, and treasured, imperiled child all in one.

Leuthar inhaled the orchid's exotic fragrance, like nothing else on earth. "Ever unchanging," he mused.

"Grown on the same vine." I gave him the lie, as I had numerous times before. Magic had never existed. It was all chicanery and sleight of hand, therefore he must accept the rational explanation. "A new bloom cut fresh from my secret garden each day."

"Someday You must show me this orchid house of Yours that grows such fabulous blossoms."

"If only I could," I replied with false regret. "But it is not for outsiders."

"Your Highness." His expression was mild, his gaze full of threat. "We are all one under the emperor's hand. There are no outsiders."

I didn't allow that to give me pause. "In this case, we are all outsiders, but for a highly trained gardener. The climate within the orchid house is so delicately balanced that even I cannot enter."

"Alas for that," he replied, making the small hairs stand up on my neck. "Take my warning, fair queen—do not fail in this charge."

"I and Calanthe exist entirely to lay ourselves down for the emperor." The welcome mat of the empire. Please trod upon us. My father had seen to that.

"I shall pass along Your reply." He held on to my proffered hand a shade too long. "And I'll include Your reply to His Imperial Majesty's missive, as soon as You've penned it."

The advantage of the alabaster makeup and painted lips is that the thinning of my smile never shows. "I can't express my delight," I replied, and pulled my hand from his unwelcome grip.

If only I could extract myself and Calanthe from the emperor's hold as easily.

8

Sondra led the way to Ambrose's new lair, while Kara remained behind to escort Salvio to his very public execution. That demonstration should convince any of the populace who still lingered in the plaza wavering on their oaths of loyalty. Some people needed to witness that their conqueror would have them killed, if necessary. It was no bluff, either. I'd have to order their deaths if they refused—I had no choice—but I'd rather terrify them into changing sides. I didn't mind being feared as a monster, since that was better than demonstrating I am one.

Once they committed, they'd discover that we'd arranged for half of Salvio's treasure to be distributed evenly among those who swore fealty to me. I didn't like them to know ahead of time, as some would say anything for financial gain. An interesting insight into human nature, that love of money drove certain personalities more than anything else. I didn't want that kind in my ranks.

Our system worked. Those wishing to pledge their loyalty to our cause did so via the waiting priests of Sawehl. We always "liberated" the local temple of Sawehl first, a trick we'd discovered early on. Anure had desecrated the temples to Sawehl and dishonored the priesthood as existing only to feed off the superstitions of the people. His

Imperial Majesty hadn't overtly forbidden the worship of Sawehl, but he'd done everything but, including taking the title *His Holiness*. The temple of Sawehl—and thus its priests—had not flourished in the empire.

Conversely, we offered them sanctuary, protection, and a hefty donation to the coffers. Sometimes all it had taken was sharing our food with the most impoverished. All they needed to do was take the pledges of loyalty and work to rebuild their parishes in our wake. Priests of every temple, cloister, and estate chapel we'd encountered gladly supported our cause.

Some priests had gone so far as insist on anointing me *Sawehl's chosen son*, the most deeply ironic honorific of all those foisted on me. As if the sun god would choose a miserable nobody who grew up in the volcanic pits of Vurgmun, son of a forgotten and immolated king, possessing only a black heart bent entirely on revenge. Of course, all of that also meant I possessed zero integrity. That sort of noble feeling belonged to Conrí, lost king of Oriel. Con, the Slave King, had no problem professing false faith, as he took advantage of every opportunity that furthered his path to revenge.

So although I hated every moment of the lie, I'd bowed my head and grated out the vows. Amazingly enough, the holy oils never sizzled when they met my unholy skin. It could be that Sawehl didn't particularly care what humankind did, which was the most likely explanation. After all, I didn't understand or concern myself with the termite mounds we passed. Or Anure was right: Magic was dead or never was. Perhaps both were equally true.

Still, the common people of the empire believed in Sawehl, and in Ejarat, even though their faith mystified me. Where had Sawehl been when Anure breached their walls, toppled their kings, executed their wizards, and burned out their farms? Anure had a point there, that the sun god had done nothing to save them. Nor had earth mother Ejarat, though Her worship had always occurred under open sky and at the hearths and homes of those who asked for Her gentle nurture in their daily lives.

There was no accounting for what people believed in. Look at how many followed me and my cause. I didn't understand any of it.

My cynicism didn't keep me from using this weapon, however. The priests in Keiost had been more eager than most, even freely giving us information on taking the walled city. Even before we showed our might, many of the populace in the surrounding towns and countryside pledged the sacred vows of fealty without hesitation. And most in the plaza had followed in those steps, messengers reported as we walked, the lines passing out the gates of the plaza. Soon they'd receive their portion of the treasure, money that had likely been theirs to begin with. But only after that. No temptation of gold should sway their hearts.

I'd give it all to them, the tainted gains that might as well be smeared in blood. But a ragtag army of peasants and slaves, along with a newly acquired, haphazard navy of fishing boats, all needed to be provisioned. Governor Slug's hoard would go a long way toward ensuring that end.

Still, we wouldn't need so much if we'd only kept the strike force small. I didn't need a full navy to take out Anure. I'd argued this all along. Assassins could accomplish what armies couldn't. "Should've kept it small."

"Kept what small?" Sondra asked, giving me the side-eye, making me aware I'd muttered that aloud.

"This." I waved a hand at the sky showing through the ceiling of the half-destroyed corridor. "All this to kill one man. Could've done it with a small strike force."

"Fifteen fugitives can't sail a ship to the heart of the empire and hope to penetrate the Imperial Citadel. We've been through this," Sondra replied, unruffled.

"Could've paid passage. Cheaper. Lower-profile."

She shrugged in her inimitable way. "One day you'll stop fighting it, Conrí."

"What?"

"You're a king. It falls naturally to you to rule. Kingdoms come to you whether you ask for them or not. It's meant. It's Sawehl's will, Conrí."

I set my teeth. Sondra loved to get under my skin, especially in pursuit of her favorite topic. She also shamelessly took advantage of my not wanting to waste breath telling her not to call me that—or explaining that I was no king. Certainly not the one she imagined in her blind optimism. "I don't want it."

She stopped, blocking the passage and glaring at me as she did only when we were alone. "Tell me, Conrí. What *do* you want—after Anure is dead at your feet?"

She'd never asked me that. I'd always thought she understood that speaking of that impossible future was off the table. We shared a vow of vengeance, a determination to reach a single, finite goal. Nothing beyond that existed. I frowned at her, but she didn't flinch. Instead she studied me, brilliant eyes somber, as if she hadn't known me since I was a boy.

"You could be emperor in his stead," she said.

It made me laugh, the surprise of it. The sheer ridiculousness that she'd even speak it aloud. The creaking guffaw burst against my ribs, straining from long disuse. I sounded like a dog that had barked and howled itself hoarse from misery, flinging itself against the chains it couldn't break.

She raised an inquiring eyebrow. The expression twisted

her scarred skin, her lovely hair gleaming like sunshine in the half-light. I choked back the laugh.

"No," I managed. "Never."

"You'd be a good ruler. Far better than he. Do you have other plans?"

"Of course not. That goal . . ." It would take too many words to explain, and the speech in the plaza had taken too much of my voice.

"Consumes everything. All possibilities," she said quietly.

She did understand. I nodded, not quite sure why she'd tested me that way. "Yes," I replied.

She nodded, too, the same way I had, but staring at her boots. Then she relented and moved on. We finished the walk in blessed silence, wending to the far side of the stone complex, into the older section. Here it was all graceful wood, bleached blond from sun and storms off the sea. Though the palace of Oriel had looked nothing like it, something in the architecture made my heart ache with bitter nostalgia. We climbed stairs that circled through the ancient tower made of golden stones. The marble was known as Simitthu, for the region where it had been quarried, centuries before. Without palaces built of the marble, that name, too, would have fallen into the mists of forgotten realms. It seemed that should mean something, but I didn't know what.

"Ambrose is through here," Sondra said, breaking into my musings, and I realized I'd stopped to gawk at the high dome of the tower that shone like the sun itself. Forgetting myself.

The alchemist's workroom and library had indeed survived the battle unscathed. Miraculously so, though Kara had been careful to direct the greatest charges away from that part of the old castle, from the tower itself. Ambrose had predicted the tower would contain the information he needed—and I'd long since stopped questioning how Ambrose knew the things he did. Probably since that first day the strange man accosted us.

It had been not long after we first regained the mainland, coming ashore in the dark hours before sunrise, after a grueling passage across the storm-tossed winter sea. No collapsing on the beach to kiss the soil of our motherland for us: We immediately set to hiding the supply boat we'd stolen. It took hours to do it right. Time well spent as it meant our continued freedom, creating a cache for that precious store of vurgsten until we discovered how best to wield our secret weapon.

We kept off the main roads as we made our way inland, following game trails to find solid ground in the swamps of the Shwem coast. In the middle of that wilderness, Ambrose had come limping up, appearing from nowhere, leaning heavily on a tall staff and leading a laden pack mule as if it were the most groomed of the empire's highways. Despite his scruffy clothing, despite the impossibility that any still existed, I knew him for a wizard. The staff sported a faceted emerald that looked genuine, and an enormous raven rode on his shoulder. I'd barely managed to stop Sondra in time, her stolen sword already swinging for the unprepossessing man's throat.

It had been a strange moment, that flash of instant realization that had me gripping her arm. Against all precaution, too, as we'd killed several others in our determination to remain undetected. The fifteen of us had been instantly recognizable as escaped slaves, in our filth and rags, our heads shorn. Some of us still wore manacles dangling links of broken chain, as we'd yet to find the tools to cut them off.

In retrospect, my unthinking reaction had likely saved

Sondra's life. Ambrose could defend himself in ways that defied rational explanation. You'd never know it to look at him, but Ambrose was powerful, and the old stories claimed that wizards weren't entirely human. I'd remembered something of my childhood in Oriel after all. Anure claimed they were all frauds and charlatans, but I recalled how the court wizards had worked magics that defied explanation. More than sleight of hand could accomplish. Something deep in me recognized in Ambrose the mantle of magic, the untapped potential of shimmering power.

I had no idea why he bothered to pretend to follow me.

As if hearing the thought, Ambrose glanced up from a pile of leather-bound tomes that threatened to topple and crush his slender frame, blond curls tousled around an angelic face, beaming at us as he had that day on the road. A smile that better belonged on some sweet blue-eyed kid. Artless, without calculation—but with that hint of mischief that made you wonder what he'd been doing so quietly.

That apparently innocent appearance didn't fool me. It helped that his eyes, those of someone much older and stranger, revealed his nature. Far from sweetly blue, the wizard had eyes green as an ancient forest, twisted, old, and shadowed. Ambrose was like one of those treacherous flowers of the Mazos jungle my tutors had told me about. With their sweet perfume they lured creatures of all types—and then trapped them in the sticky vines beneath, slowly consuming their hapless prey.

I often knew how that must feel, though Ambrose, for whatever arcane reasons of his own, had revealed his nature to me and asked to be our ally. He'd set out on the prompting of some foresight he'd never explained in detail to find us in those roadless swamps, offering his advice and guidance. We would have been lost—literally and metaphorically—without him. The physical protection our swords offered wouldn't have been needed if he'd only stayed where he'd hidden all those years. No, he wanted something else, and when the day came that he finally named his price, I only hoped I could pay it.

"Conrí!" Like Sondra, Ambrose refused to call me anything else. He bobbed his head and rose—then hastily grabbed a book he'd nearly toppled from the pile. Merle the raven spread his wings, cawing caution from his nearby perch. Ambrose continued speaking without pause. "I'm not often wrong, as you know—"

"That is, never," Sondra supplied, and Ambrose winked at her.

"Well, and I'm technically not wrong now, so my reputation is intact, but there's even more here than the portents foretold. I could happily study all this library holds for years and never finish. And the notes left behind! You should see this incantation." The rapid movement on his withered leg giving him a sideways scuttle, he hurried to a workbench littered with dusty glassware, and rummaged through a pile of scrolls.

"About the Abiding Ring?" I asked leadingly, trying not to make the question too abrupt or pointed. Sondra glared at me in exasperation anyway. After that first meeting, and not killing him, she'd developed a soft spot for Ambrose. Not romantic. I wasn't sure Sondra was any more capable of wanting that than I was, both of us so profoundly broken. Sometimes she acted almost maternal toward the wizard. Protective. Equally surprising, as I'd have said she wouldn't have the heart for that, either.

But for all that Ambrose wielded powerful abilities beyond understanding, he was also hapless. Sondra had assumed the responsibility for ensuring the wizard stayed out of trouble. Which apparently included shielding him from me.

"No, but so interesting!" Ambrose stabbed a finger in the air, seeming entirely unbothered. Still, he gave the incantation a last longing glance and set it aside—and picked up a bound set of documents. Returning to the desk he'd been working at, he tapped a page, turning it so I could see.

It looked like a bookkeeper's accounts, with rows and columns of figures. I raised an eyebrow, trying to be patient. "Mathematics are the new runes?"

Ambrose chortled as if that were a fine joke. "I wish! The currents of the future would be considerably more clear via that method. Imagine if I could determine a way to weight the probability of a potential event occurring and factor that in with the probability of other events. I could then derive an indicator value that we could apply to current actions to create a risk-versus-benefit ratio for decision making. Hmm." He dragged over a scrap of parchment and scribbled a few quick numbers.

Sondra and I exchanged glances. She tucked a stream of golden hair behind her ear with a frown for my obvious impatience. I cleared my throat.

Ambrose glanced up, eyes distant. "What? Oh right. Not this just now. *This!* This thing." He tapped the ledger again. "The Abiding Ring is as good as yours."

Disappointment hit me hard as battle rage. "'As good as'? It isn't here then."

"No." Ambrose focused on me. Looked confused. "Whyever did you imagine the Abiding Ring would be in an abandoned alchemist's tower in Keiost, of all places?"

I set my teeth against the grinding frustration at him echoing my own thoughts about Keiost. "'Take the Tower of the Sun,'" I quoted slowly, "'claim the Abiding Ring.'"

"Ah-ah." Ambrose waggled a finger in the air, and Merle made a chiding series of chuckles. "'Claim *the hand that wears* the Abiding Ring.' In prophecy, as in poetry, exact wording is key."

"Fine," I bit out. No wonder I hated poetry and prophecy in equal measure. "Show me the hand wearing it and I'll cut it off and claim the fucking ring already."

Sondra put a hand over her face, but Ambrose only laughed at me. "There will be no dismemberment necessary, Conrí. This will be another battle entirely. A more delicate form of claiming."

"Unless Anure is wearing the Abiding Ring and claiming it along with his hand will result in him dead at my feet, I don't really care about some piece of jewelry." Harsh perhaps, but the crash of disappointment and frustration had sapped me of what little energy I had left. This was clearly a waste of time that I could be using to wash and sleep.

"It's not 'some piece of jewelry,'" Ambrose corrected, as if I'd tracked shit on his fine carpet. "It's called the Abiding Ring because it's actually alive. Rather than a jewel, this text describes it as an orchid, a living blossom, affixed to a ring and never removed while the bearer lives. I don't think I should have to explain that this strongly implies a magically enforced bond."

Sondra and I exchanged wry glances. Ambrose tended to wax dogmatic on the subject of magic, as if anything associated with it should be self-evident and any ignorance on our parts came from deeply personal failings. We came from very different worlds. Of course, none of us understood where Ambrose had been before he found us—and likely wouldn't even if he hadn't refused to discuss it.

"They could simply harvest a new flower each day, to

perpetuate the myth," Sondra pointed out, ever pragmatic—and just as suspicious of magic. "People will look the other way, as most love an enchanting story more than tepid truth."

"*Or*"—Ambrose drew out the word with significance—"it's the same blossom, magically sustained. The *Abiding Ring*."

Somehow I'd thought that the "abiding" part of the ring had to do with conferring immortal powers on the bearer. Maybe that had been wishful thinking, as indestructibility on my part would be useful in killing an emperor known for not stirring his corpulent ass from the security of his well-padded throne, deep within a purportedly impregnable compound.

That the ring *itself* might be immortal . . . Well, fuck it all. The fury and frustration I'd so far kept leashed swelled up. How under Sawehl's gaze could such a thing be even remotely useful? For *this* I'd killed, suffered, and ordered the deaths of countless others? How the gods laughed at me, a broken and foolish king with no kingdom, reaching an inevitable dead end in a golden tower overlooking the sea, my real enemy an unreachable distance beyond. I needed an object of power, something to lend me the magic I lacked, to supplement the brute force and a meager gift for strategy that were all my father had to give me.

Rage, like on the battlefield, turned my vision red.

"Con." Sondra gripped my shoulders with one hand, for once dropping the title from my name, calling me out of the rage. I should remember that Ambrose wasn't the only man among us she nurtured, even though she kicked my ass in equal measure. "We've come this far. Farther than we ever thought we could. We'll find a way to kill him."

She understood. Probably she felt the same.

"Will this flower ring help me kill Anure?" I demanded of the wizard, managing to sound relatively sane.

Merle croaked at me chidingly, but Ambrose held up a hand as if in solemn vow. "Would I lie to you?"

An interesting dodge, as I fully expected that Ambrose would lie—and cheerfully—if he thought it served his purposes. Whatever they were.

"Since the ring isn't here," I tried again, "do you now know *where* it is?"

Ambrose grinned, face suffused with delight. He spread his hands at the array of documents.

"Calanthe."

9

I finally returned to my chambers after a day of the usual court activities—must keep up good appearances, after all—followed by endless conversations and meetings with my advisers. Exhausted and beyond grateful to begin the process of shedding my colorful shell, I moved through the corridors, flanked by Tertulyn and trailed by the vee of my junior ladies. The sounds of revelry unleashed in the wake of my retiring poured through various doorways to private halls, and portals to the pleasure gardens.

I ignored them, as always, but the music, laughter, and other noises were like forbidden liquor leaked from a cracked vessel onto the table. It would be so easy to dip my finger, just a dab of a brush, and taste it.

Of course, I could not—and the force of my wanting to took me by surprise. I enjoyed my small rebellions, mainly with Tertulyn or a few of my other ladies, those who seemed pleased to minister to my well-being in that way. Tertulyn brought me tales of the more exotic diversions of the Night Court, and sometimes demonstrated those she could, to our mutual delight. Any that didn't involve stretching my sacred hymen, that was. Anure, in his male blindness, might assume me to be a virgin so long as I was never alone with a man, but I wouldn't put him past having me physically inspected if it came to an actual wedding.

As the current balance depended on his belief in my chastity, and my endgame depended on making it to his marriage bed, I didn't dare risk compromising my apparent virginity. That also meant I could never be sighted at the Night Court games. That night, however, I wanted far more than the sweetly therapeutic attentions of my ladies. What, I didn't know.

At the time, I put it down to the trying day. Later . . . well, I wondered if that unaccustomed temptation was my first warning of things to come. Or one of the many, rather.

Once secluded with me in my quiet rooms, Tertulyn and Calla immediately relieved me of the crown, setting it in its niche with reverence. Ibolya and Zariah took my wig and carried it to the anteroom for cleaning. As soon as Nahua and Orvyki had the biggest pieces of the gown off me—fortunately for my crumbling patience, the undressing takes far less time than the dressing—I collapsed in my favorite chair with a groan, scrubbing at my itching scalp.

And that's when I felt it.

My wedding finger burned excruciatingly hot, the orchid's petals going from their usual violet and orange to fuchsia threaded with black. Had I been able to, I might have stripped off the orchid ring and flung it across the room. Instead I snapped up straight, holding my arm rigidly away from my body, staring at it. The burning ceased—thankfully—as if it had only done it to seize my attention, and now it seemed to be flexing its elaborate petals, almost like a sea creature moving in a tidal pool, far more violently than it had earlier in the day.

It had been unusually active lately. Another bad sign. That moment in court, it had fluttered like this while I was parsing Leuthar's elaborate lies. I might've put the move-ment down to a wayward breeze if the room hadn't been still as death. It was very real, though I didn't know how to inter-pret the messages. *Oh, Father—so many things you never bothered to teach me.* If only Anure hadn't been so thorough in exterminating the wizards and other magic workers.

"Your Highness—are You all right?" Tertulyn sounded alarmed and I nodded to reassure her, though I wasn't cer-tain at all. My gaze fell on the carved wooden box sitting on the table.

The candied dates from Anure. I'd always hated the cursed things. The one time I tried them, the sugared crust made them hard as rocks and so sweet my teeth ached even without the impact. I had never been certain if the impe-rial toad made a point of sending them to me because he didn't know how much I loathed them—or because he did and enjoyed taunting me. *See? Even my tokens of affec-tion will bring you misery.*

Most days I found strength in hating him for it, in the knowledge that I saw through his poisonous games, no matter his intention. But this time . . . perhaps it had been the arguing with the scholars and advisers, their implicit accusations of my cowardice and assumptions of my youthful—or female—lack of intelligence, or the simple headache of wearing the wig and crown so long, but the presence of this gift made me feel ill and weak. *Get it gone.* My gaze snapped back to the orchid. Had it . . . spoken? No. Surely the orchid would speak in a voice like Calanthe and Her other creatures. This must've been my own thoughts. I listened anyway, but heard nothing more.

"Euthalia." Tertulyn lifted my other hand, taking my at-tention from the orchid. "Who should I send for? Castor? Healer Jeaneth?"

"No," I breathed. Even as brilliant a scholar as Castor

wouldn't know how to handle the ring. He'd long ago told me no one knew much about the orchid ring, corroborating my childhood impression that my father had been secretive about it. And of course, Father hadn't expected his death, so he'd had little time to tell me about the ring and its properties, even if he'd been so inclined. He'd sent the wizards of Calanthe away before Anure arrived, and perhaps he'd thought one or more would return. He'd died before Anure showed his worst face and ended that hope entirely.

No, I was on my own in this. I should stop hoping for things to be otherwise. "Open that box."

"The dates? But You hate them," Tertulyn protested.

"Do it. Open it, then stand back."

She did as I asked, first setting aside Anure's pink-ribboned love letter she'd put with it for me, then opening the box, automatically facing it away from her so the hinged lid protected both of us. *Never open a container facing you.* Another old superstition, and one that served us well in this instance. Nothing happened, however, except that the ring fluttered on my hand, like an anemone filtering tainted water into clean.

The knowledge entered my head, as if I'd thought of something, or remembered an old lesson. Not a voice, exactly, but not my own thoughts, either. I knew it this time with certainty. *The dates are treated with a potion to encourage passion and obedience.*

How so very interesting: an enchanted dust to control me from the emperor who declared magic did not exist. And one that I detected, not through science, but through my magical means. Ah, the circles of the real and imagined we travel, round and round, getting nowhere. "It's poison," I said flatly, deciding no one needed to know the details—especially in my court where such a potion would be irresistible to those less principled. "We must get rid of it."

"I'll send them to the compost, Your Highness," Tertulyn replied, perfectly obliging, and not at all betraying that she might think I behaved oddly. Though I knew by the set of her lips that she did. Of all my ladies, only Tertulyn wasn't Calanthean. That made her a good companion for me in some ways, but deaf and blind in others.

"Not the compost." I had no idea how to dispose of a magical thing. What if the taint could spread? I imagined the magic perfusing the compost, and thence everything fertilized with it. Plants sucked up nutrition via their roots—why not magic? "Close it up and send it to Castor. I'll pen a note."

While my confused ladies waited, I wrote instructions for Castor to investigate with caution and keep the box quarantined. Then I sent all of it away with Calla, trusting to her sensitivity to Calanthe's murmurs to keep her safe, beyond relieved to have the thing gone from me. The orchid on my hand settled into its usual static loveliness, quiescent again with the departure of the cursed dates. Tertulyn and my remaining ladies finished removing my remaining garments and makeup. The lashes are the worst, requiring a solution to dissolve the glue, which stings my eyes unbearably. Washed clean and blessedly unencumbered but for my robe and ring, I dismissed them all but Tertulyn.

She sat and smiled, pouring us both some sweet wine. "Time for our bedtime story?" she asked.

"We may need something stronger than wine." I grimaced, picking up the loathsome love letter. "I'd rather burn the vile thing."

"Shall I fetch the brandy?"

"No." I didn't want to start on the path of escalating what I needed to sedate myself enough to read what Anure thought passed for words of affection. Though, knowing what he'd tried to do to me with the dates, I might regret that decision. "Darling Flower of my Heart," I began aloud, and paused for a cleansing sip of wine before continuing.

Darling Flower of my Heart,

How I long for you, my innocent rosebud. With every day that passes I dream of your fair skin and how I might mark it as my own. I'll plant violet blossoms to bloom where my hands have gripped your flesh. Roses will flower pink and crimson from the touch of my teeth. How you'll writhe and cry for me as I wring my pleasure from you, my virgin bride. It must be soon. I cannot wait any longer to possess you. With every day, every dream of you, I grow afraid that another will pluck the blossom that is mine alone.

Are you true to me?

You must be, for my disappointment if you are not will be a rage to burn all the empire and sink your pretty island into the sea.

Thus is my love for you, darling rosebud.

I have a plan—a special surprise—to at last bring us together, to make you my empress, mother of my heirs. Capture the rebel dogs for me. Do not fail me in this or I shall have to deal with you personally, and without the honor of marriage.

I will summon you soon and we shall come together in eternal bliss—one way or the other.

Don't make me come after you. I wouldn't want to mangle my pretty prey in chasing it down.

All my love,
His Imperial Majesty

I drained my glass and Tertulyn refilled it. "So poetic," she commented. "He puts Brenda's sonnets to shame. Of course, hers are considerably less brutal."

I laughed, needing the release of the tension around my heart and lungs. "I don't know—he's so inventive with the flower analogies."

"So many rosebuds for him to violate!" She snorted and sipped her own wine.

But our usual humor fell flat in light of the viciousness of the missive. This letter, like the potion on the dates, represented movement. The dates must have been intended to reinforce his instructions in the letter, the third blow to seal the other two. Anure's final, most poisonous threat.

"Do you think he knows? What You really are?" Tertulyn asked after a silence.

I gave her a repressive look. We didn't discuss such things, even in private. "Who knows what our emperor does and doesn't believe." My casual dismissal came out more tremulous than I'd intended.

"Are you all right, Euthalia?" Tertulyn asked softly.

I smiled at my oldest friend. She only worried for me. "Wonderful. Aflutter with anticipation for My wedding night. A girl never forgets her deflowering—especially when it comes with bruises and bites."

"It won't happen," she assured me. "Even His Imperial Majesty wouldn't dare make You less than first wife."

"He's thought of some way around it." I studied the letter again, trying to still the fluttering wings of fear by employing rational sense. I needed to be smarter than Anure. *What are you planning, toad?*

She bit her lip. "You're so good at holding him off. You'll think of something—You always do."

"I always do, yes." But the words rang hollow in my ears. Abruptly I missed my father, a great aching pit of loss opening inside me. He would've known what I should do. Without him, I had no one to call on, no one to save me. I could only do my best to rescue myself from this dire future. If I delivered the Slave King and his rebellious minions to Anure, he might be pleased enough that I could extract a reprieve from impending doom.

Regardless, Calanthe's well-being and continuation took precedence. If Anure did call our waiting game to an end, I needed an heir to pass the orchid ring to.

Once I did that, I could face my own death with, if not equanimity, then a certain relish in taking Anure with me and saving Calanthe at the same time.

"Let me tend to You, Lia," Tertulyn offered with a soft smile. "It will relax You and keep all Your sacred flowers intact."

Her deft fingers and soft kisses would help to relax me, but it wouldn't be enough, not with that feeling that I needed something else, something *more*. Besides, with the images Anure had put in my mind, even without magical reinforcement, the prospect of being touched sexually . . . no. Tertulyn cared for me, but even we had so many layers of formality between us. I didn't want to be tended. What I longed for, what I craved somewhere inside my ice-encased heart, was for someone to hold me and tell me I wasn't alone, that everything would work out for the best. To touch me out of love, and tenderness.

I rarely allowed myself such sentimental yearnings, and it was a mark of my exhaustion on every level that such thoughts entered my mind.

"Not tonight," I told her. "You may go, to the parties or your own bed, as you wish."

"Shall I help You into bed?"

I shook my head. "Take the rest of the wine with you." Otherwise I'd likely drink it all.

Once she left, glad to have no witnesses to my despair, I allowed myself to lay my head on the table for a moment, sagging under the weight of it. If my eyes watered, that had to be vestiges of the glue-removal solution. Surely my heart had long since frozen too hard for something as tender as tears.

Then I straightened, went to the window. This side of the palace looked out only on the cliffside gardens and the sea. The rosy moon's light traced long pathways across the calm waters, as if I could step out and walk along them, escape to the horizon and never look back. The scent of night-blooming jasmine rose up, filling the air along with the soft notes of the owls and nightjars calling.

I'd never walk away. Couldn't, as all this fell to me to protect, and only my death would part me from Calanthe. Which meant I had to fight.

Resolved, I took myself to my solitary bed, praying to Ejarat to spare me the nightmares, if only for the one night. I wasn't sure I could bear much more.

If I broke . . . what then?

Two of Anure's warships sailed away the next morning—leaving Leuthar and his personal ship behind, and taking the provisions I so generously, if involuntarily, gifted them—and the waters of Calanthe breathed in relief, which meant I did, too. As soon as I felt them leave my seas, I convened my advisers and set my plans into motion. They involved a great deal of waiting, but such is the concubine's lot in life, to spend her days waiting to find out how she'll be used. Whenever possible, I employed my wiles to pump Leuthar for information, and he remained singularly unforthcoming. Either Anure had kept him ignorant or Leuthar had developed a caginess I hadn't noted before.

I placed my bets on ignorance since Leuthar always

seemed more inclined to indulge in the most degenerate pleasures of the Flower Court than to extend himself to work at anything. If I were Anure, I wouldn't trust the man, either. But then Anure trusted no one. For that matter, neither did I.

I also leveraged something I'd held in store to keep Leuthar thoroughly distracted. It's not always easy to judge when to access those things saved for lean seasons. What seems to be an emergency today might be eclipsed by a far worse one in the future. I went with my intuition—and the newly acquired voice in my head, which meant either magical assistance from the ring or encroaching insanity. No reason it couldn't be both.

I summoned the Lady Delilah, something I never did. She had "ruled" the Night Court since long before my birth. We rarely crossed paths, in fact, as she slept during daylight hours to better fuel her nocturnal revelries. She also expressed zero interest in Calanthe's internal politics, preferring instead to focus on exploring the world of sensual pleasure and her own intimate games of power and control. I couldn't imagine how she hadn't exhausted the possibilities in her nearly five decades, but according to Tertulyn's reports, Delilah managed to keep her delights endlessly renewed.

I didn't trust Delilah enough to make her one of my ladies, but she could be depended upon for behavior predictable within a certain set of boundaries. She took being the emperor's vassal to heart and eagerly displayed her desire to please our cruel overlord by indulging Leuthar as proxy. Her ambitions likely reached to some fantasy of bedding Anure himself.

Though I strongly questioned her taste, the single-mindedness of her scheming made her useful. She also made a study of Leuthar's various perversions and displayed

remarkable inventiveness—so Tertulyn relayed to me—
in catering to them.

Delilah and I maintained a relatively simple truce: She
didn't hurt anyone, she fed information to me via Tertulyn, and I turned a blind eye, allowing her full sovereignty
over her shadow kingdom. I leaned a bit on that scale by
asking her for this favor, so I didn't do so without careful
consideration.

Still, the odd whispers of the ring, along with a possible army of feral wolves descending on my peaceful shores
with an explosive weapon that had dropped the walls of
Keiost like fragile glass, convinced me that the lean season
had arrived in full force.

Delilah agreed to assist, though she clearly disliked being called to attend me, and I rewarded her generously.
Hopefully she wouldn't withhold valuable gossip from
Tertulyn in retaliation. I funded a small project to supply
Leuthar with a new vice, yilkas, a powdered seed that produced exotic dreams when smoked. Combined with sensual pleasures—and fortunately Leuthar possessed enough
physical charms to lure plenty of willing partners in
that—a person could lose days, even weeks, in that haze
if carefully tended. Leuthar wouldn't be in any state to
observe my preparations to elude Anure's grasp while
fulfilling the letter of his demands.

I also fostered an air of increased frivolity in the court,
and throughout Calanthe, increasing the gifts to the Morning Glories and making sure they heard plenty of chatter
about good things to come. We laughed off rumors of rebellions and dire whispers of the Slave King. If all went
well, Anure's forces would deal with the threat, and we
would indeed go on, if not in true prosperity, then at least
as well as before.

The emperor would reward me—and all of Calanthe—

for our loyalty. The worst would not come to pass. If this Slave King slipped through Anure's grasp, I would marshal the true might of Calanthe against him, and only hope that that Anure would never catch wind of the power we held in check.

In the meanwhile, I wanted my people strong and happy. Their joy was Calanthe's, so I did my part in keeping that flow untainted.

Every night I dreamed of Calanthe falling into the bloody sea and the chained wolf becoming that cursed man asking *me* to help *him*. No—actually demanding my cooperation, while my true responsibility burned around me. And every morning, in the sanctity of the dreamthink—when I could wake in time—I carefully put it all back to rights again, banishing him and that pitiable wolf to the anguished night where they belonged.

Begone ye foul specters. In the dreamthink, I have all the power. I wave my hands, my orchid ring a blaze of exotic splendor, its fragrance a faint counterpoint, shedding daylight and spice.

The wolf and man both vanish, taking their chains and pleas with them.

Calanthe blooms in serenity, the sea restored to blue.

There. All restored to harmony. I only wished it could last longer than the next nightmare, or that I could be like my ancestors and work those spells and ones even greater as the tales told.

As it was, I did what I could to disguise how each passing night eroded my foundations. I am the queen of masks, the image of all my people hope for. I wore blithe happiness like a wig or flower-strewn gown, covering the wrenching terror and dread that plagued me.

I knew. I understood it with that part of myself that had found the dreamthink and heard the message from the orchid. The wolf would soon be at my door, dragging his broken chains behind, along with all that went with him.

I would have to kill it. Put it out of its misery. But only as a last resort. Just as joy and pleasure fed Calanthe and her deep magic, murder and violence would poison her.

I'd carefully laid my plans, and then sat back to wait. If he brought his war to me, I'd capture the threat. Lock it up in quarantine and forever lose the key. And I knew just the tools to employ.

10

"Calanthe. Surely you don't mean the pleasure island?" Sondra spoke into our astonished silence, which made me feel more sane—and helped me not growl in Ambrose's delighted face.

The inside of my skull itched with frustration. Better that than dull disappointment. Calanthe. I had no intention of wasting my time on some pretty, flower-strewn island of traitorous weaklings when I could have Anure's neck in my grasp. Fuck the Abiding Ring.

"Calanthe," I ground out. "They rolled over to become Anure's pets. None of our usual approaches would work." I was the king of the miserable and oppressed for a reason. The fat and happy denizens of Calanthe, hand-fed by the tyrant and having their soft bellies stroked by him . . . they had no reason to throw in with us and every reason to betray us. I coughed, a burning scrape of my throat. Things were simpler when I could swing my rock hammer at them. "That island would be no foothold, but a disaster in the making. I won't do it," I got out. The throat-soothing potion was wearing off. Too bad I'd drunk all of it.

Ambrose's face fell. "But the Abiding Ring—"

"We can't possibly attack Calanthe," Sondra explained

for me. She, at least, understood me well enough to speak for me. "We'd be wiped off the beaches and tossed back into the sea before we could mount our vurgsten charges. The population won't welcome us. Even if we succeeded in conquering and occupying Calanthe, the emperor's entire navy would be staring at us across a relatively narrow channel. He'd come down on us like the fist of Sawehl and we'd be trapped on a tiny island with no resources. Old King Gul welcomed Anure with open arms, and the people there have never suffered any privation. They won't love us, because we wouldn't be saving them from anything. We wouldn't have the support of the temples, or any of our usual inside allies. We might as well sail directly into Yekpehr, wave at the emperor, and let him kill us quickly."

I nodded. At least the direct approach gave us a shot at Anure. Stopping at Calanthe would be suicide. I didn't mind facing my own death—I looked forward to it, in fact—but I'd vowed to take Anure with me.

"Aha!" Ambrose wagged a finger at me and tapped the ledger again. "I perceive your doubts and am undaunted. You will succeed in defeating Anure once you have Queen Euthalia on your side."

Euthalia. Why did I know that name? I didn't and did. It was familiar in that odd way of dreams, when you meet someone in them that you know as well as yourself, and only realize on waking that they're a stranger, that you've never met them at all. A trick of the mind. I'd never heard of this Queen Euthalia. Judging by Sondra's expression, she hadn't, either—and Sondra had memorized all the royal bloodlines as part of her education as a lady, before Oriel fell.

"Never heard of her," I said, hardly growling at all. There. Polite and mostly patient.

"Gul's daughter." Ambrose raised and lowered his

brows in a gesture I belatedly realized he intended to be salacious. "Old King Gul," he clarified, "now feeding the fishes his people send to the emperor by the shipload."

"The emperor drowned Gul?" Sondra echoed my surprise. "But Gul was his ally, nearly from the beginning. Even for the emperor it makes no sense to kill such a staunch supporter. And despite his other excesses, Anure at least has hesitated to bring bad luck on himself by directly killing a king."

"You lot really did miss out on a lot, didn't you?" Ambrose shook his head in bemusement, then held up apologetic hands when I scowled at him. "I know, I know—no news in the mines. The emperor didn't kill Gul, just what he loved most. It's said the old fellow died of heartbreak as in the ancient tales. In Calanthe, they consign their dead to the sea, with full observance and regalia. The emperor even attended and spoke the prayers to Yilkay. Gul's daughter is queen of Calanthe now. Euthalia."

"Don't remember a daughter," I mused. It shouldn't feel like a lie, because—despite the dreamlike feeling of familiarity—I'd never heard of her. Of course, Calanthe had always sounded like a fairy-tale place when my tutors spoke of it. The Isle of Flowers. Untouched paradise. Blah blah blah.

"I remember her name now," Sondra said slowly. "She was a little girl, the flower princess, when . . . well."

When my family was slaughtered, Oriel pillaged, the rest of us sent to the mines—and this flower princess lived happily in her paradise. Right.

"She must be young still," Sondra added with an opaque glance at me.

"Mid-twenties," Ambrose inserted, nodding with enthusiasm. "And said to be very beautiful. Of course, Calanthean women are noted for their beauty, but she's apparently exceptional even in that frame. Common knowledge has her engaged to the emperor—"

"Then she's an enemy," I broke in. Why were we even talking about her? She had to be either an idiot or as corrupt as Anure to marry the toad. Both possibilities made her no one I wanted anything to do with. "No one I want as an ally," I clarified aloud.

"Reserve that opinion," Ambrose replied with good cheer. "There's more to her than you assume. Somehow she's managed to avoid making it an official engagement—beyond the betrothal promise her father arranged—or marriage. She's held Anure off for years. They call her the virgin queen."

Sondra snorted. "In her mid-twenties with the famed pleasures of the Court of Flowers at the least crook of her finger? Not possible she's a virgin."

I didn't know how Sondra could be so frank about such things. Just thinking about the things I'd seen . . . well, I couldn't because it made me ill to call up those images. And my sister's screams, how she called for help and no one answered.

A light flush graced her sharp cheekbones when she read my expression. "Apologies, Conrí, I—"

I held up a hand to stop her and she clamped her lips shut, glancing away, chagrined. She knew better than to bring up such things around me. I was honestly surprised *she* could bear to.

"The point," Ambrose continued in a more sober vein, "is that Queen Euthalia has no official lovers to claim her loyalty, regardless of her actual virginal status. She maintains the appearance of keeping herself for Anure. She has no close companions, other than her ladies-in-waiting."

"One of them could be her lover," Sondra pointed out.

"But as you've noted, the Flower Court is far from prudish. If she loved one of her ladies, the tales would likely tell."

"Or more than one," Sondra replied. "I could repeat some stories about Calanthe that—"

She stopped when I cleared my throat, yet again.

Ambrose knew no such delicacy, pointing a finger at Sondra. "I know some orchid tales, too. Let's exchange stories later when the company is less forbidding."

I only wished I were that forbidding. Then they wouldn't have gone down that precarious path in the first place.

Ambrose gave me a slight bow of apology, tapping the ledger again. "The old alchemist suspected that Euthalia is quite intelligent though she doesn't always display it directly. He made something of a study of her. She apparently attracts luminaries of all sorts of arts and sciences to Calanthe, promising them sanctuary and her patronage. This confirms information I've gleaned from other sources, by the way."

Ambrose's "sources" could be what the moonlight told him, for all I knew.

"Friends of mine," he clarified, reading my frown. "Human ones, who received invitations of this sort."

"But not you?" This whole conversation irritated me. I was tired. And frustrated. This strange sensation that I knew this pampered queen and had forgotten something important didn't help. It felt like trying to remember a name I knew well and had blanked on for no reason.

Ridiculous, as we'd obviously never met—we'd been children at the same time, in distantly separated realms. Though we'd shared similar stations in life back then, by the time we'd each passed our first decade, our life paths had dramatically diverged. Calanthe, the land of sniveling cowards, had turned up its belly at the emperor's first frown. She'd never suffered a day in her life, in her court

of pleasures and flowers. While Oriel had fought the noble fight and fallen.

Brutally unfair. Clever or silly, she deserved my hatred.

"I did indeed receive just such an invitation," Ambrose
said, somewhat loftily, and I reined in my gnashing
thoughts to recall what question he answered. "A round-
about sort of missive, but quite clear and sincere. I, however, had *other* plans." He finished that with a sniff and a
pointed glare. "And you're grateful for it, not only because
you have me to guide you, but because of this." That same
tap on the ledger.

Feeling anything but grateful—and knowing Ambrose
wouldn't relinquish this bone until I'd considered every bit
of what the wizard found so significant—I made a show
of bending over the page. Then sighed, squinting at the
crabbed writing, the words like bricks in a wall of text. A
painting in the center of the page caught my eye as much
easier to contemplate.

A blossom of extraordinary loveliness—a kind I'd never
seen before—and attached to what appeared to be a ring.
I'd never seen such a thing, not even made of jewels, and
this looked to be an actual flower. The Abiding Ring, no
doubt.

The usual aspect of the ring, the bit that went around
the finger, was painted as a twining vine. I couldn't tell if
it was a clever design rendered in metal or a part of the
flower. Surely it couldn't be real, no matter what Ambrose
claimed. And yet the artist had captured it so that it nearly
moved on the page, shaded in with fiery oranges that bled
into dusky indigo, like the final splash of a sunset—or the
intense sky before the sun rose. I fancied that a delicately
sweet fragrance rose from the page. Amazing to smell anything but sulfurous vurgsten. And ridiculous. A painting

of a flower would have no scent, even if my ravaged sinuses allowed me to smell anything at all anymore.

Still, though I knew it to be an illustration—flat, and on paper—the flower evoked a loveliness beyond our world, the petals almost moving, as if in an unseen breeze. It seemed so real and alive that I had to touch it, pulling back at the last moment at the sight of my callused finger, the nail twisted and forever growing broken from when I hit it with a pick long ago.

When I was a boy, I'd imagined Calanthe as a magical fairyland. This flower ring spoke to that part of me I'd thought crushed and lost forever.

I wiped at the moisture coming from my nose. Bright blood left a smeared streak on my hand. Great. I dug a cloth from inside my leather cloak. "Fucking nosebleed."

Both Sondra and Ambrose gazed at me, concern on her face and avid interest on his.

"I'm fine," I said, waving at them to ignore me.

It happened sometimes—to all of us—and though I understood that the mines had done that to me, too, along with my damaged throat and stiff lungs, it still felt like a weakness. Hard to look stern with a bloody rag clamped to my nose. This one probably came of being in the humid sea air, breathing all the vurgsten from the detonations, not to mention exhaustion and bending over the table in this dusty, stale tower room, packed with such an array of potions. Plenty of good reasons to have a nosebleed now, however inconvenient.

No reason for Ambrose to be looking so pleased. I gave him a quelling glare and stabbed a finger at the illustration. "Why am I looking at a picture of the Abiding Ring, now?"

Fascination sharpened the deep green of Ambrose's

eyes with brighter glints. "This is an excellent sign," he commented.

"What is?" I snapped. "It's a fucking nosebleed, not a portent."

"Ah-ah. You're trespassing on my expertise, Conrí. Observe." Ambrose lifted the ledger and took it to his raven, lifting it as if for inspection. The great bird cocked his head, feathers gleaming black as the obsidian stones of Vurgmun, and focused one orange eye on the illustration of the flower. He arched his wings in interest, lowering his beak nearly to touching and making a series of soft caws.

"Magic," Ambrose finally said, with some impatience, when Sondra and I stared at him blankly.

Sondra glanced at me, sharing my bemusement. "Or that old ledger has some nasty shit on it. I've seen what Merle eats."

Ambrose sighed heavily, tossing the ledger on the desk. "Thickheaded fools," he said, throwing up his hands at Merle, who echoed the gesture, spreading his wings as if he felt the same. "We are surrounded by ignorance." The raven croaked, bobbing his head.

"Fools *you* sought out," I remarked and Sondra snickered. I checked the cloth. Still bright red, so no stopping yet. I reapplied the cloth, clamping down on the bridge of my nose.

With another dramatic sigh, Ambrose placed palms on the desk and leaned straight-armed on it. "Listen to me, then, King of Fools. The presence of magic evokes a physiological reaction in sensitive beings. Merle knows it when he smells it. You inhaled the residual magic of the Abiding Ring and reacted by oozing blood. You're sensitive to it. That's a very important sign."

I didn't know about that. I could make anyone ooze

blood with my rock hammer. No magic required. But I didn't say so. The wizard could debate anyone into the ground, ending with all of us agreeing that the sky wasn't actually blue. I could use up a lot of my voice arguing about whether I could sense magic—and how a king isn't like a raven—and I'd only lose. Better to keep it simple. "I don't understand."

"The prophecy says you need to claim the hand that wears the Abiding Ring," Ambrose explained in a tone of exaggerated patience, "mention of which comes directly after the information about taking the Tower of the Sun."

I nodded, curtly. I knew that.

"Here is a picture of an orchid ring, worn by the monarchs of Calanthe, which I found here in what *has* to be the Tower of the Sun—even you thought so, Conrí—*and* the ring in the illustration possesses so much magic that even an image of it gives you a nosebleed."

"Everything gives us nosebleeds," Sondra objected in staunch solidarity. "It's a painting. In a book." She gave me a cagey glance, assessing how much more of this I could take, no doubt. "Even if the flower ring is magic, an image of it wouldn't have magic."

Ambrose gave Sondra a look of disgusted impatience. "And you're supposed to be the smart one. *Obviously* an image—properly rendered, of course—of a magical object will mirror the powers of the original." He nodded at Merle, who croaked what sounded like agreement. "This one was correctly done. My predecessor in this tower collected only the best."

"Why aren't you bleeding then?" Sondra shot back, raising her brows in anticipation of scoring the point.

But Ambrose shook his head in sorrow for her ignorance. "I'm an experienced and powerful mage, my lovely lady. Some of us possess weapons and defenses other than big hammers and bags of rocks."

I glared at him, which slid right off, as he beamed at me impishly. "Is there a point?" I asked.

"Yes!" Ambrose jabbed a triumphant finger in the air. "*This* must be the Abiding Ring spoken of in the prophecy. Whoever holds the throne of Calanthe wears it as part of the badge of office. It's passed from one ruler to the next on their deathbed."

"Or it's just a flower," Sondra argued. "The Isle of Flowers would obviously have no shortage of blossoms. Every kingdom and ruler has a bit of mythology to shore up the royal right to the throne."

"Not every one, surely," Ambrose returned cheerfully. "This nosebleed confirms what I've seen in the tides of the future all this time. Conrí will marry Queen Euthalia."

I choked. "*Marry* her?"

"With her at your side, Conrí, and the magic of Calanthe to aid you, you will triumph." He finished that absurd statement with a grand flourish that had Merle flapping wings and dancing from foot to foot.

I stared at him, contemplating the many possible replies to that outrageous series of statements. When I'd been a young prince I'd been aware I'd one day make a marriage of state. You'd think no longer having an actual kingdom should free me of that particular onus. Never mind that I could hardly be allowed to touch a woman, much less consummate a marriage.

"*Why* must I marry her?" I ground out.

Ambrose rolled his eyes. "Were you not listening to the part about it never coming off her finger while she lives? You can't take it from her."

"Then I'll take her prisoner and make her wield it for me."

Ambrose actually laughed in my face. "Magic doesn't work that way, Conrí."

"All right, then I'll kill her and take it once she's dead."

Ambrose gave me a look of the long-suffering. "You can't smash everything with your hammer or blow it up with your stinking rock. You must seduce, not coerce. Marry the queen, marry the ring, work in concert to bring down Anure."

"To kill her fiancé. She won't be happy about that."

"She'll change her mind once you win her heart."

I snorted out a laugh at the impossibility of the likes of *me* winning any woman's heart, much less a beautiful one, a queen of a land known for its sensual excesses and erudition.

Sondra studied Ambrose a moment longer, then seemed to come to a decision, because she shrugged and turned to me with a sardonic grin. "Well, we always knew you would have to marry for the sake of duty someday. Looks like we know who it is now. At least you'll finally get laid."

I nearly snarled at her, which only made her grin spread. At least someone was amused by this turn of events. Laying hands on the opposite side of the desk, I leaned in nearly nose-to-nose with Ambrose, who—to his credit—didn't flinch.

"How am I supposed to do this?" I attempted to keep the tone mild, but loaded the question with all my doubt at this patently ridiculous idea.

Ambrose only beamed. "I have faith in you, Conrí. You'll find a way. It's what you do."

I didn't bother to point out that I'd never done anything like this.

11

"Thank you, all, for attending Me upon such short notice." The men and women ringed around my private walled garden nodded back, expressions ranging from wary interest to avid curiosity. I'd planted the seeds to evoke their excitement via invitations hand-delivered by my ladies. The notes had been prettily done, discreetly worded—and the folded shapes of the missives conveyed much more to the discerning eye. A little intrigue never hurt to stimulate intellect in types like these, and I preferred to keep as much of my plans secret as possible, including that this meeting occurred at all.

Leuthar should be thoroughly occupied. Lady Delilah had been more than pleased at the extra infusion of royal coin to make her already elaborate party—with the emissary her guest of honor—a carnival of sensual entertainment. With Delilah's devotion to monopolizing Leuthar's attention, he shouldn't happen upon this gathering.

Even if he did, it would look like another of my chaste, and therefore boring, salons. Delilah's wasn't the only party going on in the palace, but naturally I attended none of them, not even the tamer ones. Even if I had the inclination, I wouldn't go. It wouldn't do to show favor to any single hostess or host, and besides, I had my everlasting virginal reputation to maintain. The habit allowed me the occasional quiet gathering of my own choosing with a select few.

If Leuthar or one of his spies were to stumble in, he'd see only a party of artists and other similarly worthless refugees enjoying my garden. The emperor indulged me in my affection for "strays," as he put it, to keep me entertained while I endured abstinence, denying myself of worldly pleasures to preserve my innocence for the day we could be together. It was a measure of Anure's arrogance that he didn't understand the might of those I'd gathered under my protection.

"Hopefully none of you are missing another much-desired gathering to attend Me," I added with a serene smile as Tertulyn and my other ladies distributed flower tea and small cakes. No servants for us this evening. I watched the faces of my guests for signs of disgruntlement. Anyone who did wish to be elsewhere would not be suited to this conversation.

Brenda cracked a smile, an odd downward-turning twist of her mouth in a square-jawed face, made more severe by her short-cut silver hair. "I 'spect the conversation here will be far more interesting," she commented.

"If only because we have conversation at all," quipped Percy, an extravagant young man who'd arrived in Calanthe bearing gifts, but emaciated, and whose still-slender frame served to display the most fanciful outfits of the court designers. Many hostesses vied for his witty presence at their gatherings, and I found it salient he chose to be here instead. I hadn't been sure of him at all.

When everyone had been served, I dismissed all the ladies-in-waiting but Tertulyn, whom I trusted as I trusted my own heart. Once the door sealed closed, I seated myself. The others watched the increased privacy with some bemusement.

"Your Highness has a knack for the enticing invitation," Castor noted with a snort. "Judging by the array of talent in this room, I assume You plan to pick our minds."

I could always count on my old tutor to bypass intrigue and lay out the bare essentials. Ah well—I couldn't ask what I needed to know by dancing around it. Indeed, the dozen or so people gathered in this courtyard were the smartest and most talented, perhaps, in all the empire.

"I've asked little of you, I believe, beyond the invitations I originally extended for you to grace the court of Calanthe with your talents. Tonight that will change. I am first asking for a vow that you will not reveal what we discuss here, made upon whatever you hold most sacred. If you cannot do this, or cannot cling to your vow, you must leave."

Though several exchanged bemused glances, and Percy seemed to be restraining a smart remark, no one stirred.

"Your Highness," Brenda said, the delicate porcelain teacup small in her rough hands, "I think I'm safe speaking for all of us here. We've accepted Your patronage with tremendous gratitude. For many of us, it likely saved our lives. None of us are stupid, so we've all 'spected that we would be asked someday to give back more than composing poems or wearing fancy outfits."

"Jealous hag," Percy replied, reaching over to pat Brenda's hand, then gave me a seated bow. "And of course, she's absolutely correct."

"Although I'm not sure what I, personally, have to offer," Agatha said. A fine-boned and delicate young woman with dark hair and a striking talent for weaving, she'd come from some distant kingdom she'd never named. Not that I asked questions of them, these people who caught word of my hospitality and made their way to Calanthe. My spies discovered all they could about my émigrés. As long as their secrets did not mark them agents of the emperor, I didn't care to know what they were. Some horrors, once known, couldn't be erased from the mind.

And after all, I had no intention of disclosing my own secrets.

"As I hinted in My invitations, I have a riddle for you all."

"The answer is 'a green mammal,'" Percy declared, and Brenda elbowed him hard. "Your Highness," he added, as if that excused his impertinence.

I didn't mind a bit, and laughed with the rest of them, equally as glad for the relief from the day's tension. It couldn't hurt for frivolous laughter to waft over the walls. And Dearsley wasn't there to frown at overfamiliarity from those of lower rank. His presence would be too difficult to explain. Besides which, he had other important responsibilities to tend to. Or he might be attending a party. I didn't expect anyone to deprive themselves of the pleasures of the Flower Court for my sake.

"I'd love for the answers to My puzzle to be so easy," I said when they quieted. "If your wit can solve the riddle I will pose, Percy, I'll reward you by granting a wish. I promise this to any of you—as long as it's within My power to give—if you can help solve My problem."

They sobered, perhaps wondering at the extent of my power. Something I wondered at times, too, much as I wished I had more of it. I'd been wary of doing more than listening to Calanthe's murmurs, as I had very little idea of how to wield the immense power there. Without a wizard to guide me, the risks outweighed the benefits. One day, no doubt—perhaps far sooner than I wished—the dangers we faced would make those risks seem laughable.

"Here is My riddle," I said, then waited for their complete attention. I didn't need to be careful of my words, as

I'd practiced this, to pose them the best possible question. "If I tell you that blood shed in violence must not touch the soil or waters of Calanthe, and if this Slave King and his aggressive minions escape the emperor's net and reach My waters, how am I to obey the emperor's command and stop them here?"

They absorbed the question in silence—and likely all its implications. Except for Percy, who asked for more wine.

"Let's take this in pieces. Do we even know who this Slave King is?" asked Agatha, finally, surprising me. I'd expected the first questions to challenge my restrictions on violence and bloodshed. Not yet. An interesting insight. And a relief.

Even I didn't know exactly what would happen if blood shed in violence touched Calanthe's awareness. It happened at times, of course, in small ways. Small incidents could be handled. Every village had its elders who heard when Calanthe flinched, and they addressed the situation, cleansed the taint, and restored the peace. The worst offenses came to me, and I dealt with them decisively—partly where I gained my reputation for coldhearted ruthlessness.

If they only knew how ruthless I'd be to protect Calanthe—and keep Her peacefully sleeping. Blood shed in violence at the level of a battle could wake powers far beyond my ability to control.

While I waited, they'd been discussing the question of the Slave King's identity with great interest. Even the wisest and most-learned gossip—just about different topics, and in greater detail.

"Does it *matter* who he is?" Brenda asked, absently, mulling the question. A poet of rare gifts, she'd also been a military strategist at some point in her life before arriving on my island. I'd recruited her for both reasons. One never knew what resources would be useful.

"Of course it matters," Percy replied, not at all flip. "Knowing where he's from would tell us how he thinks. What he plans."

"I can fill in some of what our honored emissary, Leuthar, omitted, whether deliberately or out of ignorance," Castor said, massaging one hand with the other. Though the evening remained warm, his joints must have been aching. I glanced at Tertulyn, and she gave him a quilted satin lap robe. He smiled sweetly at her. "Thank you, dear. I did a bit of research, Your Highness, and determined that the 'mines to the north' referred to must be on the volcanic peninsula of Vurgmun."

I frowned and he waved a hand at me. "It would not have been in Your studies. I had to dig out, shall we say, a recently acquired text to determine this much."

Brenda coughed quietly into her fist. As she'd been nodding along with Castor's words, I gathered she'd been the source of the text. The other advantage of inviting smart and artistic people to come live in your palace—they brought interesting things with them.

"For many decades, or longer," Castor continued, "the volcanic activity made the island of Vurgmun uninhabitable. As it cooled, explorers from several remote northern kingdoms discovered that rocks from this place, known as vurgsten, possessed interesting properties."

"I know something about it," Brenda inserted, leaning her forearms on her knees and clasping her hands. She had a habit of looking me directly in the eye, unusual for the people who normally surrounded me, but I didn't mind it. "The stuff can be used to start fires, extend burning. Get enough of it and the correct triggers, it can be applied with explosive force. This should sound familiar."

Anure's secret weapon. "Why isn't this commonly known?" I asked.

"Not that much of it to be found." She shrugged that off, an irritated twitch. "Or wasn't. Before. Mostly seen as a carnival trick; street wizards used it for the pop and sparkle."

"But if mines were discovered that supplied sufficient quantities," I filled in, "the emperor would've used such a weapon—and would've kept it secret, so only he could take advantage of it."

"Using prisoners is excellent for secrecy," Percy put in.

"That, and vurgsten is nasty stuff," Brenda said. "Willing miners would be scarce."

Castor nodded. "It's logical to assume this Slave King escaped from these mines with a good supply of vurgsten and the knowledge of how to use it. If he's clever, which he must be to have made it this far, he's maintained a supply chain that excludes the emperor—and he's using it to good effect in his campaign."

"Plus he's not dead," Brenda noted. "Tough guy. Definitely not stupid."

"And what do you suppose his ultimate purpose will be?" I posed the question yet again, hoping for a far better one from these minds than the one Leuthar had given me.

Percy gave up his indolent pose, looking excited. "That piece is supremely obvious."

"Enlighten Me." I said it drily. I had my guesses, but I wanted theirs. These people had been out in the world and I hadn't. Likely I never would leave Calanthe. If the day came that I did . . . well, it would mean terrible things, and not just for me.

"If he was a slave," Agatha said, her face shadowed with some memory, "then he can have only one true desire.

That's what Percy means." Brenda, head bent over her hands, nodded, not looking up.

The air in the closed garden had noticeably thickened. "And that is?"

"Revenge." Percy flipped a careless shoulder, but his gaze burned dark. "That's why the emperor is afraid. This Slave King is coming after him. Judging from what we've heard so far, he just might be able to take the fucker out finally."

Brenda lifted her head to level a glare at Percy, and he threw up his hands. "Oh, let's not pretend we don't all agree in this circle. We've vowed not to spill what's discussed. Her Highness is very careful in Her dance, but we all know why we're truly here."

"And why is that?" I asked, forestalling Tertulyn's move toward Percy with a minute shake of my head.

Percy gave me a thin smile, the ghost of his usual insouciance. "We're Your secret weapons. Your living treasure, carefully hoarded until the day we might be useful to destroy Anure."

Everyone shifted under the weight of the stupefied silence. Superstitious, perhaps, to fear speaking treachery aloud, even in relative security. And yet I knew of no traitors who'd been roasted on Anure's spit because they'd been too careful.

"Apologies, Your Highness"—Percy sounded bitter— "if I spoke aloud what we know to be true."

"You're forgiven, as the fault must be Mine in creating this false apprehension," I said, in my steadiest voice. No room for doubt here. Yes, I had deliberately collected these people, and trusted their motivations to a certain extent, but I could allow only so much. Any of them could be Anure's spy, an edged blade that could turn in my hand. "Let me be very clear that you are incorrect. I have one respon-sibility, one desire, and one agenda: to protect Calanthe."

I let that sit, with no further explanation. The prospect of vurgsten, this stone-rending weapon, being used on Calanthe and what it would do to Her . . . it made me ill to contemplate. The wolf, breaking its chains and the cliffs shredding themselves into the sea. That man, holding out his hand—I dispelled the visions with a shake of my head so sharp I nearly toppled the wig and crown, something I hadn't done in years. Forgetting myself.

"Let us return to the charge I give you all. How do I keep this Slave King away from Calanthe?"

"Then You won't aid him in his revenge?" Percy asked softly, something of the iron character that had enabled him to survive showing in his handsome face. "It would be Your vengeance, too. And mine."

"And mine," Agatha agreed. More echoes of agreement, even from others who'd stayed silent thus far.

"Not mine." I snapped that out crisply, certain and sure. "The self-styled Slave King is less than nothing to Me. Given the freedom, I would have ignored his presence in the world." The man, tangled hair coiling in the wind, holding out his hand. The nonsense stuff of nightmares. What I wouldn't give to remain untouched by his taint.

I took a breath, then accepted the mild wine Tertulyn handed me, steadying myself.

"I do not have the freedom to do anything but what I'm doing," I said more smoothly, my poise back in place. "No doubt you all have heard of the emperor's charge to Me. Should the Slave King come this way, I must not let him pass. I must act to stop him or suffer the emperor's punish-ment."

"Seems to me Calanthe is in peril either way, Your

Highness," Brenda said, staring me down. "Seems the noble choice would be to throw in with the Slave King."

"To what end?" I countered with infinite patience. High ideals were fine for philosophical discussions, but rarely applied to the real, extraordinarily cruel world. "Easy for you—for all of you—to contemplate sacrificing that which is not yours, that which might be precious to you only for certain reasons, your safe harbor in the storm. What if this Slave King is simply another Anure, possibly even worse?"

"He can't be worse," Agatha muttered with uncharacteristic ferocity.

"Oh, but he can," I assured her. Funny that I could be more cynical than they, but I had studied the ways of brutes and tyrants. "Anure is predictable within his framework. We are only guessing at the motivations of this unknown rebel, one who employs a weapon so destructive it topples city walls and the imperial forces fold before it."

"Better the devil we know than the devil we don't?" Brenda mused, not really asking.

"Better no devils on Calanthe at all," I retorted.

"How can You not want the emperor gone?" Percy demanded. "Even You—"

Brenda hushed him, but I answered. "Whether I want him gone or not is immaterial. It is simply not relevant. Look around this garden. How many of you come from kingdoms that no longer exist? Whose people are crushed, enslaved, forgotten, and dead. Your monuments have sunk into the sea, your libraries are burnt, your accomplishments dust. I want many things I cannot have, but I at least have the wisdom to recognize that. To fight the emperor is to be annihilated. We've all witnessed that truth repeatedly." I stared them down, sorry to upset them, but gratified to see my point making its way home. "My father taught Me that long ago. To fight Anure is to be crushed. We cannot win against him."

"You call it wisdom, what others call cowardice," Percy shouted at me.

Brenda and Agatha shushed him, casting me leery glances. I wouldn't punish him for the outburst. I'd heard all those accusations before—and far worse. However, I didn't have to accept the blame he wanted to cast on me. "I will not take Calanthe down that path while the orchid ring resides on My finger. Any of you who wish to call Me coward for that, I won't argue. But I will ask you to depart from the realm that succors you."

I let that promise hang in the air while it thickened enough to make them shift in their seats. I didn't much care to use that against them, but Calanthe mattered more to me than they did. A monarch must always keep her priorities straight. "I might point out," I said with considerable ice in my tone, "that if Calanthe had not survived, you, my dear Lord Percy, would have no refuge."

"No, Your Highness," he replied with some shame. "I wouldn't and I'm grateful."

"I don't want your gratitude. I want your cleverness. Solve My riddle."

Tertulyn regarded me with a calm face but widened eyes. Not like me, to voice such a direct threat. Those cursed dreams. My fingers ached with the physical memory of breaking themselves on the wolf's chains, and I curled them into my palms, even though I knew they were perfectly fine. The orchid ring fluttered, as if in a warm breeze.

The group was quiet in a significant way, Agatha drawing a shawl around her shoulders, though if anything the night was warmer, still and humid. The gesture again evoked that man with his leather cape and tangled mane, holding out a hand. Haunting me. I couldn't avoid the clear import of the dreams, that the wolf, the man, and the rebel they called the King of Slaves were all one and the same.

But I would not break my fingers on his chains. I would not jeopardize Calanthe for his cause.

I. Would. Not.

The circle of people sat quietly, as if expecting me to say something more.

"If it comes to battle, I will do the emperor's bidding and fight this Slave King. That is not up for negotiation or discussion, as I have no choice in the matter. The question is: How do I prevail without violence, no blood shed—theirs or ours—on the soil of Calanthe? If none of you can answer it, then we may all go and engage in more productive activities." My voice came out weary. "How many times must I ask this question?"

"Can we ask," Brenda offered, quite tentative for her, which made me think I'd come across harsher than I'd intended, "why no violence? I ask," she hastily added, "because You have the home ground, and defending with decisive force is the most direct solution."

"You can ask, but I cannot answer." Not even for this would I divulge Calanthe's secrets.

"How about defining our terms then." Agatha had a thoughtful look, at work on the puzzle at last. "Your Highness, You've said both 'no violence' and 'no blood shed.' Is one factor more important than the other?"

They watched me with keen attention. "An excellent question," I replied with some relief that I could specify. "Blood shed accidentally, ritually, or with compassion—including to feed others—is allowed. Blood shed in violence is not."

"Interesting." Percy had recovered his former insouciant

poise. "Then the other piece, 'on the soil of Calanthe'—is that literally only dirt or would, say, the palace floors still count?"

Brenda nodded her approval, eyes on me.

"The territory of Calanthe," I answered, feeling better all the time that I could explain this much of the restrictions. "So the entire island, the actual soil, and the nearby waters, within a certain perimeter."

"I'm guessing this perimeter isn't obvious, as no one has made note of it." Brenda made it a statement, raising her brows slightly in case I'd need to correct her, but I didn't. "So we have a choice of shedding blood outside the perimeter . . ."

"Or cutting off the head without shedding blood," Percy finished.

Brenda and Percy exchanged a long look. An unlikely friendship there, but one like mine with Tertulyn, full of unspoken understanding.

"I think we might have a solution, Your Highness."

I might've sagged in relief, if not for the rigidity of my corset. "Tell me."

12

"We have messages from the scout ships, Conrí." General Kara strode into Salvio's meeting room, Sondra hard on his heels, her face set, mouth flat.

I wouldn't be in Keiost long enough to stop thinking of them as Salvio's rooms and start thinking of them as mine. A good thing, too. I didn't much care to give the appearance of taking the place of the late, unlamented imperial governor, particularly by literally sitting in his chair. When I fought my way free of the mines and led my people into the battle to simply reclaim our lives, I hadn't realized that the bloodlust of conquest leads to desks covered with paperwork.

Many a would-be conqueror might be dissuaded if only they knew.

Still, the wages that war delivers are dull ones. By taking Keiost, I'd become ruler of it. Despite Sondra's determined efforts to discover any surviving members of the former ruling family, she'd turned up no one. While we kicked our heels, waiting to make the next move, my conscience—and my father's voice, which might be the same thing—spurred me to do what I could to set Keiost on a better track to protecting and feeding its people.

And though it made my skin crawl to sit where the slug

had planted his fat butt, Salvio's library and meeting rooms at least contained all the relevant documents for running the city and surrounds. I'd also found his correspondence with Anure. Helpful, though I loathed touching what they had, as if some disease of the soul might leach off and make me the same as them.

Even without that, poring over the things made my head ache. My lessons had been violently halted not long after my tenth birthday—and I began an education of a different sort, in the mines of Vurgmun—and I'd never been a diligent reader before that, which made reading an exercise in frustration. Especially as I couldn't quite swallow my pride to ask for help. As always, I kept my rock hammer and bagiroca nearby, and more than once I'd been tempted to grab either or both and bludgeon the wooden desk—and all the documents along with it—into splinters.

Witness my great restraint that I hadn't.

So Kara and Sondra's abrupt entry came as a relief, despite their tense expressions. I lifted my head from the tally sheet I'd been studying. Numbers I could understand. Though no amount of adding and subtracting would change our fleet of fishing vessels and pleasure boats into a navy able to carry an army of fifty thousand to attack and subdue Calanthe.

Ambrose could prattle on about how I'd be seducing the flower queen and fulfilling magical prophecies, but we had to get past her defenses first. On several levels, I thought humorlessly to myself. Still, the first would be the physical defenses of the island. I sincerely doubted I could just sail into Euthalia's harbor and say, *Hello, forget your imperial fiancé and marry me, a dog of an escaped prisoner instead.*

I doubted any of this absurd plan would work, regardless, but I knew my primary job and capabilities: get us *into* the harbor with all important limbs and organs attached. Before that, getting us *out* of Keiost with same.

Kara's and Sondra's faces spoke of bad news, but not the unexpected kind—and of the variety that made him worry and her gloat. I might not be able to read fancy legal language, but I could read people.

"What do our scouts say—that Anure is sending ships to retake Keiost?" I guessed.

Sondra nodded, eyes steely with anticipation, and Kara handed me the scrap of paper he carried. "Word just came via messenger bird from the deep-sea fishing boats we sent out."

I liked notes from scouts sent via birds—short words, to the point, and no embellishments. "Two warships, three days out," I read. Then grunted and tossed it in the fire. Though summer in Keiost was hardly chilly, my blood had boiled thin in volcanic heat of Vurgmun. Having a fire nearby to keep the aches out of my bones was a temporary luxury, but one I savored as fair compensation for playing governor instead of doing what I did best. Now the time had come to vacate this oversoft seat.

I grinned, slow and satisfied. This was the best news we'd gotten in a while. "So kind of Anure send me ships."

Sondra cracked a thin smile. "And here I was starting to get bored."

Kara looked between us. "Have either of you ever *seen* even one of Anure's warships? They can carry nearly a thousand soldiers and come equipped with siege engines that can sink a ship and level the walls of Keiost. Two of them is no laughing matter. And that's if he didn't equip them with vurgsten, which he will have done."

I tapped my tally sheet. "I have fifty thousand soldiers and a fleet of one hundred and thirty-three boats."

Kara's eyelids nearly peeled back in his attempt to

restrain his incredulity. "Conrí," he said through his teeth, attempting to sound deferential when I knew he truly wanted to set me back on my heels. A good two decades older than I, Kara had been the most senior of us to survive the mines. Sondra liked to joke that he did it by turning himself into rawhide and that he wasn't a flesh-and-blood man anymore. Never in his hearing, though. She respected him too much. And despite her thorny ways—and vicious glee in killing those who deserved it—Sondra still had a kind heart beneath it all. Kara cleared his throat. "Conrí. You have fifty thousand people answering to you, yes, but they include priests and clerics, mothers of small children and scholars. Easily ten thousand *are* children—"

"Eleven thousand nine hundred and eighty-three," I corrected, tapping the tally sheet again. "At last count, yesterday."

"Eighty-five, then," Sondra put in very seriously, carefully not letting Kara see her amusement. "Twins were born in the night."

I grunted appreciation, picked up the ink pen, and corrected both that number and the overall total. When I glanced up again, Kara had dropped all deference and positively glared at me. "The point is," he gritted out, "for able-bodied fighters—less the experienced ones out of commission from the taking of Keiost—you have in the neighborhood of eight thousand."

My tally had it at slightly less, but I nodded genially. "More than Anure's possible two thousand."

"How are you going to put eight thousand soldiers—"

"Seven thousand nine hundred and forty-two," I said helpfully.

"—on a hundred boats!" Kara finished as if I hadn't spoken.

"And thirty-three."

He fumed at me. "Split the hairs all you like, that's still . . ." He frowned, calculating.

"About fifty-nine and two-thirds per boat," I offered.

"Can we put two-thirds of a soldier in a boat?" Sondra mused.

Kara ignored her. "Some of these are one-person boats." He didn't wave his hands, as Ambrose might, but clenched them by his side. "Pleasure skiffs and fishing boats facing down warships is a recipe for disaster. Not a matter for joking. You weren't at Soensen. You haven't seen what—" He broke off, jerking his gaze to the window, throat convulsing as he worked to master himself.

"That's why we won't face them, General Kara," I said, plainly and with no inflection, hoping to break through whatever he saw in his memories. The man wouldn't want sympathy, though I felt bad for teasing him. Some things could never be funny, dark as our gallows humor got at times.

"We have no way to launch vurgsten in small proportions," he continued, as if I hadn't spoken, bringing himself back to the present. "Spears and swords do no good poking at a warship from a rowboat."

"That's why we won't face them," I repeated.

"You don't understand—what?" He finally caught himself. "What do you mean?"

"I mean to do what we do best. Steal Anure's warships—that will allow us to put nearly two thousand of our soldiers on them, thus only forty-four and two-thirds on the boats we have—and escape." The prospect filled me with glee. Salvio's chair wouldn't suck me in after all.

Three days wasn't much time, but we'd worked on tighter time lines. Much of the work had been done before word

of Anure's punitive force arrived. The walls had been repaired, at least to all appearances, though crews labored
night and day to shore them up to the needed depth along
with the height. Those who wished to leave had been given
their portions of wealth and supplies. Those who wished
to stay kept the rest.

Those who stayed would in turn offer the same choice
I'd given them, and either the city's population would swell
by Anure's two thousand, or the graveyard's would.

I laid my trap carefully, relishing this part of the game.
While Ambrose muttered in his tower and tinkered with
my fate, I'd exercise control over what I could—before I
became chained again, this time to the wizard's plans for
me to marry a woman I'd never met, one engaged to my
worst enemy.

Anure's warships sailed into Keiost two days later. The
flagship pulled into the harbor while the other blockaded
the exit to the sea. We'd left only a few ships at anchor—a
few fishing boats and a merchant ship—while the bulk of
our small fleet crouched on the other side of the peninsula,
sails blackened and oars wrapped in muffling. I don't know
what Anure's men thought they accomplished by trapping
the few ships they had, but Kara's experience, however
bleak, had predicted them correctly. They'd done it simply because those were their orders. Original thinkers and
the self-motivated didn't last long under Anure's thumb,
and these officers came from a loyal mold, slavishly following standard tactics. And they'd grown soft and fat living off Anure's enforced peace. They played into our
hands, soon to be trapped in turn.

I wore the clothing of a fisherman, my hammer and bagiroca inside a cart hanging with fresh fish, watching the
ships arrive with the open speculation of any man interested in supplying the emperor's fleet. Around me other

fighters pretended to go about the daily business of the city, wearing the guises of peasants, merchants, and other folk. Not far off, Sondra wore a fancy gown and a hat streaming colorful scarves as she openly flirted with her second, the man dressed in a dapper fashion he'd otherwise never be caught dead in.

The walls of Keiost reared above us apparently undamaged—we'd coated the newer stones with dust and grime to make them match the rest—the gates invitingly open. We'd found one of Salvio's flags and it flapped merrily in the wind, proclaiming the imperial governor to be in residence. A sharp eye would notice the absence of children, the elderly, and the infirm. Every single person in sight sported the hale physique of our most experienced warriors, even with no weapons in sight. I doubted Anure's officers thought much about the composition of a real population, however.

Regardless, I hadn't been about to risk anyone who wasn't a fighter in this charade. They all hid deep inside the walls, defended by a well-armed and armored force out of sight.

I wheeled my cart toward the dock, holding up a nice fish as I maneuvered for the perfect position, picturing these ship captains and their officers with the faces of the guards exiled to Vurgmun with us. Those had softened in their own way, but like root vegetables badly stored, with callused skins and rotten centers. They'd grown accustomed to having total power over us. In the time it took them to assimilate that the balance had shifted, that their cowed prisoners had slipped their chains and seized the weapons—well, that had taken them entirely too long.

The flagship captain wasn't entirely stupid. Before they docked, they sent volleys from the catapults on deck, slinging small rocks—not vurgsten—to clear the pier itself, then immediately deploying armed soldiers who ran down the gangplank or rappelled down the steep sides of the warship to wade ashore. My fighters pretended to panic, crying out their shock and pain as they yielded ground. I tossed my fish on the ground in apparent fear, pulling my hammer and bagiroca from the cart as I ducked behind it. Crouching there, I picked up one of the stones they'd shot at us, tucking it into my bagiroca. What they threw at me, I'd use against them.

The coastal breeze carried their shouts to one another, echoing across the deserted waterfront. They should be confused as hell. By the tenor of the questions and orders called, they seemed to be. The emperor's soldiers formed a line along the pier, saluting as the captain—easily identifiable by the number of shiny embellishments adorning his fancy uniform—disembarked and conferred. As I'd hoped, he headed in my direction.

The volley of rocks had halted all activity, naturally, and now the people gathered near, feigning curiosity, their readiness palpable in the air as they positioned their hidden weapons. The captain needed only be unobservant and overconfident a few moments longer . . .

"You there!" he called to me.

"Yassir." I peered out from behind the swinging fish, keeping my hammer hidden from view—and keeping my face averted. Once he got a good look at me, he'd know me for no one from around this part of the realm.

"Is all well here?" he demanded.

"Sir?" Just a little closer.

"We heard of an attack at Keiost." He frowned at the walls and the flag snapping in the wind.

That moment gave me the opening I needed. With a roar to signal the others, I swung my rock hammer at the man's head, splitting it like a melon before he finished his gasp of shock. Alert and ready, my people drove for the soldiers on the dock, taking the nearest by surprise. Shouts aboard the ship rang out, bodies flying overboard to bloody the water. The work of more of my people, who'd quietly swum out and climbed aboard the far side.

Keeping an eye on the ship uselessly blockading the mouth of the harbor, I bashed a path through the soldiers who'd taken up guard stations. Sondra led a charge of ul-ulating female warriors in lovely gowns up the gangplank, cutting down Anure's men too ingrained in traditional thinking to strike a woman.

I signaled to the battalions inside the gates, and several hundred more fighters joined us. Before the day had grown hot, we'd subdued both ships. The other ship had been taken with even fewer losses of life, having surrendered quickly to our two largest vessels, pinning it between them from inside and outside the harbor.

By evening, all had been offered the choice, going to either execution or detainment to test their submission. I didn't trust any to travel with us—transferred loyalty tends not to stick all that well in close proximity to Anure—and barely agreed for them to remain at our backs.

I wouldn't have, except most of the sailors and many of the infantry soldiers turned out to be slaves. We freed them, of course, and time would tell what kind of lives they'd find for themselves.

Another day to scour and resupply the ships—and to load our stores of vurgsten—and we set sail, though not with quite as many fighters as I'd hoped. We'd lost some in the battle of the waterfront—not many, but I begrudged every one—but I more begrudged the battalion Kara talked me into leaving behind to guard the city and its new immigrants.

Running cities takes far more work than conquering

them. At least governing Keiost would fall to someone else now. I stood at the wheel of the flagship, not being useful as I knew nothing about sailing, but savoring the brief sense of freedom. "Send the message to Queen Euthalia," I told Kara. "Let her know that Anure's loyal commanders found no sign of rebellion and will be docking at Calanthe to enjoy the delights of the Isle of Flowers for some rest and relaxation."

If only taking Calanthe would go that smoothly.

The prickle of unease in my bones told me it certainly wouldn't.

13

By the time the alert arrived that the Slave King had eluded the ships Anure sent to destroy him, I had long since passed the point where I might've been surprised by the news.

In the nightmare scenes of violence, in the foggy acceptance of the dreamthink, I'd been fully expecting his arrival every day. My dreams had tumbled dense with ocean waves and swimming wolves, their chains dredging the bottom, turning the clear water to muck. Even the dreamthink had been barely enough for me to calm the sea again, to put all the blossoms back in their places.

In the bright light of day and verifiable reality, I hoped I was wrong, that the cursed rebel would never reach Calanthe. It turned out my heart hadn't gone as cold and hard as I'd thought, because it tore me apart internally to be in the position of hoping Anure's forces would win. But as much as I hated Anure and would love to see him brought down, I loved Calanthe more.

My father had said it long ago, and had been proved right countless times over: No one had the power to defeat Anure.

Tertulyn was painting my lips on a bright and beautiful morning when a servant girl delivered the message. Knowing immediately what news the missive brought, I held out a hand in wordless command. Calla, after a bare pause, handed it to me. I scanned it. They—quickly discerning my mood—hastily escorted away that morning's Glory. Cursing inside my head, I read it again. How stupid did this Slave King think I was?

"Call Dearsley to attend Me," I commanded as soon as the girl was gone. "Immediately."

Calla hesitated. "But Your Highness is not yet dressed."

"Then dress Me," I bit out. Really, was it so hard? I'd already risen to my feet. Tertulyn, anticipating me, cast aside the paints and snapped orders at the junior ladies, bidding them to make haste even as Calla gathered her skirts and actually ran for the outer chamber to pass word. By the time Dearsley arrived—out of breath, uniform disheveled from his own interrupted dressing—they'd gotten me into my gown, and also put the wig and crown on me. Because Ejarat frown on me that I should smudge my appearance just because we faced a battle that might destroy Calanthe.

I handed Dearsley the scroll, my ladies crouched around me, busily sewing me into my garments.

He paused almost immediately, lifting a gaze full of dread to mine. "They found no sign of rebels—and they plan to disembark *here*?"

"So says this apparent captain of the emperor's warships," I replied, summarizing aloud for my ladies. "They *claim* they arrived at Keiost to find the city empty, the populace fled—along with all of the treasury—and the harbor bare of ships. Everything more seaworthy than a rowboat was gone." I hissed in useless fury. How could Anure have been such a bloody fool to fall into whatever trap had taken two warships? And who was this man who thought I was such an idiot that I'd believe this missive?

Paling, Dearsley dropped his eyes to the scroll again. "Did he say when—"

"The story is that they arrived at Keiost *four days* ago. They've been sailing around and around and sending scouts around and around the countryside, *searching*! As if they might have somehow overlooked a vast army and wagonloads full of blazing rocks." Dearsley didn't deserve my fury, but I couldn't get my nails into the person who thought to sucker me with this. "They say they only thought to send Me a messenger bird yesterday." I threw up my hands, something ripping, Nahua making a sound of dismay.

Eyeing me, Dearsley scanned the document again. "You don't believe it."

"Oh, I believe these rebels evaded Anure's might—but the rest . . . of course I don't." I had to be careful here. Citing mystical knowledge would hardly make me seem like a capable queen. And while I trusted my ladies, I wasn't so silly as to think they didn't gossip. "If you want to bring a ragtag army of escaped prisoners from Keiost to within striking range of the emperor, what do you need?"

Dearsley frowned.

"And you only have fishing boats. Maybe a few merchant ships," I clarified.

"You think he captured the warships?" Dearsley whispered, horrified.

"It's the most likely explanation." And it confirmed what the ring murmured, the images from the dreams. "They shouldn't have tried to trick Me with this *Oh, we forgot to notify You* tale. Anure's captains would have sent Me a message as soon as they knew this Slave King slipped the net." The insult to my intelligence gave a convenient path for my terror-fueled fury. I would show this rebel just who he thought to dupe with such transparent lies.

Dearsley closed his eyes. "Then the Slave King, if he's headed this direction . . ."

"Is likely already here, with two warships and a considerable force besides," I finished. I'd known it. Even if they hadn't yet touched the waters Calanthe considered Hers, I'd known. I should've prepared more than I had. Strike that. I'd prepared everything I could. I had to trust to the plan now. "Am I done?" I asked the ladies. I needed to be moving, not be decorated.

"One more moment, Your Highness." Tertulyn spoke smoothly, but with a hint of pleading in it.

My ladies danced around me, inserting the flowers and jewels to adorn the gown and wig. I forced myself to hold still. One more minute could hardly make a difference. Still, let the courtiers and politicians, those who read everything into my gown color and the placement of the jewels by the corner of my mouth, make what they would of my less-than-crisp display. "Enough with this," I declared.

"Your Highness." Tertulyn curtsied deeply, waving the ladies away. "Just a touch more on the makeup, if you will."

I flicked my fingers in permission and transferred my gaze back to Dearsley, the thick alabaster paste crackling between my brows. "Call a meeting of the Defense Council, in the map room. Also, send notice to all the lookouts, fisherfolk, and bird-masters. Full reports, even the least little thing unusual. Even if it doesn't look like a warship. I want to know everything."

"Yes, Your Highness. I shall assemble them." Dearsley took off at a jog, trying to tidy his clothing as he went.

"We have a Defense Council?" Tertulyn murmured to me as soon as he'd gone, coming at me with paint palette once again in her hand, her brush working to re-create the shadows of my cheekbones from the blank slate.

More able to bear the delay as I could do nothing more until Dearsley assembled everyone, I slid my gaze to Tertulyn. How had she not been present for those conversations? Tertulyn was ever by my side, knowing my mind as her own. Except lately, when I'd been sending her to Delilah, employing her to watch Leuthar, discover nuggets of information from the courtiers, sift truth from conjecture and exaggeration—and plant rumors of my own design.

"We need to mount a defense to keep the invaders off our land," I explained. I shouldn't have to explain myself, but I knew—much as I trusted the discretion of my ladies—that what they understood would filter to the rest of court and thence to the larger population.

"But it's against the old laws for blood to be shed in violence," Calla said. She came from an old Calanthe family and knew the traditional ways. Following Tertulyn's lead, she'd darted in to add a few more stitches to the hastily donned gown. I'd chosen scarlet the night before. On a whim, I'd thought. But perhaps some part of me had known. It could be the waters even beyond Calanthe whispered to me of who traveled through them.

"Thus *defense*," I replied mildly, reassuring her as if I spoke to a Morning Glory. "There are ways and ways to repulse an enemy without violence. Trust in Me to protect Calanthe." Even with my ladies, I hadn't shared the full, audacious plan.

"These are violent men, I hear," Ibolya, who rarely spoke, put in. "They will not be hindered by less than violence."

If it were not for Anure's demand that I confront the army of rebels, I could've arranged it so the Slave King's forces went around us. Like the ocean currents that eddy out past the island, or the tropical storms that circle, giving us their rain and then spending their fury on the open sea, his violence should have been redirected.

But Anure had neatly cornered me and I couldn't help wondering if he intended it as a test. Outsiders didn't fully understand why Calanthe had yielded without a fight—because such knowledge could be turned as a weapon against us. Anure lacked full knowledge of how my father had sent him away, but he was no fool.

But neither was I. "Then we shall turn them with something stronger than violence, which has ever been Calanthe's gift."

A sigh ran through them, and they smiled in relief. I envied them their restored faith.

"Where is the emperor's emissary?" I asked the gathering in the map room as I swept in, my ladies trailing behind me in two rows of three.

"Sleeping off last night," Dearsley replied congenially, "as is most of the palace, Your Highness. It's early yet."

True. I checked the glance of the sun against the tiled floor. Early indeed, for all that I felt already behind the game. Excellent, however, that Delilah had done her job in removing Leuthar from the board. I surveyed mine: the map of Calanthe.

The map room sits high in a tower of the palace, open to the air, enjoying a view in every direction of Calanthe. Arches lead onto a circular balustrade made of the white stone that is Calanthe's spine and skeleton. Etched into the rail are arrows pointing to landmarks, with descriptions carved beneath. Under the graceful dome, the internal space is empty of furniture or anything else that might interfere with the intricate mosaic map of the island beneath our feet.

Everyone there stood in the sea, according to the map—

an unwritten custom that always tickled me, as if treading upon the image of Calanthe might be rude when we walked upon Her in reality every day of our lives.

When the school groups come to tour, the children have no such qualms. They run, crawl, and pounce upon the great map of their home, embracing Her, even laying their cheeks against the jeweled tiles that show where their house or village might be. Very different from today's grim mood.

"Reports. Please." I added the pleasantry to the demand as an afterthought. No sense losing all vestige of civilized behavior.

My various advisers shifted, glancing at one another, most moving back a step to indicate they had nothing of interest or usefulness. One fellow I didn't know ended up stranded alone, left high and dry by a receding tide. Plainly dressed, fingering his broad-brimmed hat, he looked to be a seaman from one of the coastal communities.

"And you are?" I inquired, gently, as I would speak to a Glory.

"Your Highness," he said, his voice as unsteady as his bow.

I nearly replied that, no, that was me, but restrained myself. Tension brings out the sarcasm in me. I try to keep it inside my skull and off my tongue.

"I'm Nestor, of the reef divers," he offered, as if he'd only just remembered.

"You have something to report, Nestor?" I encouraged him.

"Yes! Yes, Your Highness. And, well, Your Highness asked that we be on the lookout for anything unusual, so I'm here to tell Your Highness what we saw. That was unusual, that is. I was coming to the palace anyway, Your Highness, and then they said to come straight here, Your

Highness, but I'm not sure that I . . ." He trailed off, looking around the imposing room with wide eyes, then fixing on me.

"The palace belongs to all, Nestor," I said as gently as I could, "just as Calanthe does. Tell Me what you saw."

"Not me or my divers, Your Highness, but the porpoises sing of an invisible ship."

"Only one?" Dearsley demanded.

"There are others, but they stay back, sailing in circles. Only one moves forward, Calanthe in her sights. Not yet in Her waters, but soon."

My finger warmed and tingled, the orchid for a moment looking to my eye like a leaping porpoise. That meant truth, I decided. Though it could mean it liked porpoises. Who knew? "Did the porpoises sing of what kind of ship it is, and how fast it sails?"

Unexpectedly, Nestor smiled at me, like sunlight filtering through shallow water. "You are a true queen of Calanthe," he said. "It's one that's been here before, but all different-smelling people aboard. It will reach our waters by midday."

And there it was.

"All right, ladies and gentlemen." Now that the moment had arrived, a strange calm settled over me. Fear is the worst in anticipation. Once there's a path to send it down, it transforms into something else and leaves you in peace. "Here is what we're going to do."

We were ready for them.

14

"There it is, Calanthe, the Isle of Flowers." Ambrose waved a hand grandly, declaring it as if he'd created the place himself. For all I knew, the wizard *had*. Ambrose might look barely older than me, but that meant nothing. The old tales spoke of ancient wizards who aged backward. Perhaps Ambrose was one of those, nearing the end of his days as he looked to be only in his third decade.

With my luck, I'd end up dragging around a mulish child or wailing infant Ambrose and still be circling Yekpehr, looking for a way to kill Anure.

Not pointing out that Ambrose wouldn't be this close to Calanthe if I hadn't stolen Anure's pretty boats to get us there, I squinted at the famed island. It looked real enough. But even from this distance, the long stretch of the island shimmered with more color than land usually did from so far out at sea. Along with the typical smoky blues and deep greens of any landmass, spots of jewel tones and pastels shone clearly. Maybe that happened as a side effect of the unnatural crystal calm of the waters surrounding the island. A memory came back in full force of the paintings in the palace at Oriel. Some of them had been a wash of color up close, but resolved into images from across the long hall. I'd spent hours one afternoon trying to solve that puzzle.

When I stood back, the people and landscapes showed with perfect clarity, even crispness. As I stepped closer, they fuzzed, then became nothing more than bits of paint dabs. I finally scratched a line on the floor with my dagger, to mark where the change occurred, and I'd stepped back and forth across it, looking for the magic.

I'd gotten into trouble for the jagged groove in the parquet floor, and my father had decided my punishment would be that no one should explain the mystery of the painting for me. I'd have to discover it for myself. And then, of course, Anure arrived, torched the parquet along with the paintings, and I never had found out the secret. Funny that I could be annoyed about such a minor thing still, after all that happened after. And yet I found myself looking for a line in the water that would mark where I ceased to see clearly.

I suspected I'd long since passed that point.

"And we're just going to sail right up to Calanthe and say hello. No scouting. Just trust that they believed we're Anure's soldiers coming to party." Sondra echoed my skepticism. We'd been over Ambrose's "plan" countless times. That didn't make either of us more confident in the craziness of it.

"Don't worry. They won't see us," Ambrose replied cheerfully. Perched on the staff the wizard held, Merle cawed an agreement. Or perhaps that was for the seabirds circling above in sunset colors of rose and flame against the midday blue sky. I'd never seen birds of that fantastic coloration.

"A big warship, even an invisible one, takes up a lot of space. They're bound to notice that," I felt compelled to point out. This felt so wrong, so backward from everything

I knew. A complete departure from the strategy that had gotten us this far. Instead of sending scouts ahead to bribe the temples, to assess the mood of the populace, suss out the discontented and recruit their help, instead of making sure we held all the elements of surprise, we were just sailing straight up pretending to be a royal visitor. Did Ambrose expect a flag-waving welcome? "This is a terrible plan."

"It can work," Kara commented. "If they do notice us, they will see us in one of the emperor's ships and think us to be from Anure and thus their ally."

"Unless they figured out we forged that message and know we didn't just dodge Anure's ships, but took them," I replied. I didn't know why I thought this Queen Euthalia wouldn't be that easy to trick. I'd built a rebellion on the stupidity of the regional governors Anure had installed. "I really don't like this plan."

"I don't like it, either," Sondra agreed.

"Don't worry," Ambrose repeated, more firmly, with some exasperation. "I have this handled. This is all how it's meant to go."

"We should've sailed straight to Yekpehr with all the vurgsten we have and blown it off the rocks," I grumbled. Stick with my strengths. I'd been a fool to agree otherwise.

"You agreed to do this part my way," Ambrose reminded me, green gaze shadowed and menacing as forest growth gone wild.

"My way has gotten us this far," I stubbornly insisted.

"Your way is to smash skulls with a rock hammer," Ambrose said, giving me a lofty look. "You can't hammer Queen Euthalia into agreeing to marry you."

That method actually sounded more likely than me somehow charming her into it.

"Maybe if she's daft from concussion she won't notice how ugly you are." Sondra grinned.

"Ha ha." Movement on the water caught my eye and I shifted for another perspective on it, telling myself I wasn't looking for a line drawn there. Water. Waves. Pink and orange seabirds. I was fully out of my depth. More the fool me for trusting in magic—or trusting in anyone but myself. Might and strategy won the day every time. Hadn't Anure proven that? I should've stuck to my strengths. I had a very bad feeling. Something was out there.

"Are you sure they can't see us?" Sondra asked. She'd followed the direction of my attention, squinting suspiciously also.

"Didn't I say as much?" Ambrose smiled with confidence and Merle cawed agreement.

I exchanged a glance with Sondra. She shook her head minutely but put a hand on her sword.

"Still . . ." she said, staring at that odd place on the water again.

"Do I tell you how to plant your vurgsten charges?" Ambrose asked, full of righteous indignation—a stance spoiled by the sea breeze tossing his unruly curls into his face. He pulled them away with some dignity. "I can disguise one ship from human eyes."

"Maybe the Calantheans ain't so human," Sondra drawled.

I might've laughed, if there had been anything funny about it. I stopped Ambrose's response to Sondra with the simple expedient of putting a hand on his head and turning it so the wizard looked in the right direction—and at the fleet of boats that had appeared, heading directly for us. I let go when he stilled in shock.

"Something has changed," he murmured. "How extraordinary."

Good thing I'd let go of his skull, as I might've been

tempted to crush it with my bare hand. We were well and truly fucked this time.

Small skiffs and coracles fanned out from the island, forming two rows and—not incidentally—creating a funnel directing our ship straight toward the island. A lilting song drifted from them over the gentle waves, sweeter than any I'd ever heard, even back in the halcyon days at golden Oriel. Not even from the silver-voiced Sondra—who now gripped the rail, sword forgotten and deeply carved grief contorting her face.

If the sound made my burnt coal of a heart ache for long ago, I couldn't imagine how she must feel, confronted with that loss. I put a hand on her back, as a kind of support, maybe. She didn't start at the rare gesture, instead sagging a little and leaning into my side, putting her head in the fold of my shoulder despite the unyielding armor I wore.

So odd, to have her feminine weight against me, and I felt like a clumsy oaf, but I slid my hand around to her shoulder. A safer place to touch my friend who'd suffered so much with me and yet hearing a song sweetly sung cleaved her like a mortal blow. We didn't speak. There was nothing that could be said—and none of us handled sympathy well. We had no place to put it.

As we sailed closer, it became clear that the boats were all piloted by beautiful young people, youths and maidens wearing flowers and scanty silks. The sheer beauty and sensual innocence of the display dug the blade further into my gut. Who were these people who sent lovely youths out to greet a warship?

So easily slaughtered with one salvo of vurgsten. Of course, our weapon remained secret and they couldn't know what it would do to them. But any ship would have arrows to rain upon them. They might be turning out to escort what they thought must be an ally—but then why disguise them until now? I scanned them for weapons, not seeing any. That didn't mean they weren't a threat.

As if reading my thoughts, Kara asked, "Shall we fire on them, Conrí?"

The ruthlessness that had served me so well for so long must have been left on the other side of that invisible line in the water. I couldn't do it. Mutely I shook my head. Even Sondra didn't argue. I think she didn't have it in her, either, if she heard anything beyond her own pain.

Ambrose had said the Calantheans were noted for their beauty. That had been an understatement. They looked like nothing from the world I knew, waving with languid grace as the ship passed, slender limbs tanned from the golden sun and robust with health. Most were nearly naked, clothed in little more than flowers and scraps of sheer silk. They wore flowers in their hair in all shades like the birds—pinks and blues and yellows, sometimes several colors on one head. Petals of all shades floated on the serene surface of the sea, making it seem like a tapestried carpet rolled out to welcome us in.

I knew better than to believe it. Like those treacherous flowers of the Mazos jungle, so sweet and pretty, they lured the unwary into honeyed, sucking death.

I struggled to fight off the charm, not quite able to. The enchanting song, loveliness, delicious redolence of blossoms in the warm and gentle air, all wrapped me up, making me want to drop my hammer, toss my bagiroca into the sea, and lay myself down in peace.

"Magic?" I ground out, pushing through the haze and startling Ambrose. He'd been muttering to Merle about prophecy, something about the currents of the future, and . . . fish? Ambrose frowned and shook his head slowly.

Then nodded. Finally he shrugged, grinning boyishly, undaunted by the scowl I leveled at him.

"There's magic here aplenty. Thicker than I've ever felt it in my life, permeating everything." Ambrose positively beamed, and I clenched a fist hard by my side so as not to punch him. "It's wonderful—like tasting a fine cut of beef when I've been on gruel for months."

"I'm delighted for you," I bit out. Beside me, Sondra snorted, straightening again and raking back her hair that snapped like a banner of pale gold in the ocean breeze. Good to see her standing on her own again.

"But I sense nothing targeted at us," Ambrose added, apparently realizing he danced on a thin line. "Look! They seem to be . . . welcoming us and guiding us in."

"Odd behavior toward an enemy they can't see," I said slowly and deliberately.

Ambrose pursed his mouth, thinking, and slowly spun the staff, Merle adjusting his footing as the jewel turned beneath his talons. "Guess I was wrong." He shrugged, as if unconcerned.

"Wrong?" I should've punched him.

"Well, I wasn't wrong before," Ambrose hastily and cheerfully said. "Everything was as it should be, but now it's changed. That's my point."

"Explain." I held on to my temper. A miracle. Or the drugging enchantment still winding around us took away my desire to fight. I should be more worried about that.

The wizard waved a hand at the sea. "There are people and forces in the world that can change the currents of events. We expect the river to flow from the mountains to the sea. If someone picks up the river in its bed, turns it around to run in the opposite direction—well, how can that be predicted?"

I stared at him. "What does that even mean?"

Ambrose stroked Merle's back, murmuring praise while the bird preened. "Merle informs me that the denizens of the sea below us observed our approach and passed the word. I didn't anticipate that anyone here could talk to the fish."

"You talk to a bird."

"Yes, but that's entirely different." Ambrose's eyes sparkled. "Isn't it exciting?"

Great. Just great. "Exciting" he called the demise of our entire enterprise. And yet the usual rage that should carry me through this—and lend fire to the need to extract us—didn't rise up. It all seemed so unreal, like a dream. Perhaps I'd wake and we'd be about to storm Calanthe, ready for another conquest, violent and bloody. Something I understood. Something I could handle. I could only hope it was a dream.

Surreptitiously, I looked down, just to be sure I wore my armor and carried my hammer, the bagiroca hanging from my belt. All as usual, and I breathed a sigh of relief. In a dream I'd likely be naked and carrying something absurd as a weapon, like a child's sweet tree-finger. I hadn't thought of those candied treats in ages. The court wizards had made them for special occasions. A memory of how magic tasted and felt—warning me of what I felt now.

As impossible as it all seemed, this was real. We were simply caught in an enchantment. I'd break it if I could—and yet I didn't want to. That, too, must be part of the magic, and I could do nothing about it.

Details of the island resolved as we drew near, meekly letting ourselves be guided—or herded—into rounding the northern spur to the long, east-facing side. The high, white cliffs shone in the midday sun like a beacon. Here and there waterfalls tumbled from them into the sea, the pools beneath the vivid indigo indicating depth. Some of the falls fanned like an exotic bird's tail, separating into fine white sprays over cascading ledges covered in emerald moss. Other falls descended in impossible and vivid shades. The pools of poisoned, sulfurous water on Vurgmun had been like that, proclaiming their toxicity with unnatural colors.

"Tainted water?" I mused. Seemed unlikely, for a purported paradise.

"No," Sondra breathed. "Not falls of water, but of flowers."

And she was right. Impossible as it seemed, huge swaths of the cliffs were draped with connecting vines blossoming in every color imaginable. The scent that had been swirling over us grew stronger, sweet and spicy, redolent of warm nights and the paradise of sensual ease.

At the most verdant section, a palace rose from the cliffs and the waterfalls of flowers, an ornate concoction of towers, balconies, and staircases. It perched right on the edge, fanciful as the ice sculptures my mother used to commission for formal midwinter dinners in Oriel, back before.

Just to the south of the palace, a great cove rounded inward protected by the point of the cliffs on one side, and a built-up fortification on the other. A city, also mainly of the white stone, with domes and spires of gold, also draped in flowers, ranged up and down the hills, cupping around an extensive harbor filled with boats of all shapes and sizes.

And there, an imperial warship sat docked—with an empty space next to it. Obviously our intended resting spot. Hopefully not one as permanent as the grave.

"It's a trap," I confirmed aloud, aware I also gripped

the rail hard enough to crack it. Here is where it would end, with us all drowned or cut down. Figured. The likes of me should never be allowed to set feet on such a paradise.

"I don't think so," General Kara said, surprising me. He'd been quiet so long that I'd nearly forgotten his presence on the other side of Sondra. "If you'd given the order to fire on them, we could've crushed those little boats at any time. None of those lads and maids appeared to be warriors, nor did any of them carry weapons that I saw."

"They could hide weapons below a false bottom," I noted darkly. What in Sawehl had made me so soft that I hadn't given the order? Take Calanthe. Take Euthalia and her Abiding Ring. Take Ambrose and his idealistic tales of seduction. A nearby young woman in a delicate sailboat with a billowing shell-pink sail waved with languid grace, smiling as she deftly kept her place in the water. Had I ever been that young, that innocent? Given the amount of pretty skin showing through the blossoms she wore, they'd have to be unusual weapons if she had them. "They played us," I said, knowing myself for the worst of fools. "Who could fire on these . . . children?"

"Anure," Kara replied, a pall of remembered horrors reflected in his face, shades of terrors witnessed.

"But he didn't on Calanthe," I reminded them. "He didn't have to because they . . ." Welcomed him in. The thought struck me with renewed horror. Had it gone like this? Did I follow in the tyrant's footsteps?

"And not exactly children." Sondra filled in the gap I left, not seeming to notice I hadn't finished my sentence aloud. "These lads and maids are quite nubile. Perhaps the Calantheans gamble less that the Slave King won't be another Anure, and more that his time of privation in the mines has left him hungry for the feasts of the flesh." She gave me an arch look. "Men have been bribed with less enticing spectacles."

A growl crawled under my breath for her ill-timed humor, and I swallowed it only because her earlier fragility still showed in the pallor of her skin and the brackets around her tight lips.

Why she so enjoyed poking me about this, I didn't know. In all truth, that part of me had burned away along with everything else tender in the boy I'd been. Sexual dalliances belonged to the world of the living, and I had nothing left in me of that. I held no illusions about that much. My stolen kingdom was a realm of scar tissue, burnt ashes, and revenge.

Which made Ambrose's insistence that I somehow court and seduce this queen of nobility, the prize blossom among hothouse roses, all the more ridiculous.

"They misfired there, because I'm not interested," I managed to say, hoping to put that conversation to rest. No such luck.

"Besides"—Ambrose studied me, all flippant behavior gone, his gaze penetrating—"your intended bride will no doubt prefer you don't dally with anyone but her."

I glared at him, ignoring Sondra, who made a choking sound as she smothered a laugh. For my part, I quelled any reply to that one. Of all the wild quests Ambrose had taken us on, this one had to take the tournament grand prize.

"Have I led you wrong yet?" Ambrose asked more quietly, even with a kind of compassion, though I didn't know what for.

"You promised an invisible ship," I reminded the wizard. Then waved my hand at the empty slip at the dock that yawned ahead. "And led me into a likely trap."

Ambrose only grinned. "Apparently I need to practice invisibility spells that work on animals, too."

Wonderful. Just wonderful.

A crew of more maids barely garbed in diaphanous clothing—if you could call it that—and merry young men who looked like they'd never wielded a sword in their lives met us when we docked.

They offered garlands of fresh blossoms as we disembarked, but I refused them. And I kept my leather cloak, though the weight of it hung heavy on my armored shoulders in the gentle heat. The welcoming committee answered no questions and made no demands, simply inviting us to come along to the palace.

As if we'd been expected.

"Does she have a wizard like you?" I asked Ambrose as we walked up a winding path, laid with white stones and bordered with flowering trees and shrubs, so densely covered the blooms hid the foliage. I tried not to sound like I wanted to kill him, though I furiously wished I'd asked him more questions like this before.

"Are you asking if Queen Euthalia might have someone with the gift of prophecy in her court to predict our arrival?" Ambrose's staff chimed as the metal end hit the stones every other step, Merle now riding his shoulder, busily pulling petals from the garland around the wizard's neck. The sound blended with the pretty song our escort sang, either nonsense words or a language I'd never heard. Though, with my education cut sadly short, I didn't recognize many. "Possible," Ambrose declared, sounding pleased by the notion.

I set my teeth. "You don't know?"

"You mean, I should be detecting them through my highly developed wizardry senses whereby we sense one another's presence in the world?"

"You can do that?" Sondra asked. The flower garland draped over her hair with lush glory, her pockmarked face almost smooth in the leaf-dappled shade.

"No." Ambrose laughed, then sobered at my expression. "I never said I could."

"Both of you—stay alert," I told them, not at all sure how they could be acting like we were heading to a party and not our likely execution. "Don't be charmed by flowers and song. These people are the enemy."

"These are not the enemy, Conrí," Sondra said softly. "And fuck you for implying I'd relax my guard and wouldn't have your back."

I had no reply to that, so I kept my silence. Kara had stayed back with the ship, a decision I now deeply regretted. Kara, at least, would have been equally suspicious of this pretty place with its pretty people. No one had asked us to relinquish our weapons. They'd only suggested we might be more comfortable without our armor, looking confused and disappointed when I threatened the girl who approached me with her flower wreath. But they didn't act afraid, which only made me more uneasy.

The only people who didn't worry about weapons were those confident in their ability to neutralize anyone who came at them. At least Kara stood ready to retreat to the rest of our fleet and rally them to our rescue. Or to continue the cause without us, in the event of our demise.

We climbed the last rise and came around the bend, the canopy of trees giving way to a sight I'd never had the capacity to imagine.

"Bright Sawehl," Sondra breathed, and I was only glad that she and Ambrose were so rapt by the sight of the palace up close that I could cover my own reaction.

It looked like something out of the old tales, or a fanciful painting. Made from the same white stone as the cliffs, it seemed carved from the rock—or grown like a plant—rather than built. With fluid, rounded lines, one level flowed into the next, archways opening into rooms huge enough to see sky beyond through yet more arches. Balconies spilled into each other, connected by spiraling staircases, all dripping with the waterfalls of blossoms.

Birds in every shade of the rainbow flew in glistening clouds, shifting direction, then settling again in orchards and sending up choruses of song. Our dancing escort sang along, harmonizing with the birds.

Feeling stunned, I walked on, unable to dredge up the least desire to turn back. As we approached the wide promenade that led up to the palace entrance, I noted the absence of other people. No guards, no walls or portcullis. No apparent doors, even. But also no courtiers lingering on the lovely lawns of tiny violet flowers, or enjoying the many pavilions and lounging chairs overlooking the crystal-clear sea. No merchants bringing in goods or gardeners working on the obviously carefully tended gardens.

"They're waiting for us," Sondra murmured, confirming my take—and that she wasn't completely enraptured. "They're taking no chances."

Perversely, it made me feel better. This Flower Queen might have enjoyed a lavish and carefree existence by licking Anure's hand and giving him her belly while others fought and died, but she wasn't without caution. Perhaps she, at least, had the wisdom to fear the threat we posed. It helped shore up my belief that we still posed one.

The vaulted entrance hall was equally quiet, leading through various empty salons, all with enormous open arches so that the sea and gardens seemed to come inside.

"I wonder what they do when it rains," Sondra muttered.

"Silly. It doesn't dare rain in paradise," I returned, and she flashed me a grin, some relief in it.

At last we reached a pair of great doors, made of carved wood, that were actually closed. That, too, felt more normal. The Calantheans wouldn't be human if they didn't want to close others out once in a while.

Our escort evaporated and we stood there a moment before the great doors. I tried not to feel like more of an idiot than I already did.

"Do we knock?" Sondra whispered.

My rock hammer would take care of these doors. Kara and Sondra had talked me into leaving it and my bagiroca on the ship and had me carrying a sword instead, calling it more kingly—and less a declaration of brute force. I preferred the heavy hammer, though. I'd grown used to wielding it in the mines. The grip fit my hand, and the wicked pick on the reverse spiked what could not be shattered. Swords had to be treated with more care. A stout kick, however, would bring those doors down. And be most satisfying.

Ambrose stopped me. "I can do this." He tapped his staff against the doors, face alight with curious interest. It made no sound, but the doors swung open, smoothly and without the hitch of normal hinges. I had no time to examine the things because a grand throne room greeted us, along with a sea of faces to either side of a long aisle.

It took a moment to assimilate it—the elaborate costumes, the heavy scent of tropical blossoms and sweet wine. The hush of courtiers, underlaid with a whisper here and there. The taut stretch of power humming in the air. It struck me forcibly. Memories of my father's court at Oriel washed through me, how it had felt just the same—full of the potency of a living realm.

It made me want to weep for all we'd lost. It made me want to rage and tear the place stone from stone.

At the end of the aisle, a set of broad white steps led up to an altar of a throne. Six ladies sat on chairs at varying levels leading up, each in a gown of a different shade, all glittering with jewels or streaming with flowers. At the apex, the Queen of Flowers reigned over them all.

A lovely traitor. Concubine to the tyrant.

I strode forward, neither hurrying nor dawdling, staring her down as the equal I should've been. No—her superior, as I never would've so merrily bent a knee to the false emperor. Sondra and Ambrose followed behind, a half step after, guarding my back and flanks. But the queen didn't glance at them. She returned my stare with a hard and crystalline gaze.

She could have been a wax sculpture of a woman, but for the living gleam of her pale eyes. Her gown of rich material spilled like fresh blood over elaborate underskirts that must've been held out with bone, wood, or wire, the way they stood in artistic forms. A high collar of worked silver rose to frame her face, with hair of the same scarlet serving as cushion to a crown that rivaled the stars for its glitter.

Amid all that, her face should have looked tiny. In fact, she might be petite under all that scaffolding. But she was far from small, her personal intensity overriding her elaborate costume. She'd coated her face with some kind of pure-white makeup that contributed to the image of her as carved from marble. Crystals glittered on extravagantly long lashes—surely fake—that weighed her lids so she should have looked sleepy. But those eyes . . . I walked right up to the bottom of the steps and, studying them, found them to be gray, with a faint shading of blue, the color of rain on a misty morning in Oriel. And those eyes were about as sleepy as a stalking mountain cat.

Her mouth, painted into a perfect bow of glossy crimson, lifted on one side, a jewel at the corner of her lips rising with it. Something amused her. Me, no doubt. One slim hand rested—no, braced—on the great arm of her throne, and she leaned forward ever so slightly, poised to pounce. On her left hand, an immense orchid glowed as if lit from within. The Abiding Ring.

I said nothing. Did not bow or otherwise defer. Neither did she. Stalemate.

The temporary détente gave me the opportunity to revise my opinion of her. This was no idle royal chit, frittering away her days in pleasurable luxury. Anure was a fool to think he'd collared her and brought her to heel.

For the first time, a glimmer of hope lightened the crushing despair I'd carried. Ambrose might be right about her. Magic sang through her, thick and heavy as honey, so strong even I could sense it, and the steel of determination shone in her like a honed blade hidden in a sheath of embroidered silk.

In respect for that, I inclined my chin, a bare deference to her territory. "Queen Euthalia," I said. "I am the Slave King. I've come to meet with you."

The other side of her mouth turned up. Not a smile, however.

"I'm so sorry to disabuse you of such a charming notion, King of Slaves," she said in a cultured voice, fluid and like the brush of a cool breeze on hot day. "But this shall be your only audience with Me, as you, and your companions, are now My prisoners."

I was going to kill Ambrose.

15

The man called the Slave King fumed like a lidded pot left too long over the flame. I half expected steam to leak from his ears, perhaps for his head to pop off entirely, spouting blood and flame to burn Calanthe to bare rock. I refused to show fear, though the first sight of him had nearly dropped my stomach through the floor.

I hadn't thought he'd be so large. He wore armor, of a kind I'd never seen, and a badly made, roughly stitched cloak of leather. *Made from the skins of his enemies*, so the rumors had said. His black hair hung loose around his face and fell down his back in ropes. It wasn't only the armor that made him look big, however. His square-jawed face spoke of strong bones, eyes a startling shade of fulminous gold intense beneath heavy dark brows. Though pitted and scarred, he wasn't entirely ugly. Not handsome or elegant, however. Even cleaned up this man would never be mistaken for anything less than a dangerous, violent brute.

Inside the corset, cold sweat ran down my spine.

He was indeed the one from my nightmares, the wolf in a man's skin. The one forever haunting me, holding out that hand, demanding and beseeching while the manacled wolf howled with a broken boy's voice. I'd known it, so I shouldn't be at all surprised. The orchid ring billowed on my finger, breathing of fate and disaster. And the presence of magic foreign to Calanthe—coming from the younger man with the Slave King. Slight, giving the appearance of youth, he leaned on a staff that oozed power. He stared at the ring, his gaze fascinated and green as Calanthe's deepest forests. A wizard? Perhaps I'd been sent a gift along with this disaster.

Interestingly enough, the Slave King's other companion was a woman, a warrior in armor. Somehow the rumors had left out that the rebels included fighting women, much less this one who must be his lieutenant. Unless she v as his lover. Possibly both.

She might've been a great beauty once—with periwinkle-blue eyes and hair the color of morning light, straight and fine as silk, that many court ladies would envy—but her complexion, like his, bore pits and scars. They both looked as if they'd been roasted over a slow flame. She returned my study, noting my makeup and clothing with something like contempt.

None of them had replied to my pronouncement, though I thought the Slave King, at least, understood my words. No matter. They couldn't argue with me, regardless. The plan had worked perfectly, to my great relief, with no blood shed. Not yet.

I waved to the guards. "Relieve them of their weapons and take them to their cells."

"Why?" the Slave King demanded, his voice startling in his hoarseness, all the more so in his anger, now that he'd given up all pretense of being polite. Though I hadn't missed that he'd addressed me as one monarch to another, with no honorific.

I raised my brows in inquiry, not playing into his hostile demand for answers.

"We came here in peace," he said. "Is this the hospitality you offer all those who seek to meet with you?"

Tertulyn laughed, bitterness beneath it, and the sound echoed through court, though with more gaiety. Everyone had turned out to see this spectacle, eager to lay eyes on the Slave King and his retinue for themselves. This gossip would feed the parties for days, if not years.

The Slave King twitched, the wolf raising its hackles. I almost imagined a shaggy coat and fangs. I would not laugh at him, as I knew well what kind of beast I'd caged. A man who employed a wizard in his cause was no blundering feral.

"Peace?" I echoed. "Did you also go to Keiost in peace? And Irst and Hertaq? Perhaps you came in peace to countless other places before you tore down their walls, murdered their people, and pillaged their stores."

"What do you know of it?" he challenged.

Truly I shouldn't allow him to show me such disrespect, but I found his direct rudeness, the stark impact of his presence almost . . . exhilarating. For all that I knew well the danger he posed, I was fascinated—and fatally curious. How had *he* found a wizard when none had answered my calls all these years?

"Clearly I know more than you expected Me to," I replied, having seen the surprise in his gaze, and in the woman's. "Also, clear logic tells Me that you acquired your armies from somewhere. There can't have been all *that* many of you who escaped from the mines at Vurgmun."

The court whispered with excitement at this revelation, while a few people smugly nodded. I hadn't expected the information to stay under wraps for long—and I hadn't needed it to. Only long enough to wield against this man who presumed to lecture me on hospitality. He didn't show a reaction to my words, but the woman did, her mouth thinning with some concern.

"Have we killed your people?" the Slave King replied. He turned in a slow circle, as if checking, making a show of scanning the walls and ceiling before he turned to face me again. "Your palace appears to be intact, no tumbling walls. Why should you fear me?"

"I don't." I allowed a pleased smile. "You are My prisoners and thus can do no harm."

"But you assume we meant harm," he countered, "when you had no reason to."

"Does one wait for a rabid wolf to ravage one before having it put down?" I reasoned. "A danger need not be experienced personally to be respected and dealt with."

He smiled then, baring his teeth like that vicious wolf I'd evoked. "Then I've caught you in a lie, Flower Queen. You do fear me—and respect me."

He'd neatly trapped me in my own words. How interesting. A keen mind lurked behind that brutish brow. Of course, he'd have to be intelligent—likely a blazingly good strategist—to have made it this far. Not smart enough to have avoided this trap, however. So ends the Slave King, and his dangerous rebellion with him.

I made a show of yawning, caging it in my nails, then waving the manufactured boredom away. "I weary of this audience. Guards, take them to—"

"What makes you think we'll go so meekly?" He drew his sword, taking a strong fighter's stance and sizing up the guards. Echoing the movement, the woman drew her sword also, pivoting so she guarded his back. The wizard, fascinated gaze still on the orchid ring, didn't move, but the raven on his staff mantled its wings, and the feeling of foreign magic they'd brought with them thickened the air.

Would the wizard have aggressive magics? Surely he would've employed them by now. Still, I would conduct this dance carefully.

"You're gravely outnumbered, Slave King," I explained, gently, as if to a child. "The three of you cannot win this fight. Better to concede and go quietly."

"I have a small army on my warship."

"You mean the warship you stole from His Imperial Majesty? That one is currently controlled by My soldiers. I believe 'small' is the operative word there." I held up my littlest finger in demonstration, allowing my gaze to stray to his groin while I lowered my brows in concern, as if seeing something distressing. My ladies, following the cue, giggled, making mournful pouts.

Interestingly enough, the Slave King didn't react as most men might. He met my eyes, the clear gold of them full of some insight. I had the unsettling sense that he saw past the formal makeup and practiced regal manner, that he could penetrate my careful masks as no one else did. Nonsense, of course. A relic of that familiarity of him walking in my nightmares, that I fancied he could.

"You who know so much about me," he said softly, almost enough to smooth the roughness that came in when he raised his voice, "you should know I won't go down without a fight."

"Tell Me," I said. "Is Vurgmun where you obtained the weapon that tears down walls?"

He paused a moment. "What do you know of it?"

"Rumors. Exaggerations." I waved a hand to dismiss all of it. "My point is that I notice no unusual weapons on you. You threaten to fight, but I'm frankly unimpressed." From the corner of my eye, I observed the wizard, the true threat in the room, but he seemed disinclined to act. Interesting.

The woman's lip curled in a snarl and the Slave King's

eyes glittered with the insult. "You have no idea what we're capable of doing. Don't test me."

I shrugged, delicately. "It seems ridiculous that you'd come so far to commit suicide, but so be it. His Imperial Majesty will thank Me for your head as much as for your life. It's your choice: Go to your cell quietly or die here and now. It's all the same to Me." I smoothed a hand down the scarlet silk of my gown, holding his gaze and reminding him that his own spilled blood would look the same.

The Slave King narrowed his eyes. Suspicion? No, testing my resolve. He glanced at the blond woman with him, apparently soliciting her opinion. Surprising, coming from a man like him. The woman, who gazed at me with black hatred, shook her head minutely. The Slave King looked to the wizard next, then flattened his mouth in irritation when the wizard only smiled with what looked like good cheer, and gestured to me. Some significance there.

"What if I go quietly—what then?" the Slave King asked, turning back to me and sounding resigned. "If I'm docile and obedient to your capricious whims, do I earn an audience with you?"

"*Another* one?" I made sure to sound astonished. "So few men attain even one audience with Me." I tsked. "The rumors of your greed don't exaggerate."

"Don't they?" He coughed. No—that was a laugh, made strained by whatever corrupted his voice. "Call me greedy then. I beg an audience with you, *Your Highness*." He used my title so grudgingly the politeness was lost, then added, "A private one."

Everybody laughed—but for the three of them—genuine delight in the sound. I allowed it, and indicated the room with a sweep of my hand, in case he hadn't noticed. "Oh my, you are so out of your depth, King of Slaves," I needled him. "Allow Me to tutor you in the etiquette you are seriously lacking. No one receives a private audience with Me. Ever."

"Not even Anure?" he shot back.

I hadn't been ready for that attack. Clever man. Too bad he'd made such dangerous choices. "Not even His Imperial Majesty."

"Difficult for a man to woo his fiancée in public, emperor or not," he pointed out, watching me with that too-astute gaze. "Surely you give him time alone with you."

I wouldn't reply directly to that, as I had no intention of discussing the threatening letters Anure sent me in the guise of love. "Difficult for a woman to maintain her reputation as an inviolate virgin if she entertains anyone in private."

He cocked his head, just barely, the wolf catching scent of its prey, holding still to track the source. "An audience with you and one of your ladies then," he offered, as if he were in a position to bargain, "and me with one of my advisers. Lady Sondra, perhaps." He indicated the blond warrior woman. "In exchange, I'll tell you about the weapon that tears down walls."

Lady Sondra gave him a glare to melt glass. He'd improvised then, not following any plan they'd made—and correctly discerning my avid interest in knowing more about vurgsten. Too bad I couldn't afford those terms. And I'd let him draw this out far too long.

"No," I said simply, sinking the weight of my decision behind it. "To answer your question, if you are indeed 'docile' and 'obedient,' going with My guards like a good dog, then you and yours will not be harmed. Those are My terms."

He clenched his jaw, eyes molten with fury. I'd pushed him too far with that mockery, his anger rising enough to make him foolish, so I threw him a bone. "I'll even release your people aboard His Imperial Majesty's warship. No one will be the wiser. They can go free."

He relaxed slightly, a frown forming between his brows. I'd surprised—and tempted—him with that. Despite the tales and his brutal, uncouth appearance, this Slave King might possess the heart of a true king. He cared about his people. How very interesting. And useful. "And the two with me?"

"They must share your fate," I informed him, for the sake of our many listeners, though I had no intention of releasing the wizard if I could keep him.

I couldn't pretend the wizard hadn't been there. But I could order him executed and then hide him. I'd done so before. Never with anyone who'd interest Anure so greatly, however. And Leuthar would likely want to send their heads along with the imprisoned Slave King. I could find a way around that. If I did, I'd try to save the Lady Sondra, too, if only because I couldn't stomach consigning any woman to Anure's horrors.

"And what is this fate you plan?" the Slave King asked, still in bargaining mode. It took me a moment to realize he addressed what I'd said, not my thoughts.

"I am to deliver you to His Imperial Majesty." I couldn't pretend to frivolity there. Even my considerable powers of subterfuge couldn't make that sound anything worse than horrible.

"I think I'd rather die here," he said, as if confiding a secret. I had to ruthlessly suppress the urge to smile in return. Surely the man couldn't be flirting with me. This man was my enemy and I'd do well to remember that.

"Your death can be arranged." I layered ice into my tone.

"I suppose Anure will reward you for my capture?"

"Or your corpse," I answered, sounding as bored as possible. "He'd be equally pleased with either."

"Then why haven't you killed me already?" He delivered the question with a bite. Far too clever by half. "You could have cut us down the moment we stepped off the ship and saved all this . . . theater." He waved a dismissive hand at the court.

I resisted narrowing my eyes, letting my lashes droop drowsily instead. He couldn't possibly know my true reasons. This Slave King simply fished for information. And sought to delay the inevitable. "Your ignorance is showing. My court has been agog to lay eyes on the escaped slave foolish enough to tweak His Imperial Majesty's nose. This has been great entertainment for us. But now I grow weary of this circular conversation. You will be removed from My presence—walking or on a slab. Your choice."

He assessed the guards, obviously measuring their distance, then his proximity to me. "Seems I could cut your throat before your guards reached me. If I'm to die, I could take you with me."

"Don't try it," I advised him, keeping an eye on the wizard, who smiled genially at me. "It will not turn out as you imagine."

He took a deliberate step forward, his unsheathed sword poised to strike. "If you think me an honorable man, that I won't strike these pretty ladies who stand between us, you're greatly mistaken. I lost my honor long ago."

A fascinating man, indeed. I wondered if he truly believed that about himself. It so clearly wasn't true—but he might think so.

"The blossoms of the Flower Court have thorns," I replied lightly. "Again, I advise against this foolish—and desperate—plan."

He growled. Actually growled, like the wolf I'd dreamed him. Surely he wouldn't.

"Conrí," the Lady Sondra said, her voice as rough as his. She looked apprehensive for the first time. "Be—"

"Shut up, Sondra," he bit out, advancing another step. "I won't wear chains again." He directed that last at me. His eyes held a world of pain and rage, and my heart pounded in understanding. We both lived as prisoners of the tyrant, even if our lives and the manner of our chains were so very different. It took everything in me to harden my heart—how had I thought it cold?—against the weakening sympathy.

My father had taught me to make decisions based on cool rationality, duty over emotion.

The Slave King took one more step and my two lowest-tier ladies, Zariah and Nahua, shifted their feet. The Slave King likely couldn't see it in them, but they were poised to intercept him. Still, I'd rather they didn't have to act.

"I'll caution you a third and last time," I told him. "And I promise: no chains." I wasn't sure why I added that, unless something about the wild, even desperate glint in his golden eyes reminded me of that wolf, its horrible howling, and how I'd shredded my dream fingers on its manacles. I might have the coldest of hearts, one that will never love, but even I am not completely impervious to another's pain. I wished I could be so callous that the scrape of sharply defined duty didn't cut so deeply. "Go quietly with my guards or suffer the consequences."

"Stop him, Ambrose!" Sondra shouted. I glanced at her, seeing real fear in her face.

The raven flapped its wings, its raw cawing an echo of

their harsh voices. The wizard, Ambrose, gave me a long look, then pointedly gazed at the orchid ring. "I think it has to go this way," he commented, almost absently.

The Slave King lunged. Zariah and Nahua moved in a blur.

Some men simply had to be shown.

16

I woke to a headache worthy of a three-day bender. A sour and bitter dry film glued my stiff tongue to the roof of my mouth, my eyes as gritty as on a windy day in Vurgmun. My body ached as if I'd been slaving in the mines. Had I somehow wound up back there? Panic gripped me—and turned my stomach.

But no. The air didn't smell like sulfur. It smelled . . . like flowers. And though warm, I wasn't baking hot. Not Vurgmun, then, and wrenching relief filled me.

But what the hell *had* happened?

The last time I'd felt this awful had been in the first village we'd taken after escaping. I'd fought hard, then indulged in a celebration in the tavern, drinking a local whiskey that scoured my stomach like lava. I hadn't stopped to consider that I'd never had liquor before in my life. Apparently the drunk had led to brawling—of the friendly variety, though no less bruising—and I'd woken up feeling like this. I'd learned my lesson then, so . . . Oh right.

Calanthe. Euthalia. That beautiful and treacherous viper of a queen.

Ah, Sawehl, I'd lost my temper entirely and moved to

attack. I wouldn't have cut her throat. Not really. I only meant to take her hostage.

And then . . . I still couldn't remember.

Concentrating, I peeled my tongue from the roof of my mouth and licked my cracked lips, then wedged my eyes open. I squinted at the bright light of the setting sun. Hours had passed. Hopefully not days. Merle, perched on a bed post next to me, flapped his wings and cawed. Sondra appeared, tucking a lock of her hair behind her ear, her expression as sour as my mouth.

"Good morning, Conrí," she said, sounding anything but genial. "Glad to have you among the living again."

Morning? That must be the rising sun then. Well, I'd truly fucked that up. That is, Euthalia had fucked me up.

"I told you he'd be fine!" Ambrose's head popped into view. "How do you feel?"

"I thought you just said I'm fine." I levered myself up, head spinning, gorge rising. I swallowed it back and swung my feet to the floor. Bare feet. My armor—and weapons—had vanished, and I wore only my pants and shirt. Wonderful. Leaning my elbows on my knees, I dropped my face into my hands, cradling my pounding head. "What the hell did Euthalia do to me—crack my skull?"

"Not her," Sondra sounded amused. "The Queen of Flowers never moved, even when you were an idiot and charged up the steps of her throne, roaring and waving your sword."

"I remember that part," I snarled.

"Do you?" Her rough voice went cool. "Then you remember that *was not* part of the plan, Conrí."

I knew it. But I couldn't admit to them how I'd cracked at the thought of chains. I hadn't thought at all. "What then?"

"Two of those ladies-in-waiting took you down." She said it as if that made sense.

"You did hit the ground pretty hard," Ambrose noted. Gently he ran hands over my head, prodding my skull. "No knots." Merle croaked an agreement. "Probably just a residual effect of the magic that knocked you unconscious. Drink this."

He nudged a fragile-looking vessel under my chin and I peered at it through the heels of my hands. Pale green and foaming. "What is it?"

"A restorative. I concocted it myself, so you needn't worry about poisons."

I took it, the delicate mug cool to the touch, but didn't drink yet. Looking around the room, I took it and our situation in. We seemed to be in a tower, since only sky showed through the arched and open windows, the rising sun framed in one of them. Probably at the top, as the ceiling rose in a high dome above us, making a poor floor for anyone wanting to be above us. No doors, only the single, circular room, a curtained screen on the far side. Three beds—two besides the one I sat on—sat at intervals around the edges, with a table on the fourth side, where pitchers made of the same material as the mug I held sat, along with platters of food.

"This is our prison cell?" I asked. Obviously, but I couldn't quite credit it.

"Nicest dungeon I've ever been in," Sondra drawled. She'd also lost her weapons and armor, wearing the light pants and shirt she'd had on beneath. Ambrose seemed only to have lost his staff, though he'd gained a walking stick of similar height. He smiled at me, gesturing to the mug I still held.

"You made this from that food?" I indicated with my chin.

"Had to," he agreed. "They took my staff and satchel—and my focus stone. These people know power items when they see them, Conrí. It was truly unwise to test the queen's bodyguards. She did warn you. Three times, even."

"But it's not unwise to eat and drink their food."

"We have been for over twelve hours now," Sondra said, with some impatience. "Did you think we wouldn't test it before giving it to you?"

I winced, rubbing my forehead. "Apologies. I'm not thinking at all yet." With resignation—after all, how much worse could things get?—I toasted her with the mug and drank the stuff, braced for another of Ambrose's vile-tasting concoctions. It wasn't bad, actually. I'd been prepared to make a dash for the window. Better to vomit on whoever or whatever lay below than stink up our nest. But it was only a little bitter and mostly minty. The coolness soothed my throat and took away the foul taste.

Best of all, the headache immediately receded and my stomach settled. I might be able to put two thoughts together. "Thank you," I said to Ambrose, giving him a nod, too. "That was exactly the thing."

"Fortunately a simple remedy to a basic nature magic. Could've been much worse!"

I decided to focus on my appreciation rather than growl at him for getting us trapped like this. And to focus on Sondra. She stood nearby, arms folded, a scowl darkening her face. Though clearly angry with me, she at least would give me straight answers. "Once more, from the top—what exactly happened?"

She sighed and threw up her hands. "Ask him!" She pointed her chin at Ambrose, who grinned back at her, and continued without waiting for him. "All I can tell you is what I saw. You charged up those steps like a crazed bull in heat. The two lowermost ladies moved so fast I couldn't track it. They looked like they embraced you, and you stiffened. Remember that guy in Irst who was on that tower in the storm and got hit by lightning? You looked like that, only without the burning, bubbling flesh."

"Small mercies," I replied drily. Feeling better, I got to my feet. "Keep talking."

"There's not much more." She raised her brows as I paced to the nearest window, then the next. A sheer drop to the gardens on one side—much too far for the vegetation to cushion the fall—and all the way to the sea at the next. I leaned out and craned my neck to look up, verifying we were indeed at the top. We could possibly climb up—and sit there to roast in the sun. "Conrí, I already checked possible escape routes. Without rope to rappel down, we'd only kill ourselves."

"Indulge me. And tell me the rest."

She huffed a breath. "You stiffened. Lost consciousness and toppled backward like a felled tree. Everybody laughed, then applauded. The guards took the sword you dropped, relieved us of weapons, including Ambrose's staff—"

"But thoughtfully gave me this walking stick to lean on," Ambrose inserted. "Quite civilized people, all in all."

"—and escorted us here," Sondra finished. "All things considered, Ambrose is correct that they've treated us with a surprising amount of civility."

"Except for their plan to turn us over to Anure, to be tortured, executed, and made into a horrific example."

"There is that," she agreed.

"Really, you have to sympathize with Queen Euthalia," Ambrose said. "She can hardly do otherwise in her position."

I ignored him. The last thing I felt for that overpainted viper was sympathy. Pacing the room, I found nothing more than I'd already seen. The screen hid only a covered chamber pot. "How did they bring us in here?"

Sondra silently pointed at the floor. Crouching, I studied the faint outline of a square hatch set in the polished stone floor. Sondra joined me. "I tried prying it open," she said, "but nothing in here that I've found is strong enough. Beneath this is a ladder that can be withdrawn, with easily a drop of three times my height to another stone floor, which is guarded."

I grunted. A tight prison, but where there's a way in, there's a way out. Ambrose had wandered over to the food table, humming and filling his plate as if he attended a party, feeding tidbits to Merle, who perched on his shoulder. "Ambrose—isn't there some spell you can work?" I tried to ask it politely. What was the point of having a wizard companion if he couldn't help us out of situations like this?

Ambrose turned and gave me a considering look. "Like what?"

"I don't know. You're the magician."

He looked pained. "Please. Wizard."

"Right. You're the wizard. Can't you fly us out of here—float us to the ground, maybe?"

"Conjure a really long rope," Sondra suggested. "Or a short rope, a lever to open the trapdoor, and something to kill the guards with."

I nodded. "Anything at all?"

Ambrose gave us a smile that looked oddly sad. "How do you think magic works, anyway?"

I exchanged glances with Sondra, who shrugged with a resigned grimace. No help there. "We don't know, do we?" I said with reasonable patience. "You've never explained."

"Much of how magic works defies explanation," Ambrose said, nodding in agreement.

I set my teeth against the urge to snap at him. "So . . . was there an answer to my question in there somewhere?"

Ambrose popped a grape into his mouth. Chewed. Swallowed. "Merle can fly," he offered. "But then, that's his nature, and he has wings."

I waited. Ambrose ate more grapes.

"So," I finally said, "you can't do anything to get us out of this."

"None of the things you asked for are things I can do," Ambrose replied. "Particularly without my staff and other tools."

Figured. I dug my fingers into my scalp, willing the solution to come to me. There had to be one. We'd escaped inescapable Vurgmun. We could escape a pretty tower in paradise.

"Besides, I wouldn't anyway," Ambrose continued.

Dropping my hands slowly, I lifted my head to glare at him. Incredulity robbed me of words for a moment, and I stared at him, speechless. "What." I cleared my throat. "What did you say?" I advanced on the wizard, who had his back turned, filling his plate yet again.

Sondra interposed herself between us. "Don't throttle the wizard, Conrí. Please."

My fingers twitched, already curled to do it. "Perhaps you didn't hear him," I said slowly. I could throttle her first, *then* him.

"I heard. But you need to *listen*." If she hadn't looked so pleading, I might not have been able to restrain myself.

"All right." I stepped up to the table, found some kind of cold poultry under a screen, and snagged a piece. Might as well feed myself while I figured our way out of this. "I'll bite. Why wouldn't you help us escape, even if you could?" I tried to sound interested, even friendly, but Ambrose winced, casting me a cautious look.

"Because we're right where we want to be?" He posed it as a question, hesitant with it.

"Is that a question or an answer?" I smiled and he took a step back.

"Conrí—don't kill the wizard." Sondra edged herself between us again.

"I haven't touched him." I said it very reasonably. I'd already stripped all the flesh from the drumstick, so I fished out another. "I'm asking Ambrose to explain."

"If you'd just *think*," Sondra muttered, "you'd know why Ambrose says we're where we want to be."

"You can't woo Queen Euthalia unless we're on Calanthe," Ambrose filled in, giving Sondra a smile of gratitude. "We did a great deal of work to get exactly here. And while your attempt to attack her will likely count as a strike against you—"

"Stupid to lose your temper like that," Sondra inserted, lowering her brows meaningfully.

"All in all, you've made a brilliant start!" Ambrose finished.

"I have?" They made no sense. The food, though, was good. I'd go to Anure's torture chamber well fed.

"Oh yes. Have some of these—they're excellent." Ambrose handed me a plate of some sort of bread smeared with black stuff. "You intrigued the Queen of Flowers. That's not easily done."

"She may be young, but she's jaded," Sondra added. "A hard shell on her. She's maybe more cynical than any of us."

I gave her a black look. "How can either of you possibly know these things?"

"I was paying attention," Sondra snapped back. "While you were flirting with her, I observed."

"As did I," Ambrose said, nodding.

Sondra snorted. "You only had eyes for the Abiding Ring."

"Extraordinary, isn't it? All we hoped for! So is the queen." Ambrose elbowed me. "Didn't I promise you she'd be beautiful? Smart, too, and cagey with it. She's perfect."

"A match like Ejarat to Sawehl." Sondra gave me a sweet smile.

I took my time chewing, at least able to use my teeth on the flesh of something. "First," I said when I finally swallowed, "I was negotiating for our lives, not flirting. Second, I don't care if this Euthalia is the most beautiful woman in the world—"

"She just may be," Ambrose mused.

"—or if she's clever or a babbling idiot," I continued, talking over him. "All I want—all I've ever wanted—is Anure dead at my feet."

"By the grace of Ejarat, make it so." Sondra touched her forehead as she murmured the vow.

"Then claim her hand," Ambrose said, all seriousness now, the sense of magic gathering around him like a cloak. "Woo her, claim the Abiding Ring along with her hand in marriage, and Anure will fall."

I took a deep and calming breath. "You promise this."

"Yes. This is what I've been telling you." He waved his hands in the air as if he found *me* exasperating.

"Can you give me any clues why *she* would want *me*?"

"You are the crown prince of Oriel. That means something in her world."

"I *was* the prince. Oriel no longer exists, nor does the crown. That title died with the kingdom that belonged to my father. I won't buy my way with a dead man's name."

"Not even to avenge him, Conrí?" Sondra asked quietly.

"Not even for that." I couldn't explain it any better. I'd no more claim Oriel than I'd dig up my father's corpse.

"Then win her on your own terms, Conrí," Ambrose said. "You already interested her without telling her who you are. You can do this."

Doubtful, but I'd followed the wizard into this trap. If I wanted out, it would be by the same path. I looked around our delightful prison. "I'm going to have a hell of a time wooing her from this cell."

"And you don't have much time," Sondra reminded me. "By noon tomorrow, if our other ships haven't heard from us, they will attack. That's likely to sour any courtship."

"That's if Queen Euthalia hasn't already shipped us off to Anure," Ambrose pointed out. "Better act quick."

I swallowed my pride and the frustrated ire. "Do either of you have *helpful* suggestions?"

Sondra wrinkled her nose. "Clean up. Let me trim your hair."

"No one is cutting my hair." She should know better than that.

"Would I do that to you?" she shot back. "I said *trim*. Just to make it neater. You're scruffy, too, and need a shave. And maybe we can ask for some better clothes. Euthalia clearly appreciates the finer things. And you, Conrí, do not look fine."

"It's true." Ambrose studied me ruefully. "When she sends for you, you should look your best."

"No private audience, remember? Why should she send for me when she can simply ship us off to Anure without dirtying her fingers?"

"It will work out." Ambrose smiled and patted me on the shoulder. "You'll see."

Closing my eyes, I wondered how I'd come to this. Maybe I'd get lucky and my own soldiers would lob vurgsten at the tower and kill me quickly.

17

"Arise, Your Highness. The realm awaits the sun of Your presence."

I swallowed my groan of protest. Though I'd woken when the rising sun hit my eyelids, instead of the meditative dreamthink, I must've fallen into sleep again. At least the nightmares hadn't returned with it. If I'd hoped capturing the rebels—Conrí, Sondra had called the man—would banish the dreaded torment of nightly hauntings, I'd been not only wrong, but grievously so. If anything, the dreams had worsened, doubling in length and intensity. I felt as if I hadn't slept at all. Now that I had the sound of his voice and the sense of his physical presence, the man had been that much more vivid, his pain enough to break a heart I'd thought incapable of sympathy.

As long as I lived, I only hoped I'd forget that look in his eyes when he vowed never to wear chains again. I had to get him off Calanthe before I forgot my priorities. I wished I could fall asleep and stay there—dreamlessly—for a hundred years.

"Euthalia—are You awake?" Tertulyn whispered in my ear. "It's past the usual hour."

I opened my eyes and stretched my lips into a serene smile. Perfectly dressed, her hair adorned today with blossoms of the deepest blue, Tertulyn stepped back, folding her hands over her heart and bowing. The other five bowed also, their delighted smiles appearing as authentic as on any morning.

I sat up, my weary body protesting. The sun had indeed risen high. Tertulyn had let me sleep far too long.

"Good morning, Tertulyn, ladies," I said, looking from the sun to Tertulyn. She only gave me an apologetic smile, making me wonder if I hadn't been the only one to over-sleep. The parties celebrating Calanthe's triumphant capture of the Slave King and his minions had been in full swing when I retired to my solitary bed, riddled with guilt and remorse. And unable to do anything to save either of us.

Now that I looked closely, I could see shadows under the artfully applied makeup of several of the ladies. Late nights all around apparently. "Who is our guest today?" I asked. As always, resorting to unthinking ritual saved me.

The Morning Glory curtsied when Tertulyn beckoned to her. The sky blue of the gown and wig suited this one, with her dusky skin and unusually light eyes.

"Welcome, Glory," I said. "Assist Me from My bed."

She only hesitated a moment before offering me her gloved hand. I took it with my left, giving her an extended opportunity to study the orchid ring. The wizard, Ambrose, had certainly been interested in it. And not in the way of most men. Ambrose hadn't seemed acquisitive or curious—he'd acted more as if he knew something about it. More than I'd dared hope for—I'd found a wizard at last, and he'd recognized the magic of the ring.

If only I could figure out how to keep Leuthar from finding out about Ambrose. He hadn't been named as a wizard in court—which at least showed circumspection and partially explained how he'd survived—so it was possible

Conrí didn't know Ambrose's true nature. After all, Anure declared magic to be a silly superstition, therefore wizards couldn't possibly exist. I'd never been able to discern if Anure believed his own edicts on magic or made them entirely to hoard magic to himself. If the former, he'd carelessly destroy the wizard; if the latter—worse for us—he would ruthlessly employ Ambrose's abilities.

No matter what, I needed to find a way to keep the wizard on Calanthe.

If I had a prisoner condemned to death handy, I could dress him in the wizard's garments and ship him off with Conrí and the Lady Sondra. Would they be happy to see their companion saved or would they protest and betray the subterfuge? If I could persuade Leuthar to separate the three, they might never know of my trick until it was too late. Still, I wouldn't condemn even the worst miscreant to Anure's brand of justice, even if I had one available, which I didn't.

And truly, if I could keep the wizard, I could perhaps keep Lady Sondra with the same trick. She wouldn't fare well in Anure's grasp. Her face might not meet his standards, but plenty in his court wouldn't care when her body promised pleasure. That might salve the eroding guilt that plagued me. Save two, and sacrifice one. If Conrí loved Sondra—as a lover or as his second—then perhaps his shade would haunt me less if I saved her.

Whatever I planned to do, I'd best do it quickly. Even if Delilah had seduced Leuthar into more excesses, he'd soon be up and about, eager to play emperor's dog and retrieve the prize. And take the credit. Right now he had only reports of what my prisoners looked like. If I wanted to take advantage of that, I needed to act. Ejarat curse me for sleeping in.

I'd save the wizard and soon forget the man with the wolf's eyes. I only wanted to wash my hands of the whole business. Ridiculous to feel any sense of guilt. Once I bathed and rid myself of the oily nightmare sweats, I'd feel better.

I touched my feet to the stone floor and used the leverage of the Glory's hand to rise. She seemed surprised—I'd likely been too abrupt—so I swept off my head scarf and handed it to her, turning away so I wouldn't have to witness her reverence. My bath awaited, so I strode for it. My impatience would hopefully be interpreted as haste due to the late hour of my rising.

While soaping my bare scalp, Tertulyn murmured, "Tonight we should set aside some time to shave Your head. It's beginning to show."

I doubted it would happen that night or the next. Not until I had Anure's prize off Calanthe. Then life could return to normal. At least, as normal as serving under Anure's tyranny could ever be. I supposed that, in my own way, I was a queen of slaves also, and a prisoner myself, with only the illusion of freedom. Would Conrí find that amusing? Somehow I doubted it.

They'd washed, oiled, and dried me, and I wore only my silk shift, sitting while the ladies tended to my nails and makeup, when one of the palace maidservants begged admittance. Curious.

"Calla, please see what she wants and send her on her way," Tertulyn directed, not pausing in smoothing the foundation paste on my cheeks.

"No," I said. Such an unusual request in unusual times might require my personal attention. "I'll see her."

Tertulyn quirked a brow ever so slightly, retrieving a long-sleeved robe for me, tying it high around my neck.

Once I'd been covered, Calla went to admit the maid. The girl entered, wearing the uniform of the lowest serving staff and curtsying low.

"Yes, dear." I spoke softly so as not to frighten her, as I would to a Glory. "You bring a message for Me?"

She didn't rise, keeping her gaze firmly fixed on the floor. "Your Highness, I work in the detention tower and . . . and, Your Highness, the guards asked me to pass along that the prisoners are requesting baths and clean clothes."

I processed that with some astonishment. "Why under Sawehl are you asking Me?"

"Please, Your Highness." Her voice trembled. "The guards, they say that Your Highness gave orders that the prisoners be given every comfort, but You did not specify whether baths and new clothing counted, and . . ." She trailed off at my silence.

"And . . ." I prompted. Tertulyn caught my eye, rolling hers.

"These are unusual prisoners, Your Highness." The girl sounded increasingly desperate. "Your Highness, they're destined for His Imperial Majesty's justice and no one wants to make an error."

No. Ejarat forfend that we should err in turning over these unfortunates to Anure's undoubtedly cruel vengeance. I flipped a careless hand, dismissing the thought. "Please rise already. I see no reason to deny the request. Give them what they need to bathe, and whatever clothing they like—though not their armor or weapons, of course."

"Your Highness, should we send for their clothing from their ship in the harbor?" The maid bit her lip when I turned an incredulous stare on her.

"All right now," Tertulyn intervened. "This is beneath Her Highness's attention. I will—"

"No, that's all right, Tertulyn. I realize we are operating without precedent here. Do not break the quarantine on their ship for any reason. It's to remain under guard, and the prisoners should access nothing from it." Who knew what the wizard might do, given the opportunity? "Provide them with an array of clothing from the palace for them to choose from."

"Yes, Your Highness."

"You'll need something large for Conrí—be sure to keep that in mind."

"Who, Your Highness?" Her clear brow knitted in anxious confusion.

"Conrí. That's what his people called the Slave King."

"Yes, Your Highness." But her frown persisted. Likely the girl hadn't seen the man, so she wouldn't realize how ill most of what we had on hand would fit him.

"And nothing too colorful—he won't like that."

"Your Highness?" The maid twisted her skirt in anxiety.

Tertulyn moved in front of me, so only I could see her face, and fully raised her brows in question. Yes, yes—I was acting out of character. I needed to get through this and I'd be able to return to my usual role and rehearsed lines. Still, I'd be serving a grave enough injury to this Slave King—even if I saved his wizard and his lady—while sending him to a fate I couldn't bear to contemplate. The least I could do was see him dressed as befit his sense of himself. The man had fought hard and won, until now.

My father had been a warrior in his day, before he gave that up for Calanthe. He'd been a big man, too. "His Highness, the late King Gul—all of his things were stored, yes?" I directed the question at Tertulyn and Calla, who both looked startled and somewhat aghast.

"Yes, Your Highness." Tertulyn recovered swiftly and replied smoothly. "Packed in cedar and preserved."

For whom, I wondered—the sons I'd never bear? If I had a way to identify and round up all of my illegitimate half siblings, I could distribute the lot to them. As things stood, it ended up being fortunate that I had the stuff still. "Let Conrí choose from those trunks. They should fit, if My eye judges correctly."

"Yes, Your Highness." The maid curtsied—an abrupt bob, quickly aborted—and fled. I looked after her thoughtfully, then became aware of my ladies' unusual silence. The Glory, sensing something in the air, looked about uneasily. Tertulyn didn't quite meet my gaze, but her mouth quirked in an unhappy bent.

"I may have had no choice but to protect Calanthe and the empire by apprehending Conrí and his companions," I said in formal tones, though I should not have to explain myself, "but we are a people who celebrate beauty and the higher aspirations of all people. I will send His Imperial Majesty's prisoners to him, but they will make the journey in the dignity befitting any human being." There, that would lay the groundwork for my subterfuge. Now I just needed bodies to put the clothing on when it came time to ship them out. If only I could use Leuthar for one.

"I loved when You called the Slave King a dog," Tertulyn quipped. "Such a joke!"

Nahua made a yipping sound, then giggled. "Did you see how *dirty* they were? No wonder they want baths!"

"No amount of soap could make them clean," Calla replied with disgust. "They've been filthy so long, the dirt has embedded itself in their pores."

"Did you see *Lady* Sondra's complexion?" Tertulyn put a light emphasis on Sondra's title, as if dubious about its origins. "Positively ruined. No wonder she's ended up with an ill-mannered brute like the Slave King. What man of refinement would have her?"

"And that's if she weren't an escaped slave and traitor!" Calla replied.

The Glory laughed with them, but with a line between her brows. What she must think of all this. Unexpected shame pricked at me. Time to send her away. Giving the Glory the usual thanks, gift, and good wishes also served to put an end to the gossiping. When the ladies renewed their efforts to prepare me for the day, they did so quietly, perhaps because I reminded them to hurry. Perhaps they sensed my displeasure.

"I'm surprised," Tertulyn murmured for my ears alone, as the others retrieved my gown, "that You would want to demean your father's memory by dressing that dog in his clothes."

I kept my face serene—necessary, so as not to disrupt her careful painting, but also to disguise my reaction to her unkind words. Had Tertulyn always been so condescending and judgmental? The Lady Sondra . . . she could be any of us. Had my father chosen to fight Anure, we, too, might have shared her fate, and lost our pretty complexions to similar trials. By the haunted look in the woman's eye, she'd endured far worse than losing her beauty.

It took me aback on a deep level that Tertulyn—the rest of my ladies, pampered and sheltered, sure, but Tertulyn, my dearest friend—had no compassion in her heart for another of her station and gender.

"I demean nothing," I replied quietly, but with an intensity that made her eyes widen and fly to mine. "They're people, like you and I but for the vagaries of fate. They deserve to be treated as such."

"Perhaps you'd feel differently if it had been *your* family they slaughtered in Keiost," she hissed, then pressed her lips together tightly.

"We don't know that," I reminded her. "I have people looking."

"Apologies, Your Highness. I forgot myself."

Yes, she did, but I didn't say so. Partly as the others returned just then, holding my gown aloft, and partly because I might feel similarly distressed in Tertulyn's position. We'd been friends so long that I could hardly hold one slip against her, particularly under such difficult circumstances.

Still, I remained silent while they sewed me into the gown and Tertulyn finished my makeup, lest I give voice to my annoyance and disappointment. Since when had we grown so callous to the suffering of others? We'd protected Calanthe and Her people, but I'd thought all knew the price we paid for our continued idyllic existence—and that most of the rest of the world, those not in Anure's pocket like we were, suffered greatly.

Apparently not, though I didn't know how to change that.

First steps first. I needed to decide how I'd deal with Leuthar, and how to trick him. I could perhaps carry off a switch—but only if Conrí wouldn't betray it.

"Has Leuthar arisen yet?" I asked, breaking a silence I realized I'd let go on far too long while I thought.

Tertulyn flicked a glance at Calla, who hurried out. "Not at last word, Your Highness," she replied with stiff politeness. "He was well into his cups until only a few hours ago—and indulging heavily in yilkas, as well—and then took to his bed with a set of lovely young triplets, two girls and a boy, new arrivals Delilah saved for a special occasion. I doubt he'll inform You of his intentions to review the prisoners until afternoon."

Her perfectly formal tone began to get under my skin, as did the pointed reminder that, as emissary of the emperor, Leuthar's authority exceeded mine as regarded the prisoners. Calla returned, moving to whisper in Tertulyn's ear.

"You may tell Me directly," I said, not sure why I did so, except my irritation—and sudden sense of losing control of the situation—made me speak before considering.

Calla looked briefly startled. "Apologies, Your Highness. The Lady Tertulyn's source confirms that the emissary is still closeted with his new toys and commanded that he not be bothered until luncheon—and then only if they aren't sleeping."

Good. "Cancel the morning's court."

"Your Highness?" Tertulyn, who'd been studiously avoiding my eyes, glanced at me in full surprise.

"Cancel the morning's court," I repeated, taking petty satisfaction in putting command in the words. She deserved it, questioning me that way. "I will interview the prisoners privately, in My courtyard." Away from over-zealous ears. "Beginning with Conrí, then Lady Sondra, then the other gentleman. Ambrose, I believe they called him."

I'd extract Conrí's promise of silence in return for saving his people, then enlist Sondra and Ambrose to the game, preparing them to hide away.

I raised my brows at Calla's hesitation and the obstinate line of Tertulyn's mouth. "Inform the guards, please, Lady Calla."

She bobbed a quick curtsy and set her basket of flowers aside, hastening to do as I commanded. Ibolya picked up the basket, working swiftly to stud my hair with flowers. I'd decided on an iridescent lavender today, to begin the journey away from the metaphorical bloodshed of the day before. Now I regretted it. Too insipid. I could hardly change my mind now, however. I'd already behaved oddly enough, and time grew short.

"I'll attend You, Your Highness?" Tertulyn asked. At least she no longer assumed. Just as well.

"No, I'd rather you take yourself to Delilah's court and keep your ears pricked for Leuthar's movements. Send Me word immediately when he pokes his head out." I'd need plenty of warning to make sure Leuthar never saw Ambrose's and Sondra's true faces.

"You can't mean to meet with this . . . escaped convict alone. A *man*. You'll take one of the other ladies."

I gazed back at Tertulyn steadily, while the other ladies exchanged excited whispers at the prospect of the gossip they'd obtain. "No, I don't think I will. There will be guards outside the walls."

"Your Highness." Tertulyn visibly wrestled with herself. "Please don't put Yourself at such risk."

"What risk?" I asked lightly, even laughing a little so the other ladies echoed it. "These people will be unarmed, escorted under heavy guard. I am not without My own defenses."

"And Your reputation?" she pointed out. "What will Your *fiancé*, His Imperial Majesty, think of You interviewing the Slave King *alone*?"

"Well, I certainly don't think he'll imagine I fucked the man," I replied, thoroughly irritated. "I'll send him a letter giving him what information I extracted during my interrogation." Oh, that was good. I'd definitely do that. "And reaffirming My love, et cetera." I waved a hand.

"I don't understand why You want to talk to this vile creature, especially at such risk," Tertulyn muttered.

I lifted a hand to her wrist, halting the jewel she had

been about to place. "I thought I'd try to discover more information about what exactly happened at Keiost."

"Oh." Her warm brown eyes filled with tears, and she bobbed a curtsy. "Oh, Euthalia, I'm sorry. Thank You."

I nodded, glad to have thought of a good excuse, the guilt for that small lie a drop against the ocean of it that threatened to drown me. I could only do my best, though.

As I stood for their finishing touches, it occurred to me with some humor that I'd somehow agreed to his absurd request. It seemed that Conrí the Slave King would get his private audience.

18

When the summons to attend the queen arrived, Ambrose gave me a small salute, otherwise not budging from his lounging position on the bed he'd adopted.

"Don't move just yet," Sondra instructed, frowning at me.

"Darling," I said, keeping an eye on the heavily armed guard who'd popped up through the trapdoor and had a sword ready. "While you're holding a very sharp knife, *he* has a very sharp sword. I think that wins." Ambrose had also produced a tonic to soothe my throat—and woo a queen—that worked better than anything he'd given me before. He ducked explaining where it came from.

Sondra trimmed along the comb, letting the hair fall into place. "Better. See? You still have plenty of hair."

I stood, brushing off stray trimmed hairs from my shoulders. Not that the dark hair would show against the black leathers I'd dug out of the trunk the guards brought up, struggling to lift the weight of it up the ladder. The clothes had been packed away in layers of silk and spilled wood shavings. Cedar, Sondra had told me, to fend off chewing insects. Go figure.

Still, I wouldn't question the gift—they were clothes worthy of a warrior and a king, whoever they belonged to—only the reason for it. The guards only shrugged and said we'd asked for clothes, here were clothes.

We had more of an argument over the manacles. "You get your audience with Her Highness Queen Euthalia," the captain of the guard informed me. "But you won't be allowed to bring Her harm. That's the price. Pay it or not."

"It's temporary," Sondra urged, giving me a pleading look. "And worth it, yes? You promised a chance to hold the torch." She glanced at the guard and back to me. "You've never backed down from a challenge, Conrí."

So I set my teeth and allowed the manacles to be locked on me. I couldn't imagine how I was supposed to woo a queen when I wore chains, but then I had no idea how I was supposed to woo her at all, so the manacles didn't change all that much.

Except that they made me feel small, weak, and worthless again. Hearing the clink of the metal, feeling the cold weight of the iron locking on—it brought back that day when we knelt in the court of Oriel for our "trial," Anure gloating on my father's throne.

It hadn't been the worst thing that happened. What came later exceeded that day in pain, suffering, humiliation. But kneeling there, in our own palace, beside my father—the king of Oriel!—with my sister missing and our nobles kneeling in ranks behind us . . .

It left the taste of ashes and rage in my mouth, and it was all I could do not to jerk up my wrists and bash that guard in the jaw. But I didn't. I paid the price of my obedient capitulation.

Yet again.

"You're next," the guard told Sondra. "Remember that you'll be meeting with the Flower Queen of Calanthe, not visiting the kitchen to scour pots."

"Oh, hey—great advice!" Sondra replied brightly. She'd

been focused on making me presentable and hadn't yet bathed.

A laugh choked out of me and I made it into a cough. Amazing that Sondra could always find a way to laugh off the worst of insults. The guard huffed but had no reply, instead pointing me to the ladder down the open hatch, ringed below by more guards with unsheathed swords. At least they'd manacled my hands in front of me, so I could hold on as I climbed down. Apparently they'd brought me up unconscious the same way they'd carried up the bathtub and trunks, via a clever rope and pulley system.

They led me down the tower and through a wing of the palace, so many guards escorting me that I decided I should be flattered. What I could do to them—or their precious queen—manacled and unarmed was beyond me. What I'd say to the queen was beyond me, too. If only Ambrose had provided me with some sort of love potion to administer to Euthalia. Shouldn't a wizard be useful that way? Though . . . he had promised that I'd have an audience with her, and against all probability I was going to one.

Made my head hurt to think about it. Besides, I needed to concentrate on wooing the queen. Sondra had stuffed my head with advice while she trimmed my hair and shaved me with a razor sharp enough to keep my attention. Give her compliments. Don't stare at her breasts. Be romantic. Say poetic things. I imagined going on one knee and reciting poetry—though the only poem I could remember was a bit of doggerel about a guy with a dick so long he could suck it. The thought of repeating that one to the icy queen made me bust out laughing—and made the guards jump.

The captain cuffed me on the head. "Be silent, Slave King."

I nearly told him my dubious honorific had been sneered much better than that, but I kept my peace, studying the palace instead. I had to admit—grudgingly to myself and never out loud—that it was the most beautiful building I'd ever seen. The palace at Oriel would forever hold a place in my heart, but it would look like a farmhouse next to the wonder of Euthalia's home.

It helped, no doubt, that they apparently had little inclement weather to deal with. Corridors and halls opened onto breathtakingly beautiful gardens—from groves of fruit trees, to masses of flowering vines, to water gardens bursting with lily pad blossoms. Some of the ponds even extended indoors, with small bubbling streams channeled through the halls, requiring us to cross bridges over them. Mosaic tiles outlined the channels in deeper colors, with patterns radiating outward, echoing the ripples of water in the floor.

The guards escorted me along one of these artificial streams—we crossed it twice—and then fully outside into a maze of gardens. I'd been suspecting that we followed a circuitous route, because I could see more direct paths than we'd followed. The guards confirmed it for me when they abruptly turned at the sight of a group of colorful courtiers, taking us into a hedge maze.

So this "audience" wasn't to be common knowledge. Interesting.

The hedge maze led to a walled garden, with a wooden door inset. The captain pounded on it with the meat of his fist. A lady pretty as a butterfly opened it, one of the queen's ladies-in-waiting I recognized from the day before. She looked me up and down, wide eyes alight with interest, then stepped aside for the captain to lead me in—not incidentally making sure I couldn't come too close to her. I opened my mouth to point out that I'd bathed and she needn't worry about me smudging her fancy gown. Then closed it again, thinking of Sondra's expectant gaze.

Who knew exercising discretion would be harder than waging war? *Just another challenge.* Right.

Queen Euthalia waited, sitting on something I couldn't see because of her overflowing gown. She'd looked as if some artist had arranged her there, a sculpture to be a centerpiece in a lovely but austere garden—all the better to display her in her spectacular glory.

The captain led me in, but the other guards remained outside the door. The only door in the sheer, high walls. Even with the manacles I could scale them, but not so fast that the guards couldn't catch me. Oh well. I wasn't supposed to be looking for avenues of escape anyway. I was supposed to be wooing this unearthly-looking woman while chained like a dog. This ought to be interesting.

"Why is he chained?" Queen Euthalia asked, sounding weary and vaguely bemused. She raised arched brows so the jewels at the corners twinkled.

"Your Highness." The captain bowed deeply, yanking me down to my knees as he did. I was stronger and could've resisted, but—prideful me—I didn't think having him beat me would add to my attractiveness in the wooing process. At least the plush grass cushioned the fall. "This prisoner is dangerous. We sought to protect You from—"

"Did I order him to be chained? Let Me help you with the answer to that. No, I did not. Take those cursed manacles off him and leave us."

The man wanted to protest. I could see it in the set of his chin and the vibration of tension through the chains he held. But he clearly didn't dare vocalize it. With quick movements, he unlocked the manacles, whispering fast and ferocious to me. "If you so much as move wrong, we'll cut you down. We'll be watching. Don't think—"

"Thank you, Captain," the queen broke in, her tone a blade of ice. "I'll call when I'm ready for the next."

He bowed again and strode out the door. She waited until the latch snicked, then a beat longer. "You may stand," she said, "or sit. Or pace." Was that a bit of dry humor there? "However you'd be most comfortable," she added, with a wave of a hand, the orchid on her finger fluttering as she did.

I stood, rubbing my wrists absently. "Thank you," I said.

"No need to thank Me," she replied. "I promised no chains. It won't happen again. Not while you're on Calanthe. We are not barbarians here."

That wouldn't stop them from chaining me again the moment we left the island, bound for Anure's even worse captivity. I took the opportunity to study her. Even up close she looked flawless. She wore pale purple, her hair several shades lighter and studded with deeper violet flowers, some trailing over one shoulder in glossy ringlets. The gown dipped low between the high silvery wings of stiff lace that framed her slender white throat, revealing delicate collarbones and a rounded bosom I quickly yanked my gaze from.

The hair had to be as fake as the lashes, also light purple and tipped with crystals. Her eyes had stayed the same—large in her piquant face, and still reminding me of rain, a pale gray, almost colorless. This close I could see darker flecks of deep blue in them, and a ring of sparkling silver at the edges.

Ambrose had said she was in her mid-twenties, but she looked younger. More like a girl in her teens under the heavy costume of her role. And she seemed different, here in this garden, alone with me. Not so . . . rigid. Though her erect posture never wavered. I wondered if it ever did.

The perfect bow of her pink mouth quirked and she
raised one brow. "Have you looked your fill?"

"You are very beautiful," I said. There. A compliment
to start the conversation. Sondra would be proud. Especially that I reined back the remark that I'd like to see her
without the costume. I would—but not the way that it
would come out sounding. What was the woman like,
under her masks?

"Why did you want a private audience, Conrí?" she
asked, as if she hadn't heard my compliment at all. Probably she heard more lavish praise and so often, it had become like background noise to her.

Hearing my true name from her lips made me feel more
stripped than losing my armor and weapons had, and I
stared at her, unable to think clearly.

"That *is* your name." She raised her brows in question,
though she hadn't posed it as one.

"Not a name anyone knows or uses," I replied tersely.

"The Lady Sondra does."

"Because she won't stop," I muttered. I'd forgotten Sondra spoke my name when warning me not to attack the
queen. Not much got past this keen-eyed woman.

"Excuse me?" The queen's perfect brows—and the
glinting jewel beside one—went higher.

Better to go on the attack.

"What about you—do they call you Euthalia in conversation?"

"No." She lowered her brows in an elegant frown. "No
one but His Imperial Majesty is allowed to address Me by
My given name. You will address Me as Your Highness."

"Euthalia is a mouthful," I commented, deliberately dis-
obeying that edict. If she had me executed for it, at least
I'd avoid whatever Anure had in mind. "And I don't want

to call you by what the imperial toad does. I bet they called you Lia when you were little."

She gave me a long look. "I begin to see the self-destructive troublemaker in you that enabled you to defy His Imperial Majesty."

"Why do you care what my name is?" I was genuinely curious.

"Because calling you the Slave King is an insult," she bit out. "Surely you realize that, Conrí."

I studied her. Her clear eyes held anger, but not for me, I thought. She might be insulted on my behalf, which was . . . extraordinary.

"I have no kingdom," I explained slowly. "I have been a slave and the people who followed me first were all escaped slaves. There's no shame in being king of people strong and greathearted enough to survive that."

She considered that, lashes lowering so the crystals glittered. "I see. But I'll still call you Conrí."

"Call me Con," I said, surprising myself, then grinned when she looked up. "And I'll call you Lia."

Narrowing her eyes, she huffed out a sigh. And suppressed that smile again. Could I truly be amusing her? "Say that around anyone else and you'll find yourself lacking a head."

"Better that than having Anure slowly carve me to pieces."

"You call His Imperial Majesty by his given name, too. Do you not have reverence for anyone?"

"No," I replied, my voice harder than I intended. "Not since my father died." I added that to soften the denial, then regretted saying so much.

"I'm sorry." She sounded sincere. "Who was he? That is, what realm did you come from?"

"Is that why you called me here, to ask about my personal history?" I returned the question. Not the right tack at all. Sondra and Ambrose would've had me answer. We could've bonded over our dead fathers, both kings of old. Absurdly, however, I found myself wanting her to like me without all that. And where that impulse came from, I had no idea.

"No. You're right—your personal history is yours and changes nothing, regardless." She tapped her nails together in her lap. They seemed to be crafted of metal, jeweled and coming to long points like the curved thorns of rose vines. She seemed to come to a decision. "I have a somewhat unorthodox proposal for you, Conrí."

"Con." She might not know that the *rí* was an honorific in Oriel, but better to save her the embarrassment if someone else did know and called it out.

She pursed her lips, growing impatient. "This is important."

"What proposal?" I asked, keeping the hope—such a foreign sensation—out of my voice. Could Ambrose have worked more magic than getting me this audience and she'd save me the trouble of this ridiculous quest for her hand in marriage by proposing to *me*?

"Yes." She studied me, her gaze frank and appraising. "I know the man you brought with you is a wizard. Don't ask Me how I know. I won't answer. But this wizard—"

"Anure says wizards don't exist," I pointed out, mildly disappointed that it wouldn't be so easy. But then, nothing ever was. Why I enjoyed needling her I couldn't say, except that she kept surprising me and I wanted some of my own back. Also, it was fun. I absorbed that with some astonishment.

She'd paused at my interruption, lips parted, and exhaled a quiet breath of irritation. "I want to keep this wizard—"

"Ambrose," I supplied.

"Thank you." She sounded both aggravated and amused, though her face revealed none of it. "I want to keep Ambrose on Calanthe."

Not at all what I'd expected. "So keep him. You are the queen here and I'm your prisoner, as you've made abundantly clear. I can hardly stop you."

She pursed her mouth over her first response, gave me a more considered one. "His Imperial Majesty's emissary, Syr Leuthar, will no doubt wish to escort you to Yekpehr. While he wasn't in court yesterday, people will inform him that there were three of you. I can hardly provide him with one prisoner when he expects three."

"One?" I seized on that. Did that mean what I hoped?

"If I can keep Ambrose on Calanthe, I should be able to keep the Lady Sondra, too. Saving her life should be enough temptation for you."

A tempting offer indeed. Ambrose could possibly take care of himself—vanish off the ship in a puff of smoke or some such—but if I could save Sondra, set her free . . . "Why would you do this?"

"Ambrose could be useful to Me. As they officially don't exist, wizards are not so plentiful that I'd willingly lose such a treasure. I would give him sanctuary here. And he'd be free to leave, of course, once it's safe for him to emerge from hiding, though I hope he'd stay."

"And Sondra—what value does she have?"

Lia gave me a hard look. "Don't pretend to Me that she means nothing to you. The relationship between you is obvious. And everyone has value, Con."

She flinched at the harsh bark of my laughter. I couldn't

help myself. "That's a pile of utter shit, Lia," I said, kind of loving that she gaped at me, her painted lips parting in shock, the expression animating her face. How would she act if I kissed her? Would she call the guards or would she . . . I shook my head. No idea where that impulse came from. No idea why it suddenly seemed deeply appealing.

But I edged close as she recovered her poise, and she didn't yell at me for my rudeness as I'd expected. "You can laugh all you wish, but I do believe in that. Everyone has value."

"Even me?" My voice came out a bit rough, despite the potion, and I suddenly, desperately wanted her answer. She gazed back at me, her eyes silvery with some emotion her face didn't show.

"Even you," she replied, her voice breathier than it had been.

"Then offer me sanctuary, too," I coaxed.

"I can't." She ground out the words, surprising anguish in her voice, especially since none of it showed. "If I'm very clever, I can find substitutes to take Ambrose's and Sondra's places—if you agree not to betray the game—but you are far too . . . distinctive. My courtiers haven't stopped talking about you, in great detail. No disguise could convince the emissary that someone else is you. Besides, *you* are the one His Imperial Majesty wants. I cannot stop it."

"But you *can*," I insisted. This wasn't what Ambrose wanted me to do, but I had to seize the opportunity. She'd softened from the woman who'd coldly captured us the day before. When your enemy shows weakness, you must take advantage as the opportunity may never come again. Besides, she didn't want to do this. I could feel it in the thrum of her voice, see it in the unhappy turn of her lush mouth. "Don't turn me over. I have an army, and ships. Throw in with us. I'll teach you about our secret weapon and you will help us take down Anure."

If I thought I'd shocked her before, it was nothing compared with her expression at my words. I could swear I caught a glimpse of pained hope. Perhaps not, because she quickly shuttered it with a mask of furious indignation.

She stood, abruptly, her elaborate skirts swishing against my thighs as she brushed past, the silk catching against the roughened skin on my hand. My fingers twitched, wanting to touch more, to reach for her. Then she was away, leaving only a cloud of subtle fragrance, like a flower that bloomed only at night.

She began pacing the confines of the small garden. No wonder she suggested the activity to me—she moved with a restless grace that clearly helped her regain calm. When she turned back to me, she'd composed herself, once again cool and remote. I'd only seen her sitting before this, and it bemused me to note she stood at least a head shorter than I—once I mentally subtracted the pile of hair and sparkling crown. Her regal bearing and intense presence made her seem so much taller. At least I dug out enough discretion not to mention it to her. Without all the trappings, she was likely slight enough for me to pick up and cuddle in my arms like a kitten.

And just like one, she paced up to me, fire in her eyes, so close I scented the warmth of her skin along with the flowers. "You *dare* speak to Me of treachery?" she hissed, leaning in more. I doubted anyone outside the walls could hear our conversation, but she whispered it anyway. Where I lacked any ability at discretion, she'd made an art form of it, not forgetting even when overcome by affronted anger.

"Oh, that's right," I goaded her. "You're engaged to Anure, aren't you? Are you in *love* with that vile toad?" I heaped scorn into the word. About as far from dishing compliments and romance as possible. Good thing Sondra couldn't witness this.

To my surprise, Lia's righteous fury faded instantly. Instead she studied me, cool and canny. She'd dropped the last mask—the non-physical kind anyway, as the formal makeup hid the subtleties of her expressions—and the real woman looked at me, her intelligence like a lethal blade.

"You're no fool, Conrí," she said softly. "Don't treat Me like one."

And I saw it all in that moment, the game she played as deftly as I planned any of my schemes. More so, as Anure didn't see her for the dangerous enemy she was. Her silver eyes glittered like a mirage of water in the desert, her beauty like the distracting flash of jewels on an enchanted sword. She used all of it like camouflage, as all the best assassins did.

And we were the same under the skin, both reckless in pursuit of our hopeless causes. I saw Ambrose's point now, that I had to persuade her to give up what had to be a suicidal plan. The urge to seize her and kiss her assailed me with renewed hunger.

I couldn't. It would be an unforgivable breach. Boorish even for me. I'd never learned elegant court manners, but I had to pierce that hard shell of hers, make her see.

I hadn't gotten this far by playing by the rules.

I leaned in, setting my hands on her narrow waist to keep her there—though I knew she'd refuse to give up ground to me—and brushed my lips against one delicate shell of her ear. She shivered, catching her breath.

"What's your endgame?" I asked, very quietly, inviting her to confide. "Marry him, then slit his throat in the marriage bed?"

19

I groped for a response to this man's astonishing nerve. His hands burned through the layers of silk and boning at my waist, the brush of his lips against my ear sending glittering shocks of awareness over my skin. He was big—I'd known that, but this close he seemed like an oak tree. The strength palpable in his grip, he held me in a way that made me want to lean in, to taste more . . .

Think! I told myself viciously.

How had he guessed so much? Because I'd slipped, foolishly taunting him not to underestimate me when I'd built all my strategy on making sure men thought me no more than ornamental. I needed to extract myself from his hands and my mistakes.

I'd bungled this entire interview. Something about Con—I'd never think of him with that vile *Slave King* epithet again, even if he seemed to take a perverse pleasure in claiming it—made me lose all my cautious habits. It was more than seeing him look so striking in my father's clothes, though that sight had blown through me like a sudden gust of wind off the ocean, full of cold spray and old emotion. It didn't help that he cleaned up unexpectedly well. Never handsome by any stretch, but Con was . . . imposing. So unlike any man I'd known, and yet so cursedly familiar.

I hadn't had a conversation this honest with another person in . . . maybe in my entire life. For all that we feinted with each other, using words like rapiers to probe the other's weaknesses, and despite the terrible stakes, part of me had been enjoying it.

I was also infuriated, terrified, and frustrated.

And aroused. I'd never felt more alive.

It shouldn't be exhilarating that he'd guessed my plan. The endgame, as he called it. What I thought of as my last resort, should it come to that. If Anure cornered me sufficiently to force me into marriage, I'd go willingly—to all appearances—and take him from this world with me. That plan wouldn't save Calanthe, however. Until I found an heir the orchid ring would accept, I couldn't let that happen. As always, I was alone in this battle.

Con had pulled back, just enough to stare into my face. His golden eyes, so like the wolf's of my nightmares, burned into mine, seeing too much. They held the same challenge, the same plea, that the animal had in my restless dreams. I should've taken warning from them. It might be too late that I hadn't.

We stood so close I'd thought he'd been about to kiss me. A startling and extraordinary insight—and I had no idea what I'd do. I should've stepped back long since, but that would be giving up ground. And now he had his hands on me. I could order him away, but I doubted he'd meekly obey. I shouldn't find that enticing.

The man didn't have a meek or obedient bone in his body and it would no doubt be his destruction. How he'd survived slavery I didn't know. They should have broken him.

"Don't do it, Lia," Con said, though I hadn't replied, his

voice rough with urgency. Always hoarse, it got more so with emotion. For a moment I wasn't sure what he didn't want me to do. "Don't marry Anure." He said it as if we were friends. As if he cared to give me heartfelt advice. "Don't do it," he repeated.

"I have no intention of doing so," I answered on a quiet breath, sounding far too serious. Risky to confirm even that much, rather than laughing in his face. This man could betray me. Somehow, though, I didn't think he would— and he seemed so . . . distressed that I hadn't found it in myself to deny it the way I should. I needed to counter his assumptions, however. Sometimes retreat is the better part of valor.

I stepped back, smoothly moving away from him, the silk of my gown cool now where his burning hands had been.

"I have no immediate plans of marrying His Imperial Highness." I was repeating myself, reaching for my usual poise on the subject. "Our engagement has been extended due to numerous extenuating circumstances."

"His other wives?" Con sneered it, but I thought that might be reflexive, because the eyes that studied me so intently held no contempt. Instead he seemed to be trying to read my mind, to ferret out my strategy. An uncomfortable sensation.

"That's one reason." I could confirm that much, as it was common knowledge. "There are several barriers to our eventual blessed union." My standard words sounded false and empty even to my ears. Con had me thoroughly rattled; it would be wisest to end this interview and withdraw. But I couldn't quite make myself do it.

"I don't believe you mean that," he said slowly, studying my face, which I knew revealed nothing, as I had it smooth and composed. I lowered my eyes, in case he could read something in them. "Why this farce?" he asked, sounding so much as if he cared that I wanted to give him a true answer. He did possess a certain charisma despite his rough manners. No wonder his people had followed him. Something about him made me want to share my secrets and rest in the comfort of his strength and determination.

Which I could not do. He thought our goals aligned, but they didn't. I didn't know how he'd retained the optimism that he could beat Anure, when I knew with absolute certainty that it couldn't be done.

"I do what I have to," I replied. "I do what I must to protect Calanthe."

"I understand that," he said, coming closer again, the wolf stalking. "But you have other options."

"Like what?" I demanded, half incredulous, half desperately wanting to know if there was an exit from this trap I hadn't been able to find.

"Marry me instead."

I opened my mouth. Closed it again without speaking. At a total loss for words as I'd never been in my entire life. And not only because of the mortal offense he'd just offered.

He returned my stare, golden eyes wide with the same shock I felt, as if he hadn't expected those words to come out. Startling, impossible, earthshaking words. The round garden seemed to spin in circles, dizziness swamping me, and if not for the rigidity of my corset and other garments, I might've sagged. Despair and delight. Wonder and horror.

The girl in me, long since buried under the weight of the crown, might have wept.

Once there had been a bright path for her, the girl I could've been. In another world, another time line, she would've had a compelling man propose marriage to her in a garden. She might've had many suitors, her choice of partners. A chance at—if not exactly normal—a marriage of minds and bodies.

No longer. Just one of the many things Anure had destroyed. Because I couldn't scream my rage at the injustice of it all, I laughed.

I burst out laughing at the great cosmic joke. Of course, it only made it more pointed that my potential husband in a marriage of state brought a woman who was mostly likely his lover with him to my court. Never mind that I'd had to make him my prisoner to please my most loathed enemy. Really, it was all too absurd to bear.

Once I started laughing, I found it nearly impossible to stop, though hurt and fury flashed across Con's face. But he didn't stomp off to nurse his wounds. Nor did he join in my laughter like a smoother courtier might, pretending to find my amusement his. He simply waited until I, gasping for breath and clutching my constricted ribs, managed to quell the hysterical laughter. When I was done, he gave me an expectant look, as if still waiting for an actual answer. I searched for a reply, realizing my outburst meant I could hardly fob him off with something bland.

Settling on the simplest reply, I shook my head. "No."

"Why not?" he shot back, hard on the heels of my denial.

I wanted to throw up my hands at him. To blister him with a setback that would peel his ears from his head. Fool. Incautious rebel. He could never understand the compromises a woman like me had to make.

Instead I paced over to the orchids wending up the old fruit tree nearby. They shimmered with delicate colors in the dappled shade, undulating along the trunk and limbs, perching on twigs like exotic birds that might take flight on ruffled petals.

"Did you know orchids can't live on their own?" I asked, though I knew it was a rhetorical question, as Con could hardly know anything about the flowers that grew only on Calanthe. "They take their nourishment from the trees, perhaps from the rain and the very air. But they cannot be planted. They're not like other flowers. Beautiful, fragile, they exist on nothing, dependent on everything."

I glanced over my shoulder at Con, who watched me with a furrowed brow. A dark and threatening man, one who'd killed without remorse. One whose actions had condemned him to death. A king of nothing. And yet he seemed to be the solid tree to my epiphytic flower.

"Interesting," he said, eyes on me and not the blossoms, "but is there some point you're making?" He ground out the words as if they hurt his throat. For all I knew, they might. I had no idea what kind of damage caused him and Sondra to sound like that.

"We are all what we're born to be, Con," I replied. "I can't marry you—even if I wanted to—because I'm engaged to the emperor. You are legally a slave, a fugitive, and a prisoner bound to answer for war crimes, among other charges. Even without those truths, I'm queen of Calanthe and duty-bound to marry to make heirs for my realm and you're a landless man with no title, no bloodline you can claim. There is no world in which we'd marry."

Even that girl I might've been had the world been different would have turned away such an offer. In truth, in that other world, we would never have met.

"There is that world," he insisted. "If Anure hadn't made his conquests—"

"But he did." I cut off that line of speculation. "The past doesn't change."

"The future does change," he countered, "and only if we change the present. Marry me and we can change the world together. I think you hate Anure as much as any of us. Don't martyr yourself. Use your power as queen of the last independent kingdom in all the empire to end his blight upon the world."

It sounded so good. Tempting. And too good to be possible.

I laughed, lightly, the bitterness in it clear to my own ears, though thankfully without the hysteria that had gripped me earlier. "Independent? You are not as clever as I thought. Calanthe and I are as independent as this orchid. On our own, we wither and die. Pretty, but ultimately insubstantial."

His gaze fell to my ring. "What of that one? It lives on, immortal though severed from its source. Perhaps you and Calanthe are like that."

I fought the urge to hide the ring behind my back. "You're wrong. It's a fresh blossom, plucked anew every day."

Frowning, he met my gaze. "That's a lie. Why would you tell a lie about the Abiding Ring?"

My breath caught in my throat and I held it there, concentrating on that rather revealing response. Perhaps the pause went on too long, but my voice came out smooth and vaguely puzzled when I managed it. "Why would you call it that?"

His mouth twisted in a wry smile. "Ask Ambrose."

"I will." The wizard did know about the ring, which meant I'd have to do whatever it took to keep him on Calanthe. Time to end this circular conversation and take steps to do what I could accomplish and forget the impossible. "Speaking of whom, will you go along with the charade? If I can substitute others for Ambrose and the Lady Sondra, do you vow that you won't betray the trick?"

"You'd trust the vow of a slave, traitor, and man demonstrably without honor?"

An excellent point, and yet . . . "I would," I told him. "If only because you love them and will do anything to save their lives."

"Ambrose got me into this trap. I'm not feeling the love at the moment," he answered.

"And the Lady Sondra?" I asked, surprised to feel a flare of jealousy for the warrior woman. "You love her."

He regarded me with a frown, seeming torn. But he met my gaze steadily. "There's no one I love more in this world."

I nodded to myself. Exactly as I'd perceived, and I appreciated that he hadn't lied to me. "Regardless of your other flaws—and you no doubt have many—you also love your people. We have that much in common."

He grunted as if I'd struck him, his eyes bleak. Then he managed that wry smile again, though it came out a shadow of its usual self. "You are . . . not what I expected, Lia."

I didn't have to ask what he'd expected. I knew. After all, I'd created that image of myself with tireless determination. Ridiculous that I should feel a tinge of regret—both that he hadn't thought much of me and that now that he knew better, it didn't matter.

"If I so swear," he continued, "will you vow to protect them?"

"As well as I can protect anyone, yes."

His smile widened. "I imagine no one wins an argument with you."

"Well, I *am* the queen," I returned with asperity. "No one usually dares to argue with Me."

I'd maybe hoped he'd laugh, but his smile faded. "Except me."

"Except you," I acknowledged. Wolf of my dreams. Destroyer of kingdoms. Rebel and doomed man. He'd reached out to the wrong person—I couldn't save him. "Do we have a bargain?"

"What about my people on the ship in the harbor?"

"They will have escaped during the night." I fluttered my lashes and shrugged as if baffled. Con's gaze went to my powdered bosom, as if he couldn't help looking, before he wrenched it away. I smiled and he acknowledged it wryly. "I thought we had it guarded," I continued in a vacuous tone, "but it disappeared to who knows where." I added a giggle, then sobered. "I assume they can easily rejoin the rest of your fleet prowling just outside my waters."

He caught himself from showing surprise, then shook his head when he realized I'd seen it. "Should I even ask how you know about that?"

I gave him an arch look, enjoying that he seemed impressed. "You can ask . . ."

This time he laughed and I found myself smiling back. A wrong and genuine one that made the trio of jewels at the corner of my mouth pull. Exchanging these confidences, bits and pieces of secret strategies, felt illicit and strangely pleasurable. Something I couldn't afford to feel. I already regretted coming to know him this well. His death, already a stain on my conscience, would weigh more heavily on me now. I'd feel a hole in my life where he might've lived. I needed to put an end to this.

"So?" I asked.

"Yes." He nodded curtly. "I can hardly refuse such an offer. Just . . ." He firmed his lips. "Treat them well. They're the best of people."

"I will." I felt that I should say something more, but came up empty. "Guard!" I called, and the door opened immediately, Xichos with his sword at the ready. He looked almost disappointed to see me intact and unbloodied. "I'll see the next now," I ordered. "Escort the lady in and take this prisoner away when you bring her."

"Yes, Your Highness." He bowed and closed the door. Con didn't move, watching me still with some grim thoughts in his mind. As if he had any other kind. Even his proposal of marriage had seemed more like a desperate challenge than anything else. Perhaps his entire existence felt to him as much of an endless battle as mine did to me. We simply fought in different ways.

"I am sorry," I told him, letting my true regret show. "I don't wish your fate on you."

"Will you mourn my death?" he asked lightly, mockingly.

"Yes," I replied. When he raised a dubious brow, I gave him my standard line. "I told you, everyone has value."

"Ah." He seemed about to say something more, but evidently changed his mind, instead bowing as he hadn't before, an echo of gallantry in it. "It's been a pleasure, Queen Euthalia. Despite everything."

I had to smile. I doubted any other man could say such a thing under these circumstances. "I wish I could say the same," I said, impetuously. Too honest, because it gave him pause.

"Am I so repellent?" he asked.

He seemed—absurdly, given his blazing confidence and arrogance—actually self-conscious, so I gave him another honest answer. Perhaps there's something about talking to a man doomed to die that makes it difficult to lie to him. "Not at all. You are also not what I expected, Con. I will mourn your death because . . ." I faltered, rather alarmed at what I'd been about to confide.

"Because?" He closed the distance between us, gaze bright and intense on mine.

I felt that strange dizziness, that longing for what could never be. A personal mirror of the longing of all the world to be something more than a maelstrom of hatred and fear. "Because in another world I might've said yes," I whispered.

The gate opened, saving me from my impetuous words, the guard escorting the Lady Sondra in, thankfully without chains. Con didn't even glance their way. "You still can," he urged, his voice quietly urgent. "You have the power to stop all of this, Lia. You're stronger than you know."

"Stand down!" Xichos thundered. "You dare disrespect the queen, you mongrel." The guards seized Con, dragging him back—though it took four of them to do it, as the big man had dug in with casual strength, gaze still fierce on mine.

"It's not too late, Your Highness," he said.

Though he was wrong about that, too. It was entirely too late.

For us both.

20

"What good is being a wizard if you can't use your magic to save my cursed life?" I snarled the question while I paced restlessly around the circle of the room as I hadn't allowed myself to do in that bloodless battle with Lia, grimly aware that our tower room and her private court-yard were about the same size, though worlds apart.

Ambrose sat sideways on the bed he'd adopted, lean-ing his back against the stone wall of the tower, Merle perched on the ledge of the open window beside him. Both Ambrose and Merle regarded me with attentive gazes, along with slightly bemused smiles. If ravens can smile.

"That's not really how magic works," he replied.

"Right—it defies explanation." I meant that to be scath-ingly mocking, but Ambrose nodded, as if a particularly dense student had suddenly grasped a difficult concept.

"Exactly."

"If it defies explanation," I reasoned, "then how can you say that's *not* how it works. If you know how something doesn't work, you know the reverse: how it does."

"Aha! Not true." Ambrose tapped his fingers together. "If a sword goes through your heart and it stops beating, then you know your heart doesn't work with a sharp object cleaving it in two. But that doesn't mean you know how the heart beats in the first place."

If my head didn't ache with impotent frustration already, that would have pushed me over the edge. As it was, I glared at him hard enough that he sat back again, subdued. "I'm not interested in debating riddles of logic." I'd had plenty of that with Lia. Tricky, clever, and foolishly obstinate woman. Had I really blurted out that offer of marriage?

Had she really said that in another world she might've said yes?

Her circular arguments made my head hurt, but those last words had pierced my heart like the sword Ambrose evoked so carelessly. I was as much the King of Regret as anything. I'd built an internal kingdom of it, cursing every bad turn that destroyed my birthright and future. She saw it, too, that world. In a world without Anure's devouring greed, Calanthe and Oriel could've been allies. Lia and I might've been encouraged to meet, to consider a marriage of state.

Perhaps this day, this meeting in the garden, had been one of Ambrose's nexus points. Maybe time and coincidence had always flowed to that conversation, where she and I met and matched wits, where we discussed marriage between us. That was the bit that made my heart—still beating, apparently, despite the many injuries to it—sting with the bitter salt on the wound. I could envision that alternate meeting. I'd have come to her as a prince, eloquent and mannered, ready to charm. And she . . . She wouldn't be determinedly engaged to a monster, planning to feed herself to it in the hope of choking it to death.

Oh, she'd denied it, but I could see her endgame as if it were mine. Not difficult to do, as my plan didn't differ much. Get close enough to kill and damn the consequences.

Though we couldn't be more different in every outward aspect, Lia and I were the same inside.

"If you're not interested in riddles," Ambrose said, genially, as if making conversation over tea, "then perhaps you'll tell me what happened. Other than that you seem to have been unsuccessful in wooing the lovely Euthalia and instead of giving you her hand, she's giving Anure your head."

I tossed him an incredulous stare. "Did you really think I'd come back here and announce our impending nuptials?" Though, for a moment there, from the wild and surprisingly reckless glint in her eye, the way she'd leaned into my touch with that sweet tremble, I'd thought she might indeed say yes.

Ambrose shrugged, all cheer, but his gaze had gone as keen as Merle's. "That *was* your mission," he pointed out. "I don't know that I've seen you fail before."

Refusing to rise to his bait, I stopped and leaned my hands on the window ledge, staring resolutely out the window at the illusion of freedom. The serene sea, the masses of flowers. *Did you know orchids can't live on their own?* She'd looked fragile in that moment, as she hadn't until then. I felt as if she'd been asking me some other question and I'd been too dense to understand. I had failed. Failed myself, failed her, failed my people, living and dead.

"She has a plan," I said, feeling the heaviness of my mortal flesh, of the chains that awaited me. "That's why she summoned us. She'll explain to you, but she's somehow divined that you're a wizard and she wants to keep you on Calanthe—apparently with the misguided notion that you'll be of some use to her."

"Is this where I point out Queen Euthalia's insight and wisdom?" Ambrose asked.

"Why waste it on a doomed man?" I said without turning. "Might as well save it up to kiss her ass, if you can find it under all those clothes. She also offered to keep Sondra."

"Really. Did she say why?"

She never had, had she? Not exactly. Instead I'd gotten sidetracked by the opportunity to convert her to my cause. "Does it matter?" I countered. "She did and that's enough for me. I agreed to the deal. You two, at least, will be safe. So are Kara and the rest—she arranged for our ship to escape during the night."

"Ah, that explains that. What did she ask in exchange?"

"Just that I go along with the charade. She hopes to send two people in your place, as Anure's emissary hasn't laid eyes on us yet, and she only needs me to pretend there's nothing wrong."

"Which people will she send in our place?" Ambrose asked, as it hadn't occurred to me to do. Something else she'd distracted me from.

I frowned at the pretty view and turned back to him. "I don't know. Does it matter?"

The trapdoor levered open and Sondra climbed through, stomping it closed again, the man below exclaiming in annoyance. "Of course it matters," she said, "which is why I told Her Highness no deal."

"*What?*" I rounded on her. Sondra stood on the trapdoor with calm insouciance, hip cocked and arms folded, ignoring the pounding from below. They had sent her clothes—something I hadn't noticed before when we passed in Lia's garden, which spoke volumes of the scrambled state of mind the difficult queen had put me in—and wore a simple gown of pale pink that somehow softened her, despite her hard expression and the look of blazing contempt in her eyes.

"Oh, don't you *dare*, Conrí." Her voice shook with quiet rage. Probably lucky for me that she'd been stripped of her weapons and her commitment to weighing the trapdoor closed kept her from advancing on me. I knew that look—and had seen plenty of men take the sight of it with them to their deaths. "I don't even know where to start."

"Then don't," I advised. "I already took the deal with the queen and you have no authority to abrogate it."

"Fancy word," she sneered. "Did you learn that from your father?"

That struck harder, sliced deeper than any blow from a weapon she might've wielded. All the more so because I probably *had* learned it at my father's knee—and in regard to Anure, too. *He's abrogated the treaties and . . .* A snatch of conversation with his advisers. With it came a fragment of visual memory, a rare image of my father at rest, if not at peace. He sat in a chair, dwarfing it with his large frame, absently stroking his beard as he studied the document he held. And my mother—her ebony hair in coils gleaming with rose-scented oil—leaning over his arm to read also as the other people around the table talked, concern and anxiety thick in the room.

Clearly I'd spied on them when I shouldn't have. How old had I been? Four or five, if my mother had still been alive. Before that moment I would've said I didn't remember her face. Now the scent of roses filled my mind, along with her fierce hugs and gentle kisses. Beyond strange for those memories to assault me now—unless my impending death brought them up. Or the encounter with Lia, who knew things she shouldn't. Perhaps she'd messed with my mind somehow.

"Can Queen Euthalia work magic?" I asked Ambrose.

"I am talking to you, Conrí!" Sondra shouted. I decided not to point out the difference between talking and shouting, and ignored her.

"An interesting question," Ambrose answered brightly, sliding off the bed and grabbing his borrowed staff. "Of course, the Lady Sondra will have to give way if I'm to have my interview. I shall see what I can discover."

Sondra regarded him sourly, some of her anger dissipating. "She's a cagey bitch. Don't go for her I'm-just-a-brainless-beauty routine."

I laughed and she transferred her glare back to me. "Did you even talk to her that long?"

"It didn't take long," she snapped. "Her Highness offered her lousy deal, I told her to fuck herself, then suggested she solve all our problems by marrying you."

My head throbbed. Scrubbing my hands over my scalp didn't help. "You didn't."

"Well, clearly you didn't get the job done." The banging beneath her feet grew louder, the voices more strident.

Setting my teeth, I tried not to growl at her. "I said I'd try. Forgive me for not accomplishing the impossible in less than an hour."

"I don't forgive you," she shot back. "You didn't even tell her who you are, you obstinate oaf!"

"I'm not him anymore," I shouted. "Oriel is gone. Lost. Ash and dust and—"

"And you told her you're in love with me." Her strident voice drowned out mine. "Why would you say such an idiotic thing?"

That pierced my fury. "I'm not in love with you."

"I know that!" Sondra waved her hands in impotent frustration, then vented it by jumping up and down on the trapdoor. Below, someone yelped and the pounding ceased for a blessed moment. "So why in great green Ejarat did you say so?"

"I said I loved you more than anyone in the world," I replied with considerable patience, "because it's the truth and so she would treat you well here."

"You don't tell a woman you're courting that you love another woman, under any circumstances." She glared and pulled at her prettily brushed hair. The pounding began again with renewed force and she turned her lethal anger on it. "I don't know how you could be that stupid," she added more quietly.

I had been stupid, and shame crawled up my spine. "I told you I'm no good at this court stuff. I'm out of my depth here and I don't know what you expect."

"You are my king and I expect you to live up to my goddamn fucking expectations, not give up like a whipped puppy and meekly go to your death!" Her voice broke and tears spilled out. The grief weakened her, and she wavered as the shoving from below lifted her.

I crossed the room, offering her a hand. "If you will, Lady Sondra."

Dashing away the tears with an impatient fist, she gave me a fierce scowl but took my hand, stepping off the rising angle of the trapdoor. Xichos stuck his head and sword through, spewing threats.

Ambrose waited patiently until he finished, smiling beatifically. "My turn?" he asked when the man wound down. Ambrose flicked a glance at Merle, who winged over to land with delicate precision on the knob of the staff. He croaked grumpily and Ambrose soothed his ruffled feathers. "I know. We'll ask for our real one. Euthalia is most rational." He cast me a glance, as if to point out all the ways I wasn't. "I'm sure she'll give it back."

"The crow stays here." Xichos pointed the sword at Merle. "Or we'll kill it."

"Step out of the way," Ambrose replied. "I have an appointment with Her Highness and I believe you've already delayed me unforgivably."

The guard looked briefly confused, then disappeared below. Ambrose turned and winked at me. "That, my dear Conrí, is how magic works."

And he descended the ladder with all the steady strength of a sound body, Merle riding the staff, majestic head held high. The trap closed, the sound of the lock snicking into place. Sondra turned and punched me.

I rubbed the meat of my shoulder. "Ow."

"Oh, that didn't hurt. Baby," she snarled.

"So much for me being your king," I remarked mildly.

"Maybe you *abrogated* that right when you gave up on us."

Weary, suddenly starving, I went to the food table and began piling food on a plate. Some sort of sliced red meat looked particularly enticing, so I tasted it. Delicious. Shoving several more slices into my mouth, I chewed and added a pile to my plate.

"This is your response," Sondra said, sounding weary, too. "You're going to stuff your face."

I swallowed and gave her a feral grin, pouring a generous mug of rosy wine. "Every doomed man deserves a last meal."

"Don't say that. It's not funny. We have to figure a way out of this."

"You do have a way out," I said, pulling out a chair to sit, my plate on the table where I could reach it. "Live on Calanthe. It's probably the last decent place left. You could do worse."

"And do nothing while Anure's emissary hauls you off?

Attend parties and orgies while you're tortured and executed, sure. Allow some poor soul to take my place and
suffer in my stead while I prance about in pretty gowns."
Sondra plucked at her pink dress, looking like she'd prefer to slice it to ribbons.

"You've earned it," I said, as firmly as I could. "We
fought. We failed in the ultimate quest, but you have a
chance now. Isn't that what we wanted, at heart? You're
out of the mines and you're free now. You can have a life
again." The one she might've had, if Anure hadn't robbed
her of it. But I didn't say that. My own regrets were too
recent and too raw.

"Do you know what she said to me?" Sondra lifted her
head, her eyes blue as fresh bruises in her pale face. "She
said I could honor you best by living well, and that I should
try to conceive your child while I could, so I'd at least have
that to carry on your legacy. That we should ask Ambrose
to enchant our fertility to guarantee it. That's why she sent
me back, so the three of us could have a moment to do that.
She plans to keep Ambrose with her, so we'll have plenty
of privacy." Her voice had gone tense, threaded with emotions I couldn't decipher. She didn't look at me, either,
sitting on the edge of the bed she'd chosen, fingers linked
between her knees, the fall of golden silk hair veiling her
face.

"When I said she should marry you, that it was fated
by the prophecy, she laughed in my face."

"Not everyone believes in prophecies. They're not exactly reliable."

"She said even if she wasn't engaged to Anure, she'd
never marry a man in love with another woman. That it
was beneath her—and it was beneath me that you held me
in so little regard."

"Did she call him by name?" I asked, curious. Otherwise I could hear Lia laughingly delivering those words as if she'd stood in the room and spoken them.

Sondra widened her eyes incredulously. "*That* is your reply?"

"She's so deliberate about calling him His Imperial Majesty, while I'm sure she's labeling him with vile epithets in her head," I explained. The grapes were good, too. Sweet and plump. Like Lia's bosom. I really wondered what she looked like under all that upholstery.

"What in Sawehl has gotten into you?" Sondra stood, came over, and went to lay a hand to my forehead—which I easily batted away.

"The prophecy is nonsense, Sondra, don't you see?" I drank down the wine, then refilled the cup. It gave me a relaxing, heady rush. Not like the harsh liquors of the towns we'd conquered, or the bottles we'd dug out of abandoned estates. Nobody left the good stuff behind. I should stay wine-drunk until they hauled me off. All that death for nothing. All my vows and certainty, gone to ash. *Sorry, Father.* "We're playing a blind game of strategy with a crazy woman. It doesn't matter what Her Highness of the Flowers thinks about me. I've lost, but at least I've lost alone and the rest of you can go free."

My cup empty, I began to pour more wine. But Sondra dashed the goblet from my hand so it shattered on the floor—and wine poured over my borrowed pants. I stood, dusting off the drenching and glanced at the glass pieces scattered across the floor. "I bet that was expens—"

Sondra punched me. Hard enough to make me bite down on the words and my tongue. I dabbed at the blood, glistening bright against the corroded gray of my fingers. "What the—"

"If you lose, we all lose." Sondra clenched her fists, restraining herself for the moment, using her words to batter me instead. "You never gave up on me before. Don't do it now."

"Then we've all lost," I ground out, waving my hands at the pretty prison, then shooting my finger at the paradise outside. "Don't be fooled by the fact that we don't stand on a bloody battlefield with the stink of vurgsten in the air. We've been defeated. We came a long way, but we're prisoners of war, Sondra. You've been ransomed. Be happy."

"I never thought I'd see you give up without a fight," she said with bitter disappointment.

"There's nothing to fight!" I roared at her. With nothing to pummel, I seized the pitcher of wine and threw it against the wall. It rained glass and fluid red as the blood on my hands. "There! Are you happy? I've attacked our prison. Has anything changed? *No.*"

"Brilliant use of a blunt object," she drawled, eyes dark with disgust.

"What would you have me use?" I demanded, fingers twitching to throttle something. I wasn't suited for this. Give me stone to pulverize. Give me soldiers to slay. Hell, give me a battle to plan. "I don't have my hammer. I don't even have that stupid sword. Here. Shall I make a bagiroca of a silk napkin and these grapes?"

"Better that than whining yourself into a drunk and acting the martyr," she bit out.

I stared at her. We'd had hard words between us—beginning when she first called me king over my father's corpse—but never had she spoken with such contempt. Fitting, I supposed, that at the end I should lose what I gained at the beginning, her regard as my first follower.

"Did you think being king would be easy?" she asked, relenting, though her sympathy ground salt in the wound she'd created with one disappointed look. "You should've told her who you are. That might make all the difference."

You're a landless man with no title, no bloodline you can claim. How could I explain how I'd wanted Lia to see value in me without calling upon lost Oriel? I didn't understand it myself. Only that claiming my decimated birthright felt like a final capitulation.

"I'm king of nothing," I replied, sitting heavily again, heartily regretting that I'd killed the pitcher of wine. King of Regret.

"You call us nothing?" Sondra shot back. "This is where it gets hard, Conrí."

"Don't call me that. You're right—I don't deserve it."

"This is where it gets hard, Conrí," she repeated. "Smashing heads is easy compared with using your own. Have you forgotten your promise to me?"

I ask only to hold the torch. "No. But I don't see how I can fulfill it, now," I admitted.

"Then figure it out," she ordered, all battlefield steel. "You have people counting on you. Your death would not be only your own. You gave up that privilege a long time ago. You don't have the luxury of giving up, because if you do, you take all of our hopes with you." She gave me that lethal smile. "Don't disappoint me, Conrí. You know what happens to those who do."

Standing there in the pink silk gown, her lovely hair cascading around her shoulders, her face set in harsh, demanding lines, she'd never reminded me more of the bald, scrawny, ash-streaked and filthy creature who'd demanded that I become king.

And I knew then what I had to do.

21

I sensed the wizard's approach well before he entered my garden. Like the golden glow of Sawehl's sun before it breached the horizon. The orchid ring seemed to stretch, then resettle itself on my finger, the band gently hugging my skin like a kitten settling delicate claws in a sleepy embrace.

Whether in deference for the wizard's twisted leg or a warrior's healthy instincts that made him wary, Xichos escorted Ambrose without the brusque treatment he'd shown Con and even Sondra. As Ambrose laboriously crossed the garden toward me, leaning heavily on his staff, I mentally reviewed the conversation with the hard woman, as abbreviated as it had been. Con's lover didn't like me—that much she'd made plain—and I hardly blamed her. As their captor and Con's judge and executioner in effect, whether I wielded the ax myself or not, I didn't expect to be loved for my actions.

And yet she'd urged me to marry the man. It took me by surprise, but I'd quickly deciphered the implications. That meant Con hadn't proposed marriage to me out of impulse or some sudden affection of the moment. Not that I'd fooled myself that he'd succumbed to some sort of romantic love-at-first-sight nonsense. Some of the younger—

and more foolish—of my ladies might coo over such stories, but if one allows cool logic to prevail, it becomes obvious that instant attraction has nothing to do with deeper emotions. It's only physical attraction. Muscled shoulders, powerful height, big and capable hands—they all spoke to the animal nature in me, that part that craves protection and . . . whatever women craved from men.

Not things I needed or could ever have.

No, any connection I imagined between us had been spun of the heightened feelings of our mutual hatred of Anure, and perhaps a shared wish that our lives and world could've been a better place. Knowing that Con had been acting on a plan they'd concocted put an entirely different spin on things.

The impression he'd given of having some personal interest in me had been manipulation, something I normally perceived more quickly than that. More the fool me for succumbing to it even for a moment. I accepted fault for my own part in falling for it, spinning those fantasies of a deep connection, a familiarity that went beyond the time we'd met.

Perhaps they'd come here for that purpose, and not to conquer. They hadn't seemed inclined to fire on Calanthe, or my people, as I'd prepared for in case the enchantment hadn't worked as I hoped. Most likely Con had used his keen strategic mind, intuiting that the silly young Queen of Flowers would be swayed by his savage handsomeness and fall, fainting and giddy, into his arms—and consequently positioning him to attack Yekpehr. Never mind that he'd decimate Calanthe in the process. What was one more ransacked and dusty kingdom to him?

It burned me no end that he'd been so close to convincing me. Years of certainty and icing my heart to think of only duty, then a few minutes in a garden with a charismatic man and I'd nearly gone against everything my father taught me.

Ambrose bowed, beaming like an honored guest visiting for tea, balancing on the staff as he made a leg with the misshapen one. An odd choice. Mocking me and my throne? The raven half spread its wings, ducking its head in mimicry of the bow.

I'd been planning to restore Ambrose's magical staff to him, but now I reconsidered. I also considered leaving him in the obeisance. Both would be petty whereas I wished to earn his confidence. Still, I'd wait until I had a sense of whether he planned to attack me before I gave him additional weapons. There. I was thinking strategically again.

"You may rise," I said, studying them both as they did. Though the wizard's eyes had been downcast, the raven's had not. Much as I could see through the eyes of Calanthe's birds during the dreamthink, Ambrose probably had at least that much ability with his familiar. Likely far more and better controlled. I so hoped he could teach me.

"So, Your Highness," Ambrose said brightly, ignoring protocol by speaking before I invited him to. "I understand I'm to be added to your Court of Curiosities."

I raised a brow at the impertinence and he shrugged with good cheer, leaning in and winking. "That's what we call it, those of us in the circles of the types of folk you collect. It's meant with affection and all due reverence for Your Highness."

I seriously doubted that. And I decided not to address the implicit irreverence. No doubt having a wizard for an adviser would come with all sorts of concessions on my part. Plus, none of Con's people were quite as they appeared, including himself. The jovial mien the wizard displayed didn't quite hide the canny and ancient being inside. Indeed, the raven had turned its head, hard orange eye on me, as the wizard apparently looked around at the flowers with an absent smile playing on his lips. He never took his attention off me.

"Ah, then, Con spoke to you of the plan. Excellent." I wouldn't have to explain it yet again—or face the sort of nastiness I'd endured with Sondra. You'd have thought I was planning to flay her alive rather than offer her a life of ease in the Flower Court.

"Conrí," he said. "I'm naturally looking forward to seeing some of my friends who've accepted your generous offer of luxurious asylum," he continued, "even as I'm sorry to refuse for my part and Merle's."

The raven croaked an agreement, bobbing his head, as if regretfully apologizing. I eyed it, wondering if Merle echoed his master's thoughts or conveyed his own. He might not be truly a bird at all.

"Not this again," I replied, having no trouble sounding utterly weary of this group of martyrs. "Con certainly has gathered himself a crew of professional victims. Let Me guess—you'd rather be tortured and executed by His Imperial Majesty, also."

"Conrí, Your Highness. The *rí* is an honorific in Oriel," he clarified. "To truncate it demonstrates either familiarity or disrespect for the crown prince."

I barely disguised my shock. Conrí, *the crown prince of Oriel*? And he'd stood there and let me malign his bloodline . . . I'd throttle the man. I swore I would.

"Is that so?" I said, smooth and barely interested. "Oriel . . . the golden kingdom in the high hills. Legendary for its prosperity, blissfully happy population—along with the noble but vicious Warriors of the Orb that guarded its borders from attack."

"Indeed." Ambrose dropped some of the clownish mask. "One of the first to fall to the upstart tyrant." He hadn't bothered to lower his voice.

"Have a care, Syr Ambrose," I warned him.

"No honorific needed for me." He stroked his familiar. "Call me Ambrose, and this is Merle."

"Ambrose," I replied with studied patience, "Merle, even I cannot protect you from the consequences of treason if your words are connected to your face."

"Can't you?" It sounded like a challenge. "I don't think the Abiding Ring would've accepted you if that were true. May I?" He extended an oddly long-fingered hand toward me, a glimpse of something beneath illusion.

Interested to test that, I laid my hand in his, the orchid fluttering its petals almost coyly, like one of my ladies simpering at a handsome courtier. *Have some dignity*, I thought at it, and it stilled, obeying for once. Merle opened his beak in a smile, while the wizard had his human gaze on the blossom. His hand felt normal. Excellent illusion then. He was more powerful than I'd guessed.

If I could learn that trick, I might be able to wear fewer clothes. An enticing thought, though minor in the grand scheme of the problems I faced.

"As extraordinary as I'd hoped," Ambrose said, releasing my hand and leaning on the staff, regarding me like one of my naturalists dissecting a newly discovered beetle. "You're not what I expected, however."

"No?" I raised a brow, going for supercilious cool.

Ambrose shook his head ruefully. "It's not your fault, your mother being taken from you so young and your father passing as he did . . . And losing your wizards, too. Well, the past can't be helped, but I did hope for more."

I squelched the need to ask what he could possibly know about my mother. Another attempt at manipulation, no doubt. He couldn't know anything of importance, I reassured myself. "I am grieved to disappoint you," I replied in a tone that froze even the most incautious of courtiers.

But Ambrose waved a hand as if in forgiveness. "I've learned to live with worse disappointments. Once you marry Conrí, that will put us on the right path. I'll be able to begin your instruction." He beamed at me, somehow making it the expression of a generous and ancient teacher despite his boyish face.

It required all my years of training in courtly impassivity not to gape at him.

"Even if I weren't engaged to His Imperial—"

"Which you're not," Ambrose cut me off. Then added a slight smile. "Don't try to trick the trickster, Euthalia. I know exactly how much of your apparent betrothal is smoke and mirrors."

"Will you assist Me then?" I asked, seizing control of the conversation. Perhaps if I'd had access to a wizard years ago, when I first ascended to the throne, too young and in the wake of my father's untimely death, I could've avoided this trap before it bound me so tightly. "Is there a way out?"

"Of course!" He smiled and straightened. I doubted he truly needed to lean on the staff at all. "Though you already have it. I've already convinced Conrí that marrying you is the best course. See, there's a prophecy that—"

I held up my hand, stopping him. "In the age of Anure, prophecies are meaningless."

Ambrose gave me a withering look. "You know as well as I do that magic is not gone from the world, no matter what the false emperor claims."

"It doesn't matter what magic remains. Even at its height, magic wasn't enough to stop Anure in the first place. If we learned nothing else, we learned that."

"Oh, child." The wizard's scorn turned to pity. "You're sorely misinformed. Magic was far from its height when Anure took advantage of the sloth and greed of the court wizards across the many kingdoms."

I stared at him, the fragments of so many lessons and advice from my father swirling in my head, reassembling into a different picture. "Even so," I replied slowly, "that may change My view of the past, but the present remains the same. Do you claim the magic of Calanthe is enough to change the entire world?"

"No." He shook his head sadly, Merle mimicking the gesture. Or agreeing. "No, you're correct there. But there's a chance, see, if you marry Conrí, that—"

"I'm not marrying him. I can't."

"But he's the rightful king of Oriel."

"Oriel is gone," I pointed out. *I am King of Nothing.* "I don't care if he's the crown prince of Oriel, I—"

"He was. Until his father died. That makes him king now."

"No, Ambrose." My voice lashed out, and the orchid ring flexed its petals with the power of it. "He is My prisoner and will face the wrath of the emperor for crimes against the empire. That is a fate of his own making. I can save you; perhaps I can save the Lady Sondra." We might have to drug her to insensibility until her liege and lover was well away, but we could do it. I owed Con that much, had promised him.

"But can you save yourself?" Ambrose asked softly, Merle cocking his head cannily.

"No. I gave up on that a long time ago when I agreed to honor My father's promises. All I can do is save Calanthe. To do that, I need you to help Me find the next wearer of the orchid ring."

"The Abiding Ring," he corrected. "That's the old name for it."

"Good to know," I answered, hard on the heels of his correction, feeling the bitterness rise. It would've been good of my father to tell me at least that much. The sun had risen high and shone down too hot. What I wouldn't give to shed these clothes and dive naked into Calanthe's cool and forgiving sea.

"As I said, your ignorance isn't entirely your fault." Ambrose read my irritation and gave me a sympathetic smile that hardened. "Though it will be if you continue to be willfully blind."

"I should let Leuthar deliver you to Anure," I hissed, anger and frustration getting the better of me. "I'm trying to help you and you only insult Me."

"Oh, my dear child." Ambrose looked sorrowful. "I don't need your help. I'm offering you mine. If you're wise, you'll take it."

I sat back slightly. The structure of my garments doesn't allow for much, but I needed a moment. "You'll help Me find an heir to the throne of Calanthe," I said, testing him.

He rolled his eyes. "Fine, fine. That will be simple once you marry Conrí. It's really the least of what we need—"

"No, wizard," I explained with all the patience left in me. "I need to transfer the orchid ring—"

"The Abiding Ring," he corrected.

"—to My heir as soon as possible so I can marry His Imperial Majesty. Time is running out."

"That's the one true thing you've said." Merle croaked an affirmation, then clacked his beak at me, chiding.

"Listen, Ambrose—" I broke off, listening to a commotion beyond the walls. The door opened to admit Tertulyn. She looked distraught, as much as she ever did.

Picking up her skirts so her dainty slippers flashed across the mossy stones of the paved courtyard, she ran to me and sank in a curtsy.

"Forgive me, Your Highness, but the emissary is awake." She caught her breath and tried to still her panting, then had to gulp in more air. Ambrose examined her with great interest.

I gazed at her, more than a little bemused. "Thank you, Tertulyn, for letting Me know he's woken, as I asked you to."

Her pansy-blue eyes flashed up to my face. "I mean he's *up*. He received a messenger bird and he's looking for You."

A bellow outside the walls. Leuthar, in a rage or excited. I closed my eyes briefly, sending a prayer to Ejarat. Then opened my eyes and pinned Tertulyn with a stare. She flushed, not only from exertion, but from . . . embarrassment? Surely not shame for an error. Unless something more had occurred.

"Why wasn't I given more warning?" I asked her quietly. Some of my anger at Ambrose leaked into my voice, because I sounded more menacing than I'd meant to.

She colored a deeper shade. "Your Highness, I—"

"Your Highness!" Leuthar called from beyond the door. "Tell Your guard to admit me. I have joyful news of the utmost importance."

I glared at Tertulyn, who blanched. How she'd failed me I didn't know, but we'd deal with it later. At the moment I apparently would have the great pleasure of an unexpected audience with the emperor's emissary, Sawehl save us. And in my favorite private garden, too. I mentally sighed for it as I could hardly refuse him, not without an excuse, and I could think of absolutely nothing. Con and his people had drained me of anything but despair. "Admit Syr Leuthar, please, Tertulyn."

She practically fled back across the paving stones. I turned my attention to Ambrose, who appeared to be in silent conversation with Merle. "I don't suppose you will disguise yourself as someone else?" I asked.

Ambrose gave me a wide-eyed, boyishly innocent look. "Why would I do that? I've never met an imperial emissary before. Sounds so exciting. Is he as impressive as his title?"

Tertulyn had reached the gate. "At least give another name," I pleaded. "Say you're one of My scholars who doesn't frequent the Night Court. There's plenty like that whom Leuthar has never met."

I'd apparently erred in not asking Tertulyn to remain because she slipped out the doors as Leuthar swept in. Perhaps she assumed my orders to keep the garden audiences private still stood, but normally she'd know that Leuthar's arrival had changed everything. I would have to find out what was going on with her. Especially as Leuthar had clearly been up and about for some time—long enough to groom himself to extravagant perfection—without her alerting me.

So not like her. And worrisome.

Leuthar pranced across the courtyard like one of my peacocks, the trailing turquoise plume of his hat bobbing as if he hoped to signal mates out at sea. He stopped before me, sweeping an ostentatious bow and completely ignoring Ambrose, who leaned on his staff, observing the emissary's approach with bright eyes and an amused smile, as if highly entertained indeed.

Then Ambrose looked at me, wrinkled his nose, and shook his head, as if in disappointment. Absurdly—especially considering how much the wizard had aggravated me—I had to struggle not to laugh. I knew better, too. Syr Leuthar might be ridiculous, but he acted for the emperor and held the power of life and death—and worse than death—over us all. Apparently the wizard didn't take even that seriously. No surprise there.

"Your Highness," Leuthar crooned, giving me a charming smile. "My sincerest apologies for my tardiness in congratulating You on Your fantastic political coup. Capturing the Slave King so handily! I only heard after You'd retired last night." He coughed delicately into a silk hankie, waving away the unmentionable time he'd spent in a drugged haze, only waking well into the night. "Once I had the glad tidings that the rebellious dogs had been taken captive, I sent a bird to His Imperial Majesty immediately to solicit instructions. I'm sure Your Highness had already done so, but it never hurts to confirm. And good thing I did!" He blinked at me in triumph. "For the message I received just a bit ago"—he pulled an ornately folded envelope of Anure's gray marbled stationery from his pocket—"implies Your bird may have gone astray. Of course, Your little birds are so small and fragile."

The emperor, and his emissaries, used large messenger birds to convey their verbose messages. They never quite seemed to understand the staying power of the smaller songbirds that migrated distances vaster than the empire twice annually. Nor did they understand that our abbreviated messages conveyed much in code. Obviously, I had no intention of disabusing them of this misapprehension.

"Oh dear." I made a sorrowful face. "I hope My poor little creature wasn't hurt or killed."

Naturally, I hadn't yet sent a message to Anure. No, because I'd been wasting time and energy trying to save those who didn't wish to be saved.

"The small things are so vulnerable," Leuthar agreed. Merle made a series of croaks that sounded like a laugh. Leuthar jumped as if poked, and eyed the magnificent raven askance, then seemed to notice Ambrose for the first time. "I don't believe we've met," he said. "Nor have I ever been in this prettyish garden." He looked about and frowned at the high walls.

"I'm Ambrose," the wizard replied, and waggled his eyebrows. "One of the rebel dog captives."

I had to lower my lashes to keep my eyes from rolling back in my head. Determined to destroy themselves.

"Captives? You mean . . ." Leuthar glanced at me, fully astonished. "I—oh my!"

"I was interrogating him," I explained and glared at Ambrose, who—along with Merle—attempted a hangdog posture, making an absolute mockery of it. Leuthar was blissfully oblivious, but the sarcasm wasn't lost on me.

"But why in His Imperial Majesty's name isn't such a dangerous prisoner chained?" Leuthar exclaimed. "Your Highness mustn't be so cavalier with Her welfare."

"Ambrose is physically unwell," I explained, giving the wizard a warning look through my lashes. "And he's a scholar, not a fighter."

"Ah." Leuthar looked unconvinced, and Ambrose obligingly leaned more heavily on his staff, giving up his playfulness and displaying every impression of frailty. Merle let one wing dangle as if broken and badly mended, putting the whole act over the top. Leuthar, however—oblivious to nuance—nodded knowingly. "And has Your Highness extracted anything useful?"

"Unfortunately, no." I shot Ambrose an icy glare. "He is most obstinate. I suspect he is mentally addled."

Merle tipped his head to the side, opening his beak and letting his tongue dangle out, forcing me to look away lest I begin laughing in truth.

"Never mind, Your Highness." Leuthar waved the

hankie, the scent of yilkas wafting from it. "His Imperial Majesty employs the very best torturers. He will soon know all there is useful from him, before he's executed. Tell me," he said, dropping his voice and leaning in to encourage confidences, "is the Slave King as fierce and brutish as they say, or is the talk all exaggeration?"

"He is not so fierce," I said, speaking largely to Ambrose, who opened his eyes wide, as if shocked I could think so. "I frankly wonder if there's much to the tales at all."

"I imagine not, as You captured him so easily. Still, His Imperial Majesty wants him, and his companions, delivered as soon as possible. Where are the other two?"

I mentally sighed, washing my hands of the lot of them. I'd tried to help them. Intention counted for something, didn't it? I refused to feel guilty. My primary responsibility, as my father had drilled into me, was to Calanthe. I owed these rebels nothing. "They are in the detention tower, Emissary."

"Excellent." Leuthar tucked the hankie away. "I'm to take them on the ship they captured on the evening tide."

"Oh dear." I fluttered my fingers helplessly. "I'm afraid it escaped."

"Escaped?" Syr Leuthar paused, alarmed, hints of anger leaking through his yilkas-induced serenity.

"In the night." I shrugged elaborately, drawing his gaze to my bosom. Unlike Con, he let it linger there and I breathed heavily, as if in distress, letting him be distracted by the show. "I don't know how." I gasped theatrically, widening my eyes. "Do you think they could know some of the old magic?"

Behind Leuthar's back, Ambrose rolled his eyes at me. Then he pursed his lips and blew some inaudible words toward the emissary. Leuthar relaxed again into his haze, smiling at me.

"Oh, Your Highness. Such flights of fancy You indulge in. Magic never existed. Our beloved emperor has labored so hard to eliminate those old superstitions. Your Highness really must try to move into the modern era and think logically."

"I shall try." I lowered my lashes modestly, allowing the crystals to chime as I fluttered them.

"Don't be too distressed. The ship can't be far and we'll recapture it in short order. I'll send His Imperial Majesty's navy after them. These rebel dogs won't be able to evade seasoned warriors as easily as they did Your soft Calanthean guards."

I smiled, closed-mouthed, swallowing my retort. I had little trouble pretending to be a silly figurehead to lull Anure and his toadies into complacency, but I found it difficult not to defend my people.

"But I have yet to tell You, Your Highness." Leuthar drew himself up, oozing pompous arrogance, and my heart chilled. "This is my exciting news—You are to accompany us! His Imperial Majesty is so pleased with You that he intends to reward Your long and lonely, virginal vigil. Bring Your wedding gown, for You are to be married at last."

By dint of great effort, I managed to shake my head sadly, mastering my fear. "Alas, I wish it could be so! But the laws of our ancestors preclude Me from becoming anything less than first wife."

Leuthar smiled, not at all nicely; it was a terrible sign that he showed that face to me. "Ah, but Your Highness, to celebrate this victory over the rebels, His Imperial Majesty intends to sacrifice his current wives. They shall be burned along with the prisoners on the bonfire to celebrate

Your marriage!" He nearly danced with joy. "You will be Empress—and I look forward to being Your closest adviser."

My stomach heaved and Merle clacked his beak savagely. I only wished I could do the same.

~ 22 ~

The trapdoor levered up. Fortunately these Calantheans made a great deal of noise, as did their locking mechanism, so I'd thoroughly hidden my escape project and lounged innocently by the window, covering the evidence with my bulk. Also fortunate, it didn't seem to occur to our guards to search our prison to see if we'd gotten up to trouble. Instead of sweeping the room as I would've had done, the guards didn't even come in, just sent Ambrose through. Merle flew through the opening and Ambrose's head followed.

Xichos only poked his head in once Ambrose cleared the ladder. "Two hours," he growled at us. "Might as well enjoy them. They're the last ones you ever will." Pleased with his wit, he cackled and disappeared below, the trapdoor closing, the lock clicking, and a bar sliding over.

I listened for more, but it was the same every time. One lock. One bar.

"One reason to stay on Calanthe," Sondra remarked. "I could teach them much more evil-sounding things to say to prisoners than that. Their repertoire is sadly lacking."

"They're very nice people here, it's true," Ambrose agreed. "What were you doing, Conrí?"

Nice people, but kind of pitiful that the wizard noticed

what Xichos hadn't. I dug out the tool I'd improvised by bending one of the metal plates, moved the bed away from the wall, and recommended digging at the inlaid jewels that decorated the windowsill.

"You're digging your way out through the wall?" the wizard asked politely.

"Making a bagiroca," I said. When Merle made a dubious caw, I grimaced. "At least it's not grapes wrapped in a napkin."

"See my knife?" Sondra showed Ambrose, looking terribly pleased with herself. She'd rolled another metal platter into a tube—by getting me to stand on it for her—and had laboriously attached the biggest glass shard from the broken pitcher to one end by binding it tightly with braided silk rope she'd made from her gown. She'd had to rip the hem off for that and for cloth for my bagiroca, so the dress now revealed most of her long legs. They'd taken away our other clothes when they brought us the fancier ones, so she'd have to fight as is. When I'd pointed out that the guards were likely to get an eyeful of her lady parts when she fought, she'd only smiled thinly and commented that it would be an excellent distraction, and that her lady parts—she'd sneered at my euphemism—were her own business.

I had to grant her that, on both counts. I even nearly made the mistake of saying I wanted nothing to do with her lady parts, but thought better of it just in time. She was still angry with me, and perhaps embarrassed, that I'd said I loved her, even to a third party. Maybe particularly to a third party.

Ambrose examined her makeshift weapon, as did Merle, who landed on his shoulder to poke his beak at it. "Will the cloth hold?" Ambrose asked.

Sondra made a face and took her "knife" back. "For a few slashes, anyway. That's all I should need to disable a guard and help myself to *his* weapons." She smiled in sunny anticipation.

Ambrose nodded thoughtfully, then examined my heap of gems piled in the center of the ragged circle of pink silk I'd laid on the bed. They weren't precious stones, but had been polished and shaped for decoration—and were the heaviest I could find in the tower. "Not your usual style," Ambrose commented.

"If you have bigger stones, I'll take them," I replied shortly. Another one came loose and I tossed it on the pile. "Either way, we're not going meekly. We're going to fight, and we have a plan to escape."

"Oh yes? Better go ahead and tie it up now," Ambrose said.

"I'd like it heavier—better impact—since I have two more hours to collect stones and plenty of room in the bag. So listen, the plan is to play scared and get the guards to come after us."

"No, no, please! Don't make me go," Sondra chimed in, pitching her voice high and piteous. I grinned at her.

"Once one or two guards come in to drag us out, we shut the trapdoor behind them and one of us stands on it while the other disables them. Or the other two, if you want to help." Merle squawked and flapped his wings. "Other three then. We take their weapons and escape this palace. We can steal some of those coracles and make it out to Kara. Once we're aboard, we'll regroup and make a new plan." Gather my army and go straight for Anure like I'd wanted to in the first place, and Ejarat could swallow Ambrose's prophecy.

I glanced at Sondra, who nodded in satisfaction. The

odds were against us, but at least if they killed us we'd have gone down fighting. That's all she needed, in truth. I felt more myself for the prospect, too.

"The middle part of the plan sounds vague," Ambrose noted.

I knew it, too, but I shrugged, chipping at the mortar. "We'll be spontaneous and seize opportunities as they present themselves. It's worked for us before."

"And may Sawehl and Ejarat watch over us," Sondra added fervently.

"Maybe you can do something to cover our tracks," I suggested to Ambrose without much hope.

"Yeah." Sondra perked up. "Do that invisibility thing until we're well away and you're safe."

"Oh, that." Ambrose shook his head. "Anure's emissary, a most obnoxious Syr Leuthar, barged in while I was talking with Queen Euthalia. She wouldn't be able to substitute someone else for me now."

"How did he know who you were?" Sondra demanded.

Ambrose blinked at her. "I introduced myself." He shrugged and held up his palms for the inevitability. "It was only polite." Merle muttered an agreement.

I just shook my head, continuing to pry at a nice big stone—the center of a flower—that gleamed with opalescent shades of purple that reminded me of Lia's gown, and the orchid on her hand. "Then you'll have to come with us. Better that way, as we need your help."

"To escape?" Ambrose asked.

"To take the attack directly to Anure's citadel at Yekpehr."

Sondra pumped a fist in the air. "Praise Ejarat—finally!"

"It's an unassailable fortress, Conrí," Ambrose said.

"And yet assail it we will," I replied grimly, changing

the angle of my prying. I wanted that stone. "Enough with prophecies and marriages and efforts at diplomacy. I'm going back to what I'm good at." Utter destruction. A man should know his strengths. And his limitations.

Voices lifted in the room below, accompanied by barked orders and the sounds of deferential salutes.

Ambrose cleared his throat. "Did I mention Syr Leuthar was coming to interview you, Conrí? He wants to inspect the prisoners personally. And take us to his ship for transport immediately after."

"What? Fuck!" The stone popped free on my curse. I added it to the bagiroca and began knotting the thing closed. It would have to do as it was. Sondra had already moved into position behind the trapdoor.

"You might've warned us," I growled, swinging the bagiroca to get a feel for its heft. Not as heavy as I wanted, but it felt familiar and should be effective enough, especially with all the skill I'd acquired at slinging it with elastic force, all the weight of my body behind it. I'd gone back to those early days when we plotted to escape the mines. I only needed my rock hammer to feel like I had then. Nothing left to lose and all the vengeance in the world ahead of me. Vengeance I would take with my own two hands and the weapons that fell easily to them.

"I *did* warn you." Ambrose sounded injured. "He never listens to me," he said to Merle, who made a sympathetic series of soft caws.

I ignored them both, listening for the telltale scrape as the bar slid away. The lock would be next.

"Go lie on the bed and look weak," I ordered him. Ambrose smiled, the enormous emerald capping his staff scattering light in all directions. His own staff. Sawehl take me that I hadn't immediately noticed he had it back. Had Lia given it to him? In exchange for what? No time to ask because the lock snicked. I moved to the farthest wall. No reason the plan couldn't still work. Guards would come ahead of the emissary, surely. If the emissary came first, then we'd have a hostage. "Get back!" I hissed at Ambrose.

"You can't leave her," Ambrose replied, pinning me with eyes gone dark with magic. It raised the hairs on my arms. Sondra cursed quietly and stepped onto the trapdoor, once again holding it down with her weight. "I won't assist unless you promise not to."

"Leave who?" I demanded.

"Queen Euthalia."

"The hell I can't. Do you *want* us all to die?"

"Anure has summoned her to become his bride," Ambrose continued.

"Fantastic. She'll get exactly what she wants then." *Though not what she deserves*, some traitorous voice whispered. Someone tried to lift the trapdoor. Cursed roundly when they couldn't. You'd think they'd learn.

"That is not true, Conrí." Ambrose shook his head. Merle flew to the staff, landing neatly on the jewel. "A bargain: I'll help you with the emissary, but only if you promise to stay and marry the Queen of Flowers."

"I asked. She refused," I gritted out, the pain oddly not all in my throat. What did I care what that capricious woman did or didn't do? She'd orchestrated everything so she could marry Anure. I'd given her an out and she hadn't taken it. I washed my hands of her. You couldn't save someone who didn't want to be saved. "I can hardly drag her to the altar."

"I'll buy you time," Ambrose said. "If you promise me. Escape the prison, but not the island."

Thumping and shouts. The trapdoor lifted Sondra up. She stepped one foot back, braced, then jumped onto it, slamming it shut again to shouts of pain from below. "Slow learners," she commented. "Next time they'll put their backs into it. Decide fast."

Ambrose looked at me. I spun the bagiroca, sorely tempted to brain him with the thing. "Fine," I bit out.

"Specifics, please."

"I won't escape Calanthe without talking to Lia," I said as fast as possible, hoping that equivocation would be enough.

"'Lia'?" Sondra instantly caught that lapse. "You already have a pet name for the Queen of Flowers? Maybe that private audience went better than you let on."

Ambrose smiled happily. "Excellent. We have a deal. If you please, Lady Sondra."

She jumped off the trap, coiling down with her improvised knife at the ready. Ambrose moved across the room. He didn't lie on the bed, but he did lean heavily on his staff, appearing terribly weary. A massive thud hit the trapdoor, and it flew up hard enough to twist the hinges. Sondra's lips curved in a feral smile of satisfaction as a soldier in the uniform of the Imperial Guards flailed, barely catching the edge, while one out of sight apparently wasn't so agile and fell with a yelp, a series of thumps, and then went ominously quiet. If we were lucky, that had been Syr Leuthar, though I doubted he'd risk his Personage without knowing the prisoners had been subdued.

The Imperial Guardsman climbed farther into the room, glared at me, then at Ambrose. "Where is the third—the woman?" he demanded.

"Right here, honey," Sondra chirped from behind him, her forearm shooting around his throat before he could turn. She jerked his chin up and drove the glass blade into the hollow beneath his ear. He spasmed, reaching for her, but she arched him back with a knee to the spine, sawing a long slice down the blood vessels in his neck. Blood spurted and he subsided with a gargle.

Another Imperial Guardsman popped through the open hatch, sword at the ready, his focus on me. With two strides I was on him, knocking the blade aside with the bagiroca and seizing him by the throat with my free hand. I caught him across the temple with a circled backswing of the bagiroca, and he dropped back down the hole like a bag of rocks himself.

Sondra kicked the trap closed, dragging the soldier's corpse across it.

"That didn't go as planned," I pointed out.

She shrugged, unapologetically. "It was the uniform. I couldn't help myself."

"I thought you were helping," I said to Ambrose.

"Shh. Don't distract me." He had a focused look, turning the staff in a slow pivot, Merle picking up his feet and setting them down again as the jewel spun, so he remained facing forward. "There. Next man through the door will be Syr Leuthar. Decide what you want to do with him quickly."

"How soon?" I asked, deciding not to ask how Ambrose could be sure—or that the emissary would be so stupid, knowing we had to be armed.

"Two minutes. Maybe three. He's not one to move with alacrity."

"Capture, disable, or kill?" Sondra asked, almost philosophically, relieving the corpse of several blades. His sword, too heavy for her, she sent sliding across the floor to me, hilt-first. "He's Anure's man," she added, "so I say kill."

I took up the sword in my left hand, testing the balance. Not great quality, but adequate. I kept the bagiroca wound in my right fist. It might be makeshift, but it worked just fine. "Capture," I corrected. "I have questions for him. And a hostage might be useful."

"You think he'll answer questions and then cooperate as we drag him down that ladder?" Sondra scoffed. "Disable, torture, then kill. I'll do it."

"Any advice?" I asked Ambrose, just in case.

He opened his eyes. "Each path has complications."

"Brilliant. Thanks so much," I muttered.

"You're welcome." Ambrose smiled at me in real pleasure.

I nodded at Sondra and she dragged the corpse off the trap, crouching again at the ready. The soldier's blood had soaked the gown on one side, so the silk went from bright crimson to a streaked edge that faded into pink, decorated with sprays of red. Blood spatter marked her face, and one of her long, blond tresses had been dipped in blood, too. With her smile of anticipation, she looked like an avatar of Ejarat, a creature out of some tale of female vengeance. I suppressed a shudder, sending thanks to Sawehl that I wasn't on the receiving end of that—and offering sympathies to Him on his dealings with such a wife.

If Sondra reminded me of Ejarat's avatar, then Lia would be the goddess herself. How would she take the news that we'd killed her men and Leuthar? Not well at all. Not that I cared, but I'd promised Ambrose I'd talk to her.

"Disable only," I hissed at Sondra as the trap opened, hoping I wasn't too late.

A tall feather of bright turquoise elevated through the hole, followed by a "helm" that would be useful only in a child's battle of soap bubbles. The emissary climbed into the room, looking around in bemusement. Sondra leapt for him, simultaneously slamming shut the trapdoor and throttling him with her forearm, just as she'd done with the other guard. The dagger she'd appropriated flashed up in a lethal arc for the man's throat.

A man who gazed round the room with a vacant and pleasant smile.

"No!" I shouted, surprised to hear Ambrose's tenor join in, along with Merle's warning caw. I don't think that we'd have stopped Sondra in time, except that something intervened, her movements going slow as if through viscous fluid. Her brow creased and her lip curled in a delayed snarl as she fought to complete the strike but couldn't.

I looked to Ambrose and found him staring at her intently, a hand raised in the air like a priest of Sawehl giving a blessing. The wizard slid me a sideways look. "I can hold her a bit longer, but best to disarm her."

I didn't question it—much as I wanted to ask why, if he could freeze people mid-attack, he hadn't demonstrated this very useful ability before this—and strode over to pry the dagger from Sondra's fingers. She almost didn't seem to notice, her attention focused on the unresisting man she throttled.

I tucked her blade in my belt and nodded at Ambrose, who dropped his hand. Sondra continued her motion at her usual lightning speed, slashing at the emissary's throat with the dagger she no longer held, spinning him away from herself in a continuation of the motion. Then her mind caught up and she rebalanced, staring perplexed at her empty hand, then at the unharmed emissary.

No fool, she immediately glared at Ambrose. "What did you do?" she demanded.

"Enabled you to obey your king's orders," he replied calmly, indicating me.

"Since when have you cared enough about that to hit me with a magic spell?"

"It wasn't a spell," Ambrose replied with injured dignity. "That's not—"

"—not how magic works," Sondra and I chimed in to finish with him.

The wizard sniffed in annoyance. "Well, it isn't. Besides, he's no threat now. I have him under control."

"And what do you want us to do with him?" I asked, handing Sondra back her dagger. She stared at it like it might turn on her, then shook her head and sheathed it. I stepped in front of the fancily dressed emissary and looked into his placidly smiling face.

"I thought you had questions," Ambrose replied mildly.

Right. "How many do I get?"

Ambrose rolled his eyes. "He's not a djinn released from a bottle. Ask as many as you like until I can't hold him anymore."

"How long will that be?" Sondra wanted to know, sidling up and drawing her dagger to have it ready.

"You'll be the first to know," Ambrose replied and sat on the bed, somewhat heavily. "A few minutes," he admitted.

"Tell us about the fortifications at Yekpehr."

Leuthar shrugged. "I'm a lowly emissary. I'm hardly privy to matters of defense."

"How much vurgsten does Anure have stockpiled?" We'd cut off his supply chain, but he'd had years to lay in supplies.

"I don't even know what that is." Leuthar leered at Sondra. "Maybe you should suck my cock and see if that tickles my memory."

She growled, low and dangerous, but smiled sweetly. "But if you're screaming and bleeding from me biting it off, will you be coherent?"

"Aw, don't be so churlish." Syr Leuthar's gaze slid over her, lingering on her bare legs. "Your face may be ruined, but your body looks pretty enough still. I could make a special pet of you. I've a dog collar that—"

He never finished the sentence, his words ending in a burble that seemed to take him by surprise, even as his eyes glazed and he crumpled to the floor, throat billowing blood from the ear-to-ear slice Sondra had dealt him. She'd moved too fast for me to see, much less stop, and stood over him, bloody knife in hand, shaking with fury. "You were saying?" she hissed.

"No more questions," I noted.

"The guards below are napping," Ambrose said. "A good time for us to leave anyway."

"Sorry." Sondra glanced at me, chagrined. "I lost my temper."

"Now we don't have to drag him around." I shrugged. If I'd been her, I would've cut his throat for that, too. We hadn't had the time to torture him into talking anyway. "They relocked and barred the trapdoor, though."

"Merle can take care of that," Ambrose said, the raven taking wing before he finished and darting out the open window. A moment later, the bar scraped and the lock snicked.

I glared at Ambrose. "Why," I asked through gritted teeth, "did you let us stay in here if you could do that all along?"

"I got you your private audience, didn't I?" He hmphed. "Not my fault you blew it."

"What else did you say to Queen Euthalia, anyway?" Sondra wanted to know, making a last check of the bodies for anything she wanted to take. "She sounded thoroughly pissed at you. I think your wooing skills need some serious work."

"I'll take the lead," I said, pointing at the stairs and deciding not to dignify that with an answer. "Ambrose in the middle, and Sondra as rear guard. Ready?"

"Ready, Conrí," they replied, each giving me their own salute. I opened the trapdoor and Merle flew through, cawing in triumphant tones.

Time to escape this pretty prison.

23

Alone, I paced the confines of my private chamber, pressing a hand to my corseted belly, willing my roiling stomach to behave and settle. It didn't help that the panicked hyperventilating made me dizzy. I made myself sit to catch my breath, but my shrieking nerves would have none of it. Leuthar's taunting words spurred me on, and I rose again, pacing.

. . . So pleased with You . . . intends to reward Your long and lonely, virginal vigil . . . Bring Your wedding gown, for You are to be married at last.

I needed to think. I needed *time* and I had none left.

Two hours.

Ridiculous that even Anure would expect me to leap to his bidding on such short notice. Bring my wedding gown, indeed! Did he imagine I kept it enshrined on a special mannequin where I petted it and dreamed of marrying the imperial toad? Probably.

A quick knock sounded—Tertulyn's special code, so I called for her to enter—and she came in, carrying a bottle of brandy and box of ice. Nudging the door closed with her hip, she set down the box, snagged a glass, and poured as she walked.

"Let me tend to You, Euthalia," she said, her smile soothing.

I took the glass but scowled at it. "I need my head clear."

"You're pale to fainting under Your makeup," she chided. "I heard everything. The whole palace has. You may be Queen of Calanthe, but You wouldn't be human if this edict hadn't knocked You back on Your heels. You don't need to be strong with me. Am I not Your oldest and closest friend? Drink."

Put that way, it sounded like a reasonable solution. I drank, the brandy burning down my throat with cleansing heat. Mutely, I held out my empty glass and she refilled it, then set down the bottle.

"Sit, Euthalia," she urged, guiding me back to the chair I'd abandoned. "Let me loosen Your stays a bit and—"

"No," I said. "I don't have time to get all dressed again. Two hours! The man gave Me two hours to board his ship. Do I even *have* a wedding gown?"

"Not that I know of and I know everything about You, according to court gossip." Tertulyn smiled, pleased that she'd made me laugh, however halfheartedly. She took a cloth and soaked it in the ice water, laying it on the back of my neck.

The scent of lavender wisped cool over my skin, and I sighed in relief, though water droplets snaked down my back, tickling as they went until they soaked into my undergarments. Sipping at the brandy, I breathed as evenly as I could. I wanted to enjoy this, to let my old friend soothe me. But we weren't girls anymore, with small spats to resolve with simple gestures and easy forgiveness.

I was queen, and that meant I had to ask the hard questions. "Where were you?"

"I got here as soon as I heard," she replied, leaving the

cloth on my neck and dabbing at my temples with another. "I only paused to gather ice, lavender water, and brandy."

"Tertulyn." I weighted her name with my disappointment and the expectation of an honest reply. Then sighed when she didn't immediately answer. "Where were you when Leuthar woke and received the messenger bird?"

Her gown rustled. "I'm so deeply sorry, Your Highness, but . . . I'm such an idiot! I fell asleep."

"Asleep?" I echoed. I'd never known her to lapse in such a way.

"I know it, and I have no excuse." She dabbed at my temples with renewed vigor, and I stayed her hand.

"Too much and you'll have to fix My makeup," I cautioned her.

"I don't mind."

"I do. I have very little time and I can't afford to squander any redoing what's already been done." Including sitting here feeling sorry for myself. Ejarat knew I'd done that aplenty. I stood, tossing back the rest of the brandy and letting the burn clear the haze from my mind. "You fell asleep."

She cringed a little as I faced her, though I thought I hadn't sounded severe, just confused. Casting her gaze out the windows, she nodded, speaking quietly. "I'm so ashamed, Euthalia, that I let You down, but I've been staying up so late, going to the parties and gathering the gossip for You, watching Leuthar all the time . . . I only closed my eyes a moment, pretending to have a wine headache from the night before, and I . . . When I woke, Leuthar had already left his quarters." She met my gaze, finally, as she finished, blue eyes damp with regret. "I'm so sorry that I let You down so terribly."

I sighed. Waved a hand. "In the end it doesn't matter. I didn't succeed in what I'd hoped to carry off."

"What were You planning?" she asked, tilting her head curiously. "I don't think You had time to tell me."

I hadn't had time, no. More than that—the orchid's petals brushed my fingers—something had made me cautious. If I'd succeeded in convincing the Lady Sondra and Ambrose to take my offer of sanctuary, I'd planned to keep the substitutions highly secret. Only Dearsley had known of my plan, as I'd needed him to find appropriate condemned prisoners for me to dress up as Con's companions. I should let him know that plan failed, though he might guess if indeed the entire palace thought I'd be departing. I'd hardly have been in a position to send substitutes for Sondra and Ambrose if I had to scurry to be ready to board the ship with the prisoners. And I hadn't even called my ladies to begin packing.

Packing. Blessed Ejarat, how could I possibly arrange to go in time? I'd made no provisions for the governing of Calanthe. Dearsley could be regent for a time, but . . . My heart picked up its frantic pace again and I regretted not letting Tertulyn loosen my stays. I couldn't *breathe*.

"Euthalia?" A polite and pretty frown furrowed Tertulyn's brow.

"We have to tell Syr Leuthar I can't possibly leave on the evening tide."

Her frown deepened. "But His Imperial Majesty said—"

"Who knows what he actually said and how much is Leuthar's political maneuvering," I snapped. "I need to speak to Leuthar, with an audience as witness. It's too late to convene court, but let's—Ah yes!—let's call for a celebratory toast. Call My ladies and everyone who can to gather in the fountain foyer. Make sure as many from My salons who are awake are there. Break out the best champagne. And tell Leuthar to attend. He's up above in the detention tower interviewing Con and the others. Quickly, Tertulyn, there's no time to lose."

But she held up a hand. "I'm so confused, Euthalia. Please, who is Con? And You want a toast—now, with Leuthar and the best champagne, but why?"

"Con is the name of the man we knew as the Slave King," I replied patiently, going to my desk and extracting my best stationery.

"I didn't know it had a name," she replied archly, adding a titter that faded as I leveled a very serious look at her.

"Conrí. Lady Sondra. Ambrose. Those are their names."

"Well, I didn't know. They didn't give them in court. I suppose You found that out in Your private interrogation. What was that about anyway?"

So many questions. Had she always asked me so many questions? Perhaps not, as she'd never had to before. "I want a toast to lull Leuthar into complacency so I can announce a ball for tonight—to celebrate My impending nuptials—and explain then how I can't possibly leave Calanthe before three days. Can I get away with claiming that many days to get ready? I think so. I'll pen the letter Myself for the bird to take to Anure."

"A . . . ball?" Tertulyn echoed, looking dazed. "For tonight, because You . . . won't be leaving yet?"

Biting back the sigh, I went to her and took her hands in mine. They were cold and wet from handling the ice. Though I wanted to tell her to keep up and do what I said, I squeezed her fingers and smiled reassuringly. "You said I'd think of something and I have. Get Calla to arrange the ball while you go order the champagne toast. Send Ibolya and Nahua to Me to run errands. And send one of My door guards to fetch Xichos for Me."

She blinked at me a moment longer, confused and wary.

"Yes, Your Highness," she replied, not moving yet. "But I—"

"No time, Tertulyn," I cut in. "Go."

She picked up her skirts and went at last. I put her odd behavior out of my mind for the moment, needing to concentrate on the correct tone for my reply to Anure. What could I say to win myself a few days of reprieve? Oh, Ejarat, now that the time had come, I didn't think I had the courage to go through with it.

Think. Don't worry about what happens when the time is up. Get the reprieve, use it to think up a new plan.

I needed to appeal to Anure's need for ceremony appropriate to a celebrated emperor. Anure's greatest weakness was fear of illegitimacy. The louder he proclaimed his right to be emperor, the more clearly the voice of his fear showed through. Anure had no royal upbringing to fall back on, no training in courtly etiquette. Even as he'd killed and destroyed the kings and queens of the noble families, he'd longed to be one of them.

Use your power as queen of the last independent kingdom in all the empire to end his blight upon the world. Con had said that. Though he was an idealistic fool, he had spoken a seed of truth there. As queen of Calanthe, the last free queen—more or less—of the known world, I would bring legitimacy to Anure's rule. I needed to remind him of that. Putting everything else out of my mind—the deaths his current wives would face, the prospect of my own suicidal marriage, leaving Calanthe alone and without an heir—I set ink pen to paper and addressed my future husband in my most elegant script.

Con wanted me to end the empire, promising me his secret weapon to tear down walls. Well, I was no warrior. But I knew how to tear down personal walls. Anure had built a fortress of his own ego, protecting the fragile thing inside thick barriers constructed of absolute power and brutal tyranny. I could breach them with my own subtle rebellion of careful words.

I wrote of our impending nuptials, how they'd inspire the empire and set the fashion for decades—possibly centuries—to come. We'd be founding his dynasty and future generations would hark back to this wedding, wanting to emulate the first and greatest of the emperors.

Warming to my topic, I moved to the extensive planning needed—and how Calanthe, isle of pleasure and all things of most-desired beauty and refinement, could supply the requirements of such a grand event. Carefully I alluded to other famous weddings and how they'd lasted for days, so ours must last longer, so as not to pale in significance. I would bring my own fresh flowers, and the best of wines.

Calla, Ibolya, and Zariah came and went, reporting on their tasks and hurrying off to execute more. Less than an hour to the celebratory toast. My letter needed to be sent before that. Fortunately, writing it helped order my thoughts for my formal—and public—set-down of Leuthar's impetuous plan. Of course, I could simply refuse to go. The emissary might try to have his contingent of Imperial Guards bodily move me—though I'd like to see him try, as my guard greatly outnumbered them. For that matter, my ladies could defend me to a point. That would cause complications, however, and blood spilled in violence to the point of murder.

And that would win me even less in the long game, as Anure would surely come down on Calanthe with all his might.

Diplomacy and calling upon the arcane world of noble females would thwart him. His Imperial Majesty wanted me to bring a wedding gown? Obviously, the wedding gown of an empress should outshine all others, past or future. I must set the finest dressmakers in Calanthe to sewing the best silk with their most delicate threads of all colors, including the fragile strands of gold and silver, to embroider the exotic blooms of Calanthe intertwining with Anure's great rock of a citadel.

Crushed beneath it would be more appropriate. I laughed to myself without humor and continued on. I'd begun to convince even myself as I spun my fictions of a wedding whose glamour would dazzle the entire empire. Such an event should be years in the planning—though I didn't dare test Anure's temper by suggesting as much— but months, surely. By the time I'd finished writing, I'd made an excellent case for waiting until spring in Yekpehr, still several months away. Hopefully Anure wouldn't counter with proposing a wedding in Calanthe, island of eternal summer. To forestall that eventuality, I added a postscript suggesting how the towers and battlements of Yekpehr could be employed in memorabilia to seal the event in memory and for all posterity.

Satisfied—at least, as best I could be for a hasty and desperate maneuver—I folded the letter myself, employing my skills to make it intricate, beautiful, and obviously from my hand. None of my ladies had returned from their current errands. How inconvenient. And odd, as they normally checked back regularly. I had asked a great deal of them in a short time, however.

I crossed my private study with quick steps, as much as balancing the wig and crown allowed, invigorated by my plan and feeling far better than my frantic pacing of only an hour earlier. Opening the door, I had already begun to ask the guard at the door to summon my master fowler when I stopped mid-word, beyond surprised to find no one there.

Impossible that my personal guards should have abandoned their post.

I scanned the hall, one that led only to my suite of rooms, in the tower that belonged entirely to me, finding no one there at all. Never in my entire life and reign had that been so. A prickle of unease crawled up my spine and I ventured out a few steps, thinking I might call for someone. Shouts rang out from farther down the bend of the stairs, along with the clang of weapons. Then a cry of pain.

Sawehl and Ejarat save me—those were the sounds of fighting.

I hastened backward a few steps; then the pounding of boots thundering down the hall alarmed me into picking up my skirts with one hand, holding the crown in place with the other, and sliding on the slick floor back into the dubious safety of my rooms. I don't move fast under the best of circumstances and these were far from ideal. Wheeling around to shove the door closed, I found it suddenly too heavy to move. Leaning my weight into it, I looked down the hall and gasped at the sight that greeted me.

Con, racing down the hall at top speed, still in my father's black, a sword in one hand and an incongruously pink silk bag in the other. His long, dark hair flew in the wind of his passage, like the wings of a great black bird, face fierce. He seemed to take up the entire hallway in his furious race, but I glimpsed Sondra running at his right flank and Ambrose at his left, carrying his staff and seeming to fly the way his draping robes covered his feet. Merle indeed flew at the vanguard, streaking past me into my rooms.

In vain I struggled to shut the door that had closed easily thousands of times. Then Con was upon me, knocking me back as he shoved the door wider to admit his bulk.

Seizing me by the arm, he caught me in time to stop me from falling ignominiously on my ass. Once Ambrose and Sondra plunged into the room, he released me and shut the door, turning the key in the lock and pocketing it.

Scanning the room, he spied a trunk and hefted it, carrying it to set before the door.

"We need more than that," Sondra said.

"I've got it," Ambrose said, giving me a distracted smile. He strode over to the door and touched the emerald on his staff to the lock. "No one will be able to open it until we're ready."

Con turned his scalding frown on the wizard. "I thought you said this was the way out."

Ambrose smiled happily and bowed to me, Merle spreading his wings to mimic a bow also. "It is," Ambrose chortled. "Her Highness is your way out. I've told you that repeatedly. Both of you. You're clearly destined for each other, so alike in your obstinacy. Forgive us the intrusion, Your Highness."

Con spun to me, as if just remembering my presence. "Are there other doors?" he demanded.

"Other doors?" I repeated faintly, with great astonishment. I realized I clutched my missive to Anure in hands gone sweaty with fear and edged away from him. He noted the movement and smiled grimly.

"Search for other entrances," he told Sondra, who saluted and obeyed immediately, heading for my inner chambers.

I found my voice and my spine. "You can't go in there," I asserted.

She tossed me a look over her shoulder and disappeared through the doorway. I turned to Con. "None of you can be in here. These are My *private chambers*," I stressed. Ejarat help me if Anure learned of this. My physical virginity wouldn't matter to him if he heard I'd been alone and vulnerable to marauders.

"Oh yeah?" Con grated out, pacing from one window to the next. "Maybe you should arrest and imprison us. Oh wait—you already did that and it didn't stick."

Impossible. "How have you escaped?" I demanded. "Where is Syr Leuthar?"

Con flashed a grin, all teeth and stark violence. "Dead."

"Dead?" I repeated. I seemed to be doomed to parrot everything he said like an addled idiot.

"I killed him," Sondra offered, striding back into the room, showing me a bloody knife. I recognized the pink gown I'd given her as a peace offering—one of Tertulyn's from last season—but it looked as if she'd soaked it in blood and lost half of it along the way. "I cut his throat," she added, pantomiming drawing the blade across someone's neck. "That shut him up. No other entrances, Conrí."

"You *killed* the emperor's emissary," I hurled at Con. Sondra was his to command. "Tell me you didn't."

"I did. Why—were you fond of him?"

"You . . ." My careful plans, years and years of delicate maneuvering, shattered around me, making chaotic ringing sounds in my ears as they fell. "You can't kill the emperor's emissary!" I ended up shouting at him.

He regarded me with a smirk. "You seem too awfully fond of telling me what I can't do, Lia. It's done. Wrap your mind around that and let's save the meaningless shouting."

I wrapped my fingers into tight fists. Never in my life had I longed to punch someone as I did him in that moment. "I told you not to call Me that."

He glanced at my fists and up to my face with a mocking smile. "Care to take a swing at me, Your Highness?"

"Perhaps give her a moment, Conrí." Ambrose came to

my side, carrying a glass of the brandy, and offered it to me. "Here, this might help."

"Thank you, I've had enough already," I replied in a brittle tone.

"Drinking in the afternoon?" Con made a tsking sound. "The depravities of the Flower Court know no end."

I laughed at that, rounding on him. "Oh, you innocent. If you think a glass of brandy in the afternoon is depraved, a little time in My court will cure you of such naïveté."

His brows lowered in a scowl and, because it was there, Ambrose holding out the glass with a gentle smile, I took the brandy and carried to my desk. Lowering myself to the chair, I sat and sipped, trying to regain my balance on every level. Scant minutes ago, I'd had a plan. Now I had . . . worse than nothing.

I needed to wrap my thoughts around this turn of events. Leuthar dead, in my palace, through violence. Oh, Ejarat, save me! "Blood," I said, lifting a now shaking hand and pointing it at Sondra's sodden gown. My thoughts whirled too loudly for me to hear Calanthe's voice. Surely if She'd woken, She'd be louder. "You spilled Leuthar's blood. In violence."

Sondra glanced down at herself, plucking at the silk and holding it away from her body, then giving me a confused frown. "Well, yeah. That's how killing people generally works."

"Where?" I demanded. "Inside the palace?"

"Lia," Con began with an impatient sigh, "we have more important—"

"*Nothing* is more important than this right now," I cut in, my words whipping out hard and fast enough to make him raise his brows in surprise. "Where?"

"In the tower prison cell," Sondra supplied crisply. "We

also killed a few guards. Mostly Imperial Guards. Your people we tried to disable where possible."

"So you haven't been outside," I clarified. Standing and taking my brandy with me, I went to the window—the one farthest from Con—and scanned the area. All looked peaceful. The orchid ring seemed undisturbed. Closing my eyes, striving for mental quiet, I stretched my senses to touch the place where Calanthe lived in my heart, murmuring to me. She seemed quiet, the songs of the birds and whispers of the fish going as usual, unaffected by this turn of events. I opened my eyes and turned back to the room to find Con and Sondra staring at me in wary befuddlement and Ambrose with alert interest. "Have. You. Been. Outside?" I asked, slowly and precisely.

"No," Con replied, biting off the word in annoyance. "We've been imprisoned in your fucking tower and fighting to get out. What about you? Are. You. Insane?"

24

Lia stared at me with such vivid rage, her eyes seemed to have darkened to thunderous gray. No longer the color of soft rain, they warned of storms, the kind to kill an unwary man. Oh yeah—Ejarat in all her power as Mother Nature. Maybe that's why they covered her in all that formal makeup, to mask the true face of the goddess.

"How dare you," she said, very quietly, her anger all the more intense for how softly and precisely she shaped her words. "You stupid, foolish man. You toy with forces beyond your imagining and then laugh it off. I should've sunk your ship the moment you entered My waters."

"Why didn't you?" I shot back. Forget my imagination. She was no goddess, only a woman, and I refused to let some petty queen and pawn of Anure's intimidate me. "I think you couldn't. You with your pretty dresses and pretty ladies prancing about on your pretty island. You only wish you had the ability to stop my army. But no." I advanced on her. She didn't straighten—the woman was never anything less than ramrod-straight, as if that stick up her ass went straight up through her crown—but she drew herself together. In a fighter, I'd expect that kind of gathering to telegraph an attack. In Lia . . . who knew? "You couldn't fight me any more than you fought off Anure. Isn't that what you Calantheans do—roll over for whoever threatens you?"

"Conrí," Ambrose said. "I think there may be more here than meets the—"

I cut him off with an upraised hand. Lia and I needed to reach an understanding. "I'm here and I think I'm in charge now. You couldn't even keep me imprisoned. So don't throw around your empty threats. In case you haven't noticed, you're *my* hostage—and you're getting us off this cursed island."

She had the audacity to roll her eyes at that. A dramatic gesture, with all those sparkling crystals on her lashes and the black paint outlining her eyes. The jewels pasted in a triangle at the corner of one eye winked at me, adding to the mockery. "Oh, I'm your hostage, am I?" she cooed, making it sound ridiculous.

I opened my arms, showing her the bagiroca and the sword, both bloodstained. Since blood bothered her so much, I might as well use that to advantage to intimidate her. But she didn't even flinch. "Yes," I said, to make it perfectly clear. "You are my hostage and if you think I won't knock you senseless to make you compliant, think again. I have people to consider."

"Consider this, Slave King," she hissed. "You are in *My* rooms, in *My* palace, on *My* island, surrounded by *My* people. Seems to Me that you're still trapped in a place where all the power is Mine. You won't make it out of here alive."

Pounding came on the doors, followed by shouts. Lia smiled, arch and serene. "And the balance of power shifts even more. Give yourself up and I'll—" She broke off, a rare frown folding itself between her brows.

The shouts and pounding continued, but the door didn't so much as shudder. Ambrose had promised it would stay shut and Sondra had guaranteed that was the only door, so I'd trust in them.

"What, Your Highness?" I asked mockingly. "Not sure what you'll do, after all? Seems like I've disrupted your plans." A carefully folded envelope made of paper painted with flowers lay on the desk. I set down the sword on the desk and poked the envelope with finger so it rotated. I couldn't read much, but I recognized Anure's name when I saw it. "What's this—a letter to our dear emperor? And here I thought you would be traveling with us."

"My plans hardly matter now," she bit out. "You've murdered the emperor's emissary along with who knows how many Imperial Guards. You realize that's an act of treason, right?"

"Sweetheart," I replied in the same tone, "I commit treason every time I draw a breath."

"No doubt. But you've just taken Me—and the last independent kingdom—along with you. You've dragged us into a war that will be our destruction and act like it's a great joke." She threw up her hands and went behind her desk, sitting again and picking up the brandy glass, staring into it. With her lashes lowered, I couldn't see her eyes very well, but I almost imagined the sheen of tears. Surely not possible from the ice queen.

I tossed the envelope to Ambrose. "Read that."

"Why don't you just ask Her Highness what it says?" Ambrose inquired, giving me a reproving look.

"Because I don't trust her," I explained. "Just read the cursed thing."

"It doesn't matter now," Lia said on a sigh.

"I'll just bet it doesn't." Why I wanted to know, I couldn't say, but I'd learned to follow my gut on such things. "I'm game, though. What does it say?"

She gave me a hard look, spinning the still-full brandy

glass between her fingers like she might toss the contents in my face. I smiled a little, almost wishing she would.

"It's plans for the wedding," Ambrose related. "You have a beautiful script, Your Highness. Mostly about etiquette, making it the event of the century."

"How long it will take for a worthy wedding gown to be created," Sondra added, reading over the wizard's shoulder. She looked at Lia. "Weeks just to find the right embroidery thread—really?"

"Wanted your special day to be perfect, did you?" I ground out. "So you could dance on our graves in your fancy dress."

Lia set the glass down hard enough to splash the brandy. "Oh, for Ejarat's sake! Are you really this obtuse? I was stalling for time. Leuthar wanted Me on the ship with you *this afternoon*. I planned to send this to Anure, then convince Leuthar that I had to stay or insult the empire with a lackluster wedding. It would've worked, too, if you hadn't gone and killed him!"

"Oh, now you call him by his name, after chastising me for not using his title?"

"I think we're past the point of formality—or being concerned about giving insult by using the man's name when I'm responsible for his emissary's *murder*."

"True. Seems to me we did you a favor," I retorted. "You don't have to get on the ship now. Much more direct method."

Her mouth fell open, then curled in a sneer very unlike her usually composed expression. "Don't you dare pretend you've done Me any favors. You and your futile rebellion have jeopardized everything I've worked and sacrificed to accomplish. I've lost every advantage I ever had. All these years of stringing Anure along, convincing him I was his ally, that I'd be his bride, all wiped out in a moment of impulse because Sondra lost her temper."

"Truth be told, I was pretty much looking for any excuse to cut his throat," Sondra inserted cheerfully. "I would've done it no matter what."

A muscle ticked in Lia's jaw, the only evidence she was gritting her teeth. A loud boom hit the outer chamber door. A battering ram, most likely.

"The door won't last long," she pointed out.

"Actually it will," Ambrose replied absently, still reading the letter. Lia had written pages. "They'd do better to knock the walls down around it, but hopefully it'll be a while before they think of that. This letter is quite brilliantly done, Your Highness. Playing on Anure's longing to be truly of the royal set. Deft and clever. It likely would've worked."

He handed her the letter and she took it calmly, but crushed the delicate paper into a ball with a fury that made me think she wished it was my neck. "Small comfort now," she muttered.

"Stop acting like this is such a disaster," I said to them both, unaccustomed guilt making me impatient. "We should all be happy not to be on that cursed ship."

Lia tapped her long, jeweled nails on the desk, eyes focused on them as if she might find a solution there. She looked the same as when I saw her earlier, though indefinably mussed. She had her usual poise, her face a smooth, composed mask, but when she finally met my gaze, her eyes sparkled with the glassiness of fear, shadowed with despair.

"I never planned to be on that cursed ship," she declared, but her voice wavered. "And I *tried* to keep you two off it," she said to Ambrose and Sondra.

"But not me," I said, sounding more bitter than I meant to. "You would've handed me over to Anure's torturers with a smile."

She transferred her gaze back to me, eyes almost metallic in their hard silvery glint. "With a smile? All right then. Yes, I'd smile because I'd be protecting Calanthe. One man's life means nothing to Me compared with that."

Particularly yours, she didn't have to say. Her words shouldn't have stung, but they did. I thought I hadn't been kidding myself about her lack of regard for me, but apparently I had nursed some sort of delusion that we'd discovered a kind of kinship, a shared understanding.

Unreasonably angry, I leaned my hands on her spindly desk and deliberately loomed over her. Not that she'd give up a shred of pride and shrink away from me. Instead she lifted her chin, eyes glittering with regal defiance.

"And the rest of the world can go up in flames as far as you're concerned," I snarled. "You've had the power to help so many and you've sat here in this palace of flowers and done nothing because you don't care."

"That's right." She firmed her mouth, pressing her lips before continuing. "All I care about is Calanthe. If I had to kill you with My bare hands to save My realm, I would."

I cast a dubious glance at her hands. "I dunno, Your Highness. You might break a nail."

"Like My ladies did when you tried to attack Me in the throne room?" she asked coolly. "Only a fool would underestimate us twice."

"Stop calling me stupid," I growled.

"Aww," she cooed. "Does the truth hurt?"

"When you two are done flirting," Sondra broke in, "we really should come up with a plan."

Lia and I both turned to glare at her. Sondra smiled back thinly. "Eventually, they *will* think of coming in an-

other way to rescue their queen and we'll have lost our advantage."

Lia folded her arms, an elegant and intricate gesture
that didn't disturb the fresh flowers on her gown or the orchid ring. "Seems I simply need to wait. Unless you plan
to kill or rape Me."

"What?" I spat. "You think that I would—" I broke off,
unable to finish the sentence.

She raised one eyebrow. "You do have a reputation."

I glared rather than continuing to sputter. If that was
what she thought of me . . .

"Everyone will assume the worst," she continued in that
cool tone, her face a perfect mask again that betrayed none
of her true emotions. Perhaps I'd imagined she had any.
"Especially the emperor. You've ruined Me."

I straightened. "We have witnesses."

Lia shook her head minutely. "Your loyal companions.
They wouldn't be believed."

"Believe this, Your Highness," Sondra said, her voice
harsh as Merle's. "I know something about rape. I would
never stand idly by and allow it to happen. Not even for
my king. I'd cut his cock off first. Begging your pardon,
Conrí."

Unwillingly, I smiled. Especially when I caught the
look on Lia's face. "She would, too."

"I appreciate your attempt to console Me, Lady Sondra," Lia replied stiffly. "But that does nothing to salve a
reputation I've spent most of My life building." She leaned
her elbows on the desk, delicately bracing the wig and
crown, groaning softly. "What am I going to *do*?"

"We should have the wedding immediately," Ambrose
said.

Lia looked up, blinked, long and slow, the crystals on
her lashes chiming musically. "There won't be a wedding.

Anure will execute Me for allowing his emissary and guards to be slaughtered, not marry Me."

"Oh no!" Ambrose laughed, shaking his head, and Merle added soft caws. "You're correct in that. But you were never meant for Anure, child. I meant for you and Conrí to marry. That will preserve your reputation and satisfy the prophecy. Although it will have to be a marriage in truth." He waggled his eyebrows at us. "No marriage in name only. Can't leave Anure any loopholes."

Lia leveled a fulminous glare on me.

"What?" I held up my hands in defense. "I didn't say it!"

"He's *your* wizard," she shot back in icy tones.

"Actually, I'm my own wizard," Ambrose said genially. Merle cawed and flapped his wings. "All right. True. I'm Merle's wizard, if anything."

"I'm not marrying Conrí." Lia declared her decision with the finality of a queen accustomed to being obeyed. Though I had no wish to marry her, either, it put my hackles up that she'd rather marry the imperial toad and sacrifice her life to him than even entertain the thought of being shackled to a brute like me.

"You asked me how to find an heir for the Abiding Ring," Ambrose said. He tilted the staff so it caught a ray of sunshine and shot a spear of emerald light at my face.

"Hey," I protested, squinting and holding up a hand to block it.

"Him?" Lia loaded a world of incredulity into the one word. "You want Me to make *him* the heir to the orchid ring and the kingdom of Calanthe."

"No, no. Perish the thought. That is not something Conrí could ever be."

I scowled at the amusement in the wizard's protest. "Gee, thanks."

"You're welcome." Ambrose bowed a little, completely

without irony. "No, I mean the legitimate children of your marriage. There will be heirs for you, I promise."

"Except that I have no intention of marrying this man." She wouldn't even look at me as she said it.

"But you will," Ambrose assured her. "It's what has to happen."

"Is it?" I asked him. If I'd truly been a king, had something to offer her, and if we lived in a different, kinder world, maybe I could've wooed Lia, convinced her that . . . what? Even if we'd met in that world, I don't know what I could've offered her. It didn't bear contemplating, as that boy, that man I might've been had disappeared along with everything else. Though I wasn't Anure by any stretch, I also didn't blame Lia for fighting being forced to take a husband like me. "Surely there's another way around the prophecy."

Ambrose gave me a long look. "You've suffered greatly, Conrí. I believe you can endure this, too."

Was that mockery? I could swear I caught a glimpse of bitter betrayal in Lia's eyes before she drowned it in impassivity. "Don't concern yourself," she told me sweetly. "I won't force you to the altar."

I ignored her and kept my gaze on Ambrose. "Do you promise that if I marry Her Highness, everything will fall into place for me to destroy Anure and end his reign?"

Lia laughed, sharp, the bitter edge riding it. "A foolhardy and grandiose ambition."

"And yours are small and petty, limited to one tiny island."

She rose to her feet and leaned toward me. "At least I kept My tiny island intact. How is Oriel these days?"

Sondra made a small, shocked sound. Even Lia seemed taken aback by her very well-aimed taunt, a glimmer of regret in her eyes.

"In ruins, thanks," I replied, for once not caring how like a dog's low growl my voice sounded. "Which is entirely Anure's fault, so I will have my revenge, regardless of your opinion. Ambrose?"

"Yes," he replied simply. "I would not mislead you about this. Marry the Queen of Flowers and together you shall destroy Anure and his empire."

I nodded, something about his careful wording bothering me. I really wanted to ask what he *would* mislead me about, but this wasn't the moment. "All right then. You might not want to force me to the altar, Your Highness, but I have zero compunction about dragging you there. That's the price of being my hostage. Before the sun sets, my sweet, you shall be the bride of the Slave King."

She paled, visible even under the makeup. At last I'd found a weakness in her formidable armor, and I couldn't find it in myself to enjoy the moment. Too bad that it was the prospect of being bound to me that did it, but as Ambrose pointed out, I'd suffered worse before this.

"You can't force Me to take vows," she asserted, but she sounded a hair less certain than before.

"You'll do it to rescue your reputation," I informed her.

But she shook her head, forcefully enough that the crown wobbled and she had to put up a hand to steady it. A hand that trembled. I felt like the brute I was.

"I'd rather be disgraced than wed to you," she replied with quiet dignity, and depthless obstinacy.

"You are the most stubborn woman I've ever met," I snarled at her.

To my surprise, she smiled, as if I'd given her a compliment. "I've often noticed," she said, in a conversational tone, "that people always call Me stubborn—though rarely to My face, I'll acknowledge—when I won't do what they want Me to do. I won't do it, Con. You can physically force

Me to the altar, presuming you find a way to hold off My guards, but you cannot make Me speak the vows."

I studied her slim and straight posture. Did she realize she'd called me by my name just then? Perhaps so, as her eyes held an appeal I might've called desperate in a less resolute personality. She thought she'd called my bluff, but then she thought I was a fool and she'd made a mistake there.

"Time for us to talk, Lia," I said, using that same conversational tone.

She raised a sardonic eyebrow. "And here I thought we had been."

I smiled without humor for her sally. Plucking up the discarded brandy, I tossed it back. I'd meant it to be mocking, to demonstrate that I could take anything of hers that I wanted to, but it went down like a dream of golden summers long since lost. Unable to resist, I poured more, sipping this time and savoring. "That's really good stuff," I admitted.

"Nothing but the best for the Queen of Flowers," she replied, voice heavy with irony.

I toasted her with the glass, sipped once more, and set it down. Much as I'd love to have more of the ambrosial liquor, I couldn't afford to slow my reflexes. There would be fighting yet to come that day—and not only with my lovely fiancée.

"Ambrose, Sondra—would you leave us alone?"

25

I nearly called the pair of them back when Ambrose offered Sondra his arm and they strolled out onto one of my balconies, as if at their leisure to admire the sights, even while the pounding on the doors accelerated. Con waited for them to go and pull the glass doors shut behind them, then turned that blazing gold gaze on me.

I braced myself. I didn't think he'd hurt me, but he had a way of getting around my arguments. In truth, my previous convictions were in tatters. All my careful plans, dashed to pieces. Furious as I was, I couldn't help reveling in the sweet relief that I wouldn't have to get on that ship. I wouldn't have to face Anure, yield to those cruel and grasping hands. Give up my life when I hadn't yet lived.

Not yet.

Con studied me, assessing me like the enemy combatant I was. So I attacked first. I raised a brow at him. "Did you want privacy so you could compromise Me in truth?"

The pounding on the doors stopped abruptly and ominously. They must be formulating a new plan.

He ignored both that and my taunt. "What will it take?" he asked. He poured me some brandy and slid it to me.

I eyed it and him calmly, offering him no opening.

"What will it take to convince you to marry me, right here, right now?" he clarified.

"Are you attempting to bribe Me?" I asked, making sure to sound incredulous.

"If that's what it takes, yes." He glanced around the room. "I obviously have little to offer you that you don't already have, but I would vow to do my best to give you whatever you ask for." He grimaced slightly. "If nothing else, I'm good at living up to my promises."

I opened my mouth, found I had no words. "Why does it matter to you so much?" I finally asked.

He looked around, spotted one of my elegant chairs, and snagged it. Tapping its seat, he seemed to be checking its sturdiness before settling his weight on it and stretching out his long legs, folding his hands over his flat abdomen. He watched me with those unblinking wolf's eyes.

"You say nothing matters to you more than protecting Calanthe? Well, nothing matters more to me than destroying Anure and his false empire."

"Everything they say about you is true," I said, pleased that he flinched, even if barely. We'd learned very quickly how best to wound the other.

"That's right." He inclined his head. "Ambrose says marrying you will get me what I want. I'm willing to give you whatever you want to make that happen."

"I want My freedom," I told him, surprising myself that I blurted it out. "And Calanthe's," I amended hastily. "Can you give Me that?"

He considered. "I took mine, by force of might, as you know. So, yes. I can promise the same freedom I have, which is something."

"The questionable freedom of an outlaw," I pointed out.

Smiling wolfishly, he acknowledged that. "Better than none at all."

I snorted disparagingly.

He sobered. "And far better than the bastardized version of freedom *you* have labored under all these years."

With no reply to that, I had to look away. Out the window to the fantastic beauty of Calanthe. For no good reason, I had to struggle not to weep.

"Lia." He waited until I looked at him again and, all seriousness, leaned forward to brace his elbows on his knees. "I promise I'd fight for you and Calanthe. I'm a good strategist, and a better fighter. Warriors more skilled than I am follow me willingly." His mouth twisted in a wry smile, as if that surprised him. "I have vurgsten in great quantities, both with me on my ships and cached in various locations. More important, I hold Anure's mines at Vurgmun with my own people, so he can't acquire more."

"He'll have plenty stockpiled," I pointed out, unable to help myself.

Nodding, he sighed for that truth. "It would be good to find out how much he has."

I laughed for the impossibility of that. "You'd need spies on the inside at Yekpehr."

His gaze didn't waver from my face. "I'm betting you have them."

Had I thought he'd believed my act, fallen for the helpless and fragile ornament I'd pretended to be? Apparently not. If nothing else, this man—this deposed and enslaved prince—saw through me in a way no one else did. I couldn't judge him for what he'd suffered at Anure's hands. He'd survived what would have broken a lesser man. So had Sondra.

"This would be a marriage in truth," I said slowly, pondering the possibility of actually doing this. "No pretenses. Even if Ambrose hadn't set those boundaries, I'd insist on them."

Con nodded once, eyes on mine. "I accept those terms."

"What about Sondra?" I asked then, working to keep the caustic jealousy from my voice and eyes. Not many marriages on Calanthe demanded fidelity of the partners or multiples, but I'd had little opportunity to explore my emotional tolerance for such things. Judging by how I felt now, I wouldn't be generous about Con continuing to be her lover.

To my surprise, he dropped his face in his hands scrubbing it, then raking his hair back. "She punched me, you know," he said conversationally, "for telling you I love her."

That sounded like Sondra, from what I'd observed. "Jeopardized the game by revealing that secret, did you?"

"What?" He looked briefly confused. "No. Because we don't love each other that way. She's my closest friend. What we went through in those mines . . ." He looked haunted, haggard, gazing out the window. Then shook it off. "I can't tell you what happened to her."

"I'm sorry," I said softly. But I could see it now, that deep connection between them, that went beyond anything as simple as friendship.

He coughed, cleared his throat. "I am not . . . good at talking. But Sondra is like a sister to me and—" He broke off again, throat working, and he studied his interlaced fingers.

"It's good to have someone like that," I said, mostly to give him time to compose himself. He'd dropped some of his hard shell to talk to me this way, and I hadn't expected to see this person through the cracks. Oriel. Something niggled in my memory. Not a crown prince, but a princess. Not Sondra, I thought, but perhaps Con's blood sister.

"Why didn't you tell Me who you are?" I asked.

His glanced up, eyes hard again. "This is who I am."

"Conrí, crown prince of Oriel."

"I was," he conceded, mouth tight. "Long ago, when such things mattered."

"They still matter," I replied.

"To you," he sneered.

"The world cares," I replied, refusing to rise to his bait. And the land cared, but he might not know that. I had no idea if the kings and queens of Oriel had observed the old ways. Even if they had, Con might've been too young still to know it.

"Do they?" Con snapped back. "Forgive me if I haven't seen much evidence of that." He propelled himself from the chair. Restless as the wolf in my dreams, as if the chains dragged at him still, he paced to the window and stared out. Then he spun and pinned me with that relentless, determined expression. "What else—or are we done?"

"We're done," I agreed. I waited, but he only watched me, also waiting. Had I expected some kind of formal proposal, the warrior bending a knee to request the honor of my hand? No, clearly he had no affection for me—or any real regard, given his contempt for me and what I stood for in his mind. "I'll marry you," I clarified, mostly to end the détente, and stood. "Let's get this over with."

At least he wouldn't be as bad as Anure. And I could stay on Calanthe. Until Anure brought his warships to destroy us. The palace towers falling into the sea, the waters boiling with blood. Fire, death, and destruction. The wolf begging me for help, and me breaking and bloodying my fingers on his chains. The dreams had been driving me to this moment all along. I supposed I should've capitulated to the demands of fate long before this.

Calanthe had warned me in the beginning, and I couldn't refuse Her.

Con watched me with that wolf's wary golden gaze, and

I realized I'd lifted my hands and stared at them, the orchid ring's petals moving with their trembling. Composing myself, I let my hands drift to my sides and I raised my chin, gathering what regal poise I could. I allowed a slight, curious smile. "Well?" I asked. "What is your plan now?"

He offered me a smile, wry and self-deprecating. "Let's just ask our pet wizard about that."

A booming thud hit the doors, making me realize how long they'd been quiet. A painting fell off the wall, clattering to the floor. "Best hurry," I advised.

With a nod of agreement, Con strode across the room and delivered the news. Neither of them seemed surprised as they returned, Ambrose congratulating me warmly and Sondra eyeing the shuddering wall askance.

Con grimaced, looking to Ambrose. "I don't suppose you thought this through, what you'd do to get us out of the corner you trapped us in?"

"I was mostly focused on making sure the marriage would occur," Ambrose admitted. Merle danced from foot to foot on his shoulder, muttering an agreement.

"We could open the doors and announce our impending nuptials to My people," I offered politely. I might've tried harder to trick Con that way, if I'd thought I could.

He barely bothered to toss an annoyed look at me. "And have your guards storm in and slaughter us? I don't think so."

Ah well. Couldn't blame a girl for trying. Old habits die hard.

"We can't stay in here forever," Sondra reasoned, pacing over to the window and leaning out to scan the walls in every direction. "Given time, we could maybe climb out, but I think we don't have time."

Another heavy *boom* resounded, and plaster shattered

where the painting had been. "Ah," Ambrose said with a note of regret, "they've figured out to come through the walls instead. Won't be long now."

"Can't you magic the wall, too?" Con asked.

"No." The wizard shook his head. "Walls aren't doors, you know."

Con briefly closed his eyes, muscle in his jaw pulsing. I tended to sympathize with his frustration. Magic users have such a different understanding of the world that their logic—while eminently reasonable to them—often seems absurd to others. Especially to a man who preferred a hammer and a bag of rocks to other weapons, I was sure.

"Do you have any helpful suggestions, Lia?" he asked, clearly attempting to be patient.

"I don't have a good solution," I admitted. Sondra made a scoffing sound, and I gave her a cool look. "This situation is of your own making. I'll abide by My agreement, but I don't know how to get through the initial exchange with My people without something terrible happening. I could try going out to speak to them while you remain inside and barricade the door aga—"

"No." Con folded his arms and dug in.

I'd figured as much, but held up my hands. "Think fast then, because they'll break through soon." The thick wall showed many cracks, the repeated thudding creating a sense of urgency I had a difficult time ignoring. If my people made it through, things would happen very fast—and not turn out well at all.

"I can marry you," Ambrose said, acting as if we'd been missing the obvious solution. Con blinked and unfolded his arms, and Ambrose shrugged modestly. "At least, I can invoke the binding vows of Ejarat and Sawehl. Will your guards recognize that, Your Highness?"

Con frowned, exchanging glances with an equally puzzled Sondra. "They should," I agreed on a sigh. "As I'm queen of Calanthe, the binding should be quite obvious, though none have seen it since My mother died and widowed My father."

"What are you talking about?" Con demanded.

I turned to him with some impatience. "Do you really want a detailed explanation or will you trust your own wizard? We're giving you what you want and saving your sorry life along with your companions'. Quit being difficult."

He glowered, taking a step to loom over me. "I am not difficult."

"Oh, sweetheart," I crooned, refusing to let him physically intimidate me. "You practically created the concept."

Boom. A hole the size of a finger opened in the wall. Con looked from it to Ambrose. "Do it."

"Ideally it should be done outside," Ambrose replied doubtfully.

"Will the balcony do? It will at least put us in the sunlight, if not on Ejarat's actual soil," I said. *Boom.* Pellets of stone fell. Excited voices echoed through the hole. Moving to the balcony would remove us a bit from the distraction of my rescuers. "Meanwhile, the Lady Sondra may use My dressing chamber to bathe and burn that soiled gown. There's a fire in there you can use. And any number of gowns. Help yourself."

The taller, more muscular woman looked me up and down. "*Your* gowns?" she asked dubiously.

"Look at the blue ones," I advised. "They come in any number of sizes and don't require the same underpinnings."

She shook her head but walked toward the bathing room. I led the men onto the flower-draped balcony over the sea, Ambrose putting his back to Sawehl's sun. Con and I turned as one to face Ambrose, who stood with his staff in front of him, grasping it in both hands. The great emerald at the tip caught the light, scattering it. Merle sat on his shoulder, looking grave.

"Conrí. Queen Euthalia," Ambrose intoned as if we stood in Ejarat's cathedral. "Please take each other's hands."

I moved to Con's right side and extended my hand that wore the orchid ring. Giving me a sideways look I couldn't interpret, Con held out his hand, palm up—and I laid mine on top. His skin was rough, callused from wielding his weapons of violence, yes, and an older hardness in it. The feel of stone and fire. He stared ahead just as stonily, clearly gritting his way through this.

Not how I pictured my wedding. But then, I'd long ago lost any sentimentality over what that might be like.

Ambrose summoned power, calling upon Ejarat and Sawehl in the old language, a prayer I hadn't heard since my childhood. The emerald lit as if from within, and Merle's orange eyes glowed. The sense of magic intensified and the orchid on my hand seemed to unfurl, growing more lavish and lush, the colors radiant, even iridescent.

Con's hand moved slightly under mine, making me think he wanted to yank his away. I glanced at him, finding him staring at the ring with an odd expression. Caught, he flicked his gaze up to mine, and I raised my brows in arch invitation. He'd insisted on this marriage and he could still back out. His eyes narrowed and, as if he read my mind, he gave a minute shake of his head, returning his attention to Ambrose.

"We stand here on Ejarat's body"—the wizard spoke the old words with reverence—"here on Her sacred isle of Calanthe, beneath Sawehl's loving gaze. They extend to You the gift of their union, to bring two together into one.

Do you both enter into this union of your own free will, with an open heart and no other obligations?"

"I do." Con's gritty voice made the vow sound harsh.

I hesitated, wondering if claiming I did this of my own free will, and with a heart that had been frozen shut for years, would be a lie—one that would violate the magical binding of the vows. Con glanced down at me. But instead of the ferocious frown I'd expected, he smiled a little. Almost ruefully. To my surprise, under the elaborate draping of the orchid, he slipped his fingers between mine, squeezing gently, in a way that felt oddly reassuring.

I supposed I had agreed of my own free will, if only for different reasons. For Calanthe. Women had wed for far worse reasons. "I do," I said, clearly and with emphasis, making up for my waffling. Where Calanthe lay in my heart, no protests rang in dissonance. So far so good.

"As Ejarat claimed Sawehl, unlike Herself and yet like, do you promise to take into your being the entirety of one who is not yourself, with all their flaws and virtues, ugliness and beauty, weaknesses and strengths?"

"I do," I confirmed first, tilting my head at Con, giving him the challenge.

He pressed his lips together as if tempted to retort. "*I* do," he replied immediately, emphasizing it as if his would be the more difficult task. My turn to narrow my eyes. He actually grinned at me.

"As Sawehl claimed Ejarat, unlike Himself and yet like, do you promise to nurture and shelter the other, to protect and support, to shed your light so that they might find their best path in life?"

Our gazes still locked, I smiled back at Con. Challenge accepted then.

"I do," we said in unison.

The binding sizzled into place, connected between the palms of our hands. Surprise lit Con's eyes, but he didn't flinch. Instead he tightened his grip on my hand. My wolf king, ever charging straight ahead into uncertainty, baring his teeth at danger.

"Your other hands, if you will," Ambrose asked. Con watched me hold out my free hand toward Ambrose, palm up, and imitated me, a line between his forbidding brows. He'd never seen a wedding ceremony in the old way, I realized.

"Brace yourself," I murmured.

He flicked me a quick look and then did brace himself as if readying for a blow. Ambrose touched my palm, drawing a line with his fingertip. My flesh parted at the touch, bright-red blood springing to the call. Con frowned harder, but his hand stayed steady as Ambrose repeated the gesture with him.

"As you've agreed to join yourselves together—one flesh, one blood, one mind, one heart—take each other's hands and seal your vows."

Con looked to me in question, so I aligned my palm to his, angling so the lines of fresh blood would meet. Understanding, he moved his hand toward mine, slowly, giving me time to match the speed. Despite everything, we found the harmony there, neither grabbing the other, but us both meeting in the middle.

Our blood touched, mingled, and the simmering nascent bond snapped into place, burning to the core of my being and then rippling outward, a stone thrown in a golden pool of light. It billowed throughout Calanthe, into the soil, through the hearts and minds of Her people, met by joyous accord from all the denizens of the air, land, and sea.

Con's bright eyes held wonder, and the possibility of joy

I didn't think to ever see in him. When he smiled, it lit his
face, the first real smile I'd seen from him, no wry bitterness, no threat, no rueful grimacing.

"For the third and final seal, as Ejarat cups you in Her
hand and Sawehl showers blessings from above, share the
first kiss of your married union."

I'd just married a man I'd never even kissed. I took a
breath to steady myself.

At least Con looked uncertain, too. I lifted my chin,
turning up my mouth for the kiss, feeling the precarious
tilt of the wig and crown, hoping the glue would hold. Instead of the ceremonial kiss placed on my lips that I'd
expected, Con turned our joined hands on our near sides
to fold up between us, stepping in to close the distance. He
also pulled our other hands in close, twining his fingers
with mine, and—all in the same movement—taking my
mouth in a hard kiss.

I hadn't expected a kiss like my ladies gave me, with
their sweet, delicate lips and reverent care. But I had no
experience to prepare me for the sheer difference of kissing a man. His beard stubble scraped my face, his lips
fierce, even savage in their hunger. I made a sound of dismay. Not exactly pain, but wincing from the crashing in-
vasion of maleness.

*Do you promise to take into your being the entirety of
one who is not yourself . . .*

I understood with brutal clarity the meaning of those
words. Not just someone not myself, but as wholly unlike
myself as I could conceive. A darker, larger, and more ferocious mirror.

He heard—or felt—my reaction and gentled his mouth,
moving his lips over mine in a more tender feeding, but
still entering into me and leaving his taste behind. And
drawing some reflected hunger out of me, for I warmed to

it, feeling his need through our bond, rising to meet and nurture that in him. I hummed at the sensation, his presence coiling deep inside me, in a part I'd thought forever cold and hollow.

His turn to make a sound, a throaty hum of surprised pleasure. The wound in my palm throbbed, our blood twining together, new vines grown on old roots.

A crash in the other room heralded the wall coming down—and yanking us apart. We gazed at each other a moment, torn from a kinder, more tender world, where we hadn't been enemies for a few precious moments.

I smiled, then had to laugh at the white makeup smeared through his beard, the crimson staining his lips. One of my jewels had come loose and snagged in the dark curling hairs, winking almost comically. A fatalistic wave of relief washed through me. I'd crossed a line from which there would be no return, and there was a surprising freedom in that. Con had offered me freedom and he'd already delivered a peace I hadn't expected.

I would never marry Anure now. The dreadful burden I'd carried for fourteen years had vanished, leaving me with a lightness of being I never recalled having.

Con stepped back, releasing our hands, leaving me feeling strangely alone, and bowed a little. "You should see *your* face," he informed me.

I clapped my hands over my mouth, realizing how utterly smudged I must be. Shouts from the other room called my name, and the doors to the room leading to my balcony slammed open, Xichos at the forefront.

"At last!" Ambrose sang out. "The wedding guests have arrived!"

26

I shook my head, trying to clear it of the dizzying taste and feel of Lia in my arms, under my mouth, against my body. And deeper inside, like the scent of flowers banishing the stink of vurgsten. *My wife*. The queen of Calanthe.

It all had happened so swiftly: the escape, the pitched fighting, being fatally trapped in Lia's rooms, then miraculously seeing the way clear to fulfilling Ambrose's prophecy, marrying Lia. I hadn't enjoyed backing her into a corner. I'd thought I'd reconciled myself to the fact that I'm a ruthless bastard capable of doing anything to avenge my father and Oriel, but this victory felt hollow. I still didn't know what I'd said that had convinced her.

Ambrose said the marriage had to be consummated and so it would. Lia said she insisted on that aspect, too, but the exchange of vows had felt as much like a battle of wills as a wedding. Viciously I wished I'd practiced this kind of thing. I hadn't even been sure how to kiss her. There had been a moment, though, when she had returned the kiss . . . Perhaps I hadn't been too clumsy and tonight would go fine.

She looked as stunned as I felt. Also uncharacteristically shaken at the prospect of facing her people so mussed. I hadn't thought when I kissed her. Probably I should've explained my lack of experience, that I'm more brute than man.

But she knew that. The way she looked at me—the way you watch a half-wild beast, readying yourself for an attack—proved that she probably understood that better than I expected. With her hands clasped over the lower half of her face, her eyes looking larger than usual, pupils dilated so the black nearly overtook the gray, silver rims around the deep pools of shock, she seemed to be searching for equanimity.

If only we'd had a few more minutes to talk before her soldiers busted down the wall. My fault there, as I'd been drowning in kissing her.

"Your Highness!" Xichos stood in rigid surprise. Another Calanthean lord stood beside him, one who'd stood near Lia's throne. Some sort of adviser then.

"Your Highness," the lord echoed, looking from her to me in disbelief. "You are . . . married to this . . . man?"

Grimly I wondered to myself what other word he'd been about to use. At least Lia and Ambrose had been correct in predicting that the Calantheans would be able to see it. Something had happened, for sure. Even as dulled to magic as Ambrose accused me of being, I'd felt the power of it. Something wrenching and changing inside the burnt places, green vines erupting through baked soil.

Lia dropped her hands, dusting them together and shooting me an opaque glance. Whatever magical connection we might have, that apparently didn't give me insight into her canny mind. I had no idea what she was thinking. She showed them the smeared blood on her palm, though to my mind her smudged, obviously kissed mouth, her face showing the scrape of my beard, made an even more undeniable declaration.

"Yes, Lord Dearsley, I am," she replied with amazing

poise, given how much I'd just torn it to shreds. I restrained
the smile that wanted to worm its way through the digni-
fied and sober mien I presented. Lia wouldn't appreciate
me gloating over how I'd melted that shield of cool calm.
I kept the gloating tucked safely away, for just me to enjoy. Perhaps it boded well for the consummation.

It wasn't easy because, for the first time since Ambrose
had proposed the preposterous plan, I entertained a feeling of . . . hope? At least a relief from dread. And loneli-
ness. No matter what happened now, Lia and I had tied our
fates together. For the first time, too, I felt a twinge of remorse that our intertwined paths would likely lead to our
mutual doom.

I was a selfish man because I couldn't help but feel glad-
ness to have some company on the road to destruction. Of
course, recognizing that I'm the lowest of humans was
hardly a startling or new discovery.

"We need to make a public declaration of the marriage,"
Lia informed them. "Including a celebration to take place
within a few hours."

"Your Highness—" Xichos hesitated, glancing at me.
"I have men dead and injured. The emissary and Imperial
Guards—"

"I know," she cut in, making it clear she knew everything that transpired in her palace. "See to your injured.
Summon Castor to clean up the blood—he knows what
needs to be done. Dearsley, would you personally oversee
that? I know I can count on you."

"Absolutely, Your Highness." The lord she called Dearsley bowed and left with impressive obedience. I could
wish my own people obeyed with so little argument.

"Send my ladies to Me," Lia instructed Xichos. "I need
a change of clothes. Move the champagne celebration to
the grand ballroom. My . . . husband will require rooms of

his own, as will his retinue. My ladies have a great deal to see to, as do you, so why are you still standing in My private chambers staring and acting as if I haven't given very clear commands?"

To his credit—or, more likely, credit to Lia's firm control of her people—Xichos snapped into a salute and cleared out his guards. Lia followed him out of the room into the antechamber, surveying the gaping hole in the wall and resulting rubble with an annoyed frown. "I should have told him to get someone to fix this."

"It's not that important," I commented. Wrong thing to say, as she spun to give me such a hard-eyed stare-down that I wondered if I'd imagined the woman who'd leaned against me and passionately returned my kisses.

"You know very little about My life and what's important to Me, Conrí," she said in cold, clear tones. "Keep that in mind."

The urge to salute or bow to the queenly command seized me, and I ruthlessly suppressed it. This would be an interesting marriage, if nothing else.

Her bevvy of ladies swept into the room, halting their various exclamations of concern and turning to eye me with the calculation of predators. Remembering how they'd easily taken me down—or not how, exactly, but that they had—I held up empty palms. One of them saw the line of blood on my palm and gasped.

"Then it's true," she said, turning what I'd call an accusing stare at her queen. Lia didn't seem to register it, but I made note of the woman, her familiarity, and the strange reaction.

"Yes, Tertulyn, I've married Conrí. Calla, I'm sorry to ask this, but the champagne toast needs to become a full ball to celebrate the wedding. I'm counting on your considerable skills to make it happen."

The lady she'd named Calla briefly bit her lip in dismay, but curtsied. "How soon, Your Highness?"

Lia looked regretful. "Two hours?"

Calla looked pained. "Could I have three?"

"Done. Whatever you need, you have My authority. Take Zariah to help. The best of everything to celebrate our wedding."

"Yes, Your Highness." Calla turned on quick feet to go, but Lia called her back.

"Make it . . ." Lia glanced at me. "Make it seem as if this had been a secret, but not a surprise. Act as if everything we've been saving for a grand occasion had been meant for this."

Calla smiled, apparently amused and excited by the challenge. "I can do that." And she hurried out.

"A ball?" I asked.

Lia flicked a glance at me. "People dress up, drink fine wine, and dance to music. A traditional form of wedding celebration."

I didn't set my teeth. "I know what a ball is. I don't dance."

"You have three hours to learn. Ibolya, would you see that Conrí is assigned appropriate chambers? Then send him a dancing instructor. We'll also need rooms for Lady Sondra and Lord Ambrose."

Ambrose came forward, leaning heavily on his staff, looking very tired. "Your Highness? If it's no trouble and you have no other plans for it, would it be possible for me to have the tower room you put us in?"

She opened her mouth, argument in her eyes, then reconsidered. The one lady—Tertulyn—handed her a damp cloth, and Lia used it to dab at the blood on her palm. The one she'd named Ibolya brought a cloth to me, too, smiling shyly.

"That's a prison room," Lia pointed out to Ambrose.

He nodded vigorously. "With an excellent view, lots of privacy, very quiet." Merle clacked his beak. "Yes, excellent egress for Merle. And it has the great advantage of being easy to keep people *out* of, as well as locked in."

Lia regarded him with bemusement. At last, a kindred spirit, someone equally unable to understand the wizard. "Anything for the Calanthe court wizard," she replied smoothly, a glint in her eyes.

Ambrose laughed. "Well played, Your Highness. Very well, as Conrí is staying, so shall I."

Lia smiled, very pleased despite the weariness in her gaze. "Orvyki, please install the wizard Ambrose in the tower, assign him servants, and see that he has everything he needs. Castor will be in the vicinity. Once he's free, he and our wizard can consult on their mutual interests." The young lady led Ambrose away, considerately moving at a slow pace and casting interested glances at the raven. She asked him something and he launched into a reply I couldn't hear. He paused to touch his staff to the door, then gallantly opened it for the lady.

Sondra had emerged from the bathing room on the other side, plucking irritably at the ill-fitting blue gown. Lia eyed her. "Nahua." She indicated Sondra. "Retrieve Lady Sondra's fighting gear and weapons. I assume you'd be happier in those?" she asked.

Sondra, taken aback as she almost never was, replied with a slow nod. "That would be . . . that's very thoughtful of you. Your Highness," she added, sounding as if she didn't mind saying it for once.

Lia nodded back, some understanding passing between them. "Nahua can assist you in finding other garments that suit your personal style, but are also grand enough for your station and court appearances. You'll find many here of similar mind-sets to yours. Nahua, perhaps find a place for her near Brenda's rooms. The finest we have. Consider the Lady Sondra My sister by marriage."

"Yes, Your Highness." Nahua beckoned to Sondra, who gave me a glance and a shrug, going with her. I didn't know what to make of it, either, that she planned to treat Sondra like my sister.

"Ibolya, do the same for My husband. He'll want his gear and weapons, so arrange to have those sent to his rooms. We'll—"

"No need to find rooms for me," I interrupted, shaking off my bemusement to focus. "I'll share yours."

Lia barely glanced at me. "No, you won't."

"There's enough of them."

"The number of rooms I have is irrelevant. You can have your own, Conrí."

"Want to argue this now?" I asked it mildly, but with enough growl to remind her that I could be as stubborn as she. We'd be sharing a marriage bed, starting that night. I had no intention of delaying engaging in battle with her on the subject until then. Most battles are won before the opposing forces ever engage, if planned correctly. Therefore I'd nullify any strategic attempts on her part to put distance between us.

Lia dearly wanted to argue the point. Her eyes flashed with frustrated ire, and she pressed her lips over what must have been several hot-tempered replies that she swallowed back. Tertulyn moved in beside her, glaring ice picks at me. "I am accustomed to My privacy," Lia finally said, choosing her words carefully. "Something I get precious little of outside these rooms."

"I see walls. Doors that can be closed to give privacy." I gave her a long look that I hoped she'd read as reassuring. "Our fates are tied. We can share this space."

She sighed, resigned. "Fine. Ibolya, would you arrange for My bath?" The young woman hurried away, looking relieved to escape, and Lia fixed me with a narrow stare. "But I expect you to observe My privacy."

"Euthalia." Tertulyn surprised me by using Lia's given name without an honorific and taking her hands. Only the three of us remained, everyone else having been dispatched to carry out the queen's commands. Tertulyn cast a look full of hatred at me and turned her shoulder, as if that could ward me away. "What in Ejarat are You thinking?" she demanded. "You can't marry the butcher of Keiost. He's the Slave King! Enemy of His Imperial Majesty."

"I can and I have," Lia responded in cool tones, extracting her hands from the lady's grip. "And you will address him as Conrí, not that vile epithet."

"But You're to marry the emperor." Deprived of her grip on her queen, Tertulyn wrung her own hands together, dropping her voice and turning her back more fully to me. "Think about what You're risking. When Syr Leuthar hears, he'll—"

"Leuthar is dead," Lia replied, cutting her off. "And I am duly married to Conrí. We can discuss this later, but I need your assistance now to prepare for a public appearance and a ball. As soon as Orvyki and Nahua are free, summon them back to help. I have no idea what I'm going to wear."

I must've made a disparaging sound because Lia moved around her lady, planted her hands on her hips, and glared at me. "Tertulyn, go review My wardrobe. Something fantastic enough for the occasion, but that I haven't worn before. Or that we can make look different enough that no one will recognize it," she directed without looking. Her lady obeyed, though throwing me one more black look before leaving the room. "If you're going to insist on being a constant hulking presence in My private rooms," Lia said, "then we need ground rules."

"We'll share a bed, too," I replied, laying down my own first rule.

She blinked at me, reassessing, then gave me an exasperated look. "I agreed, didn't I? Is that what this is about?"

"What what's about?"

"You insisting on living *here*."

"This will be a real marriage," I informed her. "Ambrose said it needed to be."

She set her jaw. "I know that. I was there, too. How is that relevant?"

Sawehl save me from negotiating with women about the intimacies of marriage. I knew less about bedding women than courting them. Sondra might give me advice if I asked. On second thought, I couldn't imagine a scenario where I could ask her that without traumatizing us both. Ejarat only knew what bizarre advice Ambrose would offer. Lia and I would have to muddle through the act on our own. Animals did it without instruction. Surely people could, too.

Lia was staring at me, finely arched brows climbing her forehead as I delayed. "You don't have to be afraid," I said, trying to sound gentle. "It can be pleasurable. I'll be careful. I won't hurt you."

Her brows fell into a crinkle of disbelief. "I'm not afraid. You're new to Calanthe and haven't seen much of the goings-on here, but believe Me, I'm far from ignorant about sexual pleasures. Just because I haven't been with a man doesn't mean I haven't had sex." She raised her brows into significant arches.

Her frankness shouldn't have put me off kilter, but it did. As did the image she put in my head. My face heated and I prayed to Sawehl she couldn't see it. Or that she wouldn't figure out just how ignorant *I* was. She was waiting for my reply, so I settled for, "Good."

When I said nothing more, she huffed an impatient breath. "My point is that we can have sex without sharing rooms."

She said that now, but I knew the disadvantage of giving up territory. Besides, I wanted her where I could keep an eye on her. Married or not, we barely knew each other and had been mortal enemies not an hour ago. "I'm staying."

She turned her head to gaze out the window, her lips moving in a silent litany. Prayers to Ejarat or cursing my name, it didn't matter. When she faced me again, she'd regained her calm poise, though the effect was entirely ruined by her bizarrely disarrayed makeup.

"Can we just get through tonight, Conrí?" she asked, as if making a formal request. "Presenting a certain image is critical for Me. You can sneer about it to yourself all you like—you can even insult Me to My face and act as if My concerns about clothing and privacy are silly female whims—but in the presence of others, you will show Me respect. In return, I'll show you respect. In case you haven't figured it out, the next few hours will be key to how Calanthe, and the entire empire, views our marriage. If you want to be recognized as My legitimate husband, a king in your own right, and worthy of commanding the forces we'll have to field when His Imperial Majesty inevitably attacks, then you need to present the correct image. We both do. Have I made myself clear?"

"I'm not stupid, Lia," I ground out, more stung than I should be.

She paused, then pressed her lips together. "No, you're not. I apologize that I spoke as if you were. I have ample evidence that you're exceedingly clever," she added in a wry tone.

The apology surprised me. I reached for her hand—the one without the orchid ring—and peeled it off her hip, holding it carefully folded between mine. "No, I'm sorry." I cleared my throat. "What do they say? The truth hurts. I hadn't thought ahead to the politics. Not my strong suit."

A slight smile curved her lips. "Well, you've had other things on your mind today, so I can hardly blame you there. Fortunately thinking ahead to the politics is what I *am* good at. Let Me do it."

I acknowledged that by inclining my head. On impulse, I followed the movement down and brushed a kiss over the back of her hand. She didn't gasp, but I felt the reaction in her, maybe through the new connection. I straightened and looked into her eyes. She regarded me just as gravely. "Maybe we can learn to work as a team," I said, then attempted a smile. "After all, the prophecy says so."

She made that indelicate snorting sound, barely audible but there. A glimpse of the woman beneath the elaborate costumes. I began to suspect my Lia might have a very dry, very sharp sense of humor. Not a trace of it made it to her regal tone when she replied, but I heard it nonetheless. "I certainly hope so, Conrí. Otherwise we'll tear each other's throats out and save Anure the trouble."

"Something to avoid," I agreed. Then cleared my throat. "I'd like my people to attend."

"Lady Sondra and Ambrose will of course attend you."

"I mean on at least the ship that was in your harbor. How far away are they?"

A cagey smile curved her mouth. "Not far at all. I may have . . . prevaricated about where I sent your ship."

I laughed, a hoarse bark of acknowledgment. "I'm glad we're on the same side now."

"Is that what we are?" She looked thoughtful. "I'll arrange for your people to be notified."

"Thank you, Lia."

"Consider it a wedding gift," she replied as she turned and left. Something made me think she laughed at some joke of her own.

27

"We're starting over," I declared after one glimpse of myself in the mirror. No wonder everyone kept staring at me, then trying to pretend they weren't. "Take everything off, scrub Me down, and begin again." It would take hours, but I had at least three. They couldn't start the celebration until I arrived and Calla would likely thank me for every moment of delay.

"You heard Her Highness," Tertulyn snapped, although Ibolya and Orvyki had already moved to lift away the crown. She took up her scissors and began the more expedient method of freeing me from my current—and exceedingly rumpled—gown by snipping the stitches and laces. The crown safely in its niche, the same pair of ladies removed my wig and I rubbed my fingers over my scalp in relief.

Glancing at the closed door, I hoped that Con would stick to the agreement and stay out there. How he'd react to my baldness I wasn't sure, but I suspected he wouldn't like it. I shouldn't care. He was my husband for the rest of my life whether he found me attractive or not. Judging by the urgent erection he'd developed while kissing me, he'd have no trouble consummating the marriage, regardless of his feelings. Still, I kind of dreaded his reaction. When I'd complimented the Lady Sondra's lovely hair, she'd told me that she'd spent most of her life in the mines with her head shorn—they all had—and she would never cut it again. She'd spoken the vow with such vicious certainty that I hadn't doubted her.

Or that Con would feel the same way.

I'd never considered that I'd have an actual husband sharing the intimacies of daily life with me. He'd have to know the truth about my nature sooner or later. Hoping to delay that conversation as long as possible was likely futile. He'd discover soon enough just what kind of "other" he'd vowed to embrace. Perhaps I could delay that awhile longer.

"Ibolya," I said, "do I have any wigs that can be shaped to hang long and loose, a more natural look and color? Something I can wear to bed."

"I can check, Your Highness." She curtsied and stepped away. Nahua took her place, dabbing the glue dissolver on my scalp and following it with a soothing salve. Orvyki asked me to close my eyes so she could loosen the lashes.

"I can't believe You're concerned about contriving natural-looking hair for *him*," Tertulyn said, showing her ire in the way she jerked at the seams of the gown as she loosened it. With my eyes closed, I could hear the venom in her voice with clarity. Nahua and Orvyki remained studiously silent, not offering opinions as they might otherwise, demonstrating how deeply they felt the tension.

"Oh yes," I replied tartly. It had been a long day in a series of long days, and wouldn't end for some time to come. "It's so odd for a woman to wish to start off her marriage on a pleasant footing. Ejarat teaches us to ignore what pleases our spouses, doesn't She? Oh wait, no. No, She doesn't."

In front of me, Orvyki suppressed a giggle, barely audible. It made me feel better. Especially as I couldn't take Tertulyn to task, not with others present. Not a native Calanthean, she wouldn't be able to sense the marriage bond as the others did, whether they understood it with their thinking brains or only through their connection to Calanthe. This pivot would seem less believable and more shocking to all those like her. I needed to have patience and work to convince them more than anyone.

"Tertulyn." Blindly I held out a hand to her and she took it, gripping it fiercely. "I'm married to Conrí. The sooner we all accept that truth, the easier it will be to adjust. I need you to lead the way, as you always have."

"I'm just so worried," she murmured fervently. "How under Sawehl did—"

"Your Highness?" Ibolya came into the room. "I've found two. One a white-blond and curling, and another raven black, very long."

"I'll need to see," I answered. Which would Con prefer? Tertulyn had a point that he was stuck with me regardless. Still, that young, idealistic girl in me whispered of wanting him to find me pretty. And here I'd thought she'd been crushed long ago. Hopefully marriage to the brutal warrior wouldn't wound her anew. I needed to be thick-skinned, tough, and resilient more than ever.

All the more so because Con and I had to present a front of solidarity if we all were to survive this.

A tug at my lashes. "There," Orvyki breathed. "You can open Your eyes, but it will sting." She pressed a damp cloth in my hands, and I dabbed at my eyes to remove the best part of the glue solvent. Tertulyn cut the laces of the corset, and the last of the undergarments fell away. I took a deep breath of relief, feeling as if I hadn't been able to since the wizard and two blood-spattered warriors burst through my doorway. Squinching my eyes open, I blinked

away the tears to study the two choices Ibolya held up. I
should go with the blond; I never wore black.

"Tertulyn, did you find a gown that will work?" Rarely
did I do this entire routine twice in one day. It occurred to
me that it would be best to choose one look for the rest of
the evening rather than change yet again. Con would no
doubt be willing to cut me out of my garments later, judging by his vehement interest in occupying my bed.

"There is nothing grand enough that You haven't worn
before." Tertulyn was shaking her head. "If we had more
time, maybe we could come up with something, but as it
is . . ." She gave me a sorrowful look that didn't quite mask
her simmering anger. And . . . jealousy? She'd called it
worry, but I wondered.

Ibolya cleared her throat, reminding me of Con when
he searched for words. She still held both wigs aloft, one
in each hand. When I gave her my attention, she threw an
apologetic glance at Tertulyn. "There *is* the gown Percy
brought You when he sought asylum. It's suitably elegant—
woven of pure gold—and unlike anything You've worn
before."

"That's not the sort of garment anyone wears outside
the Night Court," Tertulyn snapped. "Her Highness has
never worn it because it's not appropriate for Her."

"Not appropriate for the virgin queen of Calanthe," I
mused. "But it would declare my change in status. I've
married the most notorious man in the empire, for better
or worse. I might as well embrace that and meet it with
My own brand of drama. Let's do that gown, with the black
wig."

"It shows too much of You," Tertulyn argued, sounding more desperate.

"I have a husband now. I won't be able to hide Myself
from him."

"More than one marriage has been consummated in the dark."

I shook my head. Ambrose had bound Con and I in the old way. Even if I kept secrets for a while, he'd find them out eventually—and any subterfuge on my part would only weaken the fragile trust between us. "I won't be able to hide behind the virgin's veil anymore. We'll use makeup to slow the knowledge, but it will get out."

Tertulyn groaned softly and shook her head as she helped me into the steaming bath. I hissed at the heat but held up a hand when Nahua went to add cool water. The hot felt good.

The dress was a bold move, but it would be worth it to shock Con. Plus I could forgo my elaborate superstructure for once. I might even be able to enjoy dancing. Dancing. I nearly groaned. "Ibolya—I diverted you earlier. We need someone to teach Conrí at least a simple dance."

"Begging Your pardon, Your Highness," Orvyki put in, "but I passed that message along because I thought Ibolya might be delayed. Percy is in the antechamber now showing Conrí the steps."

Imagining the brooding and taciturn Con learning to dance from the extravagant and flip Percy made me smile as I leaned back in the meltingly hot water. Tertulyn cleaned the last of the makeup from my face. "I don't know how You can look happy," she muttered.

I cracked open my eyes, seeing that the other ladies were on the far side of the room, helping Ibolya with the gown, wig, and needed accessories. "Let me find humor where I can, Tertulyn," I replied. "My choices are not always My own. You know that."

"No, Your choices should be for *us*," she hissed back. "You've been fascinated by that man from the beginning. I know You better than anyone. You can't lie to me."

"Actually, Lady Tertulyn, I'm not going to justify My-self to you at all," I replied in icy tones. So much for my practicing tolerance. Wisely, she subsided at that, and did not speak again, except as related to my getting dressed.

Calla and Zariah hadn't returned, nor did I expect them to, with all they had to arrange. Another advantage of the dress Ibolya suggested: I wouldn't need so many ladies to help me into it. Once the four with me had dried and oiled me, I asked Ibolya to see to coordinating clothing for Con, since she'd done so well choosing mine.

"He must look regal," I told her. "If he balks or gives you any trouble, remind him that he promised Me."

Tertulyn looked sour, but Ibolya agreed with eager delight. She gave Orvyki and Nahua some last-minute advice on the body makeup, then departed.

None of my ladies besides Tertulyn had dragged their heels at helping me ready for this pivotal event, and they'd all shown unusual initiative. Perhaps I'd relied on Tertulyn too much, neglecting opportunities to award responsibility to my junior ladies.

The polar opposite of every court gown I'd ever donned, this one allowed me to wear nothing underneath. The fine webbing of the gold threads clung to my body from rib cage to hips, allowing for nothing but my skin beneath. Just above my pubis, the skirt flared into a spiraling swirl of cascading mesh, slit in numerous places to reveal my legs to upper thigh. The flexible metallic curlicues of the bodice cupped my breasts and connected with hooks low on my back, leaving my shoulders bare.

Tertulyn did my makeup, as always, but with a much lighter touch and blending the usual paint to match my natural skin as so much of it showed. She glued on long black lashes to match the wig, lightly tipped in gold. For my mouth she grudgingly agreed a glossy scarlet worked best, with only a trio of gold jewels at the corner of each eye.

Orvyki wove a chain of delicate golden orchids to hang round my neck, with one larger to nestle between my breasts, while Nahua draped my long hair with a golden net, studding it with more of the orchids. At last Tertulyn knelt to fasten the elaborate gold laces that held the arched shoes with thin dagger heels onto my feet. I had to take a few practice steps, as they were unusually high, but then I posed for them.

"Well?" I asked. "Honest opinions, as there's time to change."

Tertulyn shook her head. "It's too extreme. Even for the Flower Court."

Ibolya had returned for the finishing touches, assuring me that Conrí would do me justice. She looked at me with shining eyes, but glanced at Tertulyn, hesitating to contradict her senior in rank.

"Ibolya?" I asked, pointedly.

"You look gorgeous, Your Highness," she gushed, clasping her hands together. "Not like a girl or the virgin queen, but like a woman. Like a sorceress queen from the old tales. Every lady in the court will die of envy, You're so beautiful. They'll never stop talking of how You looked tonight." Orvyki and Nahua chimed in with fervent agreement.

Perfect. If Anure had to hear of this massive betrayal, I might as well give him and his court plenty to chew on. Keep his spies busy with my outrageous costume and they'd perhaps pay less attention to the import of this alliance.

"We just need to add the crown," Tertulyn noted, at least discreet enough not to argue further.

I hesitated, as it would create quite the visual gulf

between Con and me. I wasn't sure I wanted to highlight our differences in station so pointedly. "I don't know. Tonight sets the tone and the people need to see Conrí as My legitimate husband." *Just get through tonight.*

"Euthalia, You *have* to wear Your crown," Tertulyn said. "Don't let this ex-slave You married diminish You already."

I opened my mouth to reproach her, but Ibolya— protecting which of us?—spoke before I could. "But, Your Highness, Conrí *is* wearing his crown."

"What crown?" Tertulyn snapped, rounding on her. "He is a King of *Slaves*, you idiot!"

Ibolya didn't flinch, displaying all the serene composure I could wish of any of my ladies—and which Tertulyn seemed to be losing entirely. "His own crown," Ibolya replied. "His people from the ship brought it. I feel quite sure You'll find it adequate, Your Highness," she added to me, "though it *is* unusual."

I nearly laughed. As if Con would have anything but an unusual crown to represent his unorthodox kingship.

"Very well then," I said. "My crown, if you please." They sprang into motion, guiding the crown onto my head and pinning it in place. Without the usual high wig, I found it easier to balance, less heavy. Perhaps my married queen look would be these long, natural wigs. For as long as that lasted, which might not be more than a few weeks, depending on how quickly and viciously Anure staged his reprisals.

"Where is My husband?" I asked.

"Waiting for you in the antechamber," Ibolya volunteered. "Percy has gone to dress for the party, and Conrí is supervising the stonemasons while he waits to escort You."

The stonemasons? Hmm. "You all may go," I told them,

"so you can also change for the party. Take all the time you need. Inform Calla and Zariah that they may do so, too, if they wish. Conrí will escort Me, so they needn't change if they don't have time. I won't need you to attend Me."

"Not to contradict Your Highness," Tertulyn said, "but it seems to me that You'll need us to attend You more than ever. You cannot trust Your safety to that man."

"That man is My husband, sealed by My own vows and by the blessings of Ejarat and Sawehl," I replied mildly enough, but letting her hear my unyielding conviction. "Our fates are tied and I have no qualms entrusting My safety to him. Now go. I'll see you at the ball. And remember: The wedding has been secret, but only a surprise to those not in the know. You may pretend to all sorts of inside knowledge that you cannot possibly discuss."

All but Tertulyn smiled at that, knowing they could parlay such hints into even better status than they usually enjoyed at the parties that would no doubt go on all night. They hastened away, Tertulyn going without a backward glance. I mentally sighed, knowing I would have to talk with her.

"Ibolya," I called, and the young woman turned back. "Dismiss the stonemasons, too. They may finish once we've departed."

She curtsied and left. I waited a few minutes, examining myself in the mirror and giving them all time to clear out. I'd rather we got this over with alone, just me and my husband, just in case he turned out to have prudish ideas. I did look different. More worldly and mature. No longer the concubine in her glass case. No matter what else it changed, my marriage had opened the Night Court to me. If Con failed to please me in bed, I could always access the delights there.

If I only had a few weeks to live, then I planned to enjoy them to the utmost.

I glided out of the bathing chamber, through the sitting room, and into the antechamber. Con had his back to me, and he crouched, chipping at something in the erstwhile hole in the wall beside the door. It had been hastily filled in with newly mortared stones. Not a permanent solution, but enough for privacy.

Touched that he'd paid attention to my complaint, I studied him while I had the leisure of him not knowing it. He'd put on the leather cloak he'd first worn into my court, and it spilled over the floor. Not elegant by any stretch of description, it nevertheless had a powerful impact. Roughly stitched together with thick sinew, the leather panels seemed taken from a variety of sources. None human, I decided, despite the rumors.

And he did wear a crown, one that also reflected his contrary nature. It might've been a pretty thing once, but the silver had been allowed to tarnish, and he'd wrapped the base in strips of leather that matched the cloak. Light showed through gaping holes where jewels had been inset and pried out. Others held a polished stone I didn't recognize, black and somehow lightless.

I understood why he'd chosen it. The crown somehow epitomized the razed and defeated kingdoms Anure had left in his wake. The tarnished silver seemed to match Con's corroded skin, harsh as his voice, and I wondered what it would take to make them all shine again.

He'd lifted his head at my footsteps, but finished whatever he'd been doing, then grunted in dissatisfaction, setting down a tool. "It's not perfect," he said, rising from the crouch and turning, "but it will—holy fucking Sawehl!"

28

Lia just smiled, wild and sensual. I expected her to lick her lips to delicately remove the blood of the hapless victim she'd consumed.

Staring at her and yet uncertain where I could politely look—Sondra's instructions couldn't have anticipated *this*—I ended up scanning her up and down, desperately wishing I had the courtly manners to carry this off. The desire pounded through me, hardening my cock, which hadn't fully relaxed since kissing her. How was I supposed to be polite to a woman I wanted to ravage? I had no idea how men—at least, the kind of man I wanted to be, not the brutal examples I'd grown up around—handled this kind of thing.

She waited, posing for me, her clear eyes—even larger and more defined with the black lashes and simpler makeup—dominating her fine-boned face. Her long black hair cascaded down her back, shining like obsidian, framing her pale naked shoulders and slim body.

Otherwise she wore practically nothing at all. Certainly nothing on her upper half, where her naked breasts, fully on display, were cupped by some kind of gold jewelry. They'd colored her nipples with gold paint, but that didn't disguise them at all. The rest of the gown—if you could call it that—clung to her flat belly and slim hips, her skin showing through the loose weave. Her skin, as smooth and unblemished as appeared only on a person who'd never exposed it to the sun. I could make out the triangle of her pubis before I yanked my gaze with ruthless determination back up to her face.

Which didn't help at all because she watched me with that same predatory amusement, daring me to find words.

I cleared my throat. "Is this . . . for wearing to bed?" Though I tried to ask the question neutrally, a hopeful note crept in. She'd been waiting for it, because she pounced.

"No, Con," she purred. "This is My ball gown. Do you like it?"

Mentally I recited a tirade of blistering curses at Ambrose. He couldn't have wanted me to marry some meek and mild princess. No. That would have been too easy.

I should lie and say I did like it. Though that wouldn't be a lie because I did like it. I more than liked it. I didn't think I'd ever seen a woman look so distractingly beautiful. Still, even granting that my memories of the court at Oriel had gone dim and tattered with time and heartache, I didn't remember any woman dressing so . . . naked.

I'd hesitated too long, because Lia pouted. "You don't like it."

I opened my mouth, hoping the words would come, then caught the glint of malicious humor in her eyes, and belatedly remembered she was not a woman to pout. Baiting me then. "I like it," I admitted, my voice gruff, the honest lust obvious. "You're a beautiful woman and even smarter than you are beautiful. I trust you know what you're doing."

She considered me, the fake sulk disappearing, a hint of surprised pleasure in the curve of her red lips. "Thank you for that, Con. Yes, I do. This gown will be shocking, but only because I wear it. You'll likely be scandalized by far worse tonight."

Sondra had tried to warn me about the Flower Court. "I'd rather be shocked by naked bodies than other horrors I've seen," I pointed out, and she sobered.

"I imagine so," she replied. Then transferred her gaze to the wall. "Thank you for having that fixed. What were you doing to it?"

Grateful to have something else to look at that wouldn't involve me fighting not to stare at her lushly bare breasts, I stepped aside so she could examine the repair work. "The stones aren't fitted right, see?"

"So you were fixing it?" She sounded entirely bemused.

"Yeah," I admitted, realizing belatedly that it likely wasn't royal behavior. I glanced at her—and had to drag my gaze up to her eyes. "I know something about rocks."

"I'll have it properly repaired tomorrow. In the meanwhile, I appreciate you taking steps to fix something that bothered Me."

"Teamwork, yes?"

She smiled, a wry, subtle curve of her painted lips. "Yes."

"What now?"

She glanced at a fancy piece on the wall, made of wheels and a swinging pendulum. "We have nearly an hour until we need to make an entrance. I hurried my ladies along and let them go early so they could dress up for the occasion, too. Right now you and I are superfluous and would only be in the way. Would you like a tour of the palace?"

"It's that or stay and consummate the marriage now."

She actually considered it, looking me up and down, gaze lingering at my crotch, where she could undoubtedly make out how ready I was. Impossible though it seemed,

I hardened more at that salacious attention. Without blushing, she met my gaze. "We could. I have nothing on beneath this gown, but you'd have to be careful not to muss Me."

My throat went tight and dry. I manfully swallowed, wishing I could as easily push down the raging desire that washed over me at her bald suggestion. And at the thought that I could slip a hand into one of those high slits that revealed her slender thighs and find her womanhood beneath. I might as well be that ten-year-old boy who went to the mines for all I knew what to do then.

I cleared my throat. "That seems . . ." Too cold. Too like animals rutting. Too disrespectful. Not something I trusted myself to do in my current state. Nothing I could articulate without sounding like a fool. "Too rushed," I settled on.

She raised an eyebrow painted the same ebony as her hair. Did that mean this hair still wasn't her natural color? "I think neither of us entertains sentimentality about this liaison, Conrí. The point is to get it done with."

Was that the point? Despite her cool and dismissive demeanor, I suspected she felt more strongly about bedding me than that. "Later," I decided. "A tour sounds good."

"You're never quite what I expect," she mused. "Shall we then?" She extended her hand with the orchid ring. After the slightest beat, I caught on and offered her my arm and she looped hers through the crook of my elbow, resting her hand on my forearm. "People will stare, but will pretend not to. Let them. Ignore any impolite enough to catch your attention. They are beneath your notice unless I introduce you. Otherwise pay attention only to Me."

"That won't be difficult," I muttered, and she laughed, quietly, but warm and real.

"This is new to Me, too," she murmured as I opened the door. "I shall be practicing ignoring reactions, too."

We stepped into the hall and her guards snapped to attention. New faces now, as her previous guards had been drawn away by the pitched battle in the hall. I'd have to speak to their commander. A serious lapse of discipline that they'd left Lia's chambers unguarded, even as well as it had worked out for me. Possibly Ambrose had something to do with it, but nevertheless.

People raced about as we strolled through the halls, the palace clearly in a frenzy of preparation. As she'd indicated, Lia ignored them all with regal indifference, pointing out various artworks and interesting bits about the architecture. As we approached, the people with no other exit scooted to the sides of the halls, bowing and averting their gazes.

"I have something to show you," Lia said, turning down another wing of the sprawling palace, this one away from the main activity.

I refrained from commenting that she'd shown me—and everyone else—pretty much everything already. A provincial attitude no doubt. What would my mother and sister have thought of Lia and the licentiousness of her ways? Oddly, I thought they both might've appreciated it. My mother had been a fiercely intelligent queen, not unlike Lia, stern and regal when in court. And my sister . . . She would've been the same. She should never have died the way she did.

It hit me then that I already knew I'd die before I let Anure have Lia. I would have to find a way to destroy him while keeping her safe.

"Through here," Lia said, and led me into a long and shadowy arcade, lit only by glassed-in narrow windows high on the walls. "We keep it dim in here," she explained, "to preserve the art." She kept walking past extraordinary paintings and portraits. So many that they hung with their frames practically touching. Something stirred in my memory, a feeling about them that seemed familiar from long ago. Could these be from before Anure?

Then I halted, feeling even more gutstruck than when I'd turned to see Lia in all her nearly naked glory. An entire wall of paintings I remembered from Oriel. And there—the portrait of my mother and father, formal in their royal gear, my sister standing beside them in the gown commissioned for the painting, her slender hand on my father's knee.

And me, beside my mother, a little boy with chubby cheeks and a bright smile, my puppy playing at my feet.

I couldn't move. Couldn't breathe. I swallowed and my throat hurt with gritty fire.

"Is it you?" Lia asked softly, watching me.

I could only nod in reply, bereft of words.

She turned her face to study the painting, giving me a kind of privacy. "Once I knew who you are, I started thinking that we had art from Oriel. Of course, as you see, we have a great deal of art from all over the empire, but I thought I'd remembered this portrait of the royal family and that you might be the young prince in it."

She paused for a long moment while I stared at my mother's alert eyes and gentle smile, my father's stern jaw and easy authority. My sister . . . I couldn't bear to look into her sweet and innocent face.

"Should I have prepared you?" Lia asked softly. "I thought it might be worse to get your hopes up and have it not be them."

"No," I said, and it came out thick and guttural. I coughed, covering it with my free hand. I took a moment to rub my eyes. Then looked again. "How is it here?"

"How are any of them here?" she replied lightly. "People

brought them. As Anure's armies rolled over the lands, some heeded the visions, the warnings. They carried what they found most precious with them, passing art, books, music, histories from hand to hand until they came here, where they'd be safe."

"They're not yours," I managed, sounding more accusing than I meant to. Seeing my family here—and other art I recalled from those long-ago golden days—had me more rattled than I'd have thought possible, as if their existence opened up a hole into a world I'd thought burned to ash.

"No," Lia replied in a careful tone. "And they're not Anure's, either, which I feel is the most important point. I do care about the rest of the world, Con. It's more than only things of Calanthe that I protect."

True. "Would you have told me, that this painting is here?"

"If all had gone according to plan and Leuthar had dragged you off to face execution? No." She let go of my arm and turned to face me, expression regally composed. "First, it hadn't yet occurred to Me, and I doubt it would have given all I had to think about. Second, would you have wanted Me to?" She studied me, then the boy in the painting, her eyes going to my sister. "I think it would've only hurt you more."

"At least you're honest," I said. Brutally so.

"Not always." She stepped away to scan the long hall, her profile lovely and remote. "I'm an adept liar, as all good politicians are, and I abuse the truth without qualm if I need to. Honesty is not always the most important thing."

"What is?" I asked. In the dimness, I could better ignore the beauty of her unclad body, curl my fingers against the itch to touch her, to discover if her velvety skin felt as soft as it looked. How I could want her, feel this possessiveness and protective urge even as she made me angry enough to see red, I didn't know.

"What is the most important thing?" She looked at me. "I already told you: Calanthe, and all that includes. First, last, and always."

I held her gaze a long moment. "Does that include me and my people now?"

Her mouth quirked in a half smile. "Ever the king. Yes. Yes, it does. It should be time for our grand entrance. Shall we?"

I offered her my arm again. She took it easily as before, as if nothing had changed between us. Perhaps nothing had. And yet she'd given me a gift by showing me that the art of Oriel—some of it, anyway—had survived, and she'd given me back my family's faces. My father, full of vigor and arrogance, not the shuddering corpse he'd become. My sister, with all the promise of the queen she might've been.

"Thank you," I said.

She gave me a glance, surprise in it. "For what?"

How to explain? I cleared my throat. So much talking today. I should get Ambrose to brew his tonic for me. "I couldn't remember their faces. Now I can."

She nodded, gliding lightly at my side as we left the long, cool hall and stepped back into a larger open area of the palace, the setting sun streaming in, setting the jewel-encrusted pillars alight with color. "What happened to them?" she asked softly.

"A long story," I said with enough finality that she should know to leave it there.

She nodded again, the movement part of her graceful walk, the balancing of the glittering crown on her head, the flow of her hair and gown, the light *tink* of her heels on the marble floor. "I can help your voice," she said, unexpectedly. "Help heal your lungs. If you like."

"I won't refuse," I allowed. "But it won't make me tell long stories."

She cast me a smile, her eyes somber. "I suppose we don't owe each other our stories. I won't ask again."

As we walked on, I somehow felt as if I'd let her down. No doubt it would be far from the last time.

29

I have an excellent sense of timing. Probably I should credit my father's relentless tutelage on the importance of that, so I could control diplomatic interactions. Rarely do I even need to glance at the spring-and-pendulum-driven clocks on the walls that keep such excellent time. I couldn't shake the feeling, however, that I'd misstepped in showing Con the art of Oriel when I did. The sight had upset him badly—enough to bring that boiling rage to the surface. A pity, as he'd calmed so much from the seething brute who first walked into my palace.

Still, we'd had the otherwise unscheduled time, as I rarely did, and it had felt dishonest to keep it from him once it occurred to me that the golden-eyed, dark-haired boy in the painting might be him. Not that I'd spent time studying that one portrait among the many that my father had collected. A task I'd taken up along with so many others. It had been the connection to Oriel that reminded me, bringing that particular wall of art to mind—and my memory had served up the image of that royal family's portrait.

Once I began thinking about it, I couldn't stop.

Not much of that happy-go-lucky child in the portrait remained in the taciturn and scarred warrior who escorted me. He looked imposing in the black-and-gold clothing Ibolya had found, with the sword sheathed on one hip and a heavy-looking leather bag hooked to his belt on the other side. The rough cloak and stark crown added the right touches, proclaiming him a warrior to be wary of, one who'd earned his scars by rushing headlong into the worst of fires. His alert and predatory gaze provided fair warning, too, constantly scanning for trouble, assessing each person we passed before he followed my instructions and looked through them with regal disinterest.

"We're approaching the ballroom now," I advised him. "We'll enter. The heralds will trumpet—it can be quite loud. I'll welcome them all and introduce you. Do you want to say a few words?"

"We'll see," he grunted. His voice had gotten rougher with emotion, possibly with so much talking, as that seemed to wear on him like someone overusing a weakened limb.

"Just indicate to Me. You do well being silent and forbidding, so you can't go wrong either way." I had meant it in all seriousness, but his lips quirked and he glanced at me in amusement. As it did every time, his gaze slid to my bare breasts, firing with hunger, before he resolutely looked away. Sometimes he looked at me as if he'd never seen a woman in such a state of undress. Perhaps he hadn't. Growing up as Anure's prisoner in the mines wouldn't have allowed for any freedom that way. Still, I'd assumed he'd made up for that by indulging during his campaign, as the plentiful rumors had claimed.

Now I thought he hadn't and wondered just how our first bedding would go. *Better than Anure*, I reminded myself, no matter how clumsy Con might be. He certainly had physical vitality to spare. Power and enthusiasm went a long way toward compensating for lack of actual skill, from what I'd heard.

"After that?" he asked, and for a moment I thought he meant after the bedding. I needed to keep my thoughts on the moment, not speculating about what this very large and rough man would be like in bed. Would he be able to temper his strength? Or would he be brutal in his obvious lust? The heat shivered through me, a needy wanting I hadn't known lay inside me. I liked his size and strength and the thought of him—

And there I went again.

"Then we lead the first dance," I replied, happy that I sounded poised and not as if I'd been speculating about his sexual prowess. "Percy showed you the steps?"

"Yes."

I thought that was all he'd say on the subject; then he glanced at me with that whiff of humor again. "He said I wasn't putting my hands in the right places. I said he had the wrong curves for it."

I laughed, embellishing on the exchange in my mind. "Oh, I can just imagine." We came to the closed doors, the guards poised there to open them at my signal. "Ready?"

"As ever," he muttered.

I nodded and they flung the doors open. As one, Con and I stepped through, stopping on the landing before descending the great curving stairs to the grand ballroom below. I took a moment while the trumpets played to scan the room, letting them absorb my transformed appearance and—for those who hadn't seen him yet—have a good look at the terrible and mighty Slave King. His reputation would have to go to work for us now.

Truly Calla and Zariah had outdone themselves. The ballroom sits on a raised bit of land, surrounded by lily ponds and formal gardens. All the glass-paned doors had been retracted on their rollers to stand open to the golden evening. Candles floated on small glass saucers on the mirror-still ponds, so the light reflected up. Other candles filled every niche of the ballroom, making everything glow with rich warmth. Spires of orchids in every color wreathed around the pillars, spilled from containers of all kinds, mostly glass, and cascaded from arches. Accenting all the golden shimmer, black silk covered the tables bearing food and drink, and trailing ribbons in shining ebony tied back the garlands of orchids.

Every gaze fixed upon us, many people busily taking notes for the letters they'd send to their correspondents. Perfect. Lady Delilah, daringly dressed in a gown made of leather cords, chains, and buckles that showed even more of her lush figure than I displayed, stared at me intently. When she caught me looking, she acknowledged it with a slight nod and approving smile. Then she transferred her gaze to Con. And licked her lips.

The sudden surge of possessiveness surprised me. I didn't much like the thought of Con exploring Delilah's favorite fetishes. I'd have to get over that, as I wasn't so foolish as to expect to control a man like him. Or rather, I'd have to focus my efforts on more important things than who my husband had sex with.

The trumpeters finished and the crowd quieted in anticipation. Servants circulated, passing around glasses of champagne to latecomers—or those who'd skirted the edges of civility by quaffing the excellent vintage before the official toast.

"Good evening, people of Calanthe!"

The crowd roared genteel approval of my greeting, calling warm wishes back, hailing me as queen and calling for long life and good health. I waited for them to settle again.

"We are delighted to share this very special celebration with all of you," I continued. "At long last, I have taken a husband. My extended and lonely vigil has been rewarded. Ejarat and Sawehl have sent Me the best of men. A warrior feared throughout the empire! A leader of armies and defender of freedom. A prince in his own right, son of the greatly mourned lost king and queen of vanquished Oriel, I give you My husband, Conrí!"

The crowd went wild. So much juicy gossip at once, they could hardly contain themselves. The muscle of Con's arm bulged under my hand, his anger palpable. I looked up at him with a suitably besotted smile and he leaned down to speak in my ear.

"Why not just stab me in the back with an actual blade?" His voice grated low and mean.

I turned my face to beam at him, as if he'd offered me a lovely compliment. "They needed to know." With my heels, I needed only rise up on my toes a bit more to give him a kiss.

The crowd loved it, even if Con glared at me. At least he didn't wipe off his mouth. Lord Dearsley climbed the steps, his expression set in a joyful courtier's smile that covered his true feelings, whatever they might be. Halfway up, he turned and raised the glass he carried.

"A toast!" he proclaimed. "To the bride and groom! To the queen of Calanthe and Her consort, Conrí."

The room exploded with the excited exclamations repeating the toast. Calla appeared at my elbow and Zariah at Con's side, each carrying exquisite glasses painted with orchids entwined with broken chains, and filled with sparkling champagne. I took mine from Calla, raising a brow at her. She gave me a smile and a slight shrug, acknowledging the risk and that she'd done her best. An impressive feat for the short amount of time. She and Zariah had changed clothes, too, also wearing black and gold.

My ladies had clearly all conspired—and done a beautiful job. When I turned back to Con with my glass, I felt unexpectedly misty at the way they'd all taken care of me on this difficult day. He'd accepted the glass from Zariah and was studying it—then looked at me with that grim humor of his. I smiled brilliantly and gave a little shrug to convey I'd had nothing to do with it. At least that drew his gaze to my breasts.

And when he lifted his gaze to mine, his eyes burned hot with more hunger than anger. Furious lust and a promise of retribution. The look sent that answering bolt of heat through me. It would be an interesting night following a tumultuous day. We could both work off the tension.

He clinked his glass to mine. Sipped when I did.

Then gave me a smile full of wicked mischief and turned to the assembly, holding up his glass. They all fell silent in rapt expectation of what the terrible Slave King might say. I held my breath, too, bracing for his retaliation.

"To my wife, Euthalia, queen of Calanthe," he declared, his harsh voice raised in a shout. "Our marriage marks a new alliance. One that will destroy the upstart emperor and dissolve his false empire forever!"

Internally, I groaned, keeping my smile fixed. I could kill him, I really could. Con held his glass expectantly toward me, fierce challenge in his eyes, smiling at my cold glare. If I refused to toast, I'd imply disagreement with my husband and undermine everything we'd spent the last hours painstakingly creating. If I accepted the toast, I declared myself a traitor to the empire.

The room itself seemed to hold its breath, waiting for my response.

"You will be the death of Me," I said through teeth clenched in a brilliant smile.

"Or your liberation from the yoke of a tyrant," he said back.

"Or both."

"Probably both," he agreed. "Will you die a traitor or a coward, Lia?"

Ah well, he had a point.

I clinked my glass to his, then drained the excellent champagne, like drinking sunshine made liquid.

"To Calanthe," I declared loudly. "And freedom for all!"

Only a few people didn't join in the shouting, and I made note of who they were. Some didn't surprise me at all.

Tertulyn was nowhere in sight.

We handed our glasses back to my ladies and descended the stairs, moving through an aisle created by the parting crowd, then into the center of a circle. I turned to face Con, who surprised me by sweeping an elegant and perfectly executed bow, then offering me his hand. Percy had done his job well.

I laid my hand in Con's, watching his broad shoulders for cues. In dancing, one must let the male partner lead, if one is a woman. You'd think it would be restful, but it truly isn't. Given my preferences, I'd rather decide the steps and movements for myself. But we were getting through this, so I waited as the strings wove their melody, rising up.

At the exact moment, Con drew me into his arms, tucking my right hand against his heart, settling his at the small of my back, fingers splayed over the top curve of my bottom. I reached up and laid my hand with the orchid ring against his cheek, cupping the hard line of his jaw, beard silky and surprisingly soft. At the next beat, he moved, taking me into the simple, sweeping steps with confident grace.

My eyes flew up to his—and I found him looking down at me with mischievous pleasure at my surprise. I relaxed more, and he smiled. I could become accustomed to enjoying his strength. He held me so securely that I didn't have to concentrate on keeping my balance. Instead I sank into the music, enjoying the swirl and rhythm, the heady sensation of being close to Con's powerful heat. His skin felt hot and enticing under my fingers, the scent of leather and spiced soap filling my mind. He must've tucked his long hair up inside the crown he wore, and I wondered how it would feel to have it spill around us as he rose over me in bed.

Though the gold paint kept my nipples pointed, they tightened still under his intense regard, swelling almost painfully against the hardened coating. Con seemed to notice, no longer pretending not to stare at my breasts, but studying them with lingering attention as he whirled me through the repeating cycle of the dance.

When his hot eyes rose leisurely to mine, I found myself blushing. I would've said that wasn't possible, but being so close to him, feeling both safe in his arms and vulnerable to him, knowing what would transpire between us . . . I felt like someone entirely new.

For the first time in as long as I could remember, I felt more like a woman than a queen.

As more instruments joined in the dance, other couples joined us on the dance floor, following the meticulous order of rank—and forcing Con to watch where we were going. It gave me some relief, to have his scrutiny lifted, but he pressed me closer so that my nipples brushed his chest and arm, making me catch my breath at the shock of arousal.

I had never felt this extremity of desire with any of my ladies. Was that a good sign or a bad one?

I had no idea.

It didn't help that I didn't seem to be able to think clearly.

"How much longer?" he asked. When I met his gaze in mute question, he turned his face and brushed a kiss against my thumb, so near the corner of his mouth. "How long before I can have you?" he clarified, unnecessarily.

My heart thudded, working to move my thickened blood. "It will surprise no one if we make our farewells after this dance."

He didn't smile, but he looked pleased, in a grim, feral way. Pressing me closer to him, he murmured, "I'm going to eat you alive."

The music swirled to a crescendo and we parted, stepping back, Con bowing again. When he straightened and tucked my arm through his again as we acknowledged the applause and congratulations, I said through my smile, "Promise or threat?"

He grinned, still with that grim edge to it. "Tell me afterward."

"I will—if you're conscious," I retorted. We strolled off the dance floor. "By the way," I added, "you have gold paint on your shirt now."

He didn't even glance down. "A badge of honor."

"Your Highness!" Percy swept up to us. "You look historically gorgeous in that dress. I knew You would. You honor me by wearing it tonight."

"Thank you, Lord Percy. It did indeed suit the occasion," I replied. "And thank you for your service assisting Conrí in learning the dance." I glanced up to find my husband watching me with opaque suspicion. "You worked miracles," I added with a sweet smile.

"Easy to do with such excellent material." Percy gave Con a flirtatious smile. "And it only took some reminding for our Conrí to recall the lessons of his youth. The excellence is all his own, I'm afraid. You didn't tell me that you hailed from Oriel, Conrí, you sly dog. I grew up in Valencia just next door. We should trade old tales sometime."

Con tensed, but nodded in his version of courtesy. "We should."

Brenda came up as Percy excused himself, the Lady Sondra with her. They both wore gowns, but ones that had been designed to look like armor, also. "Your Highness. Conrí." Brenda bowed, then slid me an interested look. "Such a fascinating day, and ball."

"Yes," I agreed, adding nothing more. There would be time for analysis—and strategic planning. "Are your rooms to your liking, Lady Sondra?"

Sondra glanced at me, tearing her gaze from some silent communion with Con. She seemed amused more than anything. "Very much so, Your Highness, thank you," she replied in her raspy voice, so like Con's. "You look lovely tonight, if I may say so. As a maid I heard tales of the extravagant fashions of the Flower Court. I'm delighted to find my imaginings fell short." She looked me over and threw a wry smile at Con. "Your Highness must promise to leave our Conrí in one piece."

Surprised to find myself equally amused, I smiled back at her. "And here I was informed that I'm to be the one consumed."

She arched her brows and gave Con a considering look. "Is that so? Ambrose *is* a miracle worker."

Con stared at her steadily, revealing and saying nothing, but she stopped teasing him. "Speaking of the devil," Con said instead of addressing her witticism, "where is Ambrose?"

Sondra rolled her eyes. "Locked in his tower."

"Ah."

"Conrí!" A tall and imposing dark-skinned man stepped up and saluted Con. Then grinned, happy and relieved.

Con grinned back, pulled his arm from my hand, and embraced the man, with much pounding of each other's backs. "Your Highness," Con said, turning to me and drawing me forward. "Kara, my wife, Queen Euthalia of Calanthe. And this is General Kara. He remained with our ship."

"Did he now?" I mused as the man bowed. Like Con, he tried very hard not to stare at my breasts. Where had these people been—a monastery for followers of Sawehl?

Kara straightened and gave Con a significant look, though I wasn't sure what it was meant to communicate. "We have a great deal to discuss," Kara said.

"Tomorrow," Con agreed. "But tonight is a celebration. A special occasion."

"It's certainly a unique opportunity to indulge in the many pleasures offered by the Flower Court," Kara said, inclining his head toward me.

"Yes," Con said. "So stay and enjoy yourself."

"Are you going somewhere?" Kara asked, and Sondra snickered.

Con glared at her, but set a hand at the small of my back, as he had during the dance. "You are off duty, but I have one more to perform. Shall we, Your Highness?"

I answered in the same lofty tone. "Indeed, Conrí."

It took a bit more than that to extract ourselves from all the well-wishers and climb the stairs, pausing once more to wave good night. Ibolya moved to attend me, Nahua and Orvyki starting up the stairs also, but I waved them all away.

"I won't need you until morning," I told Ibolya. "Have you seen Tertulyn?"

She shook her head. "No, Your Highness. Shall I find her for You?"

"No. You all enjoy the parties tonight. You did well today. Especially you, Ibolya. You have My gratitude."

Beaming with surprised pleasure, she curtsied. Con and I walked on, guards saluting as we passed, guests who were going from one party to another pausing to offer congratulations. I allowed it now, though I kept the exchanges brief, if only in deference to Con's palpably simmering impatience. As we climbed to my rooms, the halls grew quieter—and the tension between us thicker.

"Your people seemed amused at the prospect of you bedding Me," I said into the dense silence between us.

He coughed, a bit of a choking sound in it, then glanced at me, absently rubbing at the gold paint on his shirt with his free hand. "Are you—" It came out gravelly, and he cleared his throat. "Are you asking for my sexual history?"

"Why, is it a long and fascinating one?" I'd meant to be flirtatious and coy, but it was the wrong thing to say.

His eyes went flat, and he stared down the hall like a man going to an execution rather than his marriage bed. "No."

Ah. As I'd begun to suspect. "Well, we hardly need to get into involved acrobatics or the more exotic sensual arts," I said. "It's a simple act, with a few basic steps, after all is said and done. We can dispense with the marital obligation quite quickly."

"And you'll show me these steps?"

"Well, I have lived in the Flower Court all My life. I'd say that, while I'm not personally experienced with a man, I know a fair amount about a woman's body and I understand the overall mechanics well enough."

He flicked a glance at me, made a sound under his breath.

"What's that?" I asked.

"You can be so . . . cold," he said. "Does nothing matter to you?"

A surprisingly painful sting from an unexpected quarter, so I fell back on my usual lines. "One thing," I replied. "Ca—"

"—lanthe," he finished with me, sounding grim.

I'd misstepped again. I should start thinking of Con as like one of his vurgsten charges—liable to explode with the least spark. Though I knew myself to be cold, so it shouldn't bother me that he knew it, too. I'd spent years developing that protective ice, and I didn't know how to melt it now. But I did know how to pretend.

We turned into the long hall leading to my rooms, the guards flanking the doors at attention. I moved in closer to Con, letting him feel the outer curve of my breast against his arm, where the cloak didn't cover it. "Truth be told," I purred, my words only for him, "I was rather enticed by your promise to eat Me alive." Truth there. And the heat would perhaps overcome all the rest of this awkwardness of bedding a stranger.

He tensed, that muscle ticking in his jaw. "Yes?"

"Oh yes." I smiled at the guards as they opened the double doors. "Good night, gentlemen," I said. "Make sure My husband and I aren't disturbed tonight."

"Yes, Your Highness." They bowed and closed the doors behind us.

My ladies had come back in my absence, Ejarat bless them in their earnestness. They'd decorated my chambers, too, with garlands of orchids tied with black satin ribbon, and they'd lit candles shielded by hurricane lamps, scattering them about the room. Sweet of them, to think of romance for me.

Though foolish, as they all knew full well how little this forced marriage had to do with any of the gentler emotions. Surprised to find myself terribly nervous, I turned to face Con, who stood just inside the doors, looking as if he didn't know what to do with his hands.

Ejarat take me, neither did I.

30

The candlelight gleamed on Lia's full breasts and taut nipples. I'd been hard so long that I ached, the tight pants that charming little Ibolya had talked me into wearing—no, sweetly threatened me into by evoking my promise to her mistress—so constricting they'd been torture.

Lia sauntered up to me, hips swaying under the revealing golden mesh. Her skin beneath my hands had been so hot that I'd been hard-pressed not to reach for more. Now that we were alone . . .

Sawehl take me—facing a charging army required less courage.

What an idiot I was, admitting to my lack of experience. What a naive fool she must take me for.

But I caught a glimmer of uncertainty in Lia's clear eyes, a hint of vulnerability I hadn't expected. It helped that she let me see it. Perhaps not so cold after all.

She smiled, coming close enough that her intoxicating scent obliterated my senses. She smelled of flowers, of course. A river of them. And something else beneath, something essentially green, like the fresh scent of a broken leaf in springtime. Moving slowly, she laid her hands on my chest, her touch warm through the silk, her nails a light scratch. Watching my face, she slid one hand down, closing it over my rigid cock. I jerked at the touch, nearly spilling after the long teasing. I grabbed her by the wrists, pulling her hands away.

"No?" she asked.

I didn't know what to say. Mostly I wanted to kiss her, to seize her and see the tantalizing bits she'd teased me with all evening.

"It might help to take the edge off," she suggested, not unkindly.

I knew what she meant. I might've declined the services any number of women and men had offered during our campaign, but they'd been explicit in what I missed by returning to my solitary tent. My cock leapt of its own accord, giving its own answer, but I didn't know if a true gentleman would accept such an offer from his queen.

"I want to touch you," I grated out. Honest, though maybe desperate sounding. Not that I'd fool her anyway. I'd gone beyond desperate with the long-ignored needs. Somehow Lia—cold, calculating, imperious, and infuriating Lia—had lit the fuse to the explosives I'd carried dormant inside me.

"Then touch me, Con." She slipped her wrists out of my hands and held her arms up in a graceful movement, like a dancer. Then paused. "Or does the body paint bother you?"

"The crown bothers me," I admitted.

She laughed, putting her hands to it. "I wear it so much I forget about it." Plucking deftly at pins that had held it in place, she lifted the crown off her head and set it aside, shaking out her hair. "Your turn."

Happy to be rid of the thing, I tossed my crown next to hers. She reached up, combing her fingers through my hair that spilled down, arranging it over my shoulders. "I like your hair," she murmured. "I like it like this."

I risked touching hers, as I'd longed to do all evening, sliding my fingers down one long lock. "I like yours," I replied. "Is this your natural color?"

She smiled a little and shook her head, reaching for the chain holding my cloak on. "This has to be hot." It gave, then fell, sliding down. Her fingers trailed down, too, wandering over my shoulders, smoothing the silk over it, as if testing the texture. She reached the belt holding the sword and my bagiroca. "Perhaps it's safe to go unarmed now?"

"With you in the room? Doubtful." My wry remark made her laugh, and she undid the buckle, lifting the bagiroca with a surprised lift of her brows.

"What's in this—rocks?" she teased.

"Yes, rocks." I undid the thong and showed her. "Some from the mines. Others from places I conquered."

She considered me. "And then you swing it to smite your enemies."

"It's a good weapon. Simple. I like my rock hammer, too. The sword is for show."

"Though you can use it."

"Well enough to get the job done."

She cocked her head, an odd smile on her lips. "You're an interesting man, Conrí."

"Is that good?"

"I think so. I hate being bored."

I laughed a little, though it came out choked. "I'll try not to bore you."

Reaching up, she began undoing the ties on my shirt, working her way down and spreading open the silk. I shrugged out of the sleeves and tossed it aside. She smoothed her hands over my chest and shoulders, exploring. Her touch roused me further, impossible as I thought that could be, my cock straining against my pants. When she met my eyes, hers were lustrous and gray as smoke in the candlelight. "Touch me, Con. I want that, too."

I put my hands on her smooth shoulders, her skin even softer than the Calanthe silks, smoother than anything I'd ever touched. Her eyes drifted closed and she trembled. "My hands are rough," I said, realizing how they must feel to her.

"Yes," she agreed, pink tongue darting out to lick her lips. "I like it. More. Touch me more."

That broke through whatever paralysis had held me back. Without conscious choice, I seized her tantalizing breasts, filling my hands with their luscious beauty. She arched like a drawn bow, throwing her head back and digging her nails into my shoulders as she cried out.

"Sorry, sorry," I muttered, though I seemed unable to let go of her now that I was touching. I tried to back off, to be gentle.

She groaned, pushing into my hands. "No," she gasped. "It's good. So good."

Needing no more encouragement, I rolled her nipples, fascinated by their hardness compared with the plump flesh of her breasts—and then rapt by the way she undulated, her face contorted in a combination of pleasure and pain.

"Is this right?" I swallowed my pride to ask.

"Just follow your instincts, warrior man," she answered on a moan. "You're doing just fine."

"I don't want to hurt you." I stilled my hands, images of things I'd seen men do filling my mind.

"Con." Lia had my face in her hands, holding me so I'd look into her eyes. Which were full of a compassion I hadn't expected. Also a reflection of the same heat driving me. Far from cold. "You're not hurting me. I'll say so if you do. This is us, you and me. And it's good."

She wore those shoes with the spiky heels that made her taller, so she only had to lean up a bit to find my mouth. Kissing me, she slid her hands behind my neck, drawing me down and into the sweet, hot redolence of her scent and flavor. My hands, still on her gorgeous breasts, moved again, making her pant and squirm. She pushed into them. "Use your mouth," she whispered.

I used my mouth on her throat first, trailing along the swanlike length of it, the powdery flavor of her makeup like another perfume. She made gasping, mewing sounds—nothing of the regal queen in them, only needy woman—that drew me on. Holding her by the waist as she bowed back over my hands, I found her nipple with my lips, kissing, then sucking.

She writhed, holding on to my shoulders with a fierce grip, nearly sobbing in pleasure. "Good. Yes. Good." She chanted the words in between incoherent cries, as if she knew I needed to hear them.

"How do I get you out of this?" I growled, plucking at the intricate metal that encased her ribs.

She laughed throatily and turned in my hands, holding her hair aside. "There's clasps, like on a necklace," she said. "But if we can't find them, you can cut it off me. Or just lift the skirt and leave it for my ladies to undo."

"I can do it," I said. After the extended tease, I was done with tantalizing glimpses. I wanted all of her skin, all of her naked. Finding the fastenings now that I could see them, I undid them easily. The bodice gave way, peeling off her and leaving its imprint behind. Following the slow slide of the threads, I eased the gown over the sweet curve of her hips, letting it fall down her thighs to pool at her feet.

Her skin gleamed in the candlelight, a pale glow. In an entranced state of wonder, I traced the lines of the small of her back, the flare of her hips, the sweet dimples at the top curves of her enticing buttocks. I pressed a kiss to the deepest curve of her back, centered at the narrowest point of her hips, delighting in the texture and shape of her.

In that gallery of art, there'd been countless paintings and sculptures of naked women, and I understood the impulse now to re-create that pure beauty. If I'd had the least bit of artistry in me, I would've wanted to paint and mold its likeness, too.

As it was, I could only celebrate the reality, the sensuous flesh of a woman. I kissed and tasted her skin, the urgent hunger demanding more and more. She moaned, writhing against my grip on her hips, her hair swinging around to veil the delicious view of her naked ass.

"Bend over," I told her.

With a shudder, she complied, laying herself over the desk she'd been working at earlier. She still had on the tall shoes, so her ass rode high in the air, a clear signal. I hadn't done this, but I'd seen it done—by animals, too—and figured if the base soldiers and hound dogs could find their way, I could, too. I pushed her hair aside, exposing her again. "Spread your legs."

Oh yeah. Her sex opened, layers of it unfurling like one of her orchids, all shades of pink warmed by the golden candlelight.

I ripped at the laces on my trousers, tearing the unfamiliar clasps—and groaned at the sweet release of my turgid cock springing free. Holding it, I touched her exposed sex, surprised to find it slick. Surprisingly hot, too. She moaned and wiggled, panting heavily. Trying to be gentle, I prodded, seeking the entrance I knew had to be there.

"Higher," she gasped.

"Show me."

She reached between her legs, sliding her fingers

through the folds. I almost couldn't take it, the sight of her delicately jeweled fingernails moving against that intimate female flesh. She dipped a finger into herself. "Here," she sighed.

I followed her finger with mine and she dropped hers on a groan of pleasure, pushing her ass back so my finger moved deeper into her channel. So tight, hot, and slick. She made those mewing sound, circling around my thick finger, her muscles clenching. My cock had begun to pulse, so close to coming, urging me to plunge into her. But it was so much thicker than my finger. No wonder the women screamed so.

"You're so small and tight," I said. "It will hurt."

"It will expand," she said, breathing hard and pushing herself against my hand. I couldn't help myself, I stroked her slickness, loving the way she moaned and undulated.

I guided my throbbing cock to her entrance, withdrawing my finger. She still looked so small and delicate compared with me. I hesitated.

She pushed back, enveloping the head of my cock with her slick heat. My vision went black at the edges. Unreal how it felt. "Just do it, my wolf," she commanded, steel in her tone. "Take me."

I plunged into her and she screamed, rearing up off the desk. Freezing, I waited for the guards to rush in and cut me down, my pants around my ankles, buried to the hilt in her, my weapons out of reach. Lia made a sobbing sound, collapsing back down, shuddering.

"Lia?" I asked.

"Don't you dare stop now," she grated out. "Finish it."

I had to anyway, the animal urges taking over. Grasping her hips, I plunged into her, backing out only enough for another thrust. I gloried in the way her body clasped me. She held on to the desk, the orchid ring on her finger seeming larger than ever, glowing with its own light.

I finished fast, the climax more wrenching than any stoked by my own hand. It gutted me, convulsive and consuming, dizzying. I released her hips to slam my palms on the desk on either side of her, so I wouldn't crush her. Seated deeply in her, I rode out the last few pulses, struggling to draw harsh breaths.

Lia moaned, a different sound from the ones she made in pleasure. Chagrined at my thoughtlessness, I pulled out, hearing her hiss of pain as I did. I stepped back and pulled up my pants to soak up my spilled seed. "Did I hurt you?"

She levered herself up, laughing throatily. "Some, but I was braced for it. You could have gone at it more gently," she observed with some rue, turning to face me. "I didn't get to climax, of course, but I didn't expect to. All in all I'm fine."

My pants wouldn't fasten again and I fumbled at the catches, glad for the excuse to look down. "I'm sorry, Lia." Still she'd known I was a brute.

"Don't be," she said sharply enough to make me look up.

I stared at her, feeling stupid on top of brutish, still clutching my pants together, while she leaned against the desk at ease in her glorious nakedness, smooth, slim body silhouetted by that cloak of black hair. Despite my words—and my intentions—I'd barely looked at or touched her at all. I'd lost my head much as I did in battle. Maybe whatever made men gentle and good lovers had died in me, burned away by the fires of Vurgmun, choked by the chains of slavery.

"You'll do better next time," she said more gently. "Don't look so stricken."

"Next time?" I echoed.

She tossed her hair back impatiently. "Yes. Though I suppose you don't have to if you don't want to. The marriage is consummated. It's unlikely you planted an heir in me, but possible. If you prefer not to repeat this experience, you can wait a few weeks to see if your seed took, but then you'll need to visit my bed again. I will require that of you." She sounded steely and regal, her eyes flashing and face composed. But I began to read her better and saw something else in her eyes—hurt? And not from the way I'd plundered her body.

I'd bungled that. I needed to not bungle this, too.

"I want a next time. And a time after that. As often as you'll have me."

She tilted her head, smiling slightly. "Yes?"

"Yes."

"Then why are you putting your pants back on, warrior mine?"

Because I'm an idiot apparently. "Next time is now?" I clarified. At least I'd asked enough stupid questions already that I could hardly do worse.

"I don't know that I'll be ready for more actual fucking, as I'm quite sore," she allowed with a smile. "But there's a lot we can do besides that. I believe you owe me an orgasm."

I toed off my boots and kicked off the pants. "I believe in fair play."

"I knew I liked you," she purred, then bent to remove her shoes. "My feet hurt, too. Let me get these things off, then we can clean up and discuss my compensation."

31

"Let me start on my debt," Con said, and knelt at my feet, nimble fingers picking at the knotted cords.

For a man with big, rough hands, he was surprisingly deft. I'd expected him to be clumsy in touching me, but no. He'd done his best to be gentle, even when he'd been mindless with lust. It wasn't his fault entirely that the deflowering had hurt. I'd been so exceedingly careful since girlhood to make sure nothing stretched my vulva. Even before I began my menses, I'd learned that Anure would expect my woman's passage to be pristine and tight enough to bleed. The emperor had a reputation for enjoying the pain virgins sometimes felt. I'd saved it for him, that pain and blood, all for naught.

My first time with Con would've been far more pleasurable if my passage had been more accommodating. Though, to be fair, he was a big man all over. He'd likely stretch any woman to the point of pain. Judging from gossip, that length and girth would provide me with considerable pleasure in the future.

Until then, I wasn't above playing on his guilt to get my satisfaction in other ways. If we were going to be tied together, then we should try to find pleasure in each other.

Once he knew my true nature, he might not want to touch me again, so I'd better take what I could until then.

I slid my fingers into his dark hair, enjoying the sight of him at my feet as he tried to relieve me of the shoes. He grunted, half in acknowledgment of my touch—and partly in frustration at the laces.

"Who tied these knots?" he demanded.

"My ladies are accustomed to tying and sewing me into my costumes so they'll last without needing repair. Usually they just cut them off at the end of the day."

"Ah." He rose easily from his crouch, muscles flexing, then strode to his weapons belt, withdrew a dagger, and returned.

I enjoyed the view as he did—both the rear and the front. A big man without the slightest softness on him. Scarred, yes, especially on his back, probably from lashes endured while he was a prisoner. A chilling thought. Certain he wouldn't want me to mention it, I focused instead on his impressive shoulders. His chest in particular bulged with muscle built from swinging that rock hammer he spoke of so fondly. And that bag of rocks. His abdomen rippled with toned muscle, too. His buttocks tight and thighs powerfully muscled.

I'd never expected to physically enjoy my husband. Really, in any way. I'd seen Anure and though some called the emperor handsome, I'd always found his puffy dissipation repulsive. An unexpected gift then, this man fate had thrust into my arms.

Con got one shoe off, grunting in triumph, and set to work on the other. I leaned over and traced along the thick muscle of his neck, then settled my palm over the hard bulge of his shoulder, squeezing, enjoying the surge of wet heat between my thighs. He stilled under the touch, as he had before when I caressed him, reminding me of an abused animal waiting to see if they'd be petted or beaten. Con had gone somewhere inside for a while there, too, a place of terrible memories.

I knew enough of Anure's soldiers and guards—and the "perks" of their jobs overseeing the downtrodden of the empire—to guess at what Con had witnessed. Con might not have wanted to give me details, but Anure's tactics varied little—always the most cruel and degrading to those who dared resist.

"There," he said, dropping the other shoe and looking up.

I raked his hair back from his strong face, caressing his cheek, giving him some of the tenderness he likely hadn't received in his tortured growing up. "You are a gorgeous man, Conrí," I told him.

He looked even more arrested, his golden eyes full of doubt and suspicion. "I know I'm scarred and ugly," he replied, terse, even a little angry, as if he suspected me of taunting him.

I shook my head, staying very serious. "Scarred, yes, but ugly? No. Didn't you see how everyone was looking at you tonight? They all hope to lure you to their beds and parties, to find out if your stallion's build delivers on its promise."

His mouth quirked, uncertain. "Does it?"

"Oh yes." I let him hear the delight in my voice. "But you're all mine."

The smile deepened and he wrapped his hands around my ankles, sliding rough palms up over my calves. "I think *you* are all mine," he countered, a wicked gleam sparking to life in his eyes.

"What an excellent arrangement," I purred, feeling the hard edge of unsatisfied desire surge up in me, letting him urge my thighs apart.

He bent to kiss the inside of my knee, then the other,

pushing them wider and opening me to his gaze. I loved seeing the hardness in him peel away, giving me glimpses of the man beneath the armor. At the moment his face lit with curiosity, and lust. So much desire I felt, as if I could feed off it. He flicked a glance at my face, assessing, then made a sound of satisfaction.

"Show me what to do."

Obligingly I spread my legs for him, anchoring my heels on the edge of the desk, so I sat on it entirely, my sex open. Having him look at me was a delightful and unexpected spice. Perhaps I'd grow inured to it, but no man had ever seen me there—and he had never looked at a woman that way—so the discovery added a titillation that had me even needier. "Do you want more light?" I asked.

He glanced up at me, wry and surprised. "Yes." But he didn't take his eyes off my face, studying me. "Do you like me looking at you?"

"I do," I breathed. "Very much."

"Good." He gave me a half smile. "I think I will never tire of looking."

That made me catch my breath, my heart giving a little thud. Who knew I'd turn out to be so vulnerable to such simple things? Picking up a small candle in a shallow saucer, I set it under the rising angle of my thigh, its flame warm on my skin. Leaning back on my ring hand, I used the other to touch my sex, parting the folds though I hardly needed to.

He watched, gaze fixed and hard with growing lust, the flickering candlelight playing on the sharp angles of his face.

"Outer labia," I said, showing him. "And inner. The vulva you know already." His mouth quirked but he didn't take his gaze away. Just to tease him a little, I dipped my finger in and out, ignoring the sting of the recently abraded tissues. It felt good, too. I might be wrong about not having him inside me again. Con wrapped a hand around my ankle, squeezing in warning. Ah yes, with his fuse so short, best not push him so far just yet. I trailed my fingers up, pulling back the hood over my clitoris. "The point of most acute pleasure." I stroked it in demonstration, my hips arching and a groaning sigh escaping me.

"I touch it like that?" he asked, his voice rough with answering need.

"Yes. Gently. It's sensitive."

I held myself open, inviting him to try, but he hesitated. "Mouth and tongue would be softer," he offered, glancing up at me and down again. "I've seen that done. For men. Does it work on women?"

"Oh yes. But I haven't washed."

"It's my seed and your fluids. I don't care if you don't."

"I don't care," I said, then gasped as he took my thighs and put his mouth on me. Maybe because I'd gotten so wound up without satisfaction, but I convulsed at the sensation. His jaw silky on my thighs, mouth rough on my sex. He ran his tongue along the folds, so much stronger than the delicate lapping of my ladies' tongues. When he fastened on my clitoris, sucking hard, I screamed.

This time he didn't falter. He also didn't let up, flicking his tongue on my turgid bud and sucking, then nipping lightly. I groaned his name, pleading, and he tightened his grip on my thighs, holding me in place for his mouth and finding the rhythm to drive me wild. Unable to hold myself up, I arched back, crying out my pleasure.

The orgasm grabbed me like a fist, wringing my entire body as I thrashed in his unrelenting grip. It seemed to go on forever, my cries escalating until I went rigid for a long and endless suspended moment.

Then I collapsed, boneless, staring sightlessly at the ceiling, swimming in a languorous sea of stars.

When my mind roused and I could think again, I opened my eyes to find Con bending over me, stroking my cheek with tenderness. He smiled when I did, a warmly open expression from him—and one that made a dimple in one cheek, softening the stern lines of his face. I reached up to touch the boyish dimple with a fingertip, wondering if he knew he had it when he smiled just right. I wasn't going to tell him. Instead I'd save the knowledge for myself, so I'd always know when he was truly happy.

Perhaps I'd pretend to myself that I was the only person he showed it to.

"I'm guessing I did it right," he said, filled with male pride.

Tempting to mess with him, but I suspected he might be too fragile on the subject still. "The best, my Conrí," I murmured, cupping his face in my hands and drawing him down into a deep and drugging kiss. I tasted myself on him, and him on me, the muskiness of shared desire, as he returned the kiss with sweet intensity. I felt as if something I'd held tight inside unfurled.

His cock thrust urgent against my thigh, and I smiled to myself. A vigorous lover indeed.

He groaned and pulled away. "Perhaps we should try a bed."

"All right," I agreed, sitting up and groaning, too. Though not in the same way. The table had been hard and Con was learning, but he'd been rough. My body ached, and I'd have bruises in the morning.

"Let me," he said, and lifted me into his arms, carrying me like a bouquet of flowers. "That way?"

"Yes." I wound my arms around his neck and savored the sensation of being held so easily. "I'm not too heavy?"

He snorted and gave me a disbelieving look. "My bagiroca weighs more than you."

"Well, it *is* full of rocks," I noted.

"Door," he said, and I reached down to turn the handle.

"Whereas I am made of flower petals and sunshine," I informed him loftily.

He whistled, long and low, turning in a circle to take in my bedchamber. It's a lovely room, crafted to be the sanctuary of kings and queens. Ringed in nearly a full circle by open, arched windows, it sits on pillars sunk into the sea, so it seems to be an island, floating between ocean and sky. My ladies had made up the bed in black silk, scattered with white and gold flower petals, the candles in the sconces round the room now burning low and amber.

"Pretty," Con said. Then went to a window, still carrying me, and peered out. "Not very defensible."

I had to laugh. "You should know by now that Calanthe's defenses are not in being a fortress."

"No," he agreed. "You going to tell me about those?"

"Yes," I replied, matter-of-factly. "Tomorrow. We'll have to start making plans for Anure's reprisal. But not tonight."

"Tomorrow is soon enough." He laid me on the bed of petals, his hands wandering over me in rough and gentle caresses. I arched into it, purring with pleasure. "Are you too sore?"

"Let's find out." And I drew him down to cover me.

By the time we slept, we'd thoroughly eliminated every bit of tension. I curled into him, as if I'd always trusted the bulwark of his body, and he wrapped around me. I fell asleep to the sweet sense of his lips against my forehead.

32

"Arise, Your Highness. The realm awaits the sun of Your presence."

I struggled from the depths of a sleep so profound and dreamless, I couldn't quite make sense of the whispered words. I blinked at Ibolya, who bent close to the bed, her face concerned. Then I glanced at the sun, risen quite high, and the slumbering bulk of Con beside me. Then back at Ibolya. She was the only one in the room.

"The Glory?" I asked quietly.

"Waiting outside the door. She's so excited, but we weren't sure . . ."

And clearly, Tertulyn hadn't been there to advise or she'd have been the one waking me. I sighed for that. She'd have to be found today, and I'd have to ask her difficult questions. I didn't look forward to that conversation. All these years she'd been my best and closest companion. I buried the sting of betrayal that she'd abandoned me on one of the most important mornings of my life.

I only hoped that her absence didn't bode a far worse betrayal.

Con stirred. Then leapt from the bed, stark naked and looking about wildly for a weapon he didn't have.

Ibolya lowered her gaze, heroically keeping a straight

face. "Good morning, Conrí," she said. "I apologize for startling you."

He relaxed fractionally, though his fingers still curled, twitching for a weapon to grasp as he scanned the otherwise empty room. Finally his gaze rested on me, bemused and chagrined.

"I didn't think to warn you." I didn't say that I'd never expected to sleep so late. I sat up fighting against the unaccustomed tangle of the long hair wrapping around me. The glue had loosened in the night and the wig sat askew. I tried to straighten it, wishing I'd warned him about that, too, but we'd had so little time for explanations. He narrowed his eyes, noticing. I sighed mentally. I'd been bold about declaring that he'd have to know my true nature, but facing the moment of telling wasn't so easy to face. Such a lovely night. The best I'd slept in years, maybe ever.

But morning always arrives to start the day again.

"What's going on?" he asked.

"There's a morning ritual," I explained. "My ladies and a young woman from the villages, our Morning Glory for the day, attend Me as I wake."

"Oh," he said, as if understanding—and clearly not understanding at all, still frowning at my wig. It no doubt looked absurd.

"It's a special honor," I continued, wanting him to focus on something else. "And something of a religious superstition. If I refuse her, she'll think she wasn't acceptable. It's very important, today more than ever, to demonstrate to the people of Calanthe that all is well, that their queen is in good health and happy."

He gave me a long, inscrutable look. "And are you?" His was voice gruff from sleep, and something else.

"Of course." I produced a serene smile.

He didn't like that answer, but I didn't know what else

he expected me to say, with Ibolya standing there. I had no script for this. What did women say to their new husbands the morning after the wedding night? Certainly nothing for the ladies-in-waiting to hear, no matter their discretion. Mutely, I maintained the smile, making it clear I wouldn't say anything more on the subject.

"Should I send the Glory away, Your Highness?" Ibolya asked hesitantly into the silence.

I raised my brows at Con. He didn't look happy, but he shrugged it off. "You said it's important."

"Let's proceed as usual then, Ibolya. Get Conrí some clothes. Once he's dressed, the Glory can come in."

"I brought Your head scarf, Your Highness. So the Glory can have it?"

No help for it. I sighed in truth and pulled off the wig, not looking at Con. "Take this then."

Ibolya hastened away, slipping out of the room and closing it behind her. Still not looking at Con, I wiped the head scarf over my scalp, cleaning away the residual glue and oils of sleep.

"Lia?" Con asked, sounding dangerous.

In this thing I turned out to be a coward. But I forced myself to turn and look at him, still standing on the far side of the bed. His eyes roved over my bald head, confused and angry.

"Yes, Con?" I asked, smoothly polite.

Ibolya knocked lightly and opened the door.

"Give us a minute," Con barked.

The door closed again with a resounding snap. I raised my brows at Con. "You needn't frighten My ladies."

He set his jaw, glaring at me. "Who shaved your head? Tell me now."

"Maybe I'm naturally bald," I retorted. I should've planned how I'd explain. Unable to sit still under his in-

credulous stare, I got out of bed. When Con and I had settled this, I'd get back in bed and start over. I stretched, my
body protesting, aching in new and strange places.

"Lia." Con was in front of me, laying hands on my upper arms. For such a big, rough-looking man, he moved
fast and quiet. "Only slaves have shorn heads—is that what
happened to you?"

"No," I assured him firmly. I'd been so concerned about
him finding me ugly, I hadn't thought that's where his mind
would go. He sounded outraged on my behalf, so ready to
race out and defend me that I felt I needed to be careful
with him. Reaching up, I put some order to his long and
tangled hair. He looked particularly ferocious with it tumbled around his face. And particularly enticing. I only
wished the same could be said of me.

"I've had to shave My head since I was a little girl, for
good reasons," I replied. "That's why I wear wigs."

He seemed taken aback, searching my face. "What reasons?"

I sighed mentally. Was he ready to hear all of Calanthe's
secrets? I supposed we'd have to plunge in. We'd tied our
fates together—whether I'd chosen this or not—and he'd
have to know things about me. I'd hoped for a little more
time than this, but so it went.

"I am the Flower Queen, bearer of the orchid ring and
heir to the Orchid Throne in more than simple right of
birth. I am Calanthe's daughter as much as My father's."

Con frowned still, but his hands stroked my bare arms
almost soothingly, encouraging me to continue.

"My mother . . ." How to explain? "She wasn't what you
think of as human. My father was mostly a man like you,
but My mother was a daughter of Ejarat, elemental."

He didn't understand. I could see it in his eyes. Con was
a man of the rocks he carried, one who'd walked through

fire and dealt in transactions of flesh and blood. I might as well tell him I could fly.

"Old magic," I said, as if that explained everything. In truth, it explained a great deal for those who knew. "From when the land and the people were extensions of each other."

He studied me, mental pieces fitting together.

"And your hair?" he asked, doggedly pursuing the question.

I wrapped my fingers in the trailing, tangled locks of his. "When it grows out, it's not a human color or texture. Anyone who looks at Me would know I'm not human. That I'm born of the ancient magic."

He picked up my hand. I'd discarded my nail tips in the dark, so as not to scratch him, and now he studied my fingertips, as if confirming something noticed in passing. "Your nails, too," he said. "They look like flower petals."

"Yes. Worse if not trimmed."

"And your skin." He stroked my arms, then rubbed a finger over one spot where our sex play had worn the makeup off, clearing it more. "Here it's like the pattern of bark, though it feels like skin."

"The patches come and go." I hesitated. "I get more as I get older."

"All right," he said, rubbing my arms once more and setting me away from him, looking me up and down.

"That's it?" I asked. "Just 'all right'?"

He shrugged a little. "You're my wife. I vowed to take all of you to me. And it falls to me to keep you safe now. If hiding yourself is what it takes, then all right."

Unexpectedly, my eyes filled with tears and my throat clogged. All those years of memories flooded into me in a storming rush of old grief, rage, and humiliation. I'd hated being bald. When my hair first changed from baby fluff and began growing in—pink, gold, silver, green, and blue, some strands wildly curling, other locks like viny tendrils, others ruffled as orchid petals—I'd railed at it. I wanted normal hair, flaxen and silky like Tertulyn's. It wasn't fair that I had to be so odd, that I had to be bald and wear the horrible wigs, that I had to cover my hands and wear gowns from neck to toe, and thick makeup on the rest.

Over the years my ladies had crafted beautiful wigs for me, developed the makeup to cover my odd skin, the jeweled nails to hide my own. They'd helped me create a veneer of the beauty I lacked on my own. Tertulyn adopted the same styles, in comfort and solidarity.

When the court began to emulate us, to don similar distortions to look like their queen and her most favored lady, I hadn't known how to feel.

All along I'd wanted to look like them. And they didn't have the wit to understand how blessed they were to be normal.

"Don't weep," Con said roughly. He cupped my face, his thumbs wiping away the tears that spilled over.

"I'm sorry I'm so ugly," I whispered.

He looked incredulous. "You are beyond lovely, Lia." Again he passed wondering fingers over the subtly patterned area on my arm, where the golden scales of bark drifted to my elbow. With infinite care, he ran a big hand over my scalp. I shivered at the caress, so strangely arousing on that tender skin. "You have a beautifully shaped skull."

I burst out laughing, wet and unladylike. "What?" I demanded.

He grinned, unbothered. "You do. Elegant. Without the wig, you're all big eyes and gorgeous mouth."

I opened that mouth to retort, but he took it in a deep kiss, one hand cupping my head and the other going around my waist, pulling me against him. His rising erection spoke clearly of his continued desire. Tempting to take him back to bed, but I was sore.

He ran his hands over my naked body, first soothing, then pausing here and there. I thought he looked for more signs of odd coloration, but no. "I hurt you," he said gruffly. "You're bruised. All over."

"I don't mind. I heal quickly—and I'm tougher than I look."

Con didn't move immediately. "Will your Glory report you in good health, seeing the marks of my hands?" His fingers drifted over a purpling bruise on my hip, where he'd gripped me in the intensity of his lust.

"Darling Conrí." I took his hardened shaft in my hand and stroked it, then squeezed hard and pinched the tip. Shock and arousal fired in his eyes. "This is the Flower Court. Every woman out there—except the Glory, who is an innocent, but even she will have heard gossip—knows that pain can intensify pleasure. They will envy My lover who wanted Me so badly he left his handprints on My skin."

His mouth twisted in a rueful grimace. "If you say."

"Yes. And you will learn to temper your touch, when to be gentle with Me and when to be rough. There is delight in both."

He grunted, unconvinced.

"And I'll learn to be tougher." No more game playing, pretending to be Anure's coy concubine. I'd revealed myself as his enemy, so I'd be the worst enemy he could have.

"You're as tough as they come." Smiling crookedly, Con looked torn, oddly subdued. "Still . . ."

"You're a strong man," I noted with a wry smile.

"A brutal one, you said." He regarded me seriously.

I gave him my full attention, so he'd know I wasn't

brushing him off with a convenient lie. "I think you can be brutal because your life has called for it. Your brutality and ruthlessness have served you and your people well—and I expect you to use them to serve Calanthe."

He smiled in feral anticipation. "Then you agree we'll fight."

"We don't have a choice." And the time for lying abed was over. We had a war to plan.

As if coming to the same realization, Con studied me, running a hand over my tender scalp and making me shiver. "Anure can't know this about you."

I wasn't sure if he meant it wasn't possible Anure already knew, or that he mustn't ever know. It didn't matter; both were true. "No, Anure doesn't know. He only knows that he wants what Calanthe has and he can't have it without Me. When the false emperor came here long ago, My father enchanted Anure just enough that his wizards couldn't detect it and—"

"Anure doesn't have wizards, or believe in magic," Con interrupted me.

"So he'd like the world to think," I said simply, letting him work it out.

Which he quickly did, judging by the light of comprehension in his eyes, and the following grim and determined frown. My Conrí understood strategy. "Go on," he said.

"If Anure's wizards couldn't detect the geas, they wouldn't know to remove it. It worked to make Anure satisfied in the betrothal. It was a stalling tactic that wasn't meant to last this long."

Con frowned, stroking a hand up and down my back. "King Gul died, unexpectedly."

"Exactly." The old grief choked me, and I leaned into Con. He embraced me gently, and it settled into me that I wasn't alone in this anymore. "Anure will come," I said.

"Then we'll be ready for him," Con answered.

For the first time, I thought it was possible that we could be. I kissed my husband, beyond glad to have him there. Then gave him a smile.

"Now get your clothes and dress, my Conrí, so I can bathe and get ready, too. Then we'll call a meeting of the Defense Council." And Tertulyn needed to be found. If she could be.

"I'll let your lady in."

"Con," I called as he strode to the door. He turned back in question. "I am happy this morning," I told him. "Far more than I ever hoped to be."

He smiled, the warmth lighting the gold of his eyes.

I got back into bed so the Glory could start my day again. The realm awaited the sun of my presence, after all.

Read on for an excerpt from the next thrilling
book in the Forgotten Empires series

The Fiery Crown

By Jeffe Kennedy

Available Summer 2020 from
St. Martin's Paperbacks

* * *

"I just thought I should mention," Ambrose replied reproachfully, more of his usual bite to it. "Since you seem to have such a high opinion of my wizardry. In case your brooding and obsessive study of this painting led your thoughts in that direction."

I set my teeth, resisting the urge to grind them. "I'm not brooding or obsessive. This is a good place to think. *Normally* no one bothers me here." If I had to kick my heels in this oppressively cheerful paradise, growing softer with each wasted moment, I could at least contemplate next steps, anticipate Anure's strategy to take his own revenge on Calanthe and her queen. "It's not like I have anything else to do."

"You could attend court, as consort to Her Highness," Ambrose pointed out blandly, and I suppressed a growl of frustration. At least my throat hurt less, since Healer Jeaneth had been treating me—one positive of having time on my hands. My voice still sounded like a choked dog most of the time, however.

"Court," I snarled the word. "I don't get how Lia can waste time on that posturing when she promised to discuss defense."

"She does have a realm to govern."

"She won't if Anure comes while she drags her feet. The woman is uncommonly stubborn."

"A perfect match for you." Ambrose narrowed his eyes at my clenched fists. "Isn't she gathering intelligence from her spies?"

I didn't answer that. That's what we waited on, theoretically, but I knew there were things Lia was avoiding telling me. I also suspected that she hoped it would all just go away. Both of us knew that Calanthe couldn't withstand a full-out, devastating attack. When nothing happened immediately after our wedding, Lia began to hope that nothing would.

I knew better. The painting helped remind me of all the dead waiting to be avenged—and what happened to those who fell before Anure's might.

Unfortunately, I was at a loss to find a way out of our current predicament.

If Anure was smart—and the Imperial Tyrant might be greedy, arrogant, ruthless, and devoid of redeeming human qualities, but he wasn't stupid—he'd simply surround the island with battleships loaded with explosive vurgsten and bombard Calanthe until nothing remained. He wouldn't care about salvaging anything; he never had. Even with the ships I'd captured and Calanthe's fleets of pleasure skiffs and fishing boats, we couldn't effectively surround and defeat Anure's navy. Besides, our own supplies of vurgsten had to be vanishingly small compared to what the emperor had stockpiled for nearly two decades at his citadel at Yekpehr.

We had to deploy our few strengths with strategic care, and being trapped on an island while the Imperial Toad scoured us off it with superior force wouldn't allow for that. Not only wasn't I closer to destroying Anure and taking my final revenge, I'd put myself and my forces in an even more tenuous position than before. I'd followed Ambrose's prophecy, and taken the tower at Keiost.

Take the Tower of the Sun,
Claim the hand that wears the Abiding Ring,
And the empire falls.

Claiming the hand that wears the Abiding Ring? I only wish it had been as simple as conquering an impregnable ancient city. Instead I'd had to find a way to convince Queen Euthalia of Calanthe to marry me. Against all probability, I'd succeeded. We were duly wed, though saying I'd claimed anything about Lia would be a stretch, and I sure didn't see the empire falling anytime soon. The reverse seemed far more likely.

I'd honed the skill of patiently waiting for my chance to strike—but doing nothing while my enemy mustered a crushing attack? It was driving me out of my mind.

"Lia's spies can tell her how much vurgsten Anure has, how many ships and troops he can send against us, and how well-fortified his citadel is, and we'll know nothing more than we do now," I finally replied to the wizard's expectant silence. "I thought claiming the hand with the Abiding Ring would lead to the empire's fall." I leveled an accusing glare on him.

"You claimed Her Highness's hand all right, but the wooing doesn't stop there," Ambrose replied with mild reproof. "You can't order a queen about like you can your soldiers."

"Don't I know it," I muttered. Since Ambrose had destroyed what little peace I'd found, I turned and strode down the long gallery. The wizard glided alongside me, making no sound though my bootsteps echoed on the polished marble of Lia's pretty palace. Ambrose could move silently as a cat when he wished, which was how he'd managed to sneak up on me. No one else could. I'd learned early on in the mines of Vurgmun to duck the ready lash of the guards, a habit that had stuck—and served me well in the years of battle since.

I'd have liked to say I'd gotten used to it, but even I didn't delude myself that much.

We emerged from the shadowed portrait gallery, a place thick with ghosts and the stale smells of hundreds of destroyed kingdoms, and into the bright, flower-scented sunlight of the main hall. Lia's palace doesn't have much in the way of walls. With the eternal summer of Calanthe's tropical weather, they don't need them. Open arcades of carved pillars framed the lush gardens, pools, and lawns surrounding the palace, with the gleaming turquoise sea beyond. Flowers bloomed constantly from lush lawns, flower beds, shrubs, and towering trees, with vines coiling over all of it. Butterflies of hues I hadn't known existed lifted in clouds, then drifted on the breeze, and everywhere birds sang, all sweetly, of course. I hadn't figured out yet if Lia had an army of gardeners to tend it all or if it just . . . did that on its own.

I'd made a deal with myself that I wouldn't ask. Not that Lia would laugh at my ignorance—not out loud, anyway—but I didn't like to remind Her Highness of what a provincial lout she'd married.

A stream burbled its way through the palace from a lagoon on one side to a pond on the other, meandering through in a trough cut into the marble floors and inlaid with little tiles in all shades of blue and green. Arching bridges crossed it in places, more for show than anything because all but the most mincing courtier could easily leap across the narrow channel. I might not have much in the way of fine manners, but even I knew it would be rude to actually jump over the thing, however, and I didn't much feel like changing my path to cross over the nearest dainty bridge. So, I turned and followed the stream outside.

Ambrose, of course, tagged along as if we were out for a companionable stroll.

"What do you want, Ambrose?" I finally asked, capitulating to the inevitable.

"Me? Oh, what a question." He let his staff thunk on the path of crushed stone, leaning on it as we walked, Merle rising and falling with the movement, like the carved masthead of a ship on stormy seas. "I want different things now than when I was an apprentice wizard," he continued conversationally. "Those ideas change over time, have you noticed? The expectations of idealistic ignorance give way to more mature dreams and goals. Not in a bad way. It's just that what we thought we wanted came from not really knowing what we could have. Once I learned more about what the world offered me, I discovered I wanted entirely different things. And you?"

"I have no idea what you're talking about." Or how I'd gone from leading armies, gaining momentum on my vengeance with each conquest, to strolling through a garden, having a conversation like the pretty lads and ladies we passed. Most of the courtiers were in court, naturally, kissing Lia's gorgeously garbed ass and passing their fancily folded notes, but the other denizens of the palace seemed to spend most of their time looking decorative in the gardens. In my black garb—granted, finer than what I'd arrived on Calanthe wearing—and carrying my weapons, I felt like a scarred monster by comparison. Given the askance looks the courtiers gave me before they deflected into other directions, they thought so, too.

"I'm talking about changing expectations," Ambrose replied, lifting his face to the sun and smiling like that one painting of a saint back in the gallery. "You, for example, can expect very different things from your life now that you're King of Calanthe and no longer the Slave King."

"The consort of the Queen of Calanthe," I corrected, hating the testy edge to my voice, already so rough compared to the wizard's fluid tones. "Not the same thing. I'm not king of anything, never have been."

Ambrose waved that off as irrelevant. "My point is, it's time for you to stop moping about in the shadows. Time to take action, my boy!"

I stopped next to a tiered fountain of roses, glaring at it while I mastered the urge to throttle the wizard. The roses at the top were bright white, then they got pinker lower down. The blooms progressed through all shades of pink and red, until the bottom ones, which were as dark as the blood that pours out when you strike a man in the liver.

Tiny purple bees buzzed around them, making a hypnotic sound that somehow seemed part of the heavily sweet scent of the blossoms. I kept an eye on the bees to make sure they planned to stay occupied with the flowers rather than attacking us. "What action do you want me to take?" I asked, sounding more or less calm. "Lia refuses to convene her defense council and *you* agreed, saying we should wait to see how Anure responded when he received news of the wedding."

Ambrose sighed heavily, then settled himself on a stone bench that circled the flower fountain, heedless of the bees that investigated the garland in his hair, though Merle snapped at one curiously. "That's what I'm telling you, Conrí," the wizard said with exaggerated patience. "We did have to wait. Now we don't. Must I forever explain these things?"

I wrapped my fingers into my palms, making them into fists so I'd be less likely to forget that I needed Ambrose and accidentally strangle him. Also, he was Lia's court wizard now, and she'd be put out with me if I killed him.

Ours wasn't a marriage of affection. Exactly the opposite, in fact, as we'd started out trying to kill each other before we even met face to face. But the ritual had been done properly, tying us together for the rest of our lives, like it or not. Aside from the sexual consummation, where we seemed to get along just fine, we mostly seemed to piss each other off. Like two bulls in a small pen, one of Lia's pet scholars, Brenda, had called us. Not a bad comparison, if unflattering. I wouldn't mind having horns to wave at Ambrose in menace.

"What changed?" I asked. My voice growled with frustration when the wizard got that sly look of his and raised a chastising finger as he opened his mouth. "And *don't* say everything changes all the time."

Ambrose closed his mouth again and raised his brows. "Well, everything does change. Change is the one dependable element of the world," he pointed out, almost primly, then hastily added as he spied the look on my face, "but I'll address the question I believe you meant to ask, which is why is now the time and not yesterday, or even earlier today? That's a complicated answer, because there are many factors you won't understand, even if I had time to explain them all."

"Ambrose."

"Patience, Conrí, what I'm saying is that Queen Euthalia has received a message from Anure."

"It took you *this* long to tell me that?" I snapped, incredulous. My blood surged hot, but not with anger and frustration like usual. Excitement and bold purpose filled me. Enough of delays and arguing in circles. Finally I could embark on the final phase of my mission to destroy Anure, everything he'd built, and everything he cared about. If the Imperial Toad was capable of caring about anything at all.

And the empire falls.

"What did the message say?"

"Oh, I don't know exactly. But the currents of possibility and probability have shifted. It's fascinating to see."

I bit back my impatience. "*How* have they shifted— have you seen how we can counter Anure's certain attack?"

A chorus of music blasted from the direction of the palace proper, along with cheers and shouts. I knew that fanfare well enough, as it always heralded the approach of the queen. Her people behaved as if her every appearance was a cause for joyous celebration. Ambrose stood, using the staff to pull himself up, a delighted smile on his face. "Aha! Here comes Queen Euthalia. She'll be able to tell you what the message says. Then you'll see."

"Something you could have told me long since."

"If you'd bothered to attend court, you'd have known already," he shot back, dropping all hint of playfulness, his words short and full of disapproval.

I didn't reply, setting my teeth together with a satisfying bite instead. Lia's court drove me out of my mind with their fancy dress and pretty posturing. I'd gone to court with Lia that first day, thinking that we'd get actual work done. We did have a war to plan, right? But no—she'd expected me to dress up and then sit there while fancily dressed idiots simpered and offered fake compliments, begging for favors in the guise of offering congratulations on our marriage.

When I lost all patience and suggested—politely, I thought—that we call the defense council into session, all hell had broken loose. How was I supposed to know Lia's Sawehl-cursed defense council was a *secret*? With everyone in an uproar, Lia had adjourned court and accused me of sabotaging her authority and precipitating panic. I'd had to point out that the threat of incipient attack by an overwhelming force *should* upset people. The argument went downhill from there.

We'd more or less gotten back on friendly, if formal, terms since. But I also hadn't gone back to court. And she still hadn't convened the defense council.

The music and cheering grew closer, so I stayed where I was. No doubt the purple bees had told Lia where to find me—or however her elemental magic worked. All I knew about her for sure was that Lia was as much flower as flesh. She kept her head shaved because if she didn't, her hair grew out like vines. So she told me—I hadn't seen that part, though I'd seen the plant-like patterns on her skin, surprisingly erotic.

There was magic there, too, but I didn't know how much. Lia had a lifelong habit of concealing her nature, so she didn't discuss the specifics easily, certainly not in public. And when we were alone . . . well, we didn't talk much.

She came around the bend of the garden path, preceded by two spritely children tossing flower petals in the air to flutter down and decorate the rocks before her. The gravel already had colorful, smooth stones interspersed throughout the rougher white ones, so the petals seemed especially redundant. But the Calantheans never saw anything they didn't try to make even prettier.

Lia led a phalanx of attendants, five ladies in waiting instead of her former six—she also refused to discuss replacing Tertulyn, who'd disappeared on our wedding day and had yet to be found—along with Lord Dearsley, and a few others of her various advisers. Two of my own people, Sondra and Kara, accompanied the entourage, gazes alert for trouble. They were dressed for court, too, though more severely than the extravagant Calanthe styles so they also stood out as invaders amongst the blossoms.

I hadn't seen Lia since I'd vacated the bed we shared before she'd dressed for the day. A weird Calanthean ritual dictated that the "Morning Glory," a young virgin, should assist the queen from her bed. Apparently Lia's father, old King Gul, had divested the glories of their innocence. When Lia had arched a brow and asked if I'd like to take up that tradition, my answer had been an easy and immediate *no*. I had zero interest in that tradition.

So, since our marriage, Lia had changed the years-old routine by having Lady Ibolya assist in getting me gone before Lady Calla brought the glory in and pretended to wake the queen all over again.

After that, the glory helped Lia's ladies complete the elaborate ritual of dressing her for the day, something I was fine with escaping. I preferred my wife—uncanny still to even think those words—without the adornments of her rank. I knew most noble ladies used their clothing and makeup as a kind of armor in their battles with the world, but Lia elevated dressing to a full scale war. A lot of the costume and makeup served to disguise her nature. She had to shave her head, so she wore elaborate wigs to hide that fact. The elaborate gowns and thick paste covered everything else.

Still, her choice of dress absolutely announced her mood. Today she was lethal.

She wore a stiff-boned corset, which pushed up her breasts to distracting levels, and narrowed her waist to a wisp I could span with my hands. The under part of the gown exactly matched her skin tone, with an overlay of sheer material with angular black lines of gleaming black beads in spiky patterns. The skirt flowed long and full over her hips and trailed behind her with a ruff of black at the bottom that scattered the petals as she walked. Even though there was a lot of it, the gown overall gave the impression that she was mostly naked, wearing only thin black lines of tiny beads. In fact, the more I squinted at it, the better I could see that some of the skirt was sheer, giving glimpses of her long, slim legs, made even longer-looking by the sparkling high heels on her feet.

She'd foregone her usual high collar, leaving her shoulders bare, the covering of her breasts more thickly beaded than the rest, with another ruff of lace coyly feathered over her cleavage. Even though I knew she'd have her exposed skin covered with thick makeup, the sight of her exquisite bosom tantalized me with memories of how she tasted. Long black gloves covered her arms from wrists to shoulders, her fingers tipped with sharp-looking nails, white with gleaming black at the ends, as if she'd dipped them in ink.

On her left hand, the orchid ring—the Abiding Ring I'd supposedly claimed along with her hand in marriage, for all the good it did me—bloomed in splendor, ruffled petals somehow sexual and magical.

The wig she'd donned to match the outfit was also ebony black—possibly the same one she'd worn for our wedding ball—but elaborately styled so that a long curl draped over one shoulder, the rest forming a coiling nest for the glittering crown of Calanthe. With Lia's makeup all in stark black and white also—even her lips were painted glossy black, diamonds glittering at the corners of her mouth, the two top points, and a larger one centered in the full lower lip—the crown of jewels in the blues and greens of Calanthe's gentle seas was the only point of color, besides the orchid on her hand.

Well, and the blue-gray of her eyes, a color that should have been misty, but came across as crystal shard-sharp as the beads on her gown as she assessed me from beneath diamond-tipped black lashes. Lia moved with swaying grace toward me, apparently unhurried, expression as coolly composed as always. But I didn't miss the tension simmering in her.

She paused a decorous distance before me, and I restrained the urge to bow. Yet another reason I'd hated court—or being with her in formal settings—was that I didn't know the rules for how to behave. When it was just us, man and woman, me and Lia, preferably naked, I knew how to handle her. With Her Highness Queen Euthalia . . .

"Good morning, Conrí," she said, her smoothly cultured voice sweet as flowers. "I trust you're enjoying My gardens? It's a lovely day for it."

I barely managed not to wince, or apologize—especially not for refusing to waste time kicking my heels in court. Instead I gave in to the urge to acknowledge her beauty by taking her hand, the one without the orchid ring, bending over it, and pressing a kiss to her fingers. As always, she smelled of flowers or the inside of a leaf, as if her petal-soft skin emanated the scent naturally. She curled those nails, sharp as thorns, against my palm. I straightened, and gave her a long, cautious look.

"Good morning, wife," I replied, not above needling her in return. Her eyes narrowed in smoky warning. "I understand there's news from our illustrious imperial overlord?"

That narrow gaze flicked to Ambrose and back to me. "Indeed, Conrí," she replied with decorous boredom. "His Imperial Majesty Emperor Anure has sent me a letter." She lifted her free hand, flicking the black-tipped nails with languid demand, the orchid ring's petals billowing with the movement, and her lady Ibolya set an envelope in the cage of them. The light-gray paper had been folded in intricate lines, then embossed in darker gray with an image of Anure's citadel at Yekpehr, the rocks jagged and menacing.

She spun the envelope to extend it to me, as Sondra might flick one of her blades. Lia's expression remained opaque, eyes guileless. "While I hate to interrupt your idyll in the garden, perhaps I could trouble you with your attention to this."

Oh yeah, Lia was pissed as hell. I could only hope it wasn't all aimed at me.